DALTON'S RUN

TODD BLOMERTH

Editor: Robin Harrison

Cover Design: Karen Phillips, Phillipscovers

Project Manager/Interior Design/Formatting:

Tarra Thomas Indie Publishing Services

to Phil, Tam, Wayne, Laura, Jeff and Jessica.
You kept me at it.

SUMMER

Chapter One

AT THREE IN THE MORNING, SOMETHING WAKES ME UP. AT LEAST I think it's three in the morning. My iPhone is dead. The house is warm. No hum of the A/C running. I flip on the light switch... nothing. What the hell? I quickly glance out the window. No porch lights. No street lights. Dammit! The faint illumination of the plug-in lanterns that come on when the electricity goes off light the way as I head down the stairs. In the kitchen, I flip on the coffee maker. At least I can get something hot in me. Or not. Dammit! Electricity off means electricity is off everywhere in the house.

I reach for my landline phone handset—it is battery charged. No dial tone. I was going to punch in my neighbor's number. Misery loves company. It's black as the ace of spades. Dead quiet except for dogs howling. I'm sweating, but it's not from the house's temperature. I feel a vague sense of dread. Something bad has happened. Or maybe is about to.

Grabbing a small flashlight, I head back upstairs into my office. No need to panic. I reach for my shoulder holster that hangs on the office door's doorknob, shove a clip in its 9mm, chamber a round, and set the safety. Shorts and sandals, and I'm outside.

Now there are voices. Mostly low. No one panicking. Just sounding worried. I tuck the pistol behind me, turn off the flashlight, and walk toward Fred Aston's house. I like Fred, even if he is from California and leans way too far to the left. He's not keen on owning a firearm. However, over a few beers, he's let loose on not trusting Big Brother—now there's a term from the past. He's kept an eye on my place when I had a business trip—when I had a job—and doesn't ask any questions on why me and the missus split the sheets. Not that it's any of his business anyway, but in this burg, everyone thinks you owe them your life history for the privilege of living here.

"Hey, Dalton." A disembodied voice addresses me. "That you moving out there?"

I inch through the grass toward his voice. "Hey, Fred. What's going on, you think?"

"Damned if I know." He leans on my chain link fence. I point the light toward the ground and turn it back on.

Jill, his wife, tucks in behind him. "Hey, Dalton."

"Hey, Jill." She's in a t-shirt and short-shorts. No bra. No makeup either. I'm tempted to turn the flashlight directly toward her. Maybe get a glimpse of her amazing breasts. Instead, I switch the light off.

"Listen," Jill whispers.

Fred and I, we listen.

Nothing. I mean absolutely nothing. Except for a few neighbors and the dogs howling, nothing. No hissing of cars out on the highway. No emergency vehicles.

It's too quiet. Fred starts to say something, then stops. A low rumble seems to push through the night air, through us, and then it's gone.

"What was that?"

"I don't know." It wasn't like a breeze. In fact, the air is calm. The quiet returns, except now neighborhood dogs are going crazy. That sense of dread is back.

"Our phones don't work, Dalton. Computers are dead. A/C not working. This is highly unusual."

It sure is.

"EMP." The letters come out of my mouth before the thought propelling them is completely formed.

"Emp?" Fred asks.

"No, E. M. P. Electromagnetic pulse."

I'm not expecting him to understand, and he doesn't. He doesn't have to. Jill is an IT engineer. She knows what I'm talking about.

"Oh shit," she says.

Oh shit, indeed.

Chapter Two

"YOU WARNED US, DIDN'T YOU?"

Jill almost sounds contrite. In the dark, I can't help myself. I grin, thinking, *I told you so.* I swallow the glee at getting something right. "Jill, even a stopped watch is right a couple of times a day." Someone said that about Winston Churchill. I stole it.

Fred makes a grunting noise. He's probably heard the saying, and isn't too impressed with my attempt at humor. I've been after the two of them to step up, take some precautions. He knows I'm gloating. We stand in the dark. More flickers of the neighbors' flashlights. People out of their houses. They're getting uncomfortable now. Several knock on adjacent house doors. Do any of these folks know what just happened? Not many, I'll bet.

Jill asks, "Care to come over for a glass of wine?"

Wine? Baby, the End Times are upon us, and I'm supposed to come drink wine? "Sure," I answer. "Why not?"

We sit on their back porch. Most of the dogs have calmed down. New sounds I don't hear in the city surround me. The susurration of wind in the leaves. The soft groan of a tree as it flexes. A whir of bat wings as they hunt for insects. I allow the wine to do its job, and for a moment the darkness seems benign. Fred and Jill are in their own worlds.

Fred breaks my reverie. "What happens now?"

Jill answers for me. "Things go to hell."

Besides an awesome rack and legs that seem endless, this woman has her shit together. Which is why I am really turned on by her. And probably why she does her best to keep me at arms-length. She's caught me staring at her as she gardens. The return look was withering and a clear signal. "Ain't gonna happen. Not now. Not ever."

Like I said, she's got her shit together.

Fred asks about EMPs. Rather than trying to recreate Wikipedia's description, I tell him, "Go start your car."

He obliges. I hear the back screen door open, then slap shut. He curses. "Garage door opener doesn't work." Then, "Oh, yeah." He enters the garage, releases the emergency latch and pushes up the metal door. His Beamer's doors won't open. Now, it's starting to sink in.

Jill's does a voice-over as Fred rattles keys, trying to insert the physical key into the car door lock assembly. "Anything with an electronic brain has probably been fried. That includes any reasonably recent cars. Phones. Computers. The whole shebang."

Fred's weight settles back in a lawn chair. "So, Dalton, since you've been warning us. What do we need to do?"

"Immediately? Fire up your barbeque pit and cook every piece of meat in your refrigerator and freezer. It's not going to keep. What you can't get cooked, slice thin, salt, rig a rack in the back yard, and start drying it."

"Anything else?"

"Got any firearms?"

"Not that again. Dalton, we don't believe in owning firearms." He pauses, then sounds pissed when Jill doesn't back him up. "Too many guns in the U.S. now. We've discussed this several times."

I'm beginning to think Fred is a fucking idiot. "Just a precaution. People may start worrying about food and shelter."

I hold my wine glass out in the dark and thank them. I feel Jill reach for it, touching my fingers in the process. Normally, I'd wonder whether the touch is accidental, or if there's more to it. Now, I'm thinking about getting back into the safety of my house.

I switch on the flashlight and the two walk me to the gate. Jill touches my arm. "Do you think it'd be a good idea if we team up until this is over with?"

I have to think about it. Right now, great tits and long legs are nice, but unless she can bring something to the table that'll help me survive, she's just a liability.

Chapter Three

I QUIT MY JOB AT THE POST OFFICE A MONTH AGO AND CASHED IN my measly retirement. Went to the local pawn shop here in Elmhurst, and bought six ounces of pure gold. I hope it's real gold, anyway. Spent a lot of time surfing television channels. All pretty much had the same reports: the Middle East gone to shit. Iran's attempt at delivering a cruise missile loaded with a nuclear warhead to Israel didn't work. Israel's response did. Towelheads claimed thousands of lives lost, including women and children. Pictures on lefty CNN indicated they're telling the truth—at least about that. Fox News said those rascals were lying, but even it admitted there'd been some 'collateral damage.' Straits of Hormuz blocked by mines, oil tankers being grabbed by Iran. American drone strikes on Persian military units causing untold casualties and lifetimes of anger toward the West.

Europe, and mostly Germany, tried to play referee. France interjected its version of a 'reasonable' resolution. But, hey, it's France. No one seriously cared what the Frogs had to say. They've sold out so many times.

In all this hubbub—all that is going on in the Middle East

life seemed to go on in Elmhurst pretty much as it always has. The grocery store remained open, its shelves stocked reasonably well. Gasoline prices doubled, but was still available. The weather was the weather. Hot some days. Cooler on others. Kids still went to school. The courts still sent out jury summonses. My notice for next week is sitting in a pile of unopened mail. I haven't taken time to throw it out with the rest of the trash.

To most, what was the big deal? Humanity had dealt with this craziness before. Would deal with it again.

I'm not betting on it this time.

I walk into the spare bedroom. Its floor is host to my various firearms: an AK47 made in what was once Yugoslavia, a semi-automatic AR15, pump 12-gauge, three hunting rifles—all scoped, a 9 mm Glock automatic, and a .357 revolver. An assortment of ammunition acquired over the years, just not lately. I used to order all I wanted online. The feds stopped that awhile back. Rumor is that they were stockpiling it. Rumor also was that our government didn't want people like me to have too much of the stuff if 'civilized society' broke down. Which is exactly the reason why I bought all I could lay my hands on. Working as a postal clerk, you learn what the Postal Inspectors are on the lookout for. That knowledge made it easier to get stuff through the mail that wasn't necessarily legal. Like dum dum rounds and +P cartridges with additional powder and punch. Figured if I was going to spend money, might as well get more bang for the buck. That's a joke.

Where was I? Oh, yeah. Weapons oiled. Those with cases, cased. Ammo separated and stowed.

The flashlight flickers. I turn it off to save battery power. I'll wait until daylight to assess what I need to do. I figure if things go bad, it'll be bad only so long. After all, this is the good old US of A. Lots of redundancies. Lots of 'can do' attitudes.

I don't sleep well. Haven't for years. Sometimes it's too

much booze and the ensuing headache and guilt. Sometimes it's the aches and pains from old college football injuries. Lately, both reasons have been aggravated by news broadcasts filled with talking heads warning of the possibility of war.

I crack open the upstairs bedroom window. Another recent change—jimmying open long-ago painted shut windows, anticipating no air conditioning. I smile, pleased with myself. Then I utter a silent oath. This little accomplishment doesn't amount to a hill of beans. It's still hot.

I strip to my shorts and lie on top of the bedspread. It's only a couple hours until dawn. Sleep eludes me. There's too much to do. I re-holster the 9 mm, turn the flashlight back on and go downstairs. Double check all the window locks. Its doubtful things will get bad immediately, but no streetlights are an invitation for some to see what they can steal. No sense in making it easy for them. I don't reach for the light switch in the dining room. Instincts are already saying that it's wasted motion.

Got on Amazon awhile back and bought something called a 'food dehydrator.' The outside freezer is darned near empty as I've been drying the hell out of everything in there. Bagging it and stacking it. MREs? At first, I kind of forgot about the necessity of food if the electricity shuts off. Fortunately, I know a stocker at the local grocery store. For a fifty percent mark-up, he sold me cases of ramen noodles and freeze-dried veggies. The dining room table is stacked high with the stuff. Enough for a couple of months anyway. For me. No family nearby so I don't fret sharing with them. Share with my neighbors? Jill and Fred are as close as I've got to friends.

They don't need to know about this stash. Not yet. Maybe not ever.

Chapter Four

I PASS THROUGH THE KITCHEN AND INTO THE GARAGE. TOO EARLY for what's left in the refrigerator and freezer to go bad. I walk around the Chevy—it's of no use to me right now. On the other side under a blue plastic cover is a 1965 BMW R60 motorcycle with sidecar. After my wife and I split the sheets, I bought this baby with twenty-three thousand dollars I'd hid from her. She got the elevator and I got the shaft in the divorce, so I didn't spend much time agonizing about lying on the asset sheets the lawyers exchanged.

The bike is a 600cc gem. The sidecar has a windscreen and fender skirt. Spare tire mounted on the back. The boxer engine runs as quietly as a sewing machine. I've had it out on the road a few times, but only after the ex moved out of the county. My lawyer cost me a chunk, and I wasn't interested in ponying up any more money if Gail— just mentioning her name gives me the willies— found I'd been playing cute with her on the property settlement. Out of spite, she'd have taken me back to court.

I wipe down the BMW's black surfaces. It's a thing of beauty. It's just gotten more beautiful. With a magneto and carburetor, it's not affected by the EMP. I think. I pull up the garage door a few feet and prop it open, then climb onto the bike's seat, check to ensure it's in neutral, and twist on the ignition switch. Glorious! No need to advertise this baby's presence, so the BMW is re-covered and the garage locked up tight.

As the sun rises, windows are opened and lawn chairs set under trees. Ice chests are dragged out and loaded with various foods. Adults ride around on bicycles. Some of the two-wheelers are small and look like they've been cadged from children.

I spend most of the day rummaging through my tools, trying to decide which are more likely to be needed the most. They go in a soft sided tool bag, along with duct tape, zip ties, and baling wire. I'm interrupted frequently. Most ask the same questions – What just happened? I try explaining about EMPs. I'm no expert, and it shows. When will things get back to normal? That I can't answer. Maybe I'm afraid to even think about it.

The afternoon torpor is broken by the sound of an old truck. It drives up and down the town's streets. Its presence is an assurance of civilization's continuity, and people act as if nearing it will bestow some gift. A fireman with a bullhorn older than the BMW barks out announcements. The town's water supply is off, but those that can are urged to bring containers to one of its wells where an aging gasoline engine is driving the pumps. Questions are shouted to the truck's occupants, but there are no answers. The driver and the bullhorn operator look exhausted and confused.

I secure the house and thump the side of a two thousand gallon fiberglass water tank that catches rainwater from the house gutters. Nearly full. The tank lid and valves are locked. One last check of the garage. It is two miles to City Hall. I open a small shed and wheel out my bicycle and pedal down Main Street. City Hall's doors are propped open. I carry the bicycle up the steps—I don't want it disappearing—and nod at the knot of people reading handwritten signs taped to the glass. Someone has been able to communicate with the state's Readiness Command. I'm guessing it's with a vacuum tube HAM radio set. Although electromagnetic pulse isn't mentioned, we are assured that, "Our nation's government is still functioning and is doing all it can to restore services."

Our nation's government? I am supposed to be relieved. Instead, I feel panic. Just how bad is the situation? Does it extend to Washington, D.C.? Clearly, I've thought about what will happen if things go to shit. It looks like I've not been too good at it. If I was a Syrian, or a Libyan, or maybe Cambodian, I'd have some genetic imprinting of man-made disasters, such as ethnic cleansing and such, and how to deal with them. As an American, I'm winging it. The whacko survivalists I've ignored all my adult life are starting to look not-so-whacko. So is Robert Heinlein. Great science fiction, but he didn't write 'how-to' manuals to deal with day-to-day challenges without starving, or dying of thirst, or getting murdered,

Obtaining my prepper stuff has been kind of fun. Beats the reality of my mundane existence. Maybe something'll happen and I'll "rise above" my mediocrity. Maybe even convince the ex that I've got some redeeming qualities that she's overlooked. Maybe not. I wipe that fantasy away with the sweat beading on my forehead.

So, what would happen if something 'happens?' Lots of chatter about it at the coffee shop, and I've enjoyed playing the devil's advocate with the seven or eight regulars. Most haven't seemed interested. The consensus has been that they're too old to care. Besides, 'we've all got guns, and we'll shoot the first (insert race or social status here) motherfuckers that try to come through the door.'

A young mother pushes through the crowd and into City Hall. She's been crying. "I've got a sick baby girl, and I need to get her to a hospital." The city administrator puts his arm around her, looking ashamed. I sense why. There's no one he can muster up than can help her or the child. He looks imploringly to the crowd as if to ask if there's someone who has transportation. There are hospitals twenty miles away. Some probably have emergency diesel generators. Some of those may actually be running and providing power.

An older man steps up and says something about an 'old pickup' to the administrator. Relieved, the young mother turns and follows him.

I'm relieved too. Relieved the old man has come to the child's rescue. I'm not prepared for dealing with this. If I'm going to get through this alive, I'm not about to be Mister Nice Guy. I don't need the burden of people asking for favors. I carry the bicycle down the steps and to the street.

Ten minutes later, I am in the house and away from imploring eyes seeking help.

Chapter Five

For the hardcore Bible thumpers, this last week has been a letdown. There's been no sign that God is coming. No one's seen the Four Horsemen or any other harbinger of doom. Nobody's died from radiation poisoning—at least not around here. No comet or meteor spotted that will guarantee a quick death and—if you believe that sort of stuff—a reckoning with the big guy in the sky.

Instead, life is grinding to a halt. I roam the house trying to envision different scenarios that'll require quick reactions. Break-ins. Fire. Those sorts of things. That leaves plenty of spare time to bicycle around the town. Mostly, I just watch. Lots of patched up two wheelers. Plenty of scroungers. Even more who like me, aren't interested in spending daytime hours in sweltering houses.

Garbage pickup doesn't occur. Rotting food is first loaded into Elmhurst's garbage bins and dragged to the street. Where it sits, stinking and drawing dogs, nocturnal varmints, and swarms of flies. The bins soon overload and garbage is set next to the bins. No garbage trucks are coming, but people try to get the stench away from their homes. Summer's scorching heat ensures this is unsuccessful.

South of town, a farmer with an ancient D4 Caterpillar tractor has cleaned out a dried-out earthen stock tank and is offering to bury any garbage. For a fee. The price is negotiable but he's not accepting paper money. Silver, gold, and food items can be exchanged. Take it or leave it. A few hardy folks use wheelbarrows and hand pulled carts to lug stuff out there. But not many. It's too damned hot. Personally, I think the goofy bastard needs to save the diesel in his farm tanks. Then again, he may not have anything he'll be able to use it with before the fuel starts going bad.

I spot little things. Trousers crudely cut into shorts. Shirts with dirty collars. We're all starting to look a little frayed. Kids of all ages sit in the shade of trees wondering what to do with themselves. With no video games and cell phones, the little fuckers look clueless.

I pedal across the north-south highway, locally dubbed Colorado Street, barely pausing to check for traffic. There isn't any. Weaving around the dropped arms of the non-functioning railroad crossing, and I'm literally on the "wrong side of the tracks." My side of town has a pretty reasonably representative mix of races. On this side of Elmhurst, all you see are poor folks of color, about fifty-fifty Hispanic and African-American. Even the trailer trash whites avoid the area, preferring the mobile home park on the Northside. Not so much because of crime, but because the housing is, well, poor.

There are some half-hearted waves and acknowledgments, as the bicycle winds back and forth through the narrow streets. Some folks I recognize. Mostly, the adults have staked out patches of shade and just stare. Funny. Well not "funny," but the poor kids on this side of town are adapting better than the richer ones in my neighborhood. Three of the kids climb a tree and nail boards across some limbs to construct a tree house. It hits me. Their parents couldn't afford expensive video games. The kids' imagination centers haven't been lobotomized.

A breeze carries a smoky whiff of cooking meats, which overwhelms for a moment, the stench of garbage. My mouth starts to salivate. Turning onto Apple Street, I see the reason. Ike Belton and Lupe Aguilar stand over an oil-drum barbeque pit. They look like two surgeons in the middle of open-heart surgery. Given their well-known cooking skills, the analogy isn't far off.

"Hey, Dalton. *Que pasa?*"

Braking, I turn the bike into Ike's driveway. "Nothing *pasa*, amigo." I gesture toward the pit. "Except this."

Ike chimes in. "Gotta get this meat cooked." A quick glance shows three briskets, their fat slowly rendering. He mops on some sort of sauce.

Several of the two friends' families walk up. No one seems especially glad that I'm staring at their supper. I shake hands with Ike and Lupe and turn back toward my bicycle. An afro-haired teenager is riding it down the street. The kid glances back to make sure I see him, and shoots me the bird. Got to be real careful here. Can't call after the little shit – not here and not now.

"Hey, I don't want to trouble you, but one of the kids took off with my bicycle."

Ike doesn't appear concerned. "One of my nephews. He'll come back. He's gotta eat." He walks around the side of the clapboard house and comes back with a can of beer. It's very cold. "Here. To cool you off while you wait."

He watches me think. *How in hell did this beer get iced down?*

With a grin he says, "I'll show you, bro." I follow him to a tub full of ice and beer cans. Ike points to a Reddi-Ice delivery truck backed under overgrown ligustrum. "Still cold inside.

Might as well use the ice while we got it." He pops the top, takes several swallows, and burps. "Damn. That's good."

I stare at the ice truck longingly. A few days since the EMP and all I've got left is warm Samuel Adams.

"Don't even think about it, bro. Lupe's got kin that worked for the company. Truck stopped dead over at the SacNPac." He gestures toward the highway. "You know how us blacks and browns are, bro. Lots of family. We pushed this beast over here. You might say we're "rationing a valuable commodity." He reaches down and hands me a beer.

"Thanks. Much appreciated." Beer never tasted this good.

The nephew rides up with a smirk on his face. About fifteen, his look challenges me with a look that says "You want a piece of me, white man? You're on my side of the tracks." He drops the bike on the ground and ambles over to the barbeque pit.

"Mmmm, Uncle Ike. Sho can't wait for a slice of that meat."

Ike doesn't even look at the boy. Instead, his right hand catches the teenager across the face, and he is sent sprawling over two lawn chairs.

Lupe helps the boy up, and then tries to straighten a collapsed armrest.

"Come here, nephew."

The little shit isn't looking so tough now.

"You apologize to this man." He gestures towards me. "Then you pick up his bicycle and set it against the fence."

Snot runs down the kid's face, and he does what he's told. Ike turns to me. "You finished with your beer?"

I nod and hand him the empty can. He hands it to Lupe and shakes my hand. "Best you be leaving now. That boy, there's plenty like him. No sense tempting fate, is there?" Ike's six feet and five inches tall. He's always spoken with a soft voice, letting his size imply any force necessary. Been that way since high school. He stands close to me. Too close. Lupe's off to one side, the goofus' head moving like a cheap bobble doll.

Ike doesn't expect an answer. He expects I'll leave his neighborhood. Now. I comply. If I cross the tracks again, I'll carry a gun.

Chapter Six

MY STOMACH'S STILL KNOTTED UP AS I RIDE PAST CITY HALL. THAT sorry motherfucker's intimidation is embarrassing. He was smooth. I'll give him that. But he made it clear I'm not welcome. I'm mad at myself. I've been predicting that the social order would change. It was inevitable. What did I expect? Hugs and kisses? I'm still pissed when I come up on Police Chief Larry Pettibone. On a horse, for God's sake.

"What the hey, Chief?"

Pettibone is narrow shouldered and heavyset. He's sweating like a mule pulling a plow. He's joined the coffee crowd on occasion, and hasn't been too pleased with my suggestions that law enforcement won't be able to deal with civil unrest in certain situations. Like this one.

"Hello, Mr. Kirby. I'm surprised you aren't packing a gun."

After what just happened across the tracks, I am too, but keep my counsel. "Where'd the horse come from?"

"Citizens have donated them. So we can patrol. Keep the peace."

I haven't heard of any seriously bad stuff. "It seems to be working, Chief."

"So far." He leaves it at that and shifts his pear-like body uncomfortably in the saddle. He's got a wife fighting cancer. He ought to be home doing what I'm doing. Taking care of Number One. I have to admire Pettibone for staying with the job. I wouldn't.

Pettibone sweeps a hand around, as if encompassing the town. "Looks like you made the right call."

I know.

"Dalton, how are you set up?"

Dalton? We're on a first name basis again? He's fishing for a favor. "I'm doing okay. Hanging in here like the rest of the town."

Pettibone knows I've done some prepping. "We're starting a citizen's police assistance force. Nothing real formal. Just some folks willing to walk their neighborhoods and make sure no one's house gets broken into. I'd take it as a personal favor if you'd help out."

"How many have taken you up on it, Chief?" I'm trying to act interested.

Pettibone mentions a number and some names. "We're going to divide the town up into patrol sectors. Nobody armed."

He loses me there. No way in hell I'm "patrolling" without a firearm. I shake my head. "Ike Belton one of your 'patrolmen?'"

Apparently not. "What'd Ike do?" Pettibone eyes close to slits.

"More like what he's doing right now." Remembering Ike's nephew sprawled ass over teakettle, I say, "Ike probably doesn't think he needs any patrolling. I'm betting he won't appreciate someone not from the 'hood walking any streets near where he lives."

"How do you know that?"

I'm not about to tell Pettibone how I know. "Something I sensed."

The Chief coughs, and spits phlegm into the asphalt. He winces and rubs his chest. "Just what I need. Someone staking out his own territory."

Uh huh. I wonder how many more "Ikes" there are doing the same. We live in a small town. My imagination suggests big cities are already going south. "What about the National Guard?"

That provokes a laugh. "Hell, the Weekend Warriors got families to take care of. Besides, what passes for government right now in the state capital and in Washington hasn't seen fit to give anyone specific orders on what they're supposed to be protecting. You haven't seen any around here, have you?"

No, no one's spotted any military of any kind. "Aren't you getting any information from anyone in government?"

Pettibone groans, checks to ensure his foot's in the stirrup, and dismounts. I take the horses' reins and walk it over to the shade of a large live oak that borders the back of City Hall. The Chief acts like he just got off a fishing trawler, swaying as he follows.

"We're getting reports, Dalton. Anson Gutierrez rigged up car batteries and an old tube HAM radio. Lots of atmospheric skips, but basically, whatever happened here has happened over quite a bit of the country." Pettibone removes his Stetson. "Honestly, I don't know who's in charge. We're getting bits and pieces of rioting in some cities. I'm surprised we haven't seen people coming this way from Lincoln City. Some stuff from HAMS—nasty confrontations with the police. Shelters running out of food."

"The governor's office is asking for calm. Promising Washington is on top of things. I don't know who's in charge either, but have no doubt it's going to get a whole lot worse."

Promising to think about his offer, I pedal off.

Jill is in her backyard, gloves on, grubbing holes in the sunbaked earth. She looks up, waves, and continues attacking the soil. Sweat stains soak her t-shirt. No bra. *Jesus Christ. The woman's magnificent.*

"Hey, Dalton."

I'm halfway in the back door when Jill walks toward the fence and motions me over. Any hope that she's interested in my charm is quickly put to rest. "Fred and I need a favor."

It's obvious she's not enjoying asking me for a favor. "Sure, Jill. Anything." Not really anything, but I'll listen.

"We wonder if we could get some water from you." She motions toward my 1500 gallon rain trapment tank. "The line's an hour long for a five gallon jug refill at the city facility. With this heat, there have been some fights. As you can see," she uses a gloved hand to sweep across her t-shirt and shorts, "We're getting pretty rank. Can you spare some?"

I knew this was going to happen. Inwardly grimacing, I ask, "How much do you two need right now?" My fiberglass tank is full, but it hasn't rained in two weeks, and we're in the dog days of summer.

Jill lifts the t-shirt slightly and uses it as a fan. She laughs. "How much do I need to take a long shower?"

My eyes are no longer on her face. Damn, woman. A screen door slaps shut, and Fred appears.

"Will twenty gallons keep you guys for a while?" I have no idea what the two want. Fred hears my offer. If he was a dog, his tail would be going crazy right now.

"Thanks, Dalton. It's really appreciated."

That's Fred. There's a small smirk of triumph on Jill's face as she turns back toward her garden. First Ike, now Jill.

Everyone seems to be honing their survival skills.

Chapter Seven

TWO DAYS LATER, A TRICKLE OF BEDRAGGLED HUMANITY BEGINS TO show. It's noticeable by the haggard faces not seen before in Elmhurst. First, a few houses have additional occupants, as families take in members. Most come from the state capital, Lincoln City, thirty-five miles up the highway. Lines grow longer at the City's water point. More fights erupt as the heat and uncertainty begin eating on nerves.

By the end of the week, the trickle grows into a steady stream. Many of the new arrivals are without a local contact. Tents sprout in the City Park and cemetery. Pettibone's officers make no effort to push people out. From the desperate looks, it wouldn't do any good if they tried – any attempt will be met with resistance.

I wake up Friday morning and spot a tent being erected in the large lot behind my house. I have to decide which battles to fight. It's behind the garage and other outbuildings, but too close for comfort. Its occupants appear to be a mother and father and two small children.

The 9mm goes in my belt behind my back as I close the back door. "Howdy."

The heavily tatted, father—I assume he's the kids' father—reaches into the tent. I pull my 9mm and hold it to my side. "Whoa. If you're going for a weapon, don't."

The man steps away and I peek inside the fabric door. A hand-made club rests on a sleeping bag. Reaching in, I grab the clumsy object and toss it aside.

"Name?"

"Josh," he says.

"Josh who?"

"Josh Cerveny." Cerveny is red headed and built like a weightlifter. I surmise he can handle himself. A defeated look passes over him. "I'm just looking for some shade and a place for my wife and kids."

When I don't say anything, he introduces them. The woman looks older than Cerveny, but it may be she's just worn down. The two children, a boy and a girl, hide behind their mother.

"Where're you from, and why're you in my back yard?"

Before Josh can answer, the woman begins to cry. "We're about give out, mister. We're close to out of food. Please..." She lets her eyes finish the plea.

"How'd you get here? Walk?"

Josh nods and points to a gardener's wagon with inflatable tires. "Pulled the kids and what little else we could take in that thing."

"Are things that bad?" Referring to Lincoln City.

Rather than answer, the woman introduces herself simply. "I'm Elsie, Josh's wife." She calls to the children, who huddle behind her. Elsie introduces them as David and Sarah, and tells me they are six and five, respectively. The two extend hands to be shaken. I'm taken by their maturity. Shyly, they retreat. I'm not an immediate threat so they wander off.

After David and Sarah leave, Elsie nods. "We were renting a mobile home on the south side near the Interstate. Things are…" Again, she lets her eyes finish the sentence. An annoying habit, but it's effective.

The best course of action is to kick these trespassers off the property. With the numbers drifting into Elmhurst, that may just be postponing the inevitable. "What'd you do for a living, Josh?"

"Welder."

"Any criminal record?"

"One DWI five years ago. Been clean and sober since."

He could be lying. There's no way to tell. He looks like he's not. He just looks desperate. I make a snap decision.

"Tell you what, Josh Cerveny. You and your family are welcome here on my property. But here are the conditions." Cerveny doesn't hesitate to agree when I list them.

Ike, Jill, and now me. We're all just making adjustments to our new living situation.

The Cerveny kids wave at me as I pedal toward town. Their dad is busy unbolting a manhole cover on my property's side street. With no running water for a functioning sewer system, the system's pipe is still better than a slit trench. Maybe a rain will sluice some of the waste at least partly away. He's stacked old plywood and two-by-fours for an outhouse that will sit in the middle of the street. That's one of my conditions. He turns and nods as I point toward the house. He understands it's his responsibility to make sure no one breaks into it or steals anything from my property. That's another condition.

Pedaling up the highway to the edge of Elmhurst, several locals are watching a thin line of humanity moving south from Lincoln City. Sam Nelson, a truck driver who raises 'free range' chickens on the side, spots me. "Dalton, we're fixing to get overrun with people from the big city. What the hell are we going to do about it?"

Short of starting an armed militia, there doesn't seem much that anyone can do, and I tell Sam that. It's not the answer he's looking for. Sam's not the sharpest knife in the drawer, but he's got a point. Some of the men in the group nod, and there's muttering about it. Sam doesn't have enough leadership skills to lead anything, but someone will eventually take that role. Just not me.

I head back toward City Hall. An *ahoogah* sounds. George Hixson rolls down the street in a 1917 Ford Model T truck. He grins like a shit-eating possum as he squeezes the rubber bulb.

Ahoogah.

I stop and he pulls over. "I knew I'd have a reason to hang onto this beauty." George slaps the small driver's side door and blows a kiss toward the antique's hood. "Hot damn, Dalton. I've got the road to myself."

George is a right wing nut case. He's collected several old vehicles. He dislikes Elmhurst and is showing off. He is inordinately pleased with himself.

I decide to take him down a notch. "George, you see all these people?" I motion toward bicycle riders and people on foot. "You keep *ahoogahing* and they're going to shove this buggy's tail pipe up your ass."

George acts surprised. He's highly intelligent so I don't buy it. "Get this off the streets, go home, and take care of your wife and livestock. Oh, that's right. Your wife had enough of your crackpot politics and left you awhile back, didn't she?"

"Pot calling the kettle black, Dalton. Least mine left because of my politics. Yours. She decided to find someone with a dick bigger than a pinkie finger. You always were an asshole. Just for that, I'm not going to offer you a ride home."

Ahoogah. He knows I wouldn't take him up on the offer

anyway. The Model T makes a quick turn. George shoots me the bird and heads back toward his small ranch.

I've rained on his parade. Fuck him. I've done him a favor. The less people know about your mobility, the better. His showing off will attract predators and may get him killed.

At City Hall, my ex-brother-in-law Billy Kaufman is reading taped up notices. Hoping he won't notice, I pull my baseball cap down lower and pedal faster. No luck.

"Dalton! Hey, Dalton! I see you! Need to talk to you!"

Shit.

I brake and turn back. "What's up, Billy?"

Billy glances at the people nearby and points with his head toward a pecan tree that offers shade and privacy. As I walk the bike over, he limps after me. Billy almost lost a leg in a motorcycle accident in his early twenties, and has been on disability ever since. "We need your help, Dalton."

"Who's *we*?"

The family he tells me. Is he kidding? The Kaufmans collectively have made it clear they've no use for me since Gail and I split up, and I tell him that.

"Momma and Daddy, they're as stove up as I am." He points to his gimp leg. "We got enough food for right now, but the three of us don't exactly get around."

True. My former mother- and father-in-law are up in age and suffer from arthritis. Still, there's no way they'd ask me for any assistance. They've got a large garden and larger pride.

Billy grabs me by the upper arm. "Dalton. It isn't Momma and Daddy that need you. Gail's in Lincoln City. She's sick, and we need someone to go get her out of that place."

"Sick with what? Meanness?"

Billy looks down at the ground, red faced.

"Sorry, I apologize." Billy's a gentle soul and doesn't need to hear me badmouth his sister "What kind of sickness, Billy?" The question comes out with great reluctance, because I don't want to know any more about Gail, her illness, or anything that takes me away from getting through the next days, weeks and months here in Elmhurst.

"She sent a note. Said she's trying to get back from Lincoln City. Says her condition keeps her from getting here."

I stare down Main Street. Gail is tough. Tougher than most of the people straggling into Elmhurst. There's no way she couldn't walk the thirty-five miles. I tell Billy that.

He shakes his head 'no.'

"She told someone that was leaving that she wasn't able to get out of the city. That she'd been too sick. Said she'd get down here in a week after she got better. Then, we get this." He holds out a note.

I recoil like it's a rattlesnake, and he pushes it into my hand. Written on notebook paper, Gail's handwriting reaches toward me like an accusatory finger.

Chapter Eight

BILLY STANDS THERE LIKE THE BIG OAF HE IS. HE'S EXPECTING AN answer from me, but he's not going to get one. Not now. Not ever. I hand the letter back to him and he refuses to take it.

"It's for you, Dalton. She wanted me to give it to you."

I have trouble with this concept. "You know where I live. Why didn't you just walk over there if that was the case. You don't seem to be in too much of a hurry to help your sister when I see you staring at notices on the bulletin board."

Billy pushes my hand away. "I did go by your place. Just now. You weren't there. Some guy with lotsa tattoos ran me off. Said he was protecting your place from troublemakers and told me to get away from there." Billy can't be making this up. He looks down at his feet, still refusing the crumpled note. Reminds me of something out of an old movie, *A Christmas Carol*, where the ghost is pointing accusingly at Scrooge.

I've got some choices. I can walk away, but knowing Billy, he'll make a scene. Not by being an asshole but by being pitiful. In front of a lot of people. Or, I can take the damned letter. If I take it, he's gonna make me promise to read it. No. He's going to make me do something about its contents. I choose the lesser of the two evils, which I think will turn out to be the worst decision I'll make. I know I'm going to regret it.

"I'll read it, Billy."

As expected, that's not sufficient. "You gotta promise you'll help Gail out, Dalton." Fucking puppy dog eyes. Some hangers-on have drifted near our conversation. Billy could have been a good car salesman. He gives me that hang dog, 'I'm so pitiful you have to love me and help me' look. Three people, all locals, hear his plea and look to me expectantly. What is this? A goddamned Greek chorus?

I need to get out of here. And now. "I promise, Billy. I'll see what I can do for your sister."

Satisfied, Billy's ad hoc supporting cast nods in unison and drifts off. I stuff the paper in a pocket and turn away. Billy has one more arrow in his quiver.

His eyes tear up. "Thanks. Dalton, I never had any bad feelings toward you. You're the only brother-in-law I ever had. Thanks." He grabs my right hand with his and shakes it. Hard. He's seals the deal with a handshake. As far as Billy is concerned, the handshake carries the weight of a Biblical covenant.

Sweet Jesus.

The ten-speed bicycle seems to have a mind of its own. Elmhurst's small downtown area centers on the Lee County Courthouse, a late nineteenth century monstrosity of mansards, oval windows and a clock tower. The clock's bell chimes. Startled, I glance up, and then remember. It's an old pendulum mechanism. As long as someone remembers to reset the weights, the clock will run forever. The three bongs of the afternoon's time are a distraction from the letter in my pocket. Three o'clock? Normally, I'd be interested. Time to go to the bank?

Time for a beer? An appointment at that time with the doctor? Now, it only confirms there are several more hours of scorching sunlight.

The letter crackles as my legs pump the pedals. Most of the businesses on the town square are closed up tight. A lawyer on the west side covered her large glass windows with plywood. Yeah, like anyone in their right mind is going to break *into* a lawyer's office. Tents dot the lawn around the Lee County Courthouse. Someone owns a cassette deck and its tinny speakers blare out Rolling Stone's *Satisfaction*. Families huddle under the pecan trees. A couple of long haired punks still have the energy to skateboard on the wide streets. I'm starting to think hard about caloric intake, and wonder what any of us will do without enough of it.

I've got someone watching my property, and don't want to deal with Gail's letter. Staying away for the rest of the afternoon is a no-brainer. One of Pettibone's officers rides on a bicycle down Commerce Street. I recognize Andres Lujan, a local boy who has had plenty of opportunities, pre-EMP, to work with a big city police department at three times the salary Elmhurst pays, but doesn't for some reason.

He brakes and waves. "Hey, Dalton."

"No protective vest?"

His shirt is soaked. "I'll chance a bullet before wearing that damned thing in this heat." He nods toward the South. "You been by the FoodMart?"

Not since a week ago, figuring it to be a madhouse. "How bad is it?" I guess the worst.

Lujan surprises me, and looks surprised himself. "Amazing so far, Dalton. Managers took it upon themselves to set up a rationing system for canned goods. Not charging folks anything. Let about ten people in the store at one time. Escort them around to make sure they're playing by the rules, and escort them out. Almost all the food's gone now. Gotta give

Chief Pettibone credit. He got the managers to lock up all the beer and wine in the reefer. Padlocked it."

"What about the liquor stores?" There are two in town, and several elsewhere in the county.

Lujan shrugs. "Don't know about the county." He snorts disparagingly. "Our illustrious sheriff couldn't find his ass with both hands, so I doubt his people have done anything about it outside the town limits. But here..." He points down past the grocery store parking lot toward a ramshackle building with *The Liquor Store* painted over the entrance. At first glance, the establishment appears shut. Without electricity, *every* store looks shut. A closer look and I spy a heavy-set black male in his seventies. Lemuel Wilkins, the owner, as he escorts a woman carrying a bottle out of the store.

"What the hell's he packing?" I point toward a gun belt and holster drooping below the man's gut. "That's too big for a pistol."

Lujan nods. "Sawed off shotgun. If the old rascal has to shoot someone, it's anyone's guess as to whether he'll die from the recoil."

Lemuel motions in a young black male, glancing around to ensure no one's sneaking up on him, and closes and locks the glass door. No way the kid's over twenty-one.

"What's he trading booze for?"

Lujan shrugs. "I'm hearing it's jewelry, food, stuff like that. Lemuel's not taking any cash money. Says he's not sure he'll ever be able to use it."

Lemuel may not have much of an imagination when it comes to naming his business, but Lemuel is a smart man.

Chapter Nine

THE SUN'S SETTING AS I PEDAL BACK WEST TOWARD MY PROPERTY.
The Cerveny family gathers around a small propane stove. Elsie
stirs a powder into a small pot. The two kids hardly look up
when I ride by. The mid-street outhouse is impressive looking.
Josh Cerveny catches me as I wheel the bike into the side door
of the garage.

"Can I visit with you for a second?"

I secure the door's lock. "Sure."

"Don't want to be a burden, but we need some water. Not
much, but with no rain, we've run out." He nods toward my
tank. "I tapped on that thing. Sounds nearly full. Appreciate it
if you'd allot some of the water. To your worker."

Damn. Water's precious. But, so's someone willing to help
protect the place. "Sure. Let's work something out. Since you're
watching the place, I'll let you all draw out ten gallons a day."

Josh Cerveny smiles grimly. "Thanks." Acting like he's entitled already.

"Unless we get some rain, the tank's going to drop in a
hurry." I hand him the keys. "We get some rain, I'll be willing to
adjust. Right now, though…Think accordingly. No bathing. No

donating any of the water to anyone." I think of Jill. Josh is a family man, but he's not blind. He'll react to her like I do. "Anyone."

He laughs and motions to the adjacent property. Yep, he's seen her.

Sweat-stained, Gail's letter is still legible. I pop the cap on a bottle of Sam Adams. It hasn't fared well in the heat, and the hoppy brew spews out onto the patio table. I jam the bottle into my mouth – can't waste the precious liquid.

Gail's missive is short and to the point. "Dalton: I'm not in any condition to get out of Lincoln City on my own. I thought I'd have the strength to do it. I tried. It didn't work. There's no one here I trust to help me. You know Momma and Daddy and their situation. Billy's first responsibility is to them. I doubt if you'll honor this request, but I'd appreciate it if you could at least try to give this information some attention. The part of town I'm in will probably turn into a hellhole pretty quickly." It's signed "Gail." No "sincerely." No "truly yours." No "your loving ex-wife." Nada.

I'm not feeling the least bit interested in doing anything for Gail. So far, things are going my way here in Elmhurst. I don't need someone else's issues to get in the way. Especially Gail's. When we split the sheets, there wasn't anyone with any sense who dared mention her name around me. No doubt, the feeling was reciprocal. After the final court hearing, my lawyer made sure we left the Lee County Courthouse by separate doors. That was mainly for *my* protection. The witch has red hair and an evil temper.

Billy said Gail was sick. The letter says nothing about an illness. Also, nothing about her 'condition.' I want to pick up a telephone and ask her, "Hey, what's the trouble? Cancer?

Chickenpox? Herpes?" I'm left to wonder. At the same time, no way would Gail ask a favor from me unless there was absolutely no one else she could ask, including the devil himself.

I'm settling in here in Elmhurst. Granted, the local food bank is depleted. There have been a few break-ins. The 'Ikes' are trying to set up territories. Nonetheless, Elmhurst is still relatively peaceful. My neighbors are still civil with each other. There haven't been shootings. No looting to speak of.

So, what do I do? I pull out a bottle of Herradura tequila and work on it for about three hours. Then fall into a restless stupor. Four hours later, I'm awake with the grand ayatollah of headaches and a heart pounding like a trip hammer. I'm on the back side of drunk and the front side of a vicious hangover. Dammit. No hint of dawn so I have several hours to ride out the darkness of the soul that goes with the boozing. I'm draped over the recliner and have to piss. I pee in the yard. My smug attitude toward hoodwinking the ex has been scraped off by the booze's poison in my system. Gail refused to give an inch in our relationship. With the tequila, there's no doubt of her culpability. With the ensuing hangover, my share of the blame rears its ugly head.

The night's heat is oppressive. I'm having no luck shaking off the bad memories. The full moon's glow displays a contrasting collection caused by the town's houses. Eerily calm. It belies the reality of our life since the EMP. For a few minutes, I choose to believe the moonlight's reality. Who am I kidding? Each dark structure holds lives struggling to overcome a situation no one really anticipated. Hell, if I'm honest, I'll admit getting 'ready' was a fun way for me to show I'm smarter than the average Joe. I go inside, drink three glasses of filtered water, and lie back down. I drift off, then jerk awake. I try again, and again, sleep is interrupted by an undefined darkness that leaves me panting and afraid.

Head throbbing, I surrender, and fire up a propane camp

stove. Adding coffee crystals to the boiling water, I ponder Gail's letter. Damn her. After eleven years of marriage, her presence haunts me. A dim glow on the horizon tells me it's an hour until dawn.

After turning off the propane valve, water stays hot enough for two strong cups of coffee. Not perked or dripped. Just the crystal stuff. Sugar spooned in from an airtight rubber container makes the stuff drinkable.

Light streams in the porch windows. Somehow, I managed to find sleep. Someone pounds on the back door. Where in hell is Josh to warn this obnoxious fucker away?

"Dalton, it's Chief Pettibone. Come on out. I need to talk with you."

What the fuck? My head throbs. My sweat smells rancid. I want to be left alone. Rolling over, I yell, "Go away. I need my sleep."

The pounding on the backdoor continues. "Get up, Dalton. I need to talk with you."

The bastard is persistent. One part of my mind gives me permission to shoot him between the eyes. The other part overrules it, at the same time pushing me toward consciousness.

"Goddammit! Leave me the fuck alone!"

My back door continues to rattle with the strokes of a fist. Where is my new watchman, Josh?

"Cerveny! Get rid of whoever's bothering me, dammit."

Cerveny's voice filters through my throbbing head. "I'm here, but this fellow says he's the town police chief and wants to see you."

I give up on sleep and angrily push away from my recliner. Pulling on a pair of worn-out shorts, I stumble out the back door. Curse words get caught in my throat. Pettibone looks at me. As do a dozen or more citizens of Elmhurst who are part of the new 'citizens patrol.'

My body can't take another avoidance session with the booze. Responsibility is staring me in the face. "Get the hell off my property!"

No one moves, and I scream the invective-ladened threat again.

Finally, Pettibone speaks. "I wasn't kidding, Dalton. We need you to help us keep order."

I don't respond because my head feels like it is about to explode with pain. Pettibone takes the pause in the tirade as an indication that I'm interested in what he has to say. "Lincoln City's troubles are coming this way. Two different groups showed up during the night. Said there're fires burning. Some areas, street gangs of various colors, cholos, Crips wannabes, peckerwoods, have had running gun battles with the cops."

Elmhurst isn't Lincoln City. This doesn't concern me. I turn to go inside.

"During the night, we had two houses burn down in Las Brisas." It's a new subdivision of what realtors call starter homes. "Kids inside and one died. The other, the owner spotted who threw the Molotov cocktail and took a shot." He shakes his head. "Only problem is whoever threw the Molotov cocktail wasn't the one he killed. The neighbor kid was just watching the fire. Homeowner's white. Kid he shot's black. We've got the white guy locked up in the basement of City Hall. Otherwise, they were going to lynch him."

This is way more information that I need. "Get off my property, Pettibone." The demand seems weak, even to me.

Pettibone turns away in disgust. "I told you people this self-centered bastard wouldn't help." It's said more for my benefit than the group he's brought with him.

I slam the door, and then come back out. "Chief!"

Pettibone's almost to the curb. He turns. "What?"

"I've got something I have to take care of first. Then I'll think about it."

I've got something I have to take care of first? Where in hell did that come from?

Cerveny looks confused. Rather than try to explain, I growl at him and he gratefully retreats. I'm left with my thoughts. No doubt, aspirin will become as precious as gold. I've got to clear my mind so dry swallow six 350 mg tablets, at the same time wondering how much one will be valued at in a few months.

The sun brings wet heat but no hint of rain. With no water hoses or sprinkler systems to alleviate the summer drought, the subtle hues of greenery and lawns are quickly changing to harsher distinctions. Grayish brown means plants are dead. Lighter browns and beiges mean grass and shrubberies are merely dying.

Years before, an old country church was torn down on the east side of Lee County. Inside were hundreds of leftover cardboard fans. Gail bought a dozen at a silent auction as novelty pieces and set them around the patio, more for conversation pieces than anything else. There certainly was no need from them with three ceiling fans and a water mister, and I told her so. The funeral home advertising "low cost funerals and Godly attention during your time of bereavement" was good for a laugh. How poor did you have to be to have a church without air conditioning? Now, I grasp one's wooden handle, vigorously moving the sodden air, and appreciate the sturdiness of the fan's cardboard and staples.

As the sweat pours off, almost involuntarily I put structure to the statement I shouted at Pettibone. *Something I have to take care of.* Not sure just what that something is, at least a partial decision is made. Gail's parents, Randall and Bertha Kaufman, own a hundred acres three miles northeast of Elmhurst. By midday, I decide I'm in good enough shape, so I load a small backpack with two plastic canteens of water and my 9 mm. The pistol's added weight won't slow me down on the short bicycle ride to the Kaufman property and it gives me a small sense of security. To get to the Kaufman's I'll cross the railroad tracks again. Not near Ike's house, but still. There are bound to be others like him out there. Within hours, news of the killing of a black kid by a white man will spread all over Elmhurst. I am already imagining a different route back home from the Kaufman's.

Cerveny and his family doze in the shade. Some tattered schoolbooks lay outside the family's tent. I contemplate telling Cerveny when I'll be back but decide to leave him alone. I won't be gone long. I avoid Main Street and City Hall and soon follow a county road's centerline out of town. Many vehicles in this area were junked long before the EMP. Seems as if every yard has at least one truck up on cinder blocks. Soon, I surmise, every pickup and car will rust in place or be cannibalized for useful parts. Radiator hoses, wheels and tires, axles. As I ride by, I play a game of guessing various things that can be fabricated from piston-driven lawn ornaments.

The Pederson Road, maintained, sort of, by the county, drops down out of the northeast side of Elmhurst into the bottomland created by Little Elm River. The timbers in the antiquated iron bridge, load limited because of its light construction, jostle me as I cross. Remembering childhood fun, I let out a loud "uhhhh" enjoying the ululation caused by the rough passage over the timbers. A mile past the river, I turn into the Kaufman property.

The Kaufman's house dates from the early twentieth century and was built by Randall's great grandfather who emigrated from Germany. Proud of his heritage, the hard-headed Dutchman always kept it in good repair. The white paint looked fresh last time I was here. That was almost two years ago. When we were still talking. The house's condition has deteriorated. Randall sits on a glider, a shotgun across his lap. Several laying hens with their chicks peck at insects in the dusty yard. Dismounting, I halloo the house. Randall's killed hundreds of dove and quail with a shotgun. They're smaller and harder to hit than I am, and I'm not sure how I'll be received.

The back porch screen door slaps shut as Bertha waves at me. So far, so good. Randall heaves himself out of the glider. I can see why the place has gone down. Gail's father can barely walk. Setting the shotgun down, he grabs a cane and waves it toward the house. I'm two for two. I lean the bicycle against a tree stump that serves as the base for a purple marten bird house mast and give Bertha a hug. Gail gets her red hair from her mother. Her nasty temper, that's purely Randall's contribution.

Randall shakes my hand. "Good to see you, s-" He almost says "son." On the other hand, it could be "son of a bitch." He's called me both.

I try to make a joke. "Hope the shotgun wasn't anticipating my visit."

"No," Randall replies. "People have been coming on the place. A calf went missing two days ago. Bet it's been butchered. People running out of food. Seem to think it gives them the right to steal from us." His face is livid. "These birds. Once they're gone, there'll be no eggs. I'll shoot any bastard I see anywhere near this place."

Bertha pats him on the shoulder. "It's too hot to talk out here. Let's get under cover." She takes my hand and the three of us walk up the stairs and into the screened porch. Soon, I'm drinking a cool glass of water. Seeing my quizzical look, Bertha reminds me of the house's old cistern. "Dalton, it's a godsend in this weather and with no electricity. We took the cover off it.

You remember, it'd been covered for years. Husband – she refers to Randall as Husband – he's replaced the old ropes and oiled the pulleys. We're using it to keep things cool. Water and food. Husband's got our cheeses and some dried meats down there. What do you think?"

I remember removing the wooden cover and feeling the earthy smell and damp cool air. "I think it works well." The water is delicious.

I used to call Bertha 'Momma B.' Not anymore. Just 'Bertha.' She's sugar and spice and all that but with a tempered steel core. I hand her the empty glass. The two look at me for several seconds. Bertha's countenance remains calm. Randall suddenly tears up.

"You read the note Billy gave you?"

I nod but say nothing.

"We haven't seen our daughter in a month or so. Said she was too busy at work. Legislature's in session. Or was." Randall shakes his head, and I notice a slight palsy in his left hand. I wonder if the old man's got Parkinson's disease.

Gail's worked for the state government since before we married. When we separated, she moved up to Lincoln City 'to be closer to work.'

Bertha puts a hand over Randall's. "We need you to get her. We can't go, what with Husband not feeling all that good. Billy, well, Billy's got a heart of gold, but he's needed here." What she leaves unsaid is that Billy doesn't have it in him to hurt someone if necessary. Clearly, the couple is sure I can. I guess that's a compliment of sorts.

A slight breeze wafts through the screen. The chickens have moved to the shade and I can hear them rustling in the bushes next to the house. "What's wrong with Gail? What keeps her from leaving the capital and coming home? There are plenty of folks walking in from Lincoln City."

Bertha lowers her gaze and takes a deep breath. "She's pregnant."

Time stands still. Pregnant? We tried for years to have children. Tests showed I was the problem. Low sperm count. By the time we figured out the problem, Gail wasn't the least bit interested in bearing any child containing any DNA from me. "How far along is she?"

Gail is Randall's favorite child. His voice quavers. "She's due in a month."

"Who's the father?" A father has responsibilities, dammit. Why would Gail be stuck in Lincoln City asking help from her detested ex-husband instead of the father's child?

Randall seems unable to speak. In fact, he looks like he's going to stroke out. Bertha clears her throat. "Dalton, she says the baby's yours."

What the fuck! I am too stunned to say anything. I think back. When in recent history had Gail and I even wanted to have sex? I stare at Bertha. "There's no way in hell that's my baby, Bertha."

Randall seems relieved by my denial. He's glad to hear his grandchild isn't the fruit of my loins, biblically speaking. I stand up, too quickly, and plop back down as I start to black out. This little session has gotten too weird. The old couple just sits. And stares into space. I have a million questions, but mostly, I want to get back on the bicycle and speed the hell away.

After an eternity, Bertha leans forward. "Dalton. Listen to me. You think my daughter *wants* you to be the one she's asking for help? After what you put her through?"

Bertha suffers from selective amnesia when it comes to Gail's and my relationship. Her she-cat daughter gave better than she took. No doubt, Gail made it clear why she never got pregnant by me.

I start to repeat myself. Bertha interrupts. "Dalton, you

always were a shit ass. But you were Gail's husband, so we chose to love you. My daughter is pregnant. Very much so. She didn't want you to even know the child was yours. Wants to raise the child without you in her life. So you tell me. Why would she lie about this? Tell me you two didn't get drunk one night." She mentions the name of a mutual friend. "You got drunk and apologized to Gail for how you'd acted. She felt sorry for you. You two went to bed."

In poker, it's called a 'tell.' My face is a tell. Bertha sees it. Uh oh. Something *did* happen that night, but I chose to forget it.

It's the first time I've heard Bertha use dirty language. She's calling me a shit ass and now wants me to rescue her daughter? "Surely there are people in Lincoln City who can help Gail."

"She's bedridden."

Obviously, medical facilities are, or were, better in Lincoln City than anything Elmhurst has. Her physicians are in the capital. Gail has friends—and quite a few—in Lincoln City. Sweet Jesus, there are a hundred reasons she shouldn't try to relocate now.

I know I will regret it but ask how to get to the apartment where Gail is staying.

Chapter Ten

PEDALING AWAY FROM THE KAUFMAN PLACE, I DON'T PAY MUCH
attention to my surroundings.

Thwack!

A rock smacks into my backpack. I hear a string of curse
words. "Asshole. Pussy. Shitface."

Well, shit!

The voices sound like children. I know many of the adults
living here. We attended the same schools. To them, child disci-
pline is a swat across the butt with a belt. No kid would get
away with this kind of behavior in normal times. Maybe folks
are starting to give up. Or it's just too hot to care. Or both.

Without turning around or slowing, I extend a middle
finger.

It's dusk by the time I get home, but no one is in the Cerveny's camping area. After locking up the bicycle, I grab a flashlight, pen, and paper out of my kitchen and head back outside
to sit on the patio. It's thirty some odd miles to the state capital.
A day and a half of hard hiking. A long day on a bicycle.
Neither make sense now. A pregnant woman isn't going to be

up for either. The list of items I think I may need to get Gail safely to Lee County grows.

On the motorcycle with no traffic, it could be a quick up and back. I calculate no more than two hours—tops. Except I'm not assuming it's going to be that easy. I unlock the garage and shine the light over the BMW. Will a pregnant woman even fit in the contraption's sidecar? If not, she'll have to hang on and ride bitch. I look at the bike's narrow seat. As pregnant as she is, I wonder whether Gail can even manage this.

I secure the garage door and return to my list. The sidecar can hold at least two hundred pounds of equipment, if it's properly packed. My backpack can hold another thirty to forty. With a full pack and holstered firearm, the ride won't be comfortable, but not impossible. Most important will be water, food, and weapons. My mind begins to roil with possible scenarios that might require more than those three basics. There's enough gasoline in the fuel tank for about one hundred and fifty miles.

I'm not going to be worth a damn to anyone unless I get some sleep, so I grab a sheet and collapse in the patio hammock. Bug spray keeps the mosquitoes off, but doesn't do anything about their persistent buzzing. After three hours, I decide to begin stowing gear. Opening the large garage door doesn't help with the darkness, but at least there is an occasional breath of air. I light a propane lantern and hang it on a bent wire extending from a rafter. I hope no one passes by to see what is going on. It's a chance I'll take.

The three-gallon plastic gasoline container fits— barely— into the leg area of the sidecar. A small soft sided tool kit goes in next. Two gallons of water in old milk jugs follow, duct taped shut and cradled in a blanket that might come in handy later.

Upstairs in the office, the AR15 with two magazines and an additional one hundred rounds seem as if they'll slide in nicely.

What next? I recheck the list. Food. In the dining room, six MREs, a couple of small bags of trail mix, two cans of tuna and some jerky fit into a cloth shopping bag. This seems like a lot of shit to be toting for a quick trip, but I'm not taking any chances.

Well, actually, I'm taking a lot of goddamned chances just going into Lincoln City. Especially with a motorcycle loaded with food and supplies. I can't shoot and drive a motorcycle. If I have to stop, I'll be a sitting duck to anyone fast enough to rush the bike before I can step off and defend myself.

And for what? I'm supposedly saving a pregnant woman who's carrying my child, even if that's an impossibility. I carefully lug everything to the garage. After an hour of adjusting and rearranging, the side car is full and secured with bungee cords. I close the large garage door, unhook the lantern, and walk into the relative coolness of the open air.

"Boss."

"Shit!"

"Sorry. Saw the light."

It's Josh Cerveny.

"Son of a bitch! You scared hell out of me." I'm angry with myself for letting him walk up on me.

"You all right?"

What do I tell him? That I'm going for a little *pasear*? I don't have any doubt he's seen the motorcycle. Time for another snap decision. "C'mere." I motion him inside the garage side door. I don't bother with the lantern, instead turning on a flashlight. "This is a 1965 BMW."

Cerveny's eyes open wider. "No kidding. It's a classic."

"What? You know motorcycles?"

"Harleys mostly, but I know what a boxer looks like. I've actually worked on them."

I look at him quizzically.

"In a prior life." He offers no further explanation.

He's pointing to the butt of the AR15. "Where're you going?"

I'm not going to explain the weirdness of a pregnant woman carrying a child that's supposed to be mine but surely isn't. "I've got to make a run into Lincoln City. Just being prepared."

"When are you going?"

"Trying to decide." Is it better in the daylight, or do I chance a night ride? Neither choice sounds good.

Josh asks what part of town I'm headed to. I tell him.

"You bringing someone back?" He nods at the sidecar.

"Yes. Someone who can't walk to Elmhurst. Because of a—I pause—medical condition."

It turns out that Josh Cerveny is familiar with the area of Lincoln City where Gail's apartment is. We sit on the patio. As the pre-dawn begins to glow, we hash back and forth the best way to dash in and out of a city with unknown dangers.

"You talked with your police chief?"

Josh saw my drunken interaction with Chief Pettibone. "Um, no. Not lately."

He laughs and I admit the question does evoke a bit of humor. "I'll swallow my pride and ask him what he knows."

"Good luck with that."

"Fuck you."

Josh laughs again, and a part of me starts to trust him a bit more. He's taking a chance ribbing me like that. He's got a pair, which I admire. The dawn brightens, and we shake hands. I decide to leave during the daylight, but first I need some sleep.

———

I'm soaked to the skin. After falling asleep on the patio, a rain came. With it, wind. Which blew the moisture in on the hammock. I strip naked, grab a bar of soap, lathering quickly. A cement birdbath fills with water, and I quickly use its rough surfaces to scrub off some of the filth on my skivvies and shorts.

The sun breaks through the clouds as I hang the wet clothing on a rusty steel clothesline I rigged up years ago. Until now, it's mostly been used for airing out blankets and sleeping bags, and for hanging bird feeders. Funny how the little things I've ignored are becoming so important.

Naked except for sandals, I walk into the darkened house. Too impatient to let my eyes adjust to the gloom, I switch on the small flashlight I carry. I notice something near the floorboard in the kitchen. Kneeling down, I rub my hands on the wood's blackened surface. Mold. Black mold. I remember when insurance companies paid out big bucks because of this infestation and its health effects.

"Shit."

I want to do something about this. There's not a damned thing that can be done. With no air conditioning and with poor air circulation in most houses, the growth of this crud is inevitable. Not sure what the risks are, I shrug and search for dry clothes.

Chief Pettibone has set up a small table in the foyer of City Hall. I guess being visible as the town's police presence is important to him. A couple of tired looking horses are tied to a tree. They look like they're desperate for something to eat. No grass is within grazing distance of their tethers.

"Chief. You got a sec?"

Pettibone looks like he just stepped on a dog turd. "Mister Kirby."

No more first name basis, I guess.

"You sobered up yet?" he asks as his left hand rubs the heart area of his chest.

My first and second inclinations are to cold cock him, but I won't. I need Pettibone's information on what to expect in Lincoln City. Rick Simpson and Israel Rios, two beefy cops stand beside him, their shirts soaked with sweat. Simpson and Rios patrol together. I've dubbed them Frick and Frack, and suggested they do a lot more than patrol together.

Salt rings on their shirts show they've been worn a lot more than one day. Acrid body odor attacks my senses immediately. Instinctively, I reach to pinch my nose, and breathe through my mouth. Frick and Frack look pissed off enough to swing at me on general principles.

"I owe you an apology, Chief." God, that was hard. "Can I bother you for a second?"

Pettibone tries to look spiteful, but truthfully, the man doesn't hold a grudge very well. After a few more seconds of disdainful staring, he says, "Sure. What do you need?"

Without going into the details, I explain I have to make a run into Lincoln City.

"Why?"

I explain that I need to get someone who's not well and needs to be in the relative safety of Elmhurst.

"Who is it?"

"I'd just as soon not go into it with you, Chief."

Pettibone pushes his chair back, and twists this way and that, unkinking his back. "Mister Kirby, we've got too many Lincoln City people wandering into town as it is. We don't need any more. Unless you can tell me who it is, I'm not inclined to give you any information."

Maybe the son of a bitch can hold a grudge. Without mentioning her pregnancy, I explain that Gail Kaufman can't get out of the city without my help. This brings a hoot from Rios. I snarl at him but ratchet my anger back. It won't do me any good to start something with any of the Chief's men. Besides, everyone in town knows how Gail and I ended up. It's probably reasonable that someone should hoot at the idea that Gail would ever consider my help. With anything.

"Chief, it's the truth. You've seen Billy hanging around here. He was looking for me. I need to try to help her out."

This brings a snicker from Simpson, or Frick. I can't take any more. "Hey you assholes. Fuck off."

Rios reaches for a riot baton. The fucker's going to try to whack me across the shins with the club. Pettibone stops him. "Hold on, boys." He turns and gently asks the two to please step outside for a bit.

Simpson makes a spitting sound toward the floor, and the two brush by me, making sure to slam into my shoulder as they pass.

"See you, Frick and Frack."

They both turn, glare, and walk away.

"You have a way with people, Mister Kirby," says Pettibone. "You just bring out the best in them."

I shrug. No disagreement there.

Pettibone motions me into an office. Not quite as dark as the others because of its large window, it holds a desk and some chairs. "Sit down. I'll tell you what I know. Which isn't much. What part of Lincoln City are you headed toward?" As he talks, he reaches into a breast pocket and removes a small pill container. Absently, he places a small pill under his tongue.

I tell him the area and he grunts. He spreads a highway map on his table, takes out a flashlight, and tells me what he's heard.

Two hours later, I'm back in the garage. Josh Cerveny helps me push the Beamer out. I twist the throttle, squeeze the clutch, turn on the switch and jump down on the starter. Three tries and the bike fires up. Cerveny hands me the backpack. Making sure the holster and 9mm is clear at my right side, I snap the chest and belly straps. He gives me a mock salute as I pull the goggles over my eyes. With the bike in neutral, I rev the engine a few times and it settles down into a sweet hum. Cerveny pulls down the garage door, then walks around and closes and locks the side entrance. Gotta give the guy credit, he's been good to have around. I just hope I have a house when I get back.

Chapter Eleven

It's important to explain what you mean when you say, "I'm going to Lincoln City." North? South? Near the river that divides the population roughly in half? Up in the hills on its west side where most of the affluent newcomers live? The rough and tumble Eastside ghettos and barrios?

Until recently, the capital was a fairly small city with a large state university. The legislature met once every two years. Lots of state agencies, but all in all, reasonably sedate. Then the technology boom hit, and the place doubled, then tripled in size. Techies at new start-ups drove up prices and taxes and pushed the middle class and poor out of many neighborhoods. A simple trip from Elmhurst became choosing the least-bad way to deal with traffic.

There won't be traffic now. Might be blocked streets, perhaps caused by the EMP as it destroyed auto and truck brains. Pettibone tells me there are blocked streets for a more ominous reason. Gangs. Pettibone isn't from Lincoln City. Apart from occasional shopping trips, or law enforcement seminars, he has little personal knowledge of the place. But our police chief has been interviewing people dribbling into

Elmhurst. The information he grudgingly provided seems credible—and frightening.

One story that those fleeing Lincoln City have verified: is a blockade of sorts on the highway leading to Elmhurst. Thugs are shaking down people for valuables and food. The thugs have turned back anyone not willing or capable of doing so. I've got to figure out a way into town where I don't have to contend with this. Goggled, armed and riding a BMW with a sidecar may give me the forbidding appearance, but the rock chunked at me earlier is a good reminder that it doesn't take much to take out someone on a two-wheeler.

The bike hums as I go through the gears. I turn west and away from City Hall. I am heading toward a small state highway that winds north through the farmlands in Lee County. I know this area. Mentally, I've charted several possible routes once near the capital but any of them could present problems. Right now, I appreciate the wind and the solitude of the open road.

As I drop down the hill Elmhurst is perched on, I look to my right and take in the rich dark green line of pecans and oaks marking the path of Little Elm River. It meanders off to the north. Its headwaters are in the karst and limestone a few hundred miles away. Little Elm River wraps around the north and east sides of our town before turning south toward the Gulf of Mexico.

Riding through the countryside, it's easy to forget that the world has changed. Fluffy white cotton bolls await the stripper. Some fields had already been harvested and cotton modules sit covered with tarps, spray painted with the owner's name. The maize heads are full and brown, with just the right moisture for cutting. I almost look for harvesters and grain trucks. Away from the press of desperate people, the land looks bucolic.

The motorcycle purrs at an easy thirty miles per hour. Wisps of smoke catch my attention. I approach a farmhouse just off the highway, and wave at several men standing around a fire. I recognize them as farmers. Most are related. All ran large operations. Four or five tripods hold ropes from their apexes, with feral hogs dangling head down. One man waves me over. I slow and pull into the lane leading to the house. Maybe I can learn something more about what's ahead.

Once the goggles are peeled off, Bob Ivey grins. "Hey, look what the cat dragged in."

There are some chuckles, but the men mostly ignore me. Several have whetstones and patiently work knife blades over their surfaces. The hog carcasses still drip blood. Ivey's neighbors glance at the BMW, then begin skinning the animals.

There is an urgency as they slice the tough skin away from the flesh. A small piglet's skin is fed to several hounds. The next pig's skin is placed in a container. Two of the men's wives give small waves, then lug the container toward the farmhouse. Ivey senses my curiosity. "We'll render the fat. Nothing's going to waste." He pauses. "Where're you going? You look like Easy Rider."

"I think you mean Road Warrior."

He looks puzzled. "Never mind." Ivey's a good guy, and I'm not going to try to explain Mel Gibson's character to him in the little time we have. Before he can ask the obvious question about where I'm going, I point up the highway. "What's up the road?"

Ivey scratches his head. "Dalton, we don't know shit. We've heard that the commies, or Chinks, or camel jockeys have nuked the country and fucked up everything, but that's it." His face flushes. "Why don't *you* tell us what the hell is going on?"

That gets everyone's attention. I pull off my helmet and try to explain EMPs. Questions come quick, and it's obvious I'm no scientist. These guys aren't stupid, but they know less than I do about nuclear physics. I finish with, "Our entire infrastructure is messed up, as you guys can tell. Whether it's just this part of the country, I don't know. I wish I knew more."

A farmer, Mercado's his last name, takes off a glove and shakes my hand. "Thanks. Appreciate what you shared with us." He re-gloves and turns back to butchering. The others drift away. Ivey nods. "To get back to your question. I'm guessing you're heading toward the capital. And no, we don't know much of anything. Some drifters walking this way—the long way around—but heading south toward Elmhurst we guess. One family. We gave them a couple cans of pinto beans. The kids looked nearly gone."

Three miles up the road, I have a choice to make. Either I keep going toward the Interstate or I wind around country roads. The Interstate will put me three miles from Gail's apartment. I choose it. The access road is cluttered with vehicles, but they're spaced so that gentle weaving is all that's needed to move forward. A big truck stop parking area is cluttered with semis. Most engines were killed as the drivers took breaks. The rigs look like burly soldiers lined up awaiting orders. The truck stop's café displays shattered front windows, but no human activity. I twist the throttle and power up the on-ramp. A group of mangy dogs half-heartedly chases the bike as I accelerate.

The Interstate had been heavily trafficked when the EMP went off. Trucks and cars coasted after the EMP went off as drivers tried, without power steering assist, to steer toward the shoulders. The BMW weaves around the empty vehicles. Up ahead, two tractor trailer rigs stopped dead in the center lanes of the four-lane highway force me to slide to the inside. As I slow, two figures jump out in front of me pointing rifles.

Things just got interesting.

Several things go through my mind as I downshift and brake. I check for a gap that the BMW can squeeze through. Wooden crates leave less than three feet. Not enough for the bike and a sidecar. There's time to shift to the far outside lane, and I jerk the bike behind the semi's trailer, hoping I'll find an opening there. Boxes, scrap metal and tree branches are strewn all the way from the semi's tractor to the guardrail. Can't do it.

Two men crawl out from under the trailer. All are armed with what appear to be metal pipes.

The BMW idles as I click through the gears and into neutral. The Glock at my hip is of no use, as I am surrounded by five bearded men, some in hoodies. Surprisingly, they don't grab the AR15, but do relieve me of the Glock. One who I take to be the leader, signals me to kill my engine, by running a finger across his neck. At least I hope that's all he means.

I turn the bike's key, and carefully place it in the vest pocket. No one is touching me. No one says anything. With helmet and goggles off, I focus on the man in front of me.

"Where are you going?" The leader's voice sounds educated.

Stupid question, but one I'd better respond to without being a wiseass. "Into Lincoln City."

The leader is tall, Hispanic, and reeks of wood smoke. He pulls his hoodie back and he now appears be about fifty, intelligent, with a scruffy salt and pepper beard. "No one gets past here without being checked out."

I push the kickstand down and ease off the bike. I don't want to get too far away. My AR15 is visible, and its presence is inviting a lot of attention. The leader makes a small hand gesture, and the others back off. I'm relieved for the moment, but troubled that one man has that kind of control over his followers. Clearly, I need to focus on dealing with whoever this is.

I take off my riding gloves and push them into a vest pocket. The right hand's nearness to the empty holster evokes two others who'd I'd first spotted, to raise rifles and point them at my head.

"Not doing anything, fellas. Just putting my gloves in a pocket. I don't have another gun hidden anywhere."

"Who are you?"

I give the leader my name and where I'm from. "Who are you?" I want some reciprocity.

Oddly, at least to me, the man extends his right hand. I take it. "Name's Medrano. I'm in charge of this checkpoint." He grins as he motions toward the bike's contents. "You've got a bunch of stuff on that beauty. Seem to know what you're doing."

How much do I disclose to Medrano? I'm still trying to digest the roadblock and the greasy men in hoodies holding me at bay. I nod. "Why are you guys blocking the freeway?"

Rather than answering, Medrano asks for some identification.

Turning to his followers, I speak out. "Reaching for my back pocket for a wallet, guys. Don't want to get shot."

Laughter from everyone. Except Medrano. His eyes don't leave my face. Opening my wallet, I pull a state driver's license and hand it to him. He compares the photo and hands it back. "Lucky for you. You are who you say you are."

"Why would I lie?" I stuff the wallet back in my pocket and notice the two men with the rifles have lowered them. Everyone seems a bit more relaxed. Still not sure where all this is going, I stand there. It sinks in that I could have been killed.

Medrano finally speaks. "We might let you by, but it'll cost you."

This is exactly what I was afraid of. "I don't have anything of value." Which isn't true. The BMW may be priceless. The AR15 and the Glock too.

Medrano senses my thoughts. "Calm down, *carnal*."

What, now this guy's using gangbanger phrases? "I'm calm. Just worried." And I am.

Medrano starts asking questions. What have I seen on the

freeway? How many miles have I traveled? Have there been other roadblocks. That kind of stuff. He appears frustrated and relieved at the same time when I can't give him anything interesting. He motions to a man holding my Glock. "Give it back to him."

I re-holster it as Medrano's men clear a narrow path for me to ride through. Medrano points north. "Better get going. We're expecting trouble."

"Who from?" I ask.

Medrano explains, finally, what's going on. "We've part of a home protection group for some neighborhoods." He names them. "Thugs been trying to take over this south part of Lincoln City. Most of the bastards are coming from that direction." He points south. "Seems like things are tough all over, but worse in Escondido. We've caught several gangs from that shithole town trying to steal stuff, and some even tried moving into our neighborhoods. We're a bit edgy. Word is that they're planning to come this way and try to push past us."

Happy my driver's license confirms I'm not from Escondido, I tell Medrano the short version of why I'm heading into the capital.

"We could use your firepower here."

Two men with rifles. Some others, not older than boys, with pipes. Yeah, they could use men and a dozen others. I decline. Medrano nods. "Didn't think so. But we'll take your AR15."

Shit. I hand him the rifle and its ammunition. Medrano's men wave me through.

There are plenty of other ways to infiltrate Medrano's area of Lincoln City besides the Interstate. I make that observation and he nods. "We're not the only ones trying to protect what's ours. We've got other roadblocks."

Anyone with some decent firepower can take his post down. Unless his *compadres* have figured out how to communicate with each other without radios, an enemy with any degree of combat training can take out each roadblock, one at a time. Easier than knocking over bowling pins. Medrano seems like a decent sort, so I spare him my views. This isn't my fight.

Two miles up the road, I pull over and idle the bike. The metal pings as it cools. I'm less than two miles from the exit near Gail's apartment. I kill the engine, remove my helmet, and just sit, looking at my hands. They are shaking uncontrollably.

Chapter Twelve

I EASE OFF THE INTERSTATE AT TEN MILES PER HOUR, PEERING INTO abandoned cars and darkened storefronts as I enter the access road. Cars block the next intersection, so I cut through the parking lot of an Arby's and head east. I calculate I'm less than a half-mile from my destination. People walk the streets, but don't appear threatening. Some kids play with a frisbee in the street and step out of the way as I motor through. One kid waves at me, and I wave back.

The complex with Gail's apartment is gated, but the entry is wide open. I turn past the stone and plaster sign for "Punto Milagro, Luxury Apartment Living" and ignore the empty guard shack. Two women sit on the hood of an Audi, smoking cigarettes. They give me directions to a building on the far end of the structures. The taller of the two looks like she is a college student. "Not many people left in this place."

She's got a natural beauty, and under the quickly fading blonde highlights, her hair shows to be a willowy brown. She's anxious to be gone herself, but her family lives six hundred miles away. She has no assurance they are alive. At least she's got a boyfriend and the two of them seem to have figured a way to eat—at least for now.

Gail's apartment is in Building G. Its parking spaces are filled with inoperable vehicles. I step off the bike, lock the ignition, and unholster the Glock. The building surrounds a courtyard. Until the EMP, the area probably looked upscale. Two dead fountains, some dying topiary and walkways that cross in the center. Several tents sit forlornly in the sun, wet clothes draped along their crests. No one is about, and I wonder where they are. I suppose they're prowling for food. All the apartments have balconies facing out into the courtyard. Sliding glass doors are open and I peer up, hoping to get an idea of where Gail's apartment is. No luck.

Building G has elevators. Stairs seem to be in this place only for emergencies. I take them to the third floor, go through the fire door and turn left. The letter said she was in Apartment G305.

The walkway is open to the courtyard. I carry my helmet and gloves in one hand, and the 9 mm in the other. 301, 302, 303. 303's door is open, and a dog growls as I pass it. Someone yells from a back part of that apartment, "You come in here, that dog'll tear your balls off."

Sweat drips into my eyes. I pause and wipe it away. The doors and windows in the courtyard are unlit. I can't see inside anywhere but know that those inside the cavities can see me. The delayed fear I felt from the interstate confrontation comes back, along with something else. It dawns on my that I'm scared as hell as what I'll find in Apartment G305.

"Gail. You there?" I tap on what looks to be a kitchen window. My voice is not much louder than a whisper. The apartment's front door stands open.

Nothing.

"Gail. It's me." A little louder.

If I'm expecting bells and whistles, I'm disappointed.

From the gloom comes a weak voice I recognize as my ex-wife's. "You came. I didn't think you'd do it."

I holster the weapon and enter the apartment. And trip over a kitchen chair laid across the entrance.

"Shit and Goddamnit."

I scramble to my feet and pull the chair upright.

"Sure glad someone wasn't here to ambush you. You look like a fool falling down like that."

Her voice is weak, but Gail still seems to enjoy me taking a pratfall. I bite back my customary insult and try to get adjusted to the darkness. "Where are you?"

Following her voice, I wind through the clutter of the apartment. Windows gently lighten a bedroom. Gail is propped up in a king size bed, fanning herself with what looks like a piece of cardboard.

"Hey, Dalton. Glad you came."

"Last thing I ever thought I'd hear you say." I move to the bed and touch the back of my hand to her forehead. Gail's burning up with fever. Her belly is distended with the unborn child and her breath is rancid. She looks beautiful.

"Come sit beside me." She makes an attempt at scooting over. I sit down and gently touch her abdomen. It is taut with child. Suddenly, something kicks at my hand and I recoil.

Gail grabs my hand and pulls it back. "That's your child in there, Dalton. She's saying hello."

She? Hello? I want to scream. It can't be my child. We'd gone through all that. I bite my tongue. Instead, I ask, "How do you know it's a girl?"

"Ultrasounds, x-rays, all the normal stuff an expectant mother goes through before giving birth. She's a girl. Her name will be Josefina."

I sit in the gloom. The bedroom is littered with towels, blankets, and dirty dishes. A portable toilet old people use sits against one wall. The stench of human waste shows it hasn't been emptied or cleaned. The urge to flee is overwhelming. Taking a deep breath through my mouth, I say, "I need to get you out of here, Gail."

I feel her nod. She mutters, "Help me get out of this bed." She grabs my left arm and tries to pull herself erect. Gail loses her grip and starts to collapse into a prone position. I take her arm and gently pull her into a sitting position.

"Whoo! I'm feeling real woozy right now." She shakes her head slowly back and forth. I get a glimpse of cracked lips.

"When did you last have any fluids?"

She points to several empty Gatorade bottles. "I think this morning. Not sure. Need to try to stand up."

Interlocking her hands, I slide them over my head and around my neck. Carefully, I pull her to her feet. With clumsy dance steps, we move to the sofa in the apartment's living room. The smell is better in here. The lighting is better. I position her sitting.

"I'm going to get some water off the bike. Don't move."

"I'm trying not to," she weakly laughs.

No one's bothered the BMW or its contents. As I unload water and provisions, I look around for some place to secure the bike. Gail's dehydration is obvious. She gulps down swallow after swallow of my water. It seems to restore some strength, so I leave her and return to the bike.

Two men, one black, one white, are trying to steal it.

I point the Glock at the white guy. He's sitting on the seat, jumping on the kick starter. "See this key?" I dangle it in front of him. "Bike won't start unless it turns the thing on. You're not going anywhere without it."

The black guy looks at me, the Glock, and the bike. "Just

give us the key and we'll be out of here." The white guy sits but quits trying to start the BMW.

"It's my bike. I'm not giving you the key. Get off it and get the hell out of here."

Whitey starts to laugh. "Look! His hands are shaking! He's scared shitless. He ain't gonna do anything. Get his key, Claude." Claude must be the black guy.

Claude seems more street smart. "Jimmie, that's a real gun with real bullets. I don't think so."

Jimmie gets off the bike and takes a step forward. I point the gun over his head and pull the trigger.

BLAM!

Jimmie ducks, realizes he's not hurt, and looks at Claude. The black guy starts to laugh. "Told you, mothafucka."

Inwardly, I'm praying that I don't have to shoot anyone. I don't know if I can do it. *Please, just leave.*

Jimmie seems to think about it, but Claude pulls the white man away. I know they'll be back. Gail and I have to leave soon, or I have to find a place to stash the bike.

Chapter Thirteen

I take the stairs two at a time then double over and try to keep from hyperventilating. I am afraid but have no intention of showing any sign of that fear to Gail. I regain a bit of composure and try to act calm as I enter the apartment.

"Are you ready to go, Gail?"

"Ready? You're kidding, right?" Her voice is barely audible. "I'm barely out of the bed. I've got to get into some clothes. I need to take some things for me and the baby." I rummage around the apartment, using my penlight to check drawers and cabinets. All the while, keeping a running banter toward Gail. "Where are some clean clothes? What can you wear? What do you need to take?"

I realize I'm babbling. A heavily pregnant woman sits on the sofa in a fetid, dark apartment, and I'm afraid for both of our lives. No. For three lives. There is a child in her womb she is claiming is mine. Whether or not "Josefina" is mine is suddenly immaterial. The child is alive. I've felt her kick. I need to hear Gail's voice. Assurance that she remains conscious. Entering her bedroom, open closet doors, pull out drawers, and am almost overwhelmed by the stench of human waste in the porta-potty, Frantically, I push out the window screen in the bedroom's exterior window. I grab the toilet's interior plastic container, ensure it will fit through the opening, and shove it out.

"Dalton!"

Gail's voice breaks through the ringing in my ears. I forgot just how loud the discharge of large caliber firearm is without hearing protection.

"What?" My response is shrill.

"I've been calling you, and you didn't answer. You're just pacing back and forth with that tiny flashlight." Her voice trails off and I realize she is crying again.

Taking deep breaths, I kneel next to her. My heart is pounding like a trip hammer. My attempts at concealing the fear is betrayed by my body's reaction to confronting the two motorcycle thieves. I have to ramp it down if I'm going to be of any use to anyone.

"Sorry. Just keyed up." To say the least.

"What happened downstairs?"

"Nothing. Why?"

"I can smell something like gunpowder. Did you shoot someone?"

I sniff my right shirtsleeve. The residue from the gun permeates my clothing. "Nope. Same shirt I was wearing last week. Went target practicing. Not much chance to wash clothes."

"Liar. I heard a gunshot. What happened?" Gail's voice is weak but demanding.

"How far along are you?"

"Quit changing the subject, damn it." I touch Gail's forehead. Her temperature has dropped. Getting out of the bedroom into some fresher air seems to have sharpened her tongue.

I stand and wait. I'm not dealing well with pointing a gun near someone's head and pulling the trigger, and I'm not going to explore any of this with Gail.

She relents. "Josefina's due date is in two weeks...I hope."

"Why are we going to Elmhurst for you to have, uh, Josefina?" The unborn child already having a name is still hard to grasp. "Lincoln City may be screwed up, but there have to be doctors here who can deliver babies."

As soon as I say it, I realize I've made a mistake. Even in the gloom I detect a fierceness in Gail's countenance. She leans forward. It's no easy task with her distended belly—she fans out her legs to do so.

"This child is not coming into life in this dying city. This child, *your* child will be born where I have family." The words come out in a staccato of anger. "You either take me home or get the hell out."

Whoa. Gail seems to be getting back into fighting form. Then, spent, she slumps back on the couch and starts to cry again. Jesus!

"We're getting out of here, Gail. I'm taking you to Elmhurst and your folks. It just made more sense that there'd be an OB/Gyn here in the big city." I can see this isn't getting me anywhere. I change the subject, quickly. "I was worried about your health and that of ...Josefina."

Gail takes a few minutes to compose herself while I search for tissues in the bedroom. The room's stink is dissipating, but not by much. I glance out its window. The porta-potty inset landed in the bushes two floors down. Its contents are strewn over the area. Some has splashed onto a car. A man is looking at the car as if it is his. Then he glances upward, trying to determine the shit's trajectory and launching point. I duck back quickly.

The ringing in my ears has faded a bit, and I follow Gail's

instructions as she thinks aloud of what she and the baby will need. Ten minutes later, two garbage bags are full of clothes, pads, medicines, and toiletries. There is no way in hell all this is going to fit unless I dump most of what I've brought and may still need to get us to the relative safety of Elmhurst. Rather than risk another outburst, I set the bags by the open apartment door.

"Can you walk down the stairs?" Because if she can't, I have no idea what the next step will be.

"I'm pregnant, not dying." Gail holds out an arm for me to grasp and pushes herself upward. "Whew." She teeters and I embrace her to keep her from falling. She recovers enough to shrug out of the bearhug and move toward the apartment door. "We gotta go, you said."

I stop her and sit her in the righted desk chair by the apartment's door. I didn't spot anyone either trip up the stairs but feel certain several people are still staying in the apartments. I loosen my belt and take off the holster, then tuck my pistol in my waistband under my shirt. No one's going to come close to me if I'm seen packing. I walk to the left and start knocking on door jambs—most doors are open to allow some ventilation. Finally, halfway around the courtyard, I get a response.

A middle-aged man and woman warily answer when I ask for help. His name is William. He reluctantly agrees, telling his wife Margaret to close and lock their apartment door until he gets back.

As we walk toward Gail's apartment, I sense his increasing reluctance to leave his wife alone. I try to make small talk. "Appreciate it, William. This won't take long at all. You're a real trooper. The lady I'm helping, she just needs more help than I can deal with. How have you and Margaret been holding up?"

He's not having any of it. Nearly at Gail's door, he turns. "I need to get back."

Desperate, I pull the Glock and point it at him. "Turn around, William."

He glances over his shoulder, sees the firearm, and stops. "Oh shit. I knew we shouldn't a helped."

"William, I need your help. Five minutes and I'll let you get back to Margaret. Please don't make me use this." I have no intention of shooting the poor bastard but wonder what I'll do if he refuses.

"Aw, Jesus."

William looks defeated. He shambles back, muttering. Still pointing the Glock at him, I grab William's arm. "C'mon, man. I meant what I said. You'll be back upstairs with Margaret in five minutes."

Gail stands in the doorway. She's managed to pull off the dirty sleeping clothes and donned denims apparently made for fat people or pregnant women. She's pulled on a loose-fitting top and gotten her swollen feet into some old penny loafers.

"Gail, this is William. William, this is Gail."

William perks up a bit. "I've seen you, lady. You're the pregnant one. I thought you'd be long gone by now."

"Nope." Quizzically as if wondering why I'm holding a gun to William's head.

I point to the two bags. "William is here to help you get down the stairs, Gail." I pause. "Aren't you, William?"

She looks at me pointing the gun at William. "You're shitting me, Dalton. You pulled a gun on this man to get him to help. What's got into you?"

She touches William on the shoulder. "Please forgive this asshole. Will you help us get some stuff downstairs?"

He nods. "I'd be glad to help you, ma'am. Just tell this man to quit pointing a loaded gun at me."

Gail glares at me. I put the Glock in the holster on the counter, then re-strap the holster to my belt. William grabs both garbage bags, while I strap on my backpack, and carefully lead

Gail to the apartment complex stairwell. It goes easily. William scurries ahead of us. On the ground floor, I thank William, reaching out to shake his hand. He looks puzzled, then turns to leave.

Gail calls after him, "Thanks very much, William."

He moves away quickly.

"You are such a prick sometimes, Dalton."

The bike is intact. The salt and pepper theft team hasn't returned. Gail looks at me. "Where did you get this contraption?"

" I bought in on a whim."

"Un huh. Sure." She lets out a laugh, then gasps. "Every time I laugh, Josefina kicks me," she says. "You want me to fit in that?" She points to the sidecar.

I size up the sidecar, then at her. I'll have to empty everything. Even then, it's going to be tight. "Yes. I'm counting on it."

Gail shakes her head and moves to a nearby bench. I guess the apartment complex put it there as part of the ambience, but its surface is covered in bird shit, and it's hard to imagine a reason for anyone in the pre-EMP days sitting there. The only view is of a sunbaked parking lot.

I grab a blue rag I've used to check the oil level, and spread it on the bench, just as she eases down. She looks surprised, and thanks me as she tears up again. It may be raging hormones, but inwardly, I smile at the sudden kindness of the response.

Ten minutes later, the area around the BMW is strewn with supplies from my backpack and the sidecar. I re-fill the gas tank. The gas can is set aside too. Gail seems to nod off. I tap her on the shoulder and hand her a water bottle. "Please drink. You're still dehydrated."

"Ah, I'll just have to pee every five minutes."

"We'll stop." I hope she won't as getting her in and out of the sidecar will be a bitch and eat up valuable time. The sun is at least halfway across the sky. We've got six or seven hours before the sky will darken. I open one of the garbage bags and stuff as much of its contents into the backpack as will fit.

"Can you hold a garbage bag in front of you?" I ask.

"Why?"

"It's the only way I know of that we'll get most of what you wanted back to Elmhurst. There's just no room."

"Let's see." Carefully, Gail stands and walks toward the BMW. "Help me into this thing."

She puts one foot on the floor of the sidecar, and I hold her arm as she moves her second leg in.

"Grab me under the arms." She lowers herself. No luck. She doesn't fit. I break into a cold sweat of desperation. This isn't good. Gail stands and points toward the unopened garbage bag. "Open it, please."

I hand it to her... She starts padding the sidecar's small seat and, in a minute, has built up the seat with at least ten inches of padding.

"Let's try again."

Gail's butt eases onto the clothing. She slides her feet down into the well and looks at me. "Will this work?"

"As long as I don't brake too fast. No way I can secure you. You're perched like a canary."

"More like a fat penguin." Another short laugh and groan. We leave a mess of scattered items on the dead grass. I strap on the backpack, helmet and goggles. I hand Gail an extra pair. "Put these on. You don't have a windscreen." I crank the bike and say a small prayer of thanks to the gods when it fires up. As it idles in neutral, I unstrap my helmet. "Try this on," I shout. She and the baby need all the protection I can provide. It isn't much.

I straddle the seat, squeeze the clutch, and tap the BMW into first gear. She glances up at me with a brave look. Actually, she looks scared shitless. I am too.

I ease in the clutch, and the bike stalls.

"Goddamit!"

Gail reaches up and pats my arm. "Calm down, Dalton."

I jump on the starter peg. No luck. "Dammit."

"Take a deep breath. It's going to be okay."

For some reason, I believe her.

Chapter Fourteen

THE BMW ENGINE'S VIBRATIONS ARE ODDLY SOOTHING. "OH, YOU beautiful thing. You're purring like a kitten. God bless kraut engineers."

"What?"

Gail shouts, a puzzled look on her face. I realize I am in a monologue with an inanimate object. "Nothing. Just talking to myself."

She nods. The bike wobbles slightly as she shifts her weight in the sidecar. I haven't discussed with her how I plan to get back to Elmhurst. Mainly because I'm not sure exactly which route to try. Is the Interstate open? The inbound and outbound lanes were blocked earlier, but does that mean there will be problems *leaving* Lincoln City? I should have asked Medrano of the risks when I was stopped and relieved of my AR15. I inwardly curse my stupidity in not doing so.

Gail's weight in the sidecar takes getting used to. I've ridden the BMW many times, and wish I'd had the foresight to put some sandbags in the bike's appendage so I could get used to the change in center of gravity and the awkwardness in turn- ing. I bounced onto the street in front of her apartment, thankful that when leaving the parking lot I had already had an angle on the turn. At the intersection of her apartment complex's street with the main divided thoroughfare I lean slightly into the turn – and almost run up into the center esplanade when the bike refuses to follow where I intend it to go. I hit the rear brakes and judder to a stop as the front tire bumps the curb.

"Shit!"

"What's wrong?"

Tense and embarrassed, I look around, anticipating trouble. The only humans visible are pushing grocery carts down the middle of the road on the other side of the esplanade. The carts are piled high with cherished and necessary contents. The newly homeless. I put the bike in neutral and kill the engine. I climb off, straighten the front wheel and push the bike backward to where I have room to ease into the turn.

"What's the matter? Don't you know how to drive this thing?"

"Not with someone in the sidecar," I confess. "You're the first passenger." "Jesus God, Dalton."

I kick the starter, take a deep breath, stand, turn the handlebars, and lean—hard—into the turn. Juddering again, the contraption clears the curb. Breathing heavily with relief, I shift up and head toward the Interstate. Reversing the route to Gail's is the shortest way to Elmhurst. We ease through the dead-lighted intersection of the access road, and, with a bit more confidence, I push the motorcycle into the turn. Shifting through first, second, and third gear, I face a decision as we near the ramp. Do we enter the Interstate?

I brake and stop at the on-ramp's entrance. "I need to check something out. Stay here." As if Gail can go anywhere in her condition. Something tells me that entering a limited access highway without doing some recon would be stupid.

"Here." I hand Gail my helmet and goggles and grab the

binoculars in the BMW's small Velcro windshield pouch. "Be back in a sec." Trotting clumsily to the top of the ramp, I don't wait for a response. The Interstate runs directly south. I hope to confirm that the manned barricades two miles ahead remain peaceful. At first, my heart's pounding ensures blurred double images. "Calm down, Dalton. Breathe," I mutter. After several tries, I'm able to focus the binocular lenses.

First, nothing. Then, the magnification pulls in several wisps of dark smoke from the direction of the barricades I'd passed earlier. Suspicious, yes, but not enough to indicate problems. I lower the binoculars and rub my eyes. Returning to the lenses, I will them to bring better clarity to what is or is not happening on our planned route.

Again, nothing. Gail stands, stretching and clutching her back. We've come less than a mile and it's obvious another thirty miles is going to be tough on her. She waves, as if to say she's okay, and I continue trying to make out what's going on to the south. More smoke, I think, but can't be sure. No sign of any human activity otherwise. A decision has to be made, and quickly.

To this point, I haven't discussed anything with Gail about how I'm getting her back to Elmhurst. I've been too panicky. The possibility that the salt-and-pepper would-be thieves would strike again forced me to get the hell out of the area. Now, I feel the urge to bring Gail into the decision-making process, even though I'm not sure whether I'm doing so because she is an adult, and it's her and the child's lives at stake, or because I want to pass the buck and unburden myself of some of the responsibility. I shake the thought off. Way too much introspection.

I trudge down the knoll to the bike. "Scouting the freeway. I came in this way. Want to make sure we can get back the same way." I pause, and then the words come out of my mouth. "Is this okay with you?" *Shit!* I cringe. I've just weaseled.

Gail doesn't take the bait, instead she hands me my helmet and says, "I'm counting on you. You know much more about this than I do."

Goggles and helmet in place, I kick-start the bike and stay in second gear as we ascend the entrance ramp. Then into third. There are fewer stalled and wrecked vehicles southbound out of Lincoln City, and we weave around them easily. After a mile and a half, I coast to a stop in neutral at the top of a small rise. Smoke is now visible assistance. Stepping away from the BMW and the engine's vibrations, I again focus the lenses on the divided highway, hoping the smoke is merely from small fires warming Medrano and his men who man the barricades against thugs from the town of Escondido.

At first, nothing. Then, small moving dots appear from the haze. Seconds later, it's apparent these are humans. And they are running—north. Two of them suddenly stagger and fall. They don't get up. Moments later, other figures appear. I take a prone position on the roadway surface so I can better stabilize the binoculars. The latest figures are the pursuers. Three of them near the two inert figures. One extends an arm toward a prone man's head. The inert figure jumps and then lays still. I've just witnessed an execution. The second prone figure also receives a *coup de grâce*.

In a moment of panic, I want to share this horror. "What's going on?" Gail asks.

"Nothing."

I tuck my head in my arms and swallow the gorge rising in my throat. *How did we get to this point?* Taking several deep breaths, I refocus. More figures stream up Interstate. Seemingly exhausted from running, some crouch behind vehicles. Gray tendrils of smoke indicate the pursuers' relentless attack. *Why in hell don't Medrano's men just get off the damned freeway and get into the cover of buildings along the frontage roads?* At least, I think they are Medrano's men. Or others like them. Regardless, the pitiful attempts at protecting their homes and families have failed.

"We can't go the way I'd planned."

"Why? What's going on?"

As Gail asks the question, I hear a soft *pop pop pop*. She's removed her helmet, so she hears it too. "What is that noise?"

"Not sure."

Gail is a country girl. She's been around firearms all her life. "Nonsense. Those are gunshots, aren't they, Dalton?"

Angry bees flit by us. Stray rounds. I doubt anyone is actually shooting at the two of us, but we are in danger of being hit. To prove the point, a round ricochets off the tarmac and into the metal bodywork of a car. It sounds like someone hitting a washtub with a stick. Another bullet flies by, obviously closer than the angry bees just heard. This one sounds as if it is tumbling. Despite the panic, my brain describes its syncopated passage— *lul Lul lul Lul lul* ...

Time to get out of here.

"Please get out of the sidecar—now!" Gail carefully steps out as I balance her. I guide her to the relative safety between two dead pickup trucks. "Stay behind these for a sec." As I wrestle the BMW backward toward the trucks' left sides, more bullets zip by. One stars the windshield of a small SUV. Gail moves to help.

"No! Stay back."

Something hits my foot and suddenly my left leg is no longer on the ground. Gail screams, and I am flat on the highway surface. *What the hell just happened?* Momentarily, nothing makes sense as my vision fades, then returns. Blood streams from a cut on my forehead. It made contact first. I try to move, but my left foot is numb. *Holy shit! I've been shot!* Panicking, I try to roll toward the trucks where Gail stands, ashen faced. She reaches out, holding her swollen belly with one arm, and grabs my jacket sleeve with another.

Dazed, I notice several figures flitting by us. Men, running. One veers toward us. I try to stand as I lunge toward him. No good. The leg still isn't cooperating.

"Mother fucker! I'll kill you! Stay away!" *Where is the Glock?*

Then the man is upon me, smothering my flailing arms. At first, all I hear is my voice. Filth spews from my mouth. Tears stream down my face as I realize the futility of my attempts to protect Gail and the child.

"Calm down, Dalton. Please!" Gail yells at me.

The man has me in a choke hold. "Stop fighting, *ese*. It's me. Medrano. I'm not here to hurt you."

"Medrano?" I choke out.

"Yeah. You gonna calm down?"

I nod and he releases me. "So this is who you were going into the city to rescue." He barks a small laugh. "You better get out of here. And fast."

I roll over. It's Medrano. His face is drawn into a rictus of fear.

"What happened?"

"The *cholos* from Escondido broke through. They're moving up the freeway."

"Where's my AR15?"

Medrano looks at me like I'm crazy. Maybe I am. "You think I took time to look for *your* fucking rifle? You are one dumb motherfucker. I'm running for my life, stop to help you, and you ask about your goddamned *gun?*"

I scoot into a sitting position. He's got a point. "Sorry." Not really. The SOB confiscated a valuable weapon.

"You need to get your lady friend and your motorcycle out of here. Now." Medrano points toward the south. "Those *pinches* ran over us like we weren't there. They killed some of my men." He begins to tear up, then composes himself. "Get up. Let's get you on your way."

"I saw, Medrano. Some of it. I'm sorry."

He suddenly grabs me in a bear hug, then as quickly releases his grip before I can reciprocate.

Gail and Medrano pull me upwards. The left foot is numb, but the leg is starting to respond to mental commands. "Not sure what's going on, but I think I've been shot."

Medrano turns me around as I lean on a truck's rear bumper. "Nothing." His hands run down the outside of my jeans. "Wait." Then, "You are one lucky son of a bitch."

I look down. My left motorcycle boot's thick rubber sole has an enormous gouge and is torn away from the boot's leather body. I can't see any blood, and renewed circulation is sending tingling waves of pain into my foot. I begin to laugh hysterically. "Well, I'll be." I have a huge grin on my face. Gingerly, I put more and more weight on the foot. I am almost dancing.

Gail brings me back to earth. "We need to go, Dalton." She reaches toward my bleeding forehead.

"Ouch! Godammit! What the hell, Gail?"

She shows me several bits of gravel she's dug out of the wound. "Quit whining." Handing me a wad of tissues, she says, "I was only trying to help."

As I wipe blood from my face, Medrano helps Gail into the sidecar. "*Oye*, Dalton, if that's your name. Get outta here, quick. I don't know what they'd do to your lady, but for sure they'll kill you and take your ride."

I point the handlebars north. As the bike idles, I quickly push on goggles and helmet. Medrano starts to leave. "Wait." He's not looking at me, but at what remains of the roadblock. "Where're you going?"

He waves off the question. I scream at him. "Stop!"

He seems as surprised as I am by my voice. "Get over here." I motion toward the bike's seat. "You ride bitch."

He starts to protest. "Too heavy."

Probably, but he's lost valuable time. "Just get the fuck on."

I rev the engine to emphasize. My plan is to drop him up the road apiece and give him some breathing room in his escape.

It's awkward as hell, but somehow, he manages to swing a leg over the seat without kicking Gail in the head. Medrano's arms reach around my waist. The springs and shocks groan with the abuse of the extra weight of him riding pillion.

The bike slowly picks up speed as the gears shift. Muscle memory seems to kick in as I remember the location of stranded vehicles passed this morning. It seems like a lifetime ago. As if to emphasize the need to escape, a truck's rear window explodes inward. Too close. Possibly even a shotgun blast.

I take a chance on one more gear shift upward and the BMW speed increases. "Where to?" We've already passed the exit near Gail's apartment complex.

Medrano yells a street name in my ear. It's just west of the Interstate, and thus farther away from Elmhurst. Shit. He hits my right shoulder—hard— and points to an exit ramp. I nod, throttle down, and weave around a van and a car. At the feeder road, Medrano points straight ahead. "Stop and let me off over there."

The bike eases to a stop, and I shift into neutral. I'm not going to kill the engine. It hasn't let me down yet, but the thought of the BMW not starting scares the shit out of me. Medrano crawls off.

"Thanks."

I engage the clutch and shift into first. I don't know exactly how, but the artery runs east and west. I know that I can connect with southbound roadways if I turn eastward. I start to ease out the clutch.

"Wait. Where's your family?" shouts Gail.

What am I hearing? I don't give a damn where Medrano's family is or where he's going. I've got a job to do.

He pretends not to hear. Gail screams, "Where is your family?" Medrano gives her a location, assuring us it's "just a quick walk away."

I nod, and again begin to ease out the clutch.

Unfortunately, Gail seems to know the area. "Bullshit, mister," she screams. "That's at least a mile from here. We've got time. We'll get you there."

What is this "we" shit? I start to protest and Gail pinches hell out of my right leg. She motions to Medrano to get back on the bike as she tugs on my jacket. "Dalton, just do something decent and get this man home."

No good deed ever goes unpunished. The bike squats on its springs, and he wraps his arms around me. "Thanks, *amigo*." There is relief in his voice.

"I'm not your *amigo*. And keep your hands away from my boys."

I slowly turn west under the Interstate—and away from Elmhurst.

Chapter Fifteen

"THIS WITCH IS GOING TO GET ALL OF US KILLED." THE ENGINE noise keeps my yelling from being intelligible. Medrano apparently hears something, because he yells, "What did you say?"

I just shake my head. *Gail is about to domino and she's forced me to give this guy a ride home.* Medrano pats my shoulder. I suspect he knows exactly what I was saying – and thinking. Probably, but he's getting a ride home from a hellish situation. He might be sympathetic, but he's not about to piss in his Wheaties. Gail is his meal ticket back to his family.

Gail points toward an entry street into a subdivision dubbed Las Colinas. The middle-class housing hardly matches its grandiose name. For a second, I wonder about the fat cats living in the Dallas area with the same name. Do their mansions still exist, or have they been gutted by mobs?

The subdivision is actually the first one past the commercial zone adjacent to the Interstate – maybe a half mile at most. It's quiet. Oddly so. I'm used to seeing people on the streets of Elmhurst. Here, it's as if the area is holding its collective breath. As if those in the tract homes know some sort of storm is coming their way.

I slow, downshift and lean into the left-hand turn. Medrano takes the cue and leans with me—it makes the turn easier than expected. I throttle up, but not for long. Several men, all armed, step from behind the subdivision's granite identity marker.

Here we go again.

Except we don't. Grins appear on the faces of the men. A teenager, I'm guessing maybe thirteen or fourteen, pushes through and leaps at Medrano.

"Hijo mio!"

"Daddy! We were so worried!" The boy bursts into tears. An attractive, dark-skinned woman yells, and embraces Medrano and the boy. A rush of sadness washes over me. I'm not sure why. Then, I realize that Medrano is fiercely loved, while I...

Let's not go there, Dalton. Suck it up.

"Where's my bicycle, Dad?"

Good question, kid. Where are Medrano's wheels? And why am I having to give him a ride? I'd seen Medrano this morning and smelled the smoke and noticed the smudges. Now, I realize his shirt is ripped in several places, and blossoms of blood show where his skin's been torn from the earlier confrontation.

"Sorry, *mijo*. I guess I lost it." He tries to smile as he ruffles the boy's hair. Medrano kneels to his son's level. "We'll get you another one, Adan, I promise." He is totally engrossed in the child's features, and runs his hands over the boy's face, then down his arms. As if by doing so, he will forever capture Adan's essence.

Medrano stands. A neighbor shakes his hand and says, "Some of the guys, they got away on foot. More on the bicycles. Some, we haven't seen yet."

I remember vaguely seeing a figure on a bicycle flash by as I writhed in pain on the roadway.

The neighbor, a stocky Anglo, continues. "We heard about..." He mentions several names, and I surmise I witnessed two of their executions. Medrano waves him away.

"Later." He obviously doesn't want to talk about it in front of the kid.

All this is peachy, but I'm further from Elmhurst than I wanted to be, I've witnessed cold-blooded killings, and haven't a damned clue as to how I'm going to avoid it happening to me and my passenger.

"We've got to go." I ask them to push me back where I can make a 180 turn without a lot of trouble.

One says, "Sure." He follows my instructions as I manhandle the bike to face east—and toward Elmhurst.

"Wait." Medrano pushes away from his wife and child. "We might be able to help get you started." He explains to those around him, "They need to get to Elmhurst."

That brings some quizzical looks.

Medrano's neighbors scuff their feet, but I don't hear anyone volunteering to help. I'll take any help I can get.

"Hey! We just gave this guy a ride back, so I'd appreciate one of you shitbirds giving us a hand." Now, where in hell that that bravado bullshit come from?

Medrano turns. "You did me a big favor just now. We're going to help you avoid what I've just gone through. Don't be an asshole." There are several "fucking a's." It looks like I'm not getting much sympathy here. Time to back off.

"Sorry. Just need to get this lady"—I point to Gail—"back to Elmhurst. I'm a little stressed, as you can tell."

Several of the men look at me as if I'm an insect. Medrano points to a wiry gray-haired man. "Jacob, we need about four or five to scout up to the Interstate. The scum that hit us this morning— they're like cockroaches. They'll have plenty of places to steal from—or worse—and we're the first bunch of residences they could go after if they choose to move away from the Interstate. Once they're off the main arteries, they'll scatter and be harder to hit. We need to see if they've gone past us or are thinking of coming this way. If so, we need to hurt them, badly. We need to show 'those people' that if they come near our families, it will cost them."

He reminds me of Robert E. Lee at this point, who only referred to the Union enemy as "those people." He looks into the eyes of each man standing. They all look scared shitless, but no one expresses an objection. Clearly, this group has its blood up after what's happened to neighbors and friends.

He puts a hand on Jacob's shoulder. "After the five of you recon the Interstate area, will you please lead these two as far as you feel safe. The lady's pregnant, and I'd like to get her out of here." He doesn't mention *my* safety—the jerk.

I have to give Medrano his due. He's more than some self-appointed leader. Like this morning, the men seem to be drawn to his calm guidance. He's the real deal. Jacob accepts this too. He's probably twice Medrano's age, and I wonder if he's some retired professor or teacher. Not a thing about him looks hard. A huddled discussion ensues, and Jacob emerges from it on a mountain bike. Four others, all with deer rifles slung, and two with holstered revolvers, ride along with Jacob.

"Follow us," he says. "We'll try not to get too far ahead of you."

Wiseass. Medrano bends and kisses Gail's hand. Shit, she's probably swooning. He shakes my hand, and I realize Elmhurst could use several dozen like him. Medrano turns to me. "I appreciate what you've done. You didn't have to do it, but you did. God go with you."

I have many questions. Like, the thugs from Escondido—the *cholos*—are they the only ones to be worried about? As big as Lincoln City is, there must be other groups just as bad or worse. Why are Medrano's men finding the courage to fight what might be others' battles? How am I going to get Gail back to Elmhurst before she decides to go into labor? Lots of questions and no answers.

Nearing the Interstate, Jacob uses hand signals to tell me to kill the engine. He points at my automatic, and says, "We're going to check things out before we get any further. We can always use another man. The scum that hit our barriers on the freeway may have come this far. If so, we'll try to do as much damage as we can without losing our friends."

It seems apparent that Jacob wants payback for his dead neighbors. He wants to kill someone. He waves his arm indicating the four that rode with him. "You want my help getting home, you help us." He points at my automatic again. "So, come with us."

"Will she be safe?"

He shrugs. "Probably. Put her somewhere she doesn't stick out. Hide the bike. I'm not going to get shot at, going blind. I can get you a lot further on, but only if you cooperate with me." Obviously, Gail's welfare isn't at the top of Jacob's list of concerns.

Point taken. The guy doesn't talk like a retired professor. I ask him about it.

"Retired professor. Also, retired military."

I dismount, and kick in the door of an abandoned muffler shop, finding a place for Gail to sit. No dead bodies, or at least no smell of decay. I assure her I'll be right back, that we can't go further without Jacob's help, that it's smart to make sure we won't get shot at or jumped when we cross under the Interstate. She nods wordlessly, and plops down in an office chair. No doubt, it was once the manager's. I wonder if she's having second thoughts about the time spent taking Medrano home.

Two of the men help me open the bay doors to the shop, and we push the BMW inside. I shuck off my heavy motorcycle jacket. It's soaked with sweat. I stash my helmet and gloves and follow Jacob and the others. Ahead is the underpass we turned onto from the Interstate access road less than an hour ago. Has anything happened since then? I see no sign of it, but the group isn't taking any chances. I'm put with two guys who give their names as Bill and Chuy. Jacob puts Chuy in charge of our little squad.

First, Jacob and the other two cautiously move south, peering in and around buildings to ensure no one is lurking on top of the Interstate's overpass or on the southbound frontage road. Five minutes later, the trio is back.

"No one on top." He taps one of his group. "Buzz, take your rifle. Get up there, crawl over and *carefully* check out the other side." He means the northbound access road, which I vaguely recall is lined with machine shops and storage facilities, and then the Mobil station where I stopped to let Medrano off. "Don't let yourself get spotted. We're going to go under the overpass in just a few."

"Frankie." That must be the other guy with Jacob. "Frankie, go up to the lip of the freeway and once Buzz is set, relay what he sees back to us."

The two move off. An eternity it seems, but probably no more than a couple minutes, and Frankie returns.

"Anything?"

Frankie replies, "No, Buzz didn't see anything and neither did I."

Jacob looks uncertain. "Frankie, get back up there. We're going to go under the freeway on both sides of the street. You guys cover for us. Don't hesitate to shoot someone—just not us." That provokes several nervous snickers.

At this point, I just want to get Gail and blast through the intersection on the Beamer. It's stupid, I know. We can't outrun bullets, but I just want a release from the tension I'm feeling

"Chuy. You take this guy, what's your name?"

"Dalton."

"You and Dalton. Go on the north side. We'll go on the south side. Anyone sees anything, yell out."

Jacob and Bill both have weapons at the ready. I wonder where to even watch. Empty buildings? The overpass's abutments? There are so many possibilities. I hear a cough and look south. No Jacob or Bill. *Where in hell did they go?* Then I spot them high on the concrete slope of the underpass. There is someone with them. Where in the hell did that person come from? The person is pointing toward the access road that goes northward. I see and hear nothing, but nonetheless, obey Jacob's hand command to come toward him.

It takes a lifetime to cross the empty intersection. Chuy and I move up on the concrete's slope. Jacob puts a finger to his lips. How can anyone *not* hear my heart beating? After witnessing the killings, my mortality is at the forefront of my thoughts. I get a better look at whoever was talking with Jacob. He's probably only in his forties but looks ancient. Several layers of clothing, and several layers of filth. Missing teeth. I'm looking at a homeless person. A real one—not one created by the EMP. For a second, I envy this ragamuffin. He's developed street smarts to live rough a long time ago. The EMP has moved him up the survival chain substantially, and he seems to be reveling in his new role.

Jacob whispers, "This gentleman—he goes by Jim—has something to share with us." The homeless guy leers. 'Gentleman' isn't how he's been described.

"Name doesn't matter" he says. "But you need be aware I saw a couple of real nasty looking fellows setting up in the service station." I lurch backward from the stench of his breath. He points in the general direction of a Mobil station on the corner, some seventy-five yards away now. I'd pulled up to the intersection next to it when Gail had made me take Medrano home. "They look like they've got AK47s."

Pretty knowledgeable for a street person. Bill raises an eyebrow.

"Afghanistan. Seen a few."

Jacob nods approvingly. "Iraq."

They fist bump. *Spare me.*

My first thought is to retreat, grab Gail and the BMW, and go around this place. Jacob is ahead of me. "Forget it," he says. "I don't know any other way to get you pointed in the right direction. Besides, we need to do something about what's at that service station. And, before more show up." He thanks the homeless guy, who pats him on the shoulder and disappears.

"We got lucky. I would have walked right toward them," Jacob says. "There'd be no element of surprise."

Well, that's for sure. I'm wondering about why that matters. Are we supposed to attack those guys? My bowels go to liquid, and I want to shit badly. How does this guy know they're bad guys?

Jacob pulls open the breach on what looks to be a Smith and Wesson .40 caliber and I catch a glimpse of the live round in the chamber. "You want to go over and say howdy to them, do you, tough guy? Ask permission to pass through with your fancy motorcycle and your woman?"

Well, no. But what Jacob is saying is that we are going to 'neutralize' them. In other words, that we kill them or run them off. Clearly, Jacob the college professor's time in the military wasn't in the Quartermaster Corps. I look at this gray-haired guy in stretch riding shorts and tennis shoes with a new appreciation. His blood is up.

I get an approving punch to the shoulder. "The homeless guy. He just walked up to them. Harmless. We're two more homeless. Just as harmless."

"That's your plan?"

Jacob nods. "You and I are the two that don't have rifles. Only choice we've got. Too much space between here"—he indicates the concrete solidness of the underpass—"and them. We're going to stagger up like a couple of drunks."

"Then what?"

"What do you think, hotshot?"

I think that someone is about to die. Chuy disappears around the south side of the embankment. He's on his way to tip the guys overlooking the intersection. Before I can digest this, Jacob slides to the sidewalk at the base of the overpass, musses his hair, tucks his Smith into his waistband under his loose shirt, and adopts a staggering walk of a alky.

Chuy returns, and he and Bill nervously re-check their deer rifles. They'll move into the open at Jacob's command.

"Your turn."

I affect the walk of a drunk. I'm so damned scared I'm not stable on my feet anyway.

We shuffle into the tarmac of the northbound access road and pretend to be holding each other up. Keeping my head down, I glance up. No movement, no warnings—nothing. Up onto the concrete of the station's pad. Jacob starts singing some ditty in a slurred voice. My throat is too dry to utter a sound, but I move my mouth as if I'm singing with him.

Past the first pump island, and two tatted men with bandanas step out of the station's office door. "Hey, you two. Stop."

Dear Jesus, can the rifles on the top of the Interstate see this far under the pumps' roof?

Both cradle their AK-47s—yep, Jim the alky was right. Jacob has one arm around my waist, and now he reaches under my shirt and grabs *my* Glock. I stand there, frozen, as he suddenly pushes me away, points, and empties the weapon's magazine into the two men. The noise is deafening.

"Holy shit!" The part of my mind that hasn't gone to mush notices Jacob has hit both men with at least two rounds each center mass. One also is missing the back of his head.

Chuy and Bill appear and grab the dead men's weapons. Jacob returns the Glock. "Hope you've got some more rounds for that thing. Nice, not having to worry about a safety to unlock." He seems unfazed. "Appreciate your help, but as shaky as you were, I didn't trust you to do what needed doing."

He's probably right. I feel somehow emasculated.

Frankie and Buzz stay put, hopefully still watching the area over with their scopes. Bill pushes into the Mobil station and announces "clear."

Jacob, now alone on his bicycle, leads the BMW under the Interstate, easily dealing with various cars obstructing the roadway. Gail points as we go by the Mobil station. She's asked what happened. I haven't been able to give an answer. Now she spots the two bodies, and the blood that has run toward the street.

"Oh, my God, Dalton."

About a mile later, Jacob stops. "I'm taking you on some back streets that'll get us out of the subdivisions and into some county roads. You may recognize them. They'll trend east and south. You should be able to find one to get you home." He shakes my hand. "Be careful."

I tap into first gear and try not to stall the BMW's engine as I ease out the clutch.

Chapter Sixteen

JACOB PEDALS HIS BIKE, HIS SPEED CONSTANT AT TEN MILES PER hour. The college professor, who is retired military and looks like a wimp, isn't. His legs pump the pedals like heavily muscled metronomes. His unemotional killing of the two men at the gas station has put my brain into a fugue state. I wonder what makes this man tick, that he just did that, and walked away, showing no sign of remorse and no indication of introspective thoughts on the taking of human lives.

He scares the hell out of me.

A few minutes east of the Interstate, Jacob motions me to pull over. I tap the gear lever into neutral and kill the engine. He dismounts and sets his kick stand. As I remove my helmet, he steps toward me and says, "This is as far as I go. Do you have a map?"

I pull the paper road map from a pouch and try to memorize the route he points out. Turn here, left here, right there. I'm so used to a GPS; I've forgotten to bring a pencil.

Gail removes her helmet so she can hear. Jacob moves to the right side of the bike, shakes her hand, and wishes her

Godspeed. I continue to stare at the roadmap. Jacob taps my shoulder and waves as he rides off.

I now can use Gail's help. I hand her the map and we try to commit the suggested route to memory. After several mental missteps, Gail says, "Give me the map. I'm the navigator. I'll tell you where to go."

I effect a glare. "You've told me where to go several times."

Gail raises her eyebrows, displays a theatrical looking moue. "Ooooohhh." she smirks then explodes into laugh. "Who? Me?"

My weak attempt at humor has relieved some of the tension. For a moment, I'm dazzled by her smile that encompasses all the muscles in her face and reaches her eyes.

We sit there giggling. The world has gone to hell and for a few moments, everything is just, well, okay.

"Yes, you. No doubt about it." I still smile as I turn the bike's ignition switch and kick start the engine.

"Wait."

"What now?"

"Give me your pistol."

"Why?"

Gail holds out her left hand. "I'll put it where I can reach it. There's no way you can steer this motorcycle and shoot a gun at the same time."

I start to protest, then unholster the gun and hand it to her.

"I killed my first deer when I was six. I don't intend to kill anyone with this thing." She waves the automatic around, and I duck as the barrel swings by my head. "But maybe I can scare someone, if I have to, and we can keep going."

It hadn't crossed my mind, but it's true. "It's a Glock. There's no safety on the thing. Please watch where you point it."

She rolls her eyes. "No shit, Sherlock." Gail racks open the slide enough to confirm there's a live round in the chamber, then wedges the automatic, barrel down, next to her in the sidecar.

BANG!

Holy shit! I kill the engine and run around to the sidecar. "What happened?" It's an automatic response, and a ridiculous one. I know what happened.

Gail is white as a sheet. "It just went off." She starts to shake. "Oh, God! Oh, God."

I scream, "Are you hurt? Are you hurt?"

She sobs, "I don't know." The illusion of the last few minutes' normality is gone. Images of her wounded, or the child inside her wounded, race at light speed through my mind. She sets the Glock on the BMW's seat. It slides off onto the ground. I shove it into my holster. Gail tries to take off her helmet. Her hands shake so badly she is unable to unhook the chinstrap.

"Oh, Jesus God, please." Her mantra continues as I pull her up and out of the sidecar, looking for blood. Gail starts to crumble, and I lean her up against the sidecar's body.

My hands are all over her clothing, feeling for some sign of the bullet's path. "Please, I need you to stand up for just a second." So far, nothing. She stares into space. "Please!" I yell. "Please!" I manage to lift her enough to turn her ninety degrees from me, and furiously use eyes and a free hand to seek where the bullet went. Her jean's left buttock is stippled and torn—but no blood. A scant sense of relief until I remember that, contrary to what I've seen in movies, gunshot wounds don't always just start pumping blood out. It depends on nearby blood vessels

Gail begins to pass out on me. "I think I'm fainting," she barely vocalizes.

I embrace her as her body sags. All I can think to say is, "It's okay. It's okay." And I think it might actually be all right. "Lift your arms and wrap them around my neck." We do an awkward dance toward the curb, where I lower her into a sitting position. Gail can't maintain it and starts to fall sideways. I try to hold her somewhat erect, but it's becoming hard.

"Whazzup, man?"

I look up. We've drawn a crowd. A cornrowed black man asks the question. He appears concerned.

"Please help me. She's maybe been shot."

He kneels, and while I explain what I'm trying to do, the two of us begin to turn Gail onto her side so I can determine the damage.

"You two, don't you be hurting that woman." A wizened black woman takes one last drag on a cigarette, flips it onto the street, crouches down, and cradles Gail's head. "You shoot this woman, white boy?"

"Jesus, no." I start to explain, but the woman is having nothing to do with it.

Gail, eyes unfocused, mutters something.

"What'd you say?"

"He didn't shoot me." Her words come out slurred. "The gun just went off."

Somewhat mollified, Gail's new best friend finds another point of attack. "Boy." She tries to stare me down. "This woman is pregnant. What's she doing on a motorcycle? Don't you have good sense?"

The crowd has grown, and there are some murmurs of agreement. I can only imagine that this is the best street theater the folks in this neighborhood have seen in a while.

The cornrowed man introduces himself. "Name's Frederick. I don't see no blood anywhere."

A pillow appears, and someone in the crowd slips it under Gail's distended belly. Gail begins to tell the woman cradling her head, "I'm okay. I think I can sit up." "No honey, you stay where you at until they finish doing whatever it is that they need doing."

The jagged tear on Gail's left flank oozes a few drops of

blood. I push on the area and she yelps. "Hey, quit pushing on my butt. It hurts."

Frederick shakes his head. "My oh my. She's not shot. The bullet creased the lady's ass, but that's all. She'll have one hell of a bruise."

This evokes several cheers from the onlookers. We carefully roll Gail onto her back, and then sit her up.

"Boy, was that stupid," she says, and starts to cry.

Well, yeah, but I'm so relieved all I can do is pat her shoulder and keep repeating, "You're okay. The baby's okay."

The wizened black woman addresses the crowd. "You all quit staring at this woman. Get your asses over here and help us lift her up." Whoever she is, she has the command presence of a drill sergeant. Several people gently ease Gail onto her feet and walk her to the BMW. I tell the crowd where we are going. Some nod in agreement, while others check out the motorcycle.

Someone taps me on the shoulder. It's a young kid. "I found the bullet, mister." He shows me the flattened slug. "It made a hole in the street."

Sure enough, directly under the sidecar seat, the asphalt has a new divot.

"You want the bullet, mister?"

"No thanks. Keep it." There's been enough gun play for a lifetime. I just want to get Gail home, before she has a baby.

Frederick and the others handle Gail like she's made of fine china. This is a rough neighborhood—or was a rough neighborhood. Now, I guess it's just like every other neighborhood. Most of the people crowding around are black, yet I sense no hostility. Gail's new guardian is in-your-face, but she leaves no doubt of her concern for a very scared and pregnant woman. I can't think of what to say. Soon, Gail is re-situated in the sidecar. Her color has returned, and she hugs several of her helpers. It seems as if they can't do enough for her. The neighborhood drill sergeant stands off to one side until Gail waves her over, reaches up and pulls the woman into a hug.

"Thank you. You are very, very kind."

The woman pats Gail gently on the head, then quickly retreats to light a cigarette. The gesture clearly has affected her, as I spot her wiping her eyes.

I shake Frederick's hand, as Gail shoves the helmet back onto her head. She cinches the chinstrap and hits my right leg. "Let's go. I don't want to have this baby on the side of the road."

Gail's pronouncement brings laughter to several.

Damn.

Quickly going through the gears gets us to steady thirty miles an hour on a narrow two lane. Houses now occupy one- and two-acre tracts. Zoning regulations loosen as mobile homes, trailers, and small commercial business structures jumble together. We pass the city limits sign and I breathe a sigh of relief. I know the way back to Elmhurst now. We have around twenty miles to go.

Gail taps me on my right hip. I think she's seen the city limits sign too. I nod, but don't look down. Another tap, this one harder. I slow and glance at her. She points at my holster. I release the grip and reach for the Glock.

It's gone. Someone in the crowd relieved me of it while I was dealing with Gail. I scream curse words and look at Gail. She throws her head back and laughs. Dammit! It's infectious. Soon, we are both howling. I can't tell whether it's because I've seen four men die, or that Gail didn't kill herself. Whatever the reasons, I realize that at this moment in time, I don't care about the missing firearm. The next few miles feel like they are all downhill.

Gail gives a whoop as we pass the Lee County marker. Less than fifteen miles to the Kaufman farm. The gas gauge reads less than a quarter of a tank. More than enough to make it there. Things are definitely looking up. The lessened need for vigilance allows my mind to wander a bit. I'll be glad to offload Gail, but there is a fleeting sadness. For a moment, I'm not sure why. Then it hits me. This has been one hell of an adventure. I am about to fulfill my promise to my ex-in-laws. I will get their daughter home safely.

"Hey!"

I glance down. Gail is pointing downward, toward her legs. What does she want? I ignore her.

"Hey!"

I downshift into neutral and brake in the middle of the narrow tarmac. "Now what?"

"I think my water just broke." She struggles out of the sidecar. Her crotch is soaked. Gail pulls off her helmet. "Oh, my God. I'm going into labor." She suddenly grabs my arm. It hurts like hell. "I'm cramping."

"Quick. Get back in the sidecar."

She takes several deep breaths. "Wait just a sec. I think this is going away. Maybe I've got some time. I don't want to be cramping sitting in that sidecar."

Hell, I don't want her to be cramping standing *or* sitting. I have no flipping idea about birthing no babies, as someone said in a movie.

"Whooh. Okay. Better now." She grabs the helmet, readjusts it, sits back down and says, "Let's go!"

And we do. The BMW shakes several times as Gail's cramping returns, and she writhes in the seat. I gesture to suggest a stop and am waved off. The plan is to get to the Kaufman place, but there is no doctor there. For a moment, I ponder driving straight into Elmhurst, but realize there is no guarantee we'll find any doctor there either.

"I'm going to cut down Sims Ranch Road to your folks," I yell. The route is shorter than heading into town and back out again on Pederson Lane, the county road, but it is also over several poorly maintained gravel roads.

"No!" she yells back. "Go up the hill and then cut over the old bridge. It's paved."

An eternity later, I cross the highway bridge over Little Elm River, and up and into the edge of Elmhurst. I cut off before the downtown district, using small city streets until, an eternity later, I come to Pederson Road. At the bottom of the hill, I aim the BMW for the narrow iron bridge east of town. I slow trying to compensate for the rough timbers' bouncing.

Kathunk, kathunk, kathunk go the timbers as I ease the BMW over their bolted surfaces.

"Oh, Jesus," Gail wails. "Get me off this damned old bridge or it'll pop this baby out right now."

A half a mile later, we're pulling into the gravel driveway at the Kaufman farm. As we near the house, I press insistently on the motorcycle's horn. "C'mon, be here, you two."

The BMW passes the chicken coop as Randall and Bertha Kaufman open the screen door. Billy follows behind.

I slide to a stop and forget to engage the clutch. The BMW jumps several times and its engine dies. All I am able to do is yell, "She's having a baby. She's in labor, and she's having a baby."

Chapter Seventeen

THE FOUR OF US HAUL GAIL UP THE STEPS TO THE PORCH AND INTO the house. Not without loud protests, however. "I can walk. I can walk." She repeats what she's told me earlier. "I'm pregnant, not dying." The objections fall on deaf ears, and soon, Gail is laid on a double bed in her old bedroom. Some of her high school cheerleading pictures are still on the wall, and a Raggedy Ann doll stares at me from the dresser top. Bertha Kaufman is all business.

"You men, help me get these filthy clothes off her."

Billy's concern shows. But he's not having anything to do with helping get his sister undressed. He stands back, eyes averted, until Bertha shoves a pile of clothes into his chest. "Make yourself useful. Take those things and put them in the washtub. We'll deal with them later." Bertha stands maybe five feet and a couple of inches, and can't weigh much over a hundred pounds, soaking wet. However, there's no doubt who's in charge.

Billy appears relieved at being released from the bedroom. His tread recedes toward the back porch where Bertha keeps her washing supplies. She pulls a rubber band off her wrist, pulls her graying brown hair into a ponytail, and mechanically doubles and redoubles the rubber band as she tells Randall to start heating water. He disappears into the kitchen. Suddenly, I'm aware I'm in a room with my ex-wife and her mother— alone. Bertha doesn't give me time to ponder my awkwardness. "As soon as we get some clean, warm water, I'm giving Gail a whore's bath."

I bark a laugh at the expression and get a nasty look for my trouble.

"We need to get her as clean as we can, for her sake and the baby's."

Where and when did she go to nursing school? I ask Bertha, "Have you ever helped with births before?"

"No, you fool. Just because we live a few miles out of town doesn't mean we're some kind of cedar choppers." Bertha calls all trashy white people *cedar choppers*. "But I've helped pull many a calf in my day. Some things are similar."

I resist suggesting that using a come-along on a human child having trouble in the birth canal might be counter-productive. Gail's taking all the banter in, and, beginning to laugh until a contraction hits. "Don't you dare suggest a come-along, Dalton."

The contraction eases, and I wonder how long this delivery is going to last.

"Go see if you can find Doc Randhawa," barks Bertha.

Gail seems to sense I'm going to object. "Please, Dalton. I know everyone will do fine by me, but it'd be nice to have a doctor here."

She's right. I heed Bertha's command.

Jagir Randhawa, MD, is a physician who lives in Elmhurst. Given our proximity to Lincoln City, there are several out-patient clinics that bring doctors in from time to time, but Jagir is the only one living in the area. Thirty years ago, when there was a shortage of physicians in rural America, some small towns like Elmhurst recruited foreign doctors. Doctor Randhawa showed up and despite offers over the years to move elsewhere, stayed. Until specialty clinics and doctors made their appearances about fifteen years ago, he treated almost everyone for about just about everything.

The gasoline I'd brought to Lincoln City was jettisoned to make room for Gail. I check the BMW's fuel gauge. There's still enough gas to make it to town and back without using precious time going by my house to re-fuel. The sidecar and motorcycle won't be a secret anymore, but I can't do anything about that now. Two things go through my mind as I pull onto the county road: Can I find Doctor Randhawa, and when's the last time this general practitioner did any obstetric work? He's pushing seventy now and near retirement. From what I recall, for years and until the EMP, women went to obstetricians and hospitals in Lincoln City to have their babies.

I barely notice the Sheriff's Office cars sitting in front of the SO office on the east side of the courthouse square. I turn onto the west side of the courthouse, the square seems to perk up as I wheel past it the two blocks to his small clinic. Several people stop what they're doing and stare. With the helmet on, I wonder if any recognize me. Word will get out soon enough. The "Closed" sign dangles from Doctor Randhawa's glass entry door. I kill the BMW and try it anyway. It's locked and I see no evidence of anyone inside. I hope Doctor Randhawa is at home. Our town doesn't have a hospital, and it's quite possible he's making a house call. I hope desperately I find him. I fire the bike up and turn south toward the doctor's residence.

The ride into town has been a respite from having to deal with something I know absolutely nothing about—childbirth. I've been gone twenty minutes from the frantic worry in Gail's bedroom. I've got to get in gear and find the goddamned doctor. I press the horn button as I turn into the driveway to the doctor's home. By the time I reach the front door, it's open and a dark-skinned woman stands there, as if waiting to see who in hell is raising the ruckus.

"Where's the doc, ma'am?" The woman in the doorway may be a relative—he's imported a bunch of his family from the Punjab, and frankly I can't keep track of them all. I don't recognize her and wonder if she speaks English. When there is no response, I slow my speech down and ask again. "Do you know where Doctor Randhawa is, please?"

"I'm sorry, sir. The good doctor is not available at the moment." Her voice has a lilting British accent that at any other time would be delightful.

Shit, it's Mrs. Randhawa, whom I've met and visited with before.

I'm in a hurry and more than a little bit embarrassed. She has a better command of the King's English that I do.

"Mrs. Randhawa, please accept my apology. My wife's having a baby. She's in labor, and I need to find Doctor Randhawa."

Mrs. Randhawa nods, as if waiting for me to continue. "Where might he be, if you know?"

"Oh sir, he is at your facility for prisoners. Your jail. I believe you will find him there."

"Thanks." I get back on the bike. She waves and shouts, "The very best wishes to your wife, sir."

I did say wife, didn't I? Too much time would be wasted trying to explain Gail's and my relationship. I wave and head toward the County Jail.

The Sheriff's Office and the Lee County Jail are co-located in a featureless rectangular building on the east side of the Courthouse. An enclosed connector yokes it to the Courthouse, uglifying an otherwise beautiful 1890s masterpiece. I find a place to stick the BMW between dead patrol cars and walk to the front door. Elmhurst Police Chief Larry Pettibone's horse, or at least the one he was mounted on painfully just a day or two ago, is tethered to the bumper of a cruiser. Someone has propped the office door open with a brick. I step inside, and it takes several seconds for my eyes to adjust to the gloom. "Anyone here?"

"Who's asking?" The response comes from the corridor leading from the office area to the jail.

"Me. Dalton Kirby. I'm looking for the doc."

Someone walks toward the front of the offices, holding a flashlight. It's Pettibone.

"What's going on, Chief?" It's no secret that Pettibone holds the County Sheriff, a goober named Leonard Baird, in contempt. "What brings you here?"

Pettibone says, "Some of us are trying to help out. We've got a situation…"

I interrupt. "Can you give me the Cliff Notes version? I need to see the doc. I got Gail back to her folks' place and she's in labor."

"Shut the fuck up, Dalton, and let me finish. Jagir's back there trying to save a man's life." He grabs a dirty handkerchief out of his back pocket and wipes sweat off his face.

I shut up.

"That EMP or whatever that was fried the jail's electrically controlled cell doors. They all unlocked. Most all the prisoners were in here on pissant stuff like DWIs, so they stayed put. Probably didn't want to get more charges filed for escape." He blows his nose of the handkerchief and stuffs it back in his pocket. "There were two prisoners being held on warrants out of state. I think from Nebraska. Authorities up there were scheduled to pick those two bastards up when things went south." Pettibone is talking about arrests made a week before the EMP attack. The Highway Patrol had pulled over a car with fictitious plates and arrested two out-of-state white males with long criminal records. The arrests made the local newspaper. "The jailers somehow managed to chain their cell door shut before they broke and ran. Both warrants are for murder and sexual assault."

He takes a breath and I know where this is headed. "Let me guess. They're in the wind and before they left, someone got hurt."

"You got it, Dalton. That's what I'm trying to tell you. Jagir's trying to keep our good Sheriff alive."

"What happened?"

"It's dark back in there and the jailers have kept some Coleman lanterns going. Been bringing in food. The two from Nebraska, they're some mean bastards and Baird, to his credit, didn't want them loose. Somehow, one picked a padlock, and beat hell out of the jailer on duty. The Sheriff was walking in when the two grabbed his pistol and shot the hell out of him."

Pettibone shines his flashlight on the linoleum floor in the hallway, illuminating blood spatters. I watch as he moves the light toward the jail entry. It looks as if someone fell, bled, tried to get up, and smeared his hands and feet all through the mess.

Momentarily, I do a tally of the death I've seen today. It stuns me, but Gail is having a baby. Her life and that of the child can be at stake.

"Can I ask Jagir something, real quick?"

Pettibone shakes his head as if to say, "you don't get it." He motions me back down the hallway. We gingerly skirt the blood and enter a central atrium. To one side is a glass enclosed room, the control picket, with a control board and video monitors – all dead. In front of it is an open area and then a row of cells. All the doors are open, and the cells empty. To the left is a holding cell often dubbed the "drunk tank." Some architect designed the cell with a skylight, probably an attempt at humanizing incarceration. Now, the late afternoon waning light, filtered by tempered glass barely helps illuminate to a macabre scene.

An EMS emergency transport gurney is being used as an operating table. Three people, two men and a woman, all whom I recognize as either paramedics or sheriff's deputies, are holding aloft battery powered lanterns. Facing away from me is Doctor Randhawa. The cell floor is strewn with blood-soaked towels. He mutters something and a paramedic's free hand produces some type of surgical instrument. I make out the unconscious form of Sheriff Leonard Baird.

Careful not to slip on the bloody towels, I inch toward the makeshift operating table. Betadine, or something like it is smeared over Baird's abdomen. Blood wells and runs from a large incision as the doctor, hands slightly quivering, seem to be probing. Is he looking for a bullet? Trying to fix a perforated bowel? I have no idea. Jagir pauses as if to get his breath, glances my way and says, "Ah, my good friend Dalton." He pronounces it *DOLE twun*. "To what do we owe the pleasure?"

I blurt out, "Gail is in labor. She's having a baby."

"Yes. Yes." Jagir turns back to the sheriff's gut. "Those in labor are usually having babies. I suppose you need assistance?"

I swallow, hard. "That was the plan, Doc. But..."

"But, indeed. As you can see that plan is most certainly needing to change, my good man." Doctor Randhawa mutters something to another person, who's been cradling the sheriff's head. He no longer takes heed of my existence.

Back outside, the sun has set. I turn to Pettibone. "Is the Sheriff going to make it?"

"What do you think?"

"I think he's going to die right there on that gurney."

Pettibone looks shaken. He pats me on the shoulder. "We've rustled up some ATVs that are running. If he gets loose and is up to it, we'll run Randhawa out to the Kaufman place, but don't hold your breath."

It's pitch black by the time I arrive back at the Kaufman residence. I kill the engine and hear a loud groan as I throw my helmet into the sidecar and run toward the house. Butterfly McQueen's famous line in *Gone With the Wind*—"I don't know nothing about birthin' babies"—rattles through my thoughts as I enter the porch. Billy is sitting in the dark. I pause long enough to ask, "How's it going in there?"

"She's hurting, Dalton. I just can't stand to see my sister like that. I feel like a coward, but I just can't be in there with her right now."

Billy's no coward. He just looks scared. I don't blame him. With no medical help, Gail could die. The baby—Josefina—could die. Or both. The bedroom door is open, and I tap on the wall and ask, "Can I come in?"

Randall's sitting on the edge of a small chair in one corner. "Where's the doctor?"

Gail's legs are spread. At first, I'm embarrassed to be looking at her naked vagina, but she's oblivious to the exposure. Gail's contraction seems to ease, and she looks over at me. I lie. "He'll be here as soon as he can. Had a small emergency that he's finishing up."

Bertha Kaufman's countenance tells me she's not buying what I'm selling. She pumps up a blood pressure cuff and puts a stethoscope to her ears. I start to say something and she shakes her head "no."

Where in hell did that device come from? It dawns on me. Randall suffers from hypertension. He's been on medication for as long as I've known him.

Bertha releases the pressure. "180 over 120. Gail, honey, this labor's giving you high blood pressure. Too high."

Her brow furrows with worry. "Did your ob/gyn ever discuss this with you?"

Gail nods. "She said there was a risk of gestational high blood pressure. I told her about Daddy. I gave her the name of his latest medication. She said we'd have to just be aware of the blood pressure maybe running in the family."

Bertha sets the cuff down and turns to me. "There's warm water on the stove, and there's soap and a towel. Wash your hands and arms, really wash them, and come help me." She turns to Randall. "Husband, go make sure he washes like I told him."

Randall grunts as he stands. He touches his daughter gently on her arm and he and I go to the kitchen. "Doc isn't coming, is he?" he whispers.

"Probably not."

My ex-father-in-law starts to cry. "I'm worried, son. This is tough going. I don't see how women get through it."

I swallow, nod, and hug him. "We'll do this. Gail'll be fine." I have no idea whether this is true, but the old man needs a dose of optimism. I scrub like I've seen doctors do on TV and Randall dries my arms and hands. Back in the bedroom, Gail begins another contraction. She bites down on a rolled towel.

"Push, baby." Bertha screams in encouragement. "I can see the baby's head."

Sure enough, the top of Josefina's head fills her vaginal opening. Gail seems to pause, and the baby's head starts to disappear.

Bertha tells Gail, "Push, honey. Push hard!"

Josefina's head reappears. "Are your hands clean?" Bertha doesn't wait for an answer. "Reach down and carefully grab your daughter's head when it appears again."

My daughter? This is really happening. I utter a prayer— *Dear Jesus, please don't let me fuck this up*—and reach where Bertha guides me.

Another contraction begins. I'm now part of the chorus. "Push. Push. Push. Push."

Suddenly, a tiny, slime-covered head starts to appear.

Bertha, God bless her, isn't taking any chances. She and I carefully grasp the baby's head.

"Gently. Gently," she says to me, then, almost yelling, urges Gail to push. "You're almost there. This baby's coming, honey. Just keep pushing!"

Randall distractedly wipes Gail's sweat-covered face and forehead as she screams and hurls colorful epithets I'm not sure *I've* even heard before. The Kaufmans seem unfazed, but I'm sure there'll be some discussion later about the salty language.

Probably just a minute passes, and the next contraction is harder. And then, as Bertha and I gently pull, a tiny wriggling, pink and purple, blood covered child appears. Bertha takes the newborn, carefully wiping its face and patting it on its tiny back. The newborn utters a squeaky cry. It's breathing! She lays the child on Gail's abdomen. "Here," she says to me. "Take this soft towel and gently wipe your daughter. Husband, get the clamp."

Billy makes an appearance in the doorway. His smile seems to split his face in two. "Hey, big sister. Way to go."

Randall reappears with kitchen scissors and a paper clamp. "I put them in boiling water, honey." The old man's face is streaked with tears. He mutters, "I'm a grandpa. I'm a grandpa." He is giddy with relief and joy.

The scissors are for cutting the umbilical cord. But a paper clamp? Bertha doesn't hesitate to explain. "To clamp the cord so the baby doesn't bleed."

Oh.

For minutes, I sit there watching Gail caress a tiny, wriggling baby girl. I find myself checking to make sure the child has all its parts. Ten toes— check. Ten fingers—check. Two eyes —check. Her scalp is covered with a thin layer of hair. It may even match my hair color. There is a final contraction and the placenta is delivered. "Why don't you cut your child's umbilical cord?" Bertha asks in an uncharacteristically gentle voice.

She hands me the scissors as she squeezes open the paper clamp and releases it near Josefina's navel.

"Are you sure?"

Gail nods. I cut through the tissue.

In that moment, whether I sired this child, I know I am forever Josefina's father.

———

AUTUMN

Chapter Eighteen

THE LAST TWO MONTHS HAVEN'T EXACTLY BEEN EASY. AN INFLUX of strangers fleeing Lincoln City, the lack of basic necessities—like food, electricity, most forms of transportation, sewage, and clean water. And of course, there's Josefina, the life changer. I wonder how long any of us can continue to live in this community.

Now October, the weather continues hot. There are, however, hints that summer is easing its grip. Some types of trees are beginning to drop their leaves. The nights are longer. Occasionally, the early morning coolness retains the smell of many cook stoves' wood smoke a bit longer. In normal times, I didn't pay a whole lot of attention to these manifestations of the Earth's wobbly rotation. Now these changes add additional urgency to a host of duties. I open the garage. The BMW no longer takes up space. It's hidden securely—I hope—in one of the Kaufmans' outbuildings. I unchain my bicycle and pedal to City Hall to meet with Chief Pettibone and others in what we've informally dubbed the "Elmhurst Neighborhood Patrol." Regular bathing is quickly becoming a thing of the past. The group meets under an oak tree next to the parking lot. I'm still not inured to the gamey smell of unwashed bodies, so the outside venue is appreciated.

Six of us, five males and one woman, stand around, and wait for Chief Pettibone.

When I got Gail back from Lincoln City, I'd grudgingly acquiesced to Pettibone's request to help maintain order in Elmhurst. Josh Cerveny is a member. He witnessed my rebuff of the Chief's first request to join, and the Chief's angry outburst afterward. He knows what I witnessed on the trip to Lincoln City, and it would have been impossible to look him in the face if I'd refused to help a second time.

Pettibone found some obscure law, dating from the days when the state was on the frontier, that allows a county judge to deputize civilians as deputy sheriffs. The Sheriff surprisingly survived his gunshot wound—barely—and agreed to deputize the whole lot of us, including the town's police chief. Leonard Baird wasn't worth a damn as a lawman before the two thugs broke out of their jail cell and shot him with his own gun. He hasn't improved, but at least seems to understand that Chief Pettibone and a bunch of deputies can give part of Lee County a measure of law and order.

The presence of members of the patrol brings the inevitable questions from a small crowd that shows up at City Hall front steps daily. The crowd's number has dwindled, I suspect because walking here burns too many precious calories. Frankie Gonzales appoints himself as the crowd's spokesman today. He gets off the steps where he's been whittling on a stick. It's my turn at bat so to speak, so I head him off before he becomes a pain in the ass to the others.

"Hey, Dalton. What'ja hear from Lincoln City? We gonna get any help?"

"Same answer as yesterday, Frankie. Nothing new to report, unfortunately."

Frankie presses the issue. "C'mon, man. You people said there might be some help coming this way."

He's right. Communication is spotty, but there have been broadcasts picked up by local HAM operators purporting to be from FEMA, assuring Americans that things are getting better —that help is on the way, eventually.

Some of the local HAM operators are survival nuts. They kept radio equipment, batteries, and solar rechargers in Faraday cages to shield them from electromagnetic pulses. It's allowed them to reach out to the outside and assess what Elmhurst's future is.

I'm still kicking myself for not having done it. At the time, I could have bought several types on Amazon, but didn't.

"Frankie, all I know is that parts of the country weren't hit nearly as bad as we were. There've been some services restored, and maybe the country will get back to some kind of normal." I pause.

Frankie shrugs his shoulders. "I think you're hiding something, Dalton."

I turn away. Frankie's a pain in the ass, and there are plenty like him. I'll suggest to the Chief that he assign someone to type up and post a daily information sheet with the bits and pieces of information gleaned from what we now call "the outside world."

Pettibone opens the meeting by asking each of us what we've seen and heard on our rounds. We meet daily, so there are no dramatic items to report. Less food to distribute in the food kitchens set up in some of the churches; more illnesses reported from foul water and lack of cleanliness; frayed nerves caused by hunger, heat and desperation erupting into fistfights and spousal assaults; some chickens stolen; a dog shot trying to enter a coop. Several people have died from conditions ordinarily preventable. Families have abandoned houses and apartments and drifted away, in hopes of better living conditions, more food, or seeking shelter from kin elsewhere. The sameness of it all dulls our sense of reality: incrementally, Elmhurst is dying.

Josh Cerveny and his wife Elsie have fit well into the community. They and their children have moved into my house. It's a pain in the butt. I like my privacy, but last month's sudden downpour came with high winds and tore hell out of their tent on the back lot. Josh and Elsie are tough enough to fend for themselves, but their two kids are better off with a real roof over their heads.

We're a mixed bunch. Andres Lujan is here. He is still "employed" by the City of Elmhurst, although he's no longer getting a paycheck. He lives on Elmhurst's southside. He's kin to most of the Hispanics, or so it seems. Certainly, he's got family scattered throughout the town, and some more throughout the county.

My neighbor, Jill Aston, pedals up on an old Schwinn. "Sorry I'm late." She's part of the organization too. Pettibone says nothing. We all cut her some slack. Fred, her husband, managed to hit his ankle with a hand axe while trying to split firewood. It's gotten infected. The few antibiotics Doctor Randhawa has scrounged up so far aren't making much of a difference. Jill spends much of each day heating water, soaking the foot, and re-dressing the wound. Fred's a bit of a weenie and a lousy patient. Her bleached blonde hair has reverted to its original dark brown. She wears no makeup—no one does. Jill's face shows her worry. She's still a natural beauty.

We're what's left of an original group of dozens of enthusiastic citizens. Hunger, illness and general malaise have whittled us down to this. Ike Belton is not part of the Patrol. This morning's discussion, like others, eventually turns toward his control of Elmhurst's east side.

"Andres, what's the word in Ike's world?" Pettibone asks.

"Not much, Chief. Word is that some kid tried to steal food from the A.M.E. Church's food line last night. I didn't get much out of anyone, but the boy got the hell kicked out of him by some of Ike's henchmen. Didn't kill him, but there are some broken ribs, at the least."

The stocks of food are dwindling fast. People are hungrier. I'm surprised there haven't been more incidents like this.

Pettibone shakes his head. His attempts at a town-wide patrol have been snuffed by Ike Belton. Belton feels he's mean enough, and black enough, that he doesn't need our help on "his side of town." It's a sore spot with Pettibone, but there are few reports of problems from that area. The Patrol gets some information from Ike's territory, mostly from Lujan's relatives and a very few of the African Americans. It's done quietly. Anyone living within Ike's reach makes it clear the information shared is being done on the q.t. Ike Belton has a nasty temper and isn't afraid to punish anyone he thinks is talking out of school.

Josh Cerveny grunts, and mutters, "I guess Belton is helping us by giving us less area to cover."

He's right. Belton's attitude to "outsiders" hasn't changed since I quickly fled from in front of his barbeque pit, months earlier. Belton also nurses a personal grudge against the Chief. When the two houses in the Las Brisas subdivision were torched with Molotov cocktails, a child burned up in one of the houses. The adjoining Anglo landowner took a shot at the black perp but missed and killed a neighbor kid—who was also black. Pettibone locked up the white landowner in the basement of City Hall to keep a mob from getting to him. That was the night before I turned down Pettibone's request for help. Seeing no court system available to sort the mess out, the Chief "discovered" the white guy "escaped" a month ago. Rumor, and it's only rumor, is that the condition of the landowner's "escape" is that he and his family get the hell out of Elmhurst and never come back. A rough justice, to be sure, but with the mess the country's in, it makes sense. Ike is convinced Pettibone was instrumental in the action. So am I. The Chief isn't talking.

Pettibone gives us our assignments. We mostly patrol at night, armed and on bicycles. Some of the patrol members have their own firearms. Josh uses my .357 magnum revolver. Pettibone retrieved a revolver from his evidence locker for Jill. After taking a load of shit about losing both the AR15 and the Glock, Pettibone scrounged up a 1911 Colt .45 for me. The damned thing weighs a ton and has a notoriously bad reputation for accuracy. The saying goes that if you want to kill someone with it, take it out of the holster, get within three or four feet of the intended target, and throw it as hard as you can—and pray you don't miss. I ought to swap the thing to Josh for my revolver, but for some reason, I don't.

A couple of us suggest additional people who might join the Patrol, and Pettibone agrees to check them out. I'm not hopeful. I think that we are all the Chief's going to get. Everyone else is too hungry, tired and preoccupied with getting through one day at a time.

With some hours to kill, I pedal home and check my water storage tank. There's some wet ground around its base. It hasn't gotten any worse, so I recruit Josh Cerveny's two kids to help me inventory foodstuffs I ordered before the EMP or scrounged afterward. Elsie seems glad to take a break, and David and Sarah eagerly follow my orders as I go through a blank photocopied checklist I'd run off and saved.

Both kids are whip smart. Elsie continues to homeschool them, and they read labels on cans, boxes and containers with ease. Soon, much too soon, we're done. I thank the two and they run off. I walk to the patio and review the inventory. My supplies are dwindling much faster than I want them to. Some is the Cerveny family. It's impossible to allow a family to live in your house and pretend its members aren't aware of a dining room and part of a basement stacked with food. The Cervenys are earning their keep. No one's broken into the house or any outbuildings, and Josh can repair just about anything. I've also provided some flour and sugar to the Kaufmans.

I sigh, fold the paper, add it to the other inventories, and glance at the sun. I pedal to Anson Gutierrez' home. He's linked up with other radio operators. The back room in his place has an array of radios, speakers, antennas, and other HAM stuff I can't describe.

"*Que ule*, Anson. Anything new?"

"Not dark. Better reception at night. We'll keep you posted." Anson is eager to show me some newly pieced-together contraption he assures will extend his transmission range. I try to act like I know what in hell he's talking about, then say my goodbyes.

The sun is dropping quickly in the west. It's time to begin our patrol.

Cerveny and I get lucky and draw the use of an ATV tonight. Pettibone's confiscated four or five of them from reluctant owners, and three are in running condition. Cerveny checks the fuel level. We head to the Elmhurst Street Department's yard to top it off. The City's gasoline bulk tank is still half full. Two turns on the rotary fuel pump, and the ATV's small tank is full.

"Where to, Dalton?"

Night patrolling means additional weapons and equipment, but it's still light out. "Let's just cruise for a bit."

We wander the neighborhoods for a while. The ATV's noise draws attention. There are almost no vehicles running, anywhere. Some folks wave. Others sit in their yards in lawn chairs and just stare. Meandering from street to street for a couple of miles, something becomes apparent. I see very few overweight people anymore. Men's belt ends flop down, a sure sign of newly punched belt holes cinching up pants. I start to make a joke about all the fat people I used to see in Walmart, when Cerveny cuts me off. "Look at that fella." He points toward a back yard.

I stop the ATV. A man in his fifties or sixties stands in an overgrown back yard is trying to chop down a pecan tree. The tree is old, and the man's axe looks dull. We dismount and walk through the fence's gate.

"Hey. Why're you cutting the tree down. He's notched the tree in a way that it's bound to fall on someone's roof.

He looks up. I recognize Leroy Carter, a retired school-teacher. "Leroy. You're gonna get a heart attack doing that."

Carter appears shocked at our sudden appearance. He glances at our firearms.

Leroy is panting and he looks exhausted. I walk to the tree. "At this rate, you'll finish about the time you turn eighty, if you don't die of heat stroke or a heart attack."

Leroy mutters something that I don't catch. I look around. He's not on his property. He's cutting down someone else's tree. "Whose house is this?" I ask.

Leroy looks up defiantly, but doesn't appear to know who I am. "We're about out of firewood at our house. Winter's coming, and we don't have enough. No one's going to miss this tree. It's been nearly dead for decades."

"Mister Carter." He was my twelfth-grade calculus teacher, and I hope calling him by his last name will jog his memory. "This isn't the way to do this, and you know it. Put the axe

down. We'll figure out another way to get you some firewood."
I haven't got a clue how this is going to happen.

Carter leans the axe against the tree. All bluster seems gone.
In high school, he didn't take any shit off me. I respected him
because he was one of the few teachers who'd get in my face
and tell me to quit acting like an asshole. His words. Now, he's
just another defeated, tired and desperate man worrying about
a future he never envisioned.

Carter shakes his head, glances at my face two times.
"You're Dalton Kirby."

I nod in agreement.

"My wife and I moved back here five years ago. Haven't see
you around." He recovers some of his grit. "Never thought
you'd amount to a hill of beans with that attitude of yours."

Fuck you, you wood stealing son of a bitch. "Well, I probably
didn't, sir. But Elmhurst is in a poor way, and you know what
they say, 'Beggars can't be choosers.'"

Unexpectedly, Carter extends his hand. "Good to see you,
son. I guess there *are* better ways of going about this."

I shake his hand and introduce him to Josh. As we leave, I turn.
"Mr. Carter, we'll figure a way to get firewood to you and others."

Back on the ATV, Josh turns to me. "What's gotten into you?
You made a mighty big promise back there. You pull that out of
your ass? How're you going to find firewood for everyone?"

I don't know, but something about cutting down Elmhurst's
trees for kindling rubs me the wrong way. There are miles of
uncut saplings in the county.

"I'll think of something."

Josh and I go to my house, and load the ATV with flashlights,
rifles, and a thermos of boiled coffee provided by Elsie Cerveny.

We weave through the city streets slowly. I'm hoping for a boring shift. I haven't seen my daughter in a day-and-a-half. It seems every time I blink, the little baby has changed.

"You're thinking about Josefina, aren't you?"

"Is it that obvious?"

"I've got two of my own, now under your roof. Don't worry. The little girl will be there in the morning."

He's got a point. Gail continues to live on the hundred acres owned by her parents. One heifer and a couple of chickens have disappeared, but the Kaufman farm appears safe. Josefina gets enough attention for ten children from me, her grandparents, uncle, and of course, her mother. Still, I can't wait to see her.

"You and Gail doing okay?"

Actually, we are. We're not living together. Or having sex. But the baby's built a bridge between us that wasn't there before. I find myself on the Kaufman's porch sometimes, holding my daughter, sipping on a glass of water, and simply, well, content. The feeling is often fleeting, but I take what I can get. Not surprisingly, Gail is a super mom. I tell Josh that. "Did I tell you I used to call Bertha Kaufman, Momma B?"

"No, you didn't."

I turn on the road into the heavily wooded City Park. The ATV's engine masks any sounds but its own. The occupants of an earlier tent city have cleared out. Either they've moved in with relatives or decided to move on. Nothing remains but trash, ashes of fires, and a scattering of human shit.

"When we were going through the divorce, I made the mistake of using Momma B when addressing her. That she-cat damned near came after me with claws." I pause. "Two days ago, I accidentally used the term Momma B. I almost shit once it came out of my mouth. And you know what?"

"What?" Josh shines his flashlight into some trees near park's entrance.

"Josh, the woman just smiled. She patted me on the arm and smiled. Amazing."

"Dalton, kill the engine on this thing."

I comply. The only noise I hear is the metal pinging on the ATV's hood as the engine cools. "What?"

"There's something down in that creek bottom." Josh points toward the tree line thirty yards away. "I think I saw people running into the brush over there." He points.

I start the engine and drive where the ATV's headlights will help illuminate the area. We step out and move carefully under the trees, staying about ten yards apart. I shine my flashlight down toward the creek bed. The crunch of gravel and pounding of feet tell me Josh is right. More than one person is using the dry creek bed as an escape route.

"I wonder what all that's about?" Josh asks.

"I'm not going down into that bottom by myself, and neither are you. If we both go, we may come back to a missing ATV. Where were they coming from?"

We move back to the edge of the tree line and Josh points in the direction he thinks the group was coming from.

We mount the ATV and slowly move up the tree line, shining our flashlights to each side of the headlamps.

"There!" Josh points toward something about forty yards away. "Are those *bodies*?"

Only one way to find out. We cautiously drive toward two lumps in the tall grass. Leaving the engine running with its headlamps aiding us, we walk toward the lumps. I shine my flashlight and make out the shapes of two men. Both are lying face down. Josh rolls the first one over on his back. He's a large white man, dressed in jeans and a motorcycle shirt. He's heavily tatted. A bullet has entered his head cheek high. He no longer has the back of his skull. Brain matter is scattered through the grass.

I roll over the second body. Another male, somewhat

smaller, with a long-sleeve shirt. The shirt is one mass of red. Two holes show where he was hit.

We go through the dead men's clothing. Neither has any ID. They don't appear to be locals. Their bodies are still warm.

Josh states the obvious. "This just happened. If we'd got here a couple a seconds earlier, we could 'a prevented this."

That's not what I'm thinking. If we arrived a few minutes earlier, there might be four dead bodies lying in the grass.

———————

Chapter Nineteen

TWO MEN EXECUTED ON THE INTERSTATE, JACOB'S COOL dispatching of thugs in a service station parking lot, the Lee County Sheriff Baird oozing life from a gunshot wound, and now two unknown males killed just minutes ago. I take a quick mental inventory and realize that with each event, I've felt less shocked. I am more and more inured to the violence.

Suddenly, I become aware that we are exposed. Josh seems to sense it too, and we both grab our rifles out of the ATV and move into the tree line. Usually, unflappable, Josh sounds scared as he asks, "They coming back?"

"I have no idea."

I reach for the radio clipped to my vest. Its transmission range is about three miles, which will suffice tonight. Lee County had received a bunch of equipment from the Feds for disaster preparedness. Unwittingly, some County worker unwittingly spared about twenty of the radios from EMP damage by storing them in the Courthouse basement. Elmhurst has been allotted five.

"Chief, this is Patrol One." Patrol One is Josh and me tonight. "Chief, you read me?"

Pettibone doesn't answer, but Jill Aston does. Six of us are out, in three patrols. She's odd man out tonight, and is at home, where she can take care of Fred's wound. She sounds like she's been sleeping. "What's up, Dalton?"

"We're at City Park and have two dead bodies."

Jill's voice suddenly becomes crisper. "Say again?"

I repeat the information, and Jill promises to track down Pettibone. I break contact.

"Shit. Shit. Shit."

"What?"

'We're hiding in the fucking trees, and I just asked the Chief to toddle over here in the dark."

I contact Jill again. "Tell the Chief to hold short of the park and to radio us. We'll come to him." I said too much, dammit. I'll be surprised if we don't get onlookers before dawn. The patrol radios are supposed to be encrypted but aren't very well. The HAMs listen in at will. Word of the killings will be all over town by morning. Shit!

We sit quietly for several minutes. The only sounds are dogs barking in the distance.

"Dalton, I think we're okay."

I agree, and we return to the ATV and move out of the City Park. Pettibone shows up on an ATV twenty minutes later.

"Let's go take a look," says Pettibone. "Whoever killed those two aren't going to be waiting for us."

I hope not.

Pettibone pulls into the grass beside us and spends a few minutes checking the bodies. I tell him we've already checked for IDs and come up empty. It doesn't stop the Chief from rifling pockets again. Finding nothing, he walks to his ATV. Occasionally, one of us shines a light out into the trees, but by this time, we're not expecting any trouble. Whoever did this isn't coming back. The waxing moon's three-quarter crescent creates a silvery vagueness of the wooded areas.

The Chief is in a philosophical mood. His ATV is parked next to ours and we use the two as comfortable seats as we await the dawn. The three of us sit in the dark, saving batteries, and trade ideas on how these unknown individuals wound up in our City Park and dead.

"Hard to believe I'm sitting out here with you jokers and two stiffs over there in the grass," he says in the dark. In my mind, I see his hand gesturing toward the cooling bodies. "If This happened in normal times, we'd have EMS and PD over here in a heartbeat. We'd have followed the perps, taken shoe-print casts, canvassed every house within half a mile from here. Asked for tracking dogs from the State, got roadblocks up. With a municipality this size, someone would have seen someone. Chances would be we'd nail a perp within a week or two. Now? Unless someone walks up to me and says, 'Chief, I know who shot those two guys found in the City Park—the shooter's name is Joe Blow,' we won't know who or why."

Josh and I stay quiet. I sense that Pettibone needs to let off some steam. He's been trying to keep this place together for weeks now. The truth is that he's doing a hell of a job, but with everything else going on, I wonder whether he senses how well he's doing. Maybe he feels there's no fixing what's broken and he's feeling the futility of it all.

Finally, he winds down. A pre-dawn breeze wafts around us. "What are we gonna do with the bodies?" Josh asks.

"That's another thing."

I guess he's not through yet.

"We'd have the bodies to the Medical Examiner up at the capital. That old butcher's got, or did have, a contract with Lee County for these types of things, you know?"

I didn't but Pettibone's question is rhetorical.

"We'd get a bunch of information, like angle of track and such that would help show how they were located when they were killed. We'd get the State boys to run lab work and get

DNA samples. Oh, well." He slumps back resignedly. "We'll fingerprint these guys and take 'em out to the cemetery and bury 'em. Who knows? Maybe something will turn up."

In an odd way, the stillness of the park is calming. Chief Pettibone seems more human. I've found out the small pills slipped under his tongue is for angina. He's got a bad ticker. He could, and should quit, spend more time with his dying wife, but won't. His and her health are off-limits for discussion.

The talk fends off the slight chill. The moon's moved behind us. We're just three men shooting the shit.

With the early morning light, we scour the area for shell casings and anything else that might be relevant and turn up four empty 9mm shells. Pettibone puts them in a plastic bag and starts his ATV. "I'll send someone with something to wrap those guys in. We'll lay them out in one of the rooms at City Hall. I'll see who we can get to take a gander at the two before they start to stink too much. Someone might know them, but I doubt it. You guys go get some sleep."

Josh and I drop off the ATV and ride bicycles home. As I pedal, I look around and wonder if anyone I see is a murderer. The dead men aren't from around here, but that's not unusual anymore. There are more people drifting in from Lincoln City every day. What the two were doing in the City Park after dark, and why they were shot, confounds me.

I lock the cable around the bike. The adrenalin rush of the night's event has drained out. My joints and my mind ache with exhaustion. I think there is a very good chance no one, except the killers, will ever know any more than what I do right now. It's depressing.

The morning temperature according to the thermometer advertising the local feed store is a cool 55 degrees. I desperately want to see Josefina, but my open-windowed bedroom is too inviting. I lie on the ragged bedspread and am asleep within seconds.

I wake as the back-door screen slaps shut. It's afternoon and the house is beginning to swelter. I pass Elsie in the kitchen. We're not cooking in there—it's too hot and often not light enough. Josh and I have moved the oven/stove combination under the patio and re-jetted the appliance for propane. Elsie still uses the counter space for slicing and dicing, and the cupboards still hold all the dishes. It is a touch of normality.

"Hey, Dalton. Josh told me what happened. Sorry about what you guys had to see last night."

"Thanks, Elsie. It's a puzzler." I'm preoccupied and it shows. She smiles as David and Sarah dodge past me on my way outside. I have things I need to do, and I need to see my child.

The bicycle's tires feel a bit low and the tire gauge confirms it. I hook up the hand pump and add some pressure. Five blocks later, I bump over the railroad tracks. I've been giving the firewood issue more thought and hope I have an answer. North of Elmhurst some three miles, George Hixson owns a hundred acres. He raises cattle as a hobby, but his real love is antique motor vehicles. I hope he's not still pissed off at me.

The bicycle coasts down the long hill toward the narrow bridge over Little Elm River on a poorly paved country road. When the county began changing some of the road designations from numbers to names, George became such a pain in the ass at County Commissioners meetings that they threw up their hands and designated it Hixson Lane.

The bottomland is thick with trees. The river is deep here, and the shadows of the foliage make its surface appear almost black. For a few moments, memories of swimming holes and rope swings and endless summer days make me smile.

The cool air disappears as I pedal away from the recollections and toward George Hixson's place. His electric gate doesn't work. I pedal by several storage sheds. The door to the largest one is open. Sacks of fertilizer are piled high on pallets. I get to the house, climb off, rub my sore ass, then, halloo the house and get no answer. I set the bicycle against a tree and walk toward a barn-like structure.

"George, you here?"

"Quit yelling, goddammit. I'm inside."

I follow the voice. Legs extend from the undercarriage of a Model T. "It's Dalton," I say.

"No shit, Sherlock." George slides the creeper out, wipes his hands-on filthy coveralls, and drops a crescent wrench on the cement floor. "What do you want?"

"Christ, George, is that fertilizer ammonium nitrate?" I've read somewhere the stuff is dangerous if not stored properly. Not that I care, but it's an opportunity to give Hixson some shit. "Are you planning on fertilizing all of Lee County, or blowing up something?"

George's face turns red, a sign that he's pissed off. I change the subject. "You still got that old Dodge Power Wagon?"

George tilts his head. "You know that damned thing hasn't worked in years. Engine froze up."

He still looks mad, but I think I've got his attention. "I need it."

"*You* need it. You gave me shit for riding a Model T into town. You come by two months later and now *you* want something? You are a cheeky bastard."

As I've said, George is a conspiracy theorist from way back. Brilliant but a few bricks short of a load. He and I have agreed to disagree on damned near everything, mainly to keep from killing each other. We've also drunk more than a few beers together. He somehow held onto his place during his second divorce, a nasty one, by being such a shitass that his wife threw up her hands and told him to take everything—she just wanted out. George was the only person I'd dared confide in when I bought the BMW and sidecar with the money I'd ratholed during my own divorce. He'd acknowledged a grudging admiration for a fellow skunk. I hope I can trade his goodwill for use of the Power Wagon.

"Shit, George, you know I'm just like you. How're you doing?"

"Doing okay, I guess. No one's bothered me, so far." George looks like he's doing more than okay. His windmill's pump rods move water into a steel tank with six-foot-tall sides. He has an old cast iron pitcher pump installed onto a hand dug well. Smoke drifts gently from a smokehouse. A couple of cats loll in the shade provided by the two-bedroom house's east wall. I take it all in.

He interrupts my reverie. "What do you want with that old junker?"

I decide to tell the truth. "People are going to cut down all the trees in town if I don't figure a way to haul firewood."

"Who gives a shit? What they deserve for living in town."

I resist the urge to remind George he was born and raised in Dallas and didn't discover country living until he was in his forties. "Well, I do, because they'll probably cut down some of mine in the process." I explain the plan to take chainsaw crews to cut fire- and cordwood out in the county on raw land.

He snorts. "Even if you can get that junker to run, what's in it for me?"

Gotcha. Now it's just a matter of how much this is going to cost.

The Power Wagon is a beast. Non-synchronized transmission, a rear-end gear ratio that ensures the thing will never break fifty miles per hour, and heavy as a house. I remember pictures of my dad beside one when he ran a seismograph crew as a young man. The one in the picture was tough looking. The truck I'm staring at in George's open shed looks like a priest needs to give it Last Rites. I openly wonder whether it can be made roadworthy before all the forests in North America are hewn down.

I pause and just stare. *I can't believe I'm begging this guy for the use of this monstrosity.*

"You want it or not?"

I do, but there's no way to move the thing. "Can we work on it here?"

George bridles. "I don't much like people, and now you want me to let someone come on my place?"

I explain, again. In the end, I've made a deal. I've only got to convince about seven people to play along by providing parts and labor to make it work. And convince Chief Pettibone that it is in the best interests of Elmhurst for him to 'donate' five hundred gallons of gasoline to the contrariest man in Lee County.

Piece of cake.

It's dusk when I ride onto the Kaufman property. My ass is sore from the bicycle seat and the Colt .45 has chafed a raw spot on my right hip from the up and down of the pedal motion. For the umpteenth time, I regret the loss of the Glock.

Billy comes down from the porch. "Hey, Dalton. You doing okay?"

We shake hands. "How's Josefina?"

He laughs. "Dalton, you could at least act like you're glad to see me."

"Okay." He's got a point. "How ya doing, Billy?"

"I'm fine, Gail's fine, Josefina's fine. Momma's fine."

Nothing is said about Gail's father Randall. I let it pass and walk onto the porch. Bertha's set out a tub with water, a bar of soap, and an old dishrag. No one goes inside without clean hands. I kick off my boots and set them to the side, then tap on the screen door. Josefina is crying somewhere toward the back of the house.

"Come in, Dalton."

Gail approaches the front door as I enter. Her hair is knotted in a bun. She wears jeans and blue work shirt. She's barefoot. I reach out and touch her hand. "How're you doing?"

"Worn out. It's your turn in the barrel."

I grin. Bertha sits in a wooden rocker rocking a squirming Josefina. "She's fussy today. Maybe she needs some daddy time." Bertha's face remains neutral, but I detect a slight tic and think she's trying not to smile. I've got a long way to go to get out of her doghouse, but I might be making some progress.

Gail returns from the kitchen mixing the contents of a bottle of formula. "I'm still breast feeding, but the little booger needs more nourishment than what I've been able to produce."

There's little of the powdered stuff left. I haven't found any formula in Elmhurst and have Elsie Cerveny and Jill Alson sniffing around for some. No luck so far.

I settle onto a sofa in the den with Josefina. I touch her cheek with the nipple and she begins to nurse hungrily on the bottle. She is beautiful. The day's temperature is dropping quickly.

After a while, Bertha says, "You need to burp her, or she'll get real fussy."

Gingerly, I place the little child on my shoulder and begin to pat her back. Suddenly, Josefina lets out a huge burp. We all laugh as I return her to the fold in my arm and place the bottle to her mouth. Bertha nods approvingly and drapes a small blanket over her granddaughter.

Soon, Josefina is asleep. Gail takes the empty bottle, winks and jokingly says, "I hate you. It's been a struggle all day with her."

Josefina is doing fine. I worry about the lack of vaccination for basic kid diseases, but Doctor Randhawa never kept any serum around. Maybe a pediatrician in Lincoln City has some, but short of a life-or-death situation, I'm not going back there. Right now, I'm just content to hold Josefina, and wonder at her features.

I bring Gail and Bertha up to date on Elmhurst, HAM accounts of elsewhere in the country, and the efforts to obtain the Power Wagon. The two dead men aren't mentioned.

Billy shucks his coveralls on the front porch and soon joins the discussion. My arm goes to sleep holding Josefina, but I'll be damned if I'll admit it. Finally, Bertha lights some candles and oil lamps and invites me to stay for supper. It's too late to ride the bicycle back to Elmhurst, and I'll sleep on the daybed on the front porch.

Billy asks if he can hold his niece. He handles the child like she is fine china. We move to the table. It dawns on me I haven't seen Randall.

"Where's Randall, Bertha?"

"He's not doing so well, Dalton."

What the hell? I look at Gail.

"Daddy's blood pressure medication ran out yesterday. He's resting right now."

Suddenly, I'm not hungry. The old man's had blood pressure problems for years. Without medication, it will go through the roof. "What kind is he taking?"

Bertha produces two empty prescription bottles and gives me their generic names—amlodipine besylate and candesartan.

I open my mouth to say something. Gail quickly cuts me off. "Don't say a thing, Dalton. We'd have done something about this before now, but Daddy thought he had several more bottles. He didn't."

We sit and eat quietly. Afterward, I help Gail and Bertha clean the dishes. Once the dishes are done Bertha takes me onto the back porch. Randall is sitting quietly on a glider.

"Howdy, Randall."

"Hey, Dalton. I screwed up, I guess."

Randall's always been quiet and self-assured. Coming from him, this statement hits me harder than I expect. "Heck, it'll be okay." I can't think of anything else to say.

"I've let my family down, son. I didn't take care of this when I should have. Just assumed it'd be okay." Randall sweeps both hands over his balding head.

He just referred to me as 'son.' In many ways, I feel like one. I love this old man. I sit in a wicker chair. Gail starts breast feeding Josefina. Crickets erupt with early evening chirrups. Bertha brings the blood pressure cuff, pumps it up and reads the gauge as Billy holds a flashlight.

"175 over 110," she announces.

Randall just nods. He seems defeated.

Finally, I pipe up. "I'll see what I can find in town, Randall."

"Even if you find something, Dalton, what happens when I run out the next time? Or the next?"

I know the answer but am determined help to postpone the inevitable.

"Billy, would you help me push the BMW out of the shed? I need to get back to town tonight."

Billy grins. "Sure, Dalton." We push the machine backward, and then turn the handlebars to get it pointed in the right direction. He hands me my helmet.

"Thanks."

"Sure." Billy looks at me quizzically. "Dalton, you're going to look for medicine for Daddy, aren't you?"

I put the key in the ignition and turn the petcock to open the fuel line. "Yeah. I guess I am."

A grin creases his sunburnt face.

"What's so funny?"

Billy pats me on the back. "You better be careful, Dalton. Someone might start thinking you're a pretty nice guy."

Damn. Not sure I need that. I give him my best scowl, fire up the engine and kick it into gear.

Chapter Twenty

THERE WERE TWO PHARMACIES IN ELMHURST. ONE WAS LOCALLY owned, the other part of a national chain. Shortly after the EMP, both were broken into. The looters were run off before they could get their hands on any controlled substances, but they managed to trash both locations. Chief Pettibone insisted that the prescription drugs be moved to a place where they wouldn't disappear. Jim Conrad, the elderly owner of the Corner Drug Store, went one step further.

"Hell, I can't guarantee I won't get broken into again, and I'm too old to stop it. It may turn out that a lot of other stuff besides dope is going to be needed. Empty my God damned store out to the walls. It's not doing me any good, and I have a feeling folks in Elmhurst may need some or all of it."

No one ever showed up at the national chain's location, so the Chief followed Conrad's suggestion with that store's inventory as well. City workers emptied out both the drug stores and secured everything in an old National Guard armory. The place is built like a fort, and Pettibone found a welder with an acetylene rig to weld bars on all the windows and reinforce the steel doors. The armory now holds an array of over the counter and prescription medications and health aids. Doctor Jagir Randhawa is custodian of those inventories.

Perhaps I'll get lucky.

The ride into town seems to take forever. I turn into Doctor Randhawa's driveway and kill the engine. In normal times, a darkened house would indicate no one is home. Not anymore. I pull a small flashlight out of the handlebar's pouch and use it to guide me to the front door. After several knocks, a female voice asks who is out there.

"It's me, Dalton Kirby. Is the doc in?"

Several locks click, and the door cracks open. "Yes?"

I shine the flashlight up, but not on the woman's face. I recognize Mrs. Randhawa. She looks haggard.

"Sorry to bother you, but I need to talk with Jagir, if it's not too much trouble." I don't care how much trouble it is, pounding on a door after dark and expecting a friendly response requires at least some courtesy.

Doctor Randhawa's voice echoes through the house, speaking some language I can't understand but assume to be Hindi. Mrs. Randhawa opens the door wider and motions me inside. The doctor holds a flashlight he shines on the locks and deadbolt of the front door. Mrs. Randhawa finishes securing it.

Mrs. Randhawa touches my arm and says, "Please, won't you follow us into the sitting room." Her British accent is oddly calming. It is part of her old-world courtesy, and I remember the doctor mentioning that his wife had attended schools in England.

I shake hands with Doctor Randhawa and follow the two. The darkness melts into a glow of several candles set on various pieces of furniture in a comfortable room. The dark large-screen television now seems like an unwelcome intrusion into the warmth of comfortable furniture, shelves of books, framed paintings and a gentle but distinct scent of curry.

"Please, Kirby." The doctor motions toward a recliner. "Sit. What brings you here at this late hour?"

I suspect it's barely eight o'clock. I quickly explain Randall Kaufman's predicament, as Mrs. Randhawa reappears with delicate china cups and saucers which she places next to the doctor and then on a small table next to me.

"It is black tea, Mr. Kirby," she says. "Would you like sugar?"

The serenity of the moment is overwhelming. I want to sink into the cushions of the chair, close my eyes, and sleep. The brief reverie is interrupted by the doctor's next question.

"What type of medication is Mr. Kaufman taking?"

For a second, I'm puzzled.

"There are many kinds of hypertension medications, Kirby."

Duh. I pull the two empty pill bottles out of my pocket. Doctor Randhawa isn't the prescribing physician. I hand them to him. He holds the labels up to a candle.

"Doctor Tao. He is a heart specialist in Lincoln City." He pauses, then asks, "How much medication does Mr. Kaufman have left?"

"Actually, none."

"None? Oh, no, Dalton. That is not good. That is not good at all."

He continues, "We dribble out medicines only when absolutely necessary. Sadly, I must inform you that since local drug stores relied on just-in-time deliveries to keep inventories to a minimum, many medications have been exhausted. There is no more like these"—he holds up the empty containers—"on hand in Elmhurst for Mr. Kaufman's condition."

Doctor Randhawa turns to his wife and lapses into Hindi. She nods, takes a candle off a countertop and leaves the room. He motions toward my tea. "Please, it is cooling. Enjoy it while it is still warm."

He takes a sip and gently sets his cup onto its saucer. "Kirby,

I will confess to you that all medications are becoming quite scarce." He holds up the plastic pill bottles. "Especially certain critical ones."

I take another sip of the tea. It is delicious. I'm suddenly angry at myself. What right do I have to this comfort, when someone I know may be dying? I set the cup down quickly and startle at the noise of its contact with the saucer.

"Sorry."

The doctor waves a hand as if to assure me he knows what I am thinking. Mrs. Randhawa appears with an old-style doctor's bag. The two move toward a low coffee table next to where I sit. He unbuckles the leather strap and spreads the bag open, then places Randall's pill bottles next to the bag. As Mrs. Randhawa shines a flashlight, he reaches into the bag and pulls out a large glass bottle of pills.

"I am going to give you thirty pills for your ex-father in law." He counts out the pills then places them in one of the small plastic containers. "These are not quite the same as what he was prescribed, but they will suffice to give Mr. Kaufman some relief." He pauses. "I know what you are thinking. 'What happens when these are gone'?"

Exactly.

"People with diabetes need insulin. People suffering from hepatitis need suppressor drugs, Mr. Kaufman and others who are in danger of a stroke or heart attack need blood pressure medications." He pushes the plastic pill bottles into my hands. "I have no answer, other than to say that unless our country restores medical services, many will die." He shakes his head. "In fact, many have already died." He smiles faintly. "Tell Mister Kaufman not to work too hard. No splitting firewood." I grin. "You seem to know Randall well, Doc."

"I came to Elmhurst as a young doctor. Randall Kaufman was one of my first patients. You may not recall this. You are very young. But many years ago, when a hurricane hit the Gulf Coast, it's winds damaged many buildings here."

I do remember, barely. "I think I was three. Mostly I remember stories, Doc."

"My first office was almost destroyed. The roof disappeared. Probably a small tornado. Randall Kaufman came into town, saw what had happened. He recruited at least a dozen local men. They somehow obtained plastic tarps. I don't know how —the demand was great. They worked two days and covered the place. And Randall made sure the place remained weather-proofed until the insurance company could get workers to repair it."

I hadn't heard that story and tell him so.

"Randall Kaufman is a gentleman. He hasn't been my patient for many years, but I still consider him a very good friend."

Mrs. Randhawa insists that I finish my tea. I stand and thank them both. They walk me to the front door.

"Thanks again, Doctor." Mrs. Randhawa touches her husband's arm and I understand. I start down the steps, and then turn. "These pills. These are meds *you* need, aren't they?"

The door closes gently, and the locks are secured. I put the medication in a pouch, start the BMW's engine and slip it into gear. The doctor has given Randall Kaufman thirty days more of health and taken as many from his own.

Randall's blood pressure is still too high, but at least he's feeling better, and Bertha doesn't seem to think he'll blow a gasket momentarily. The family's gratitude is almost more than

I can handle since I haven't done anything but delay the inevitable. And that inevitability hangs over the Kaufmans like some sword from a Greek tragedy. I return the BMW to the Kaufman's shed, and crash on a day bed on the porch.

After breakfast, I pedal directly to Anson Gutierrez' house, on the north side of town.

"You got a second, Anson?" I peer through his front screen door and hope I don't piss him off.

"Shit fire!" Anson yells. "I just got to sleep. Leave me the hell alone!"

The floor reverberates with Anson's angry stomps as he walks toward me, pulling up a pair of dirty khakis.

It's mid-morning, but he looks like he just crawled out of bed. Which he has. Anson's HAM license works well with him being a night person. Better communication, and sometimes something called 'skip' at night, lets him reach through the airwaves to various places in the United States and, sometimes, to other parts of the globe. Since the EMP, he and his HAM operators, at least the ones whose rigs didn't get fried, are our ears and voice to the outside world. Which is why I'm here bothering him.

"You of all people, Dalton. You know damned well you shouldn't be bothering me."

Well, yes, but I need his help. I explain Randall Kaufman's situation and give him the names and dosages of the two medications.

"I'll see what I can do tonight," he says. "That is, if I'm not too damned tired to get on the air. I hear a lot of calls for meds. There are three possibilities."

I try not to grin at Anson's attempt to shame me. Isn't gonna happen. "What are they?"

"I'll get lucky and someone will have some extra meds that will work for Randall. Or, I'll strike out, but eventually some other HAM will track the stuff down. Or, most likely, no one will have any luck, or admit to being able to score what you need."

"Sounds like you're in the drug market, Anson."

"I am. This is just like trying to score dope on the street."

"Thanks for trying." I turn to leave.

"Oh, and another thing."

"What?"

"What are you willing to pay?"

I have no idea. "Pay? Who's got money that's worth anything, Anson? What's it going to cost?"

"No idea, but you better be thinking fast about what you are willing to trade, because nothing I find is going to wind up in your hands out of the kindness of someone's heart. There's a shortage of that commodity right now."

Anson waves off my goodbye and grumbles as he shambles back toward his bedroom and interrupted sleep. As I walk the bicycle to the street, I sense a slight movement and turn to see two young boys in the adjacent yard. Both are barefoot and shirtless and are listlessly kicking a partly deflated soccer ball back and forth. One looks over and raises an arm to wave. He ignores his chum's pass and the ball thuds against the yard's sole tree.

"Hi, mister." The kids walk toward me. "You were talkin' with the radio man, weren't you?"

"Yes, I was." I look closely at the two. Both appear Hispanic. "What are you guys up to?"

The talker ignores my question. "Is anyone gonna send us some food, mister?"

The kids' arms are thin, and their ribs are visible. "How old are you two?"

The talker tells me he's Robert and he's ten. "Jose, he's nine. Why?"

Jesus. Robert's eyes are sunken back in his head. "When's the last time you guys had anything to eat?"

Jose picks at his nose as Robert says, "Momma made tortillas this morning. We each got two." He fidgets, as if embarrassed. "We had some beans and rice too."

Jose stops his nose picking. "Not much though. We're hungry."

They are more than that. They're malnourished. Badly. "My name's Dalton. I'll ask Mister Gutierrez, the radio man, if he can find out something tonight, okay?" It's a bullshit response, but all I've got.

They nod solemnly. Jose pulls the stalk off some Johnson grass and begins to chew on it. I ride away.

I arrive home and find Elsie Cerveny in the garden. She's furiously grubbing with a hoe, tending rows of seed potatoes.

"Hey, Elsie. How're you doing?"

Startled, she looks up. "Oh, Dalton. Scared me. Guess I was wrapped up in my own thoughts." She looks worried.

"Where is everyone?"

She's given the two children a break from her home schooling, and Josh is in the garage, repairing a small engine. After a few minutes of pleasantries, I walk toward my back door.

"Dalton?" Elsie puts aside the hoe, and, wiping her hands, motions toward my patio. "Can you talk for a minute?"

Uh oh. "Sure."

After a couple of moments, she asks, "You know we're running out of food?"

My stash of MREs, canned and dried foods wasn't intended for the additional four people now under my roof, but I haven't spent much time worrying about it. "Sure, Elsie, but we'll make do."

She shakes her head. "Not so sure about that. We've got this garden, but its produce will only stretch so far. The growing season is about over with for most vegetables. We've been hit by cutworms and other bugs that will reduce what we get out of the ground." She pauses. "We're eternally grateful to you for what you've done for us, but the plain truth is that you don't have enough food for all of us through the coming winter."

She's probably right. No, she *is* right. "You got any suggestions?"

"No, but you need to hear that if it gets down to it, we're prepared to move elsewhere. You've got to deal with a new baby, and neither Josh nor I have any idea what the Kaufmans have for food supplies."

Elsie's suggestion that she and her family are prepared to leave comes as a jolt. "You guys aren't going anywhere." As I say the words, I'm surprised at how strident they sound. Somewhere in the last weeks, our relationship has changed. The family is here because Josh had some skills I needed. Now, I appreciate the presence of Elsie, Jacob and Sarah as well. "We'll figure something out."

"Dalton, we know you started in better shape than most folks, 'cause you sort of prepared for this stuff. But, if you haven't noticed, folks are going hungry. Unless something changes quickly, all of Elmhurst is going to be in a pickle."

Maybe it's been gradual, or maybe I've been around it so much I haven't noticed, or maybe paid attention. I tell her of Robert and Jose and their gaunt and undersized appearance.

The conversation lapses into uncomfortable silence. Josh appears from the side of garage, wiping his hands on an oily rag. He asks, "How is Josefina?"

Elsie has yet to see the child. "Yes, Dalton. How's your daughter? And the rest of the family?"

I launch into a recitation of Josefina's amazing traits. I smile and realize my friend has moved us away from a painful subject. One that I can't continue to ignore.

"Elsie, you're right. We are going to be in a pickle. I mean what I say. Your family is far safer here than elsewhere."

We've been assuming what we're going through will end. That things will get back to some sort of normal. Elsie is voicing what I haven't wanted to deal with.

She volunteers to re-inventory every foodstuff on the property. Our informal and haphazard rationing is going to become more disciplined. The Kaufmans will need to do the same.

I give Elsie a kiss on the cheek. "Thanks." I've got other matters to deal with.

I walk next door and knock on the Aston's door. Jill looks so haggard I don't take my usual peek at her breasts. She motions me inside. Fred sits on a kitchen chair by the living room window, his foot elevated onto another chair.

Fred smiles. "Hello neighbor. Good to see you. You've been scarce lately."

I have been. Our friendship was mostly based on my attraction to Jill. The attraction is still there, but things have changed. I have changed.

"Sorry. Things are crazy, as Jill's no doubt told you. How's the ankle healing?"

Fred's smile remains intact, but his voice is strained. "Getting better, Dalton. I'll be up as good as new soon." He lifts the clean dishtowel covering the wound. It oozes pus. It is red and angry looking. He looks at the wound, then looks me directly in the eye, as if to dare me to say otherwise.

I glance at Jill. She stands behind Fred's chair and gives an almost imperceptible shake of her head, as if to confirm that Fred's cheerful assessment of the wound's condition is very wrong.

Oh, Jesus. First Randall. Now Fred.

We shake hands, and I promise to drop by more often. Jill walks me outside. "It's infected. There's no more antibiotic available, according to Doctor Randhawa."

Jill's got enough on her plate, so I don't share the results of last night's visit with the good doctor. "Are you still soaking it?"

She tears up and nods. "Fred knows what's going on, I think. We just pretend otherwise. I know you think he's a bit of a softy, but my husband is showing me he's tough inside."

Yes, I have thought that. Now, I just saw some grit he didn't have before. Or, maybe I didn't care to notice.

Pettibone and Andres Lujan stop their discussion when I walk into the City Hall alcove. I push aside my worries for Randall and Fred and focus on George Hixson's truck. I leave out the promise for five hundred gallons of gasoline and explain Elmhurst's need to get the Power Wagon up and running. Pettibone looks skeptical.

Andres smiles. "Some of my cousins are damned good shade-tree mechanics." He spools off several names, some I recognize as recent guests of the state penitentiary. "They're all sitting on their asses right now. If you can keep Hixson from calling them names, I think I can get them to ride their bicycles out there and try to get the thing running. They love old trucks."

"Thanks, Andres. That'd be great."

"If they get it going, those *pinche vatos* are going to expect that they'll be the ones to operate it."

I cock my head as if to ask why they'd want to take that on.

Andres laughs. "When they're not doing the good deeds for the local folks, they'll figure out some way of using the truck to do a little business of their own."

I don't even want to know what that entails. I glance at Pettibone before I answer. "Sure, that'll work."

Now I've got to figure out how to get five hundred gallons of gasoline, make Hixson refrain from his racist remarks, and pray that bunch of outlaws don't get caught using the Power Wagon hauling contraband. Piece of cake.

I shake hands and pedal back over to Anson's house. I need him to get on the airwaves to ask for two types of medication now. I'll drop off two MREs for Robert and Jose and their family when I get there.

Chapter Twenty-One

ANSON GUTIERREZ HAS ALWAYS BEEN A BIT OF A LONER. I HOPE he'll let me sit in on his nightly radio session. I can't sleep, and besides it's an excuse to drop the MREs off next door to Robert and Jose I pedal back to the north side of town. I chain my bicycle to Anson's front porch post, and walk next door

"Hello the house." I holler out my presence. When it starts to get dark, most folks understand courtesy and a healthy dose of self-preservation dictates you announce your presence before you near a darkened structure.

Nothing. I try again. Finally, a male voice responds. "What do you want?"

"I don't want anything." I explain I met Robert and Jose earlier in the day. "I have something for the family."

What sounds like a jam stick clatters to the floor, and the badly weathered door opens. A heavily bearded Hispanic, skinny as a rail, exits the house and shuts the door behind him. He inspects me in the dark as the thump of children's feet running emanates from inside. Robert appears from the re-opened door. "Pops, it's the guy who was next door at the radio man's house."

I extend my hand, the man shakes it, and says, "Guillermo Sosa."

"Mr. Sosa, these are for the family." I hand him the MREs. "It's not much but I suspect you guys aren't eating all that well right now. They're easy to fix, and maybe they'll help fatten up the boys a bit." Sosa stares at me as he takes the MREs I play it as a joke, but I hope that the two boys get at least some of the food.

Holding the packets, Sosa says, "I can't take this from you. You have a family too."

"Not so much, Mr. Sosa. I'm divorced." That doesn't cover the whole story, but it's enough. Guillermo Sosa is a proud man, but he's got a house full of hungry people.

"There are six of us here. The youngest is three. My mother, the boys' *abuelita*, she's eighty-six. Thank you." He shakes my hand and thanks me. Robert waves goodbye and the door closes.

That out of the way, I return to Anson's house. Tonight, he's secured the house's front entrance with more than the screen door. Through the now-closed wood door, I hear voices and electronic howls and static. Taking a deep breath, I beat on the door jamb and yell out, "It's Dalton. Let me in."

Inside, Anson keys a mike and talks loudly to another HAM operator. I rap on the jamb again and am surprised when he unlocks the door and waves me inside without a fuss. He's clearly preoccupied, and he returns to his various rigs to continue some discussion. The living room is full of solar panels I assume Anson is repairing or adding to his rooftop array. I clear some technical manuals off an old kitchen chair and carry it to the small room Anson uses for his HAM equipment. To my untrained eye, the place looks like a disaster area. A large calico cat rubs against my leg as it tries to enter. Anson gently tosses a toy mouse into the kitchen and the cat runs off. Apparently, the calico isn't allowed into the sanctum.

Anson twiddles dials, digital readouts blink, a small wattage lightbulb glows, and a portable generator the City salvaged and loaned him hums outside. While Anson takes notes, I stare at all the QSL postcards plastered on the walls and ceiling. They acknowledge radio contact between Anson and other HAM operators. Most are from familiar places: Saint Louis, Juneau, Vancouver. Some are more exotic. I spot one from Ulan Bator, Mongolia and another from Alejandro Selkirk Island, the supposed basis for Defoe's *Robinson Crusoe*. I'm impressed.

Anson signs off and asks, "Why are you back?"

I hand him a slip of paper. "Some antibiotics. Please check on this too. If any of your compadres can get ahold of something strong to treat an infected wound, it'd be appreciated."

"Can it be veterinarian grade?"

Huh? "Of *course* it can. It's the same stuff. Why?"

"Andres Lujan. His cousins." He rattles off several names. "I'm hearing they 'might' have broken into a vet's clinic." He mentions a small town twenty miles south of Elmhurst.

"How in God's name do you know this?" I shake my head, dumbstruck.

"The Lujans are family. Those guys are cousins of mine, too."

My laughter is loud, even to me.

"What's so damned funny? It's going to cost you, but at least you'll get it, and I won't have to waste my time on the radio trying to find it."

Anson shakes his head and promises to spend some of his time asking for Randall's blood pressure medicine. He's not aware of the deals I've been working for a firewood hauler. I can't stop giggling. Elmhurst is entrusting the operation of its soon-to-be running Dodge Power Wagon to a bunch of burglars. And I'm about to abet their misdeeds by begging medicine off them for my neighbor with a badly infected foot.

Josh stirs as I unlock the backdoor. I wigwag a flashlight beam and whisper my name, then head for my bedroom finally falling asleep as the dawn breaks. Anson and others will continue to provide what information they obtain about the EMPs. It looks like there were many, many distinct EMP incident across the United States and North America. Which explains why so little has been done at a national level. Some areas apparently weren't damaged, but no one is sure what that means for the rest of us. Unless someone shows me differently, I'm convinced that Elmhurst and its citizens are on their own for a long time to come.

I wake up to Josh yelling up the stairs. I may have slept three hours. "Dalton. Dalton. Need to talk with you. You awake?"

"I am now." Groaning, I pull on some shorts and slip on old huaraches. "What's going on?" Josh looks deeply troubled. Elsie's teaching the kids their lessons in the front of the house. "Let's go outside."

"You okay, Josh? Family okay? What is it?" The words tumble out. I follow him to the patio. Josh is normally a cool customer. Something bad has happened. I grab a lawn chair. "Okay, what's going on?"

Josh sits across from me. "I worked patrol last night, on rotation. There was a small house fire."

"Why wasn't I called?" We all help on those incidences.

"Not a big thing. It petered out on its own. We found five dead people in the house though."

A flood of questions follows. How? Where? Who?

"We're keeping it quiet, per the Chief's instructions. I don't know why. Half the neighborhood"—he mentions the subdivision— "saw or heard what happened." "Well, what *did* happen?"

"A whole family's been murdered. A whole goddamned family. All shot at point-blank range. Chief wants you to come to the scene."

I nod okay.

"It's not like those two we found in the park. This is a mother and father and three kids. The kids look the age of David and Sarah." Josh's face dissolves into tears, and he hides his face in his hands. "Oh, Jesus. It's awful, Dalton."

Josh has never shown this kind of emotion before. I follow silently to the city's ATV.

Ten minutes later, Josh delivers me to a fairly new development on the southwest edge of town. Large lawns, hedges, sprinkler systems, alarm company signs indicate a stable, affluent neighborhood. He turns onto Cosgrove Terrace. The short street is a cul-de-sac. At the end of the street there is nothing except farmers' fields and scattered stands of scrub oak. A large two-story house with attached two-car garage sits between two empty lots at the top of the circle. Several small groups of adults and children stand on various lawns of the Terrace's few occupied lots. Chief Pettibone and two of the citizen patrol, Jill Aston and Andres Lujan, huddle in a discussion at front door.

"I'm staying outside, Dalton. I've seen enough for right now. I'll keep any crowds away."

I nod, squeeze his arm, and walk through the yard's desiccated grass. "What's up?"

A stupid question, and the trio's expressions confirm it. Pettibone answers. "We've got a whole family dead in that house. Adult male's head caved in. The rest of the family executed." He points toward the front door, and I follow him inside. Jill's face is streaked with tears. Andre tries to look cool, but his hands are shaking uncontrollably. As I pass them, he makes the sign of the cross on his body. *Oh brother.*

The adult male, as Pettibone describes him, is someone I know. Make that knew. "Geez, Chief, that's Rick Simpson."

Former Elmhurst Police Officer Rick Simpson's body lies feet toward the front door, head in the tiled foyer. He's wearing a t-shirt and boxer shorts. Nothing on his feet. There's a dent in his forehead the size of a hammer peen. Which makes sense, as a ball peen hammer lays next to the body. To make sure of death, whoever hit him also put a bullet into his head. His left eye socket is mangled where the bullet went in, and the tiles around his head are soaked in blood and viscera. I start to heave and find a wastebasket just in time not to add to the mess.

Pettibone stands staring at the body of his former police-man. The Chief is ashen faced. I worry about his heart.

"Simpson was an asshole, Chief," I say, remembering the run-ins at City Hall. "But no one deserves this." I spit acidic phlegm into the wastebasket. "No one."

The air is dank. The blood isn't totally congealed. A fly lands on what was Rick's left eye. I want to turn toward the front door and leave. But don't. Pettibone is as white as a sheet. He needs the support of at least someone, and I seem to have drawn the short straw for this review of hell. Pettibone steps around the body. "This way." He turns to the left and into a large den/kitchen area.

Pettibone glances back as if to ensure I'll follow. "I'm coming Chief." Simpson quit Elmhurst Police Department when he didn't get a paycheck. I thought he'd left town. "Why's Simpson still in Elmhurst, Chief?"

"Missus Simpson's mom and dad's house. The McCades. Retired. Moved here to be closer to the grandkids, then decided they liked the open road better. Simpsons were sort of renting it while the McCades travelled around the good ole USA in a big-ass motor home. I guess the in-laws couldn't get back, so why not stay put?"

Because he and his family are dead, that's why.

The second part of the horror show takes place in the kitchen. A slight, sandy haired woman wearing short pants and a sleeveless blouse is slumped in a corner. I assume she is Simpson's wife. Her three children are massed into a small clump next to their mother's body. All have been shot once it the head. I think of Josefina and have to grab a chair to sit on. With head between my legs, I take deep breaths, through my mouth. The coppery smell of blood mixes with urine and human feces, released when the bodies' muscles relaxed.

Pettibone squeezes my shoulder. Nothing is said. My eyesight clears and I force myself to assess the situation.

"How old are the children?"

Pettibone answers. "They were eight, six, and three. Two girls and a boy. Simpson had a hard time making it on a cop's salary. His wife"—he nods at the sandy-haired woman with blood running from her forehead and pooling in her lap— "she taught school in Lincoln City."

He points to empty 9 mm shell casings on the kitchen countertop. "We picked these up."

Someone with an automatic shot these people. "Why, Chief? Dear God. Who would do this? Did someone have it in for this family? Or maybe Simpson?" The thought crosses my mind that Simpson may have crossed some line in law enforcement that exacted a sordid revenge.

"I think I know why. Come 'ere, Dalton." Pettibone walks past me and back toward the foyer. He stops at a door that opens under the stairs going up to what I presume are the bedrooms. A draft of cool, damp air envelops us as Pettibone shines a flashlight toward a darkened staircase leading downward. "One of the few houses around here with a basement."

The unfinished wood on the risers echo as we descend the ten or so feet. Pettibone's flashlight reveals rows of well-built metal racks. They are empty.

"What was in here, Chief?"

He doesn't respond but walks toward a small desk with a computer terminal on it. Next to the printer is a folder. He opens it to several paid invoices. The McCades bought a shit-load of foodstuffs from survival food companies. "Patriot Supply Corporation—serving Americans who prepare for the future" says one. "Liberty Survival—Your First Choice in Food for the Tough Times Ahead," reads another. The invoices list canisters of dried rice, whole wheat flour, freeze-dried fruits and vegetables, MREs. The numbers are staggering.

"Someone cleaned this place out." As if to prove his point, Pettibone points his flashlight at the concrete floor where dried carrots and beans lay.

"And they killed a family in the process? What kind of animals are we dealing with here? They could have just tied them up and taken the damned stuff." My voice trembles with anger.

"Yeah, they could have. But God help us, they didn't. Let's get the hell out of here." Pettibone trudges up the stairs slowly, as if carrying the weight of the world on his shoulders. I shade my eyes from the painful intensity of the sunlight as the Chief closes the door behind us.

Fresh air helps erase the grim inside. Andres stretches crime scene tape as Josh joins us under the shade of house's porch. Pettibone says the obvious. "Anyone with any food in Elmhurst is at risk."

Josh nods and interrupts my un-voiced concerns for those living in my house. "They were in some sort of truck." He guides us behind the house. Tire tracks go off in the stubble of unharvested maize and toward distant stands of large trees. "They came in and went this way."

I glance at the sun. Early afternoon. Enough time to start tracking, although I hold little hope of success. Too many hours have elapsed. Pettibone says, "I'm going to have to go looking for those people. Who wants to go with me?"

"You're not going anywhere, Chief." I want to pull the words back but it's too late. The Chief looks down. I try to recover. "Chief, this place'll fall down around our heads if you aren't here to keep an eye on things." Which is true, but not the real reason, and he knows it. He looks off in the distance. I feel dirty. Inadvertently, I've demeaned a good man. "I apologize, Chief."

He just nods his agreement. "Take the ATV with extra fuel. You may get lucky."

Josh immediately volunteers. Jill says, "You can't go alone. I'll go."

Both would too, but neither are going to. Josh's family is at risk because of the foodstuffs I've stored. Jill's got a husband with a horrible infection to take care of. "Give me and Andres a second, will you two?" I pull him off to the side. "Where are those no-good cousins you told me about?"

Andres' nose flares. "You think they did this?" He almost shouts. Jill and Pettibone turn and stare.

"No goddamit." And I don't. His outlaw cousins are thieves, not killers. "I need to get ahold of them, fast, on another matter." I speak softly. "*Another* of your cousins—Anson—mentioned something about them stealing veterinarian grade antibiotics." I explain the veterinarian office break in. Andres' face flushes. He calms down, and his expression indicates he doesn't know what I'm talking about—or is a damned good actor. "Jill's husband needs some of what they've got. Now!"

"Those *pinche putos*. They're worthless."

"Maybe so, but right now they may have stashed some antibiotics that can save Fred Aston's life."

He glances at Jill, then nods. We walk back toward the other two. I explain to Pettibone and Jill, "Andres and I'll be going, but first we need to get lanterns, flashlights, long guns and ammunition."

Andres agrees and tells me, "You go home with Josh. I'll swing by City Hall and grab shotguns, and ammunition. And..." He pauses, glances at Jill who is already walking toward an ATV. "I need to make a quick stop—by myself—before we go." He winks as he walks away.

Chapter Twenty-Two

"WHAT WAS THAT ALL ABOUT?" JOSH ASKS AS HE STEERS THE ATV back toward my house. "And who says it's your fight and not mine?" Even though I'm sitting right next to him, he doesn't wait for an answer. He barks another question. "Yeah, I've got a wife and kids and yeah, I need to make sure this kind of thing doesn't happen to one of them." He slams a hand on the steering wheel. "Another thing. Who made you boss around here? Pettibone? I don't think so. You forget, amigo, that I was there when you made an ass out of yourself in front of him when he needed your help. Several people stepped up to the plate before you decided you were going to show one damned bit of interest in helping out around here."

Ouch. "You through yet?"

"Fuck no, I'm not through yet, Dalton!" He cranks the ATV's wheel hard to make a turn. I fly half-way out and desperately grab for a support stanchion.

"Stop this fucking thing! You damned near killed me, Josh. What the hell?"

The ATV's engine idles as he coasts it to the curb. "Sorry. Didn't mean to do that."

He's still red beet with anger. If Josh's wife and kids weren't with him, I'd be inclined to kick his ass off my property, the ungrateful SOB. "Let's talk before this blows up in front of Elsie or the kids." I go over the reasons that Andres and I should being the ones to search for the killers.

He stops me. "This is bullshit. You've got a new daughter, and a father-in-law who's in bad shape. It's daytime, for God's sake. No one's going to attack anyone in town during the daylight hours. And what were you and Andres talking all hush-hush about?"

I step out of the ATV. A couple of scrawny kids stare at us. "You through?"

Josh raises his hands in mock surrender. "Talk."

"One question at a time. I was telling Andres about some of his sorry kinfolk who might have access to some antibiotics that could save Fred Aston's life." As the story of Anson Gutierrez' hunch about the location of stolen veterinarian supplies comes out, Josh seems to simmer down. He's hardly mollified, however.

"You think just two of you are going to lasso a bunch of stone-cold killers? What are you gonna do? Tie 'em up and put them in jail to await trial? Oh, I forgot! There is no jail. There is no justice system. So, what happens when you and Andres waltz your happy asses into their camp, or wherever the hell they are?" He affects a highly educated Englishman's vocabulary. "'Good day, gentlemen. We are arresting you. Please raise your hands so that we might truss you up. Soon a jury of your peers will decide your fate, based upon the evidence we will collect…'"

I can't help it. I begin to laugh. Which pisses him off.

"You think I'm shitting you? What do you think you two are going to be able to do by yourselves, besides get shot all to hell?"

He's got a point. Several, in fact. I haven't thought this

through very well. I crawl back onto the ATV seat. Josh quietly resumes driving, but more slowly. Minutes later, we pull into the driveway. Elsie and the kids are playing some sort of game in the back lot. Andres pulls up behind us. He's grins like a Cheshire cat, wagging two white cardboard boxes at me. When Josh turns around, Andres tries to lower his arm quickly as if he's dropped something on the floorboard. He kills the ATV engine.

"What's in your hand, Andres?"

"Nothing, Josh. Why?"

"Cut the shit. Dalton told me."

Sheepishly, Andres steps out and walks toward us. "You were right, Dalton. Those pricks did break into that vet's office." He holds the two boxes up so I can see the labels.

"What'd you do to get this stuff? Pull a gun on them?" I ask.

Andres looks exceedingly proud of himself. "That's exactly what I did. I told Felipe—he's the oldest of those pricks—that I was going to blow his *huevos* off, and then I pulled my *pistola* out and shoved it down his pants."

Maybe it's the potential danger we are going into, or Josh's anger that has abated—somewhat—but whatever the cause, we all burst into laughter. This draws the Cerveny family over. Andres is well liked, and the kids immediately give him a hug. He gives Elsie a peck on the cheek. Momentarily, it feels as if nothing out of the ordinary has happened.

Elsie peers into the small bed of Andres' ATV at the array of weapons and ammunition. "What's with all the firepower, guys?" She looks dubious when Andres gives a nervous laugh and makes up some bullshit story about taking the rifles home to clean them.

"Yeah? You cleaning the shells and bullets too?"

Shit. Elsie's nobody's fool.

Josh intercedes with an *I'll explain it all to you in a minute* look. Casting a doubtful eye at us, Elsie shoos David and Sarah into the back yard, then rejoins them.

"You gonna tell Elsie about the dead kids, Josh?" Andres asks.

I inwardly cringe at Andres' bluntness. I have no idea how Elsie will handle something this horrible and threatening to her own children.

Josh ignores the question and faces me. "We aren't finished with our discussion, Dalton. Two people aren't enough. I need to go with you."

I explain that there is no guarantee of getting back before nightfall, that Andres and I will be careful. "Name one person besides you that you'd feel comfortable going with us right now?"

The reality is that the Elmhurst Neighborhood Patrol consists of seven people. Jill Aston has a seriously sick husband, and Josh has his family (and the contents of my house) to guard. The other three in the Patrol are in their seventies. I have no doubt they'd volunteer, but after seeing the Simpson family's bodies, there's no way I feel even remotely comfortable with their abilities.

We bounce several names. Rios, the cop. Nope, he left town. Someone from the East Side like Ike Belton? Not enough time, and doubtful results.

"What about Chief Pettibone?" Josh asks.

I turn to Andres. "Please take this stuff next door to Fred and Jill. She'll know what to do with it."

Andres nods, tucks the two boxes of meds under his arm, and jogs toward my neighbors' house. He looks relieved to be away from the confrontation between Josh and me.

"No doubt the Chief would go with us. Hell, he'd go alone. But he's got a bad heart, and a wife with cancer. He's in his sixties but looks eighty." I'm angry with the delays. "And, we're wasting time."

I head toward the house to retrieve weapons and equipment. The spare bedroom is now occupied by the Cerveny kids, so I've moved its contents into the dining room. David and Sarah know not to enter that room. I grab ballistic vests, ammunition, a thirty-ought-six scoped hunting rifles, and the AK47. I change into camouflage and a boonie cap and begin to lug everything to the driveway.

Before I can leave the house, Elsie Cerveny confronts me at the back door.

"Josh told me what happened with the Simpson family." Her freckles stand out more distinctly because of the pallor in her face.

"It's bad, Elsie." I move to get by, and she blocks my path. "Why aren't you taking Josh to help find the killers?" She makes it clear it's a rhetorical question. "Stop trying to be some kind of manly protector. You're chasing horrible, horrible killers. Two isn't enough. We'll be okay while you three are gone."

Three? My anger flares again. "Since when did Josh start needing you to fight for him?"

Elsie is clearly stung by my retort.

I mutter an apology. I'm not sure what to say.

"Josh has earned the right to be with you."

"What?" I draw the question out. "The right to possibly get killed?"

"We're in Elmhurst. We take the good with the bad." Elsie steps back. She's got tears in her eyes.

I step outside. Josh is kicking a ball around with his kids. "Josh!"

"What?" He gives a questioning look at Elsie.

"Help me load stuff." He looks angry until I show him two ballistic vests. "We need another one."

His countenance changes as he understands what I'm saying. He taps the ball to Jacob and smiles. "Come to your senses, huh?" Elsie wipes her eyes and brushes by him. His face turns grim. "She can be persuasive, can't she?"

I shrug.

"I didn't put her up to this, Dalton. I just told her what just happened, and your plans, and why you don't want me to go. She just turned and made a bee line to the house."

I believe him. "Let's finish loading, okay?"

I unlock the drain valve on the rainwater tank, fill up two one-gallon plastic jugs, drop a purifying tablet in each, then re-cap them.

Jill appears from her backyard. Her smile almost splits her face in half. Clearly, she's been crying. Andres follows behind. "I am so grateful. Andres told me how he found the antibiotics."

I look at Andres. "Oh? Where'd he says he got them?"

Andres' smile disappears. He makes frantic hand signs behind Jill's back.

Clueless, Jill continues. "He's amazing, Dalton. To walk into an abandoned office building and find all this stuff. It's a miracle."

Abandoned office building? Andres' eyes send me a desperate message: *Please play along. Don't tell her the truth.*

I nod, looking solemn. "It surely is a miracle. Andres is amazing, and we're mighty blessed. He's got the instincts of a tracking dog. Amazing fella."

Jill turns and gives Andres a huge hug and kiss on the cheek. "Thanks, Andres. You may have saved Fred's life." She moves toward the driveway and the ATVs. My face is red, as I try desperately to keep from breaking into laughter. Andres stops long enough to punch my arm.

I whisper, "Can *I* kiss you, too?" He shoots the finger but mouths a 'thank you.'

Josh joins us. Fortunately, Andres' ATV is a four-seater with a zip off canvas top and sides. Josh suggests we remove the top and siding. Soon, the roll bar and structural steel is bare, and we lash shotguns and rifles to them. Andres rummages through a tote bag and pulls out three radios.

"Three?" I ask.

Andres says, "Chief helped me load stuff at City Hall. Said we might need these."

Josh grins. "Three, huh? Not two. Three." Chief's a smart man. Smarter than some others I know."

I ignore the zinger. We check to see the handsets are charged, then clip them to breast pockets or web gear.

There is a quick round of hugs. Josh tells David and Sarah he'll be back soon. Jill gives Andres another kiss. She will return the other ATV to City Hall.

Josh and I are still giving Andres hell when we turn onto at Cosgrove Terrace. As the McCade house nears, all talking ceases. I stare at the crime scene tape and hope the Simpson family's bodies have been removed. The Chief assured us it would be taken care of. I'm just thankful I didn't have to move one of the kids. A quick glance reveals the grim faces of Josh and Andres.

I steer the ATV over the curb, and we follow wide tire tracks away from town. The tracks indicate one heavy vehicle, probably a truck of some kind, came in and went out the same way. Andres sits in the front seat. He leans out to ensure we don't lose sight of the tracks. Josh follows suit.

"Don't seem to be worried about anyone following them." I speak loudly over the noise of the ATV.

The tire tracks don't follow any recognizable trail. They drop off the rise most of Elmhurst is perched on, and pass through the maize fields in the fallow flats, and then into a scattering of scrub and post oaks. I brake and Andres looks at me quizzically until I gesture toward the firearms. We double check to ensure they're within easy reach. I unholster the clumsy Colt 1911 .45 and rack the slide to ensure there's a round in the chamber. Josh opens my .357's cylinder.

"Wanna trade?" Josh asks. I shake my head no. I don't want to admit it, but I've gotten comfortable with the clunky automatic.

Andres pats his holster, then slides the assault shotgun's receiver to confirm its readiness. He places it between his legs, barrel down.

An old topography map shows this part of Lee County largely unpopulated. Andres points to where we are on the map. "According to my granddad, my family used to sharecrop out in this area. Cotton, corn, maize." He mentions an Anglo surname that I recognize. At one time, the family owned thousands of acres, and sharecropped some of it out, mostly to poor blacks and Hispanics.

"Those folks sold out decades ago." I can't recall whether any distant family members even live in Elmhurst.

There is no sign of farming now. Large ranch holdings replaced farms and small tenant operations years ago. Small trees grow on fields long left dormant. We continue tracking westward, and the sun hits us with mid-afternoon heat. If the tracks continue this way, we'll soon have the sun in our eyes.

We follow the tracks down into a small, drying wallow. Feral hog prints tattoo the mud around the water hole. I accelerate up a small incline and out of the swelter of the wallow's brush. A barbed wire fence has been cut midway between two mesquite posts. The wire is pulled back and twisted on posts to allow a vehicle's passage.

Josh observes, "Whoever did this didn't seem in too big of a hurry."

The ATV's odometer shows we've traveled seven miles.

Now in sandy loam, the tires' markings stand out, and I say a silent prayer of thanks that there hasn't been any rain to erase the tracks. Another half-mile, another fence cut, and the tracks reach a graveled county road running north and south. We stop.

"Shit!" mutters Andres. I kill the engine and we tramp around the area west of the road. There are no tire tracks.

The sun is at the four o'clock position. Larger trees and heavy brush loom ominously on either side the county road. Josh and I go north, and Andres walks south on the road looking for evidence of a truck's passage. Andres suddenly whistles. I look south in his direction and he waves frantically, then starts toward the ATV.

"What'd you see?"

"Hard to say, but I think that truck went south." He points. Barely visible are fresh tire marks.

We walk another hundred yards, staring at gravel and dirt. Similar markings on hardpan where gravel has thinned confirm Andres' beliefs.

"Damn, Andres. You *do* have the instincts of a tracking dog."

"Aw shit, Dalton. Are you ever going to let me live that down?"

"Not in this lifetime." We chuckle and walk back to the ATV.

We confirm our location on the map. I gesture north and south. We've hit County Road 203. It meanders through an old oil field, and Ts into another road.

Andres points to the T junction. "This is Brushy Creek Road." We trace the five miles to the junction.

Josh says, "Glad you guys grew up around here. Makes me feel a little safer." He holds the AK47 across his chest, eyeing the dense vegetation.

Trees begin to break the sun's rays. Andres says, "I've been on this road before. High school. Beer drinking. Gets spooky after dark."

Josh retorts, "It's spooky now."

I turn the ATV south. Sweat soaks my shirt, and it's not all from heat. I begin to imagine gunfire from the woods shredding us before we know what's hit us. Andres' face is a sheen of sweat. I am not the only nervous one. Three miles further south, we again check the Topo map.

Andres points at a pip, about a half-mile west after the County 203 tees with Brushy Creek. "Know what place this is?"

I can't be sure, but I recall a large ranching operation. I shake my head. "Don't know, but there used to be a large house and outbuildings." I squint. The map has tiny letters "FL" adjacent to tiny indicators of buildings. "Feed lot?" I ask.

We nod in agreement. "There was a big feed lot for years and years. It hasn't been in operation for a long time."

Andres and I wrack our brains trying to remember terrain, roads and structures. I ask, "Is there someplace we can watch this place to make sure no one's there before we get there? Better yet, before anyone can see us?"

Neither of us knows the answer, so we drive south another two miles and stop inside the edge of the wooded area. To our south less than a half mile, there is a stop sign where the county roads meet. Sighting down long leg of the right triangle, I count a brick ranch house, a grain storage tank, and three outbuildings. The largest of the outbuildings is, or was, an implement shed. The land between us is bare of trees, but the pastureland hasn't been cut or baled. Dotted here and there are small pump jacks once operating stripper, or low production, wells. None of the rusted pump jacks are seesawing, and I wonder when crude oil filled two tank batteries that still set adjacent to Brushy Creek Road.

"You see any cattle?" Andres asks.

"No." None near the house. None in the pastures. Not

surprising, given the situation. Probably sold, butchered, and eaten by now.

We spend several minutes using binoculars to scope the property. Josh asks, "You see any movement? I don't."

I'm puzzled. Why would cold-blooded killers only come this far from Elmhurst? With the right transportation and fuel, they could be hundreds of miles away by now. And why would the killers cut cross-country where their tracks remain visible, instead of taking hard-surfaced roads? I voice that to the others. My earlier bravado is fading. We've made it our duty to track the Simpson family's killers, but a small part of my insides tells me I'll be very relieved if we're not forced to confront them.

Josh says simply, "Maybe they don't give a shit. Maybe they don't think anything will happen to them. Maybe they're from around here."

He has our attention.

"Maybe, two hundred miles away doesn't make any sense. I mean, the world's gone to shit. People are dying. Dalton, you've seen it weeks ago. Gangs taking over large chunks of territory. Maybe whoever we're after isn't afraid of anyone, because they think they're meaner, badder, than any law." Josh eyes seem focused on something Andres and I can't perceive.

I have never seen Josh like this. I sense he is opening a door to a part of him he's not sure he wants opened. The silence sits on the three of us like a millstone.

Josh cocks his head. "Dalton, I told you I had one DWI. I lied. I spent six years of my life in an Oklahoma penitentiary for killing a man."

Andres shuffles uncomfortably. All I can say is, "Josh, I took you at your word, but now…" I pause.

He shrugs. "I was eighteen, I was with the wrong crowd. There was a fight, outside a honky-tonk. The cops scooped up everyone who might have had anything to do with a fight where a man lost his life. I was there. I saw the fight. I egged it on. But that was all." He exhales loudly. "The jury didn't see it that way. That was a long time ago."

This is hardly the time for confessions. At the moment, I don't care about Josh's past. I tell him that.

"The point of this story isn't my youthful misdeed. It's that in prison I was around people that don't think like you do, Dalton. Or you, Andres. There are men who will kill you for a cigarette, and then walk away and sleep like babies." He points toward the ranch house. "The people we're looking for think nothing of squashing the life out of a human being—like a cockroach." Tears run down his face. Suddenly embarrassed, Josh wipes his eyes and raises his binoculars.

The afternoon's lengthening shadows seem an appropriate setting for Josh's revelation.

Andres pats Josh on the back and goes back to looking through his binoculars. I'm still processing what I've heard. Not about Josh, but about the caliber of men we are probably up against.

"Still lots of daylight left. All we want to do is get safely past the built-up area. Let's concentrate on that right now," I say.

Suddenly, Andres asks, "You see that?"

"Where?" Josh asks.

Still looking through his binoculars, Andres points toward the implement shed. "Saw a flash. Like a car or truck door swinging shut. Sun caught the movement on the window glass." He describes a location partially shaded by the corrugated metal of the grain tank and the late afternoon's shadows.

"There!" Josh exclaims.

I sense movement but can't make it out.

Josh asks, "How close can we get in this ATV without being seen or heard?"

After about a hundred yards where we are exposed, County Road 203 is below eye level from the structures as it dips slightly behind the roll of the prairie. Andres replies, "Once past the open spot, we can make it to Brushy Creek intersection."

I wonder out loud whether it is much ado over nothing. Anyone, including the owner, can be occupying the structures.

Josh asks, "You want to take a chance on that?"

"Nope."

It takes fifteen minutes, driving at walking speed to avoid stirring up dust. I kill the engine just before the stop sign. Because of a slight depression, the ranch structures aren't visible the half mile or so to our right. Deep bar ditches line each side of Brush Creek Road. Andres walks down into the south side ditch to confirm it is dry.

A strong westerly wind rustles Johnson grass and coastal Bermuda. We don ballistic vests, grumbling as we help each other secure the straps. They're heavy and hot. They'll stop a pistol round, but not a bullet from a high-powered rifle. Several swigs of water, and then we take turns ensuring we each have readied ammunition, and secured weapons.

Operating mostly by hand signals, we agree to cross the road surface and steer the ATV into the bar ditch. Once there, I keep in its low area, and we edge closer to the buildings. The wind's direction and strength encourage me that the ATV's sound won't carry, and that we can inch closer and not have to lug ammunition as far. Josh walks ahead, while Andres stands on the ATV's seat to signal when the change in elevation allows him to see the top of the highest structure, the grain storage tank.

A quick hand motion and I kill the engine.

Andres carries a single bandolier of shotgun shells, a mix of OO buckshot and slugs. I sling the 30-ought-6 over behind my back. It's bolt action, holds five rounds in the internal magazine. I carry the other twelve-gauge shotgun with a similar load, and bandolier. A box of twenty 150 grain bullets weighs down an outside pocket of my camo pants. Josh stuffs four thirty-round magazines in his pants leg pockets and lugs the AK47 with two thirty round magazines taped back-to-back for easy reload.

The hand-held radios come with wired headsets. Either by dumb luck or the Chief's foresight, the rarely used accessories were included in the with the handsets. Each of us turns off the external volume and ensure the headsets work.

"Ready?" I whisper. My mouth is as dry as cotton and the blood pounds in my ears.

Josh merely nods.

Andres gives a little grin. "No. You?'

"Hell no. Let's do this." I'm scared shitless.

We inch toward the structures. To our left is a barbed wire fence, its top two strands missing.

Josh softly speaks into the headset. "Circling around so I'll be at your ninety. I'll tell you when."

I give him a thumbs up, and he carefully steps over the remaining two strands and moves south through the mesquite that has invaded what was once a pasture. Andres and I crouch, scurrying quickly the last distance to a badly weathered wood fence. We are now maybe forty yards from the house.

I drop belly down. Andres does the same. At first, I see no movement through the binoculars. The place looks vacant except for a large truck tucked behind the grain bin which sits on metal legs, once used for feeding penned cattle about to be sold for market or auction.

"Shit," whispers Andres as he makes a sudden movement. "Fire ants." He rolls several feet and frantically brushes off the little bastards.

Damn. Scared hell out of me.

Once he settles down, I point toward the partially hidden truck. "Think that was what you spotted?"

Andres nods yes.

The truck, lightly rusted, has slats instead of solid sides surrounding its bed. It's partially covered with an old tarpaulin, and it's hard to tell what's in the bed.

Suddenly, there is laughter, and two men appear from the back of the house. One of them climbs into the truck's bed and lifts a rectangular cardboard box over the side.

"Oh, Jesus Christ," I whisper. Even without the binoculars, I recognize the container. "Those are MREs." The heavily tatted man on the ground, takes the container and sets it on the ground. The two begin to readjust the tarpaulin. As they do, metal containers for corn, wheat and soy, become visible. Then more cases of MREs. The items match those described in shipping receipts in the McCade basement.

Josh's voice comes through the headset very softly. "In position. I saw the two on the truck." "Josh, remember those two who broke out of jail?"

Andres and I peer through our binoculars. Light breaks into jagged fragments as the sun begins to dip below the trees. Finally, the tatted man, stays stationary in the beam of light as he ties down one corner of the tarpaulin. His face matches the Sheriff's Office booking photo. He is one of the two prisoners from Nebraska that shot the sheriff.

We've found the Simpson family's killers. The question is, what do we do next?

Chapter Twenty-Three

I ROLL ONTO MY BACK TO TAKE THE TENSION OFF MY SHOULDERS and elbows. Andres continues watching through his binoculars. I take a few deep breaths and try to concentrate on the layout of the place, hoping the effort will slow my heart rate.

The large ranch house, tractor shed, grain tank, and outbuildings are fenced in an enclosure about two acres in size. Andres and I are on the east side of a large steel pipe holding pen. There is no cover to our west for the hundred yards or so to the large ranch house. The horizontal lengths of pipe fence on the west side obscure our sightlines but provide little protection.

I press the PTT and ask quietly, "Josh, where exactly are you?" The throat mic's strap is unfamiliar. It feels like a noose strangling me, and I loosen the Velcro strap.

Josh's voice comes through the earbud in my left ear, and for a moment its clarity and high volume are enough to make me roll over and raise my head to make sure his words can't be overheard. Andres is clearly more experienced with the comm devices and he gives me a knowing smirk. I turn the headset volume down.

"On the east side of the tractor shed. I'm through the barbed wire fence and behind the building itself. Its back wall is about ten feet inside the fence line."

In my mind's eye, I see Josh half-way across the south side of the property, hidden by a large wood and corrugated metal structure. He's now closer to the truck than Andres and me.

What now?

"Josh, is it safe for Andres to move your way?"

"Send him," Josh says. "Andres, stay away from the east fence until you get on the south side. The back is thick with trees. They won't see you in the heavy growth." Josh tells Andres to cover behind the tractor shed on the end nearest to where he and I are now. "Andres will be about thirty or so feet from me when he gets set. It'll give both of us clear shots toward the truck and the back porch of the house."

Andres gives me a thumbs up, crab-walks backwards, and disappears into the mesquite.

That leaves me to wonder how in hell am I going to get near the house without being seen. The one-story brick building is set off from Brushy Creek Road about fifty yards. I recall spotting a two-car detached garage on the west side of the house. I can't see it from here. The pipe-fenced pen ends about forty yards from the residence. It's all open ground between where I lie and the side of the house. The house's windows facing me reveal nothing, except to confirm they aren't covered by venetian blinds or drapes.

Shit.

I look to my right. Brush Creeks Road's north-side bar ditch may be the answer. I push the PTT and whisper my plan. Josh and Andres acknowledge only with the click made from tapping their talk buttons. I scamper away from the property, then quickly cross Brushy Creek Road and lie flat in the depression of the bar ditch. With the rifle slung across my back and the shotgun held in both hands, I slither into the bar ditch.

Sweet Jesus, no rattlesnakes, please. I begin the ordeal of belly crawling toward and across the front of the house.

A lifetime of effort later, Andres asks, "Where are you, Dalton?"

I pant into the mic, "Let me check." Sweat and dust sting my eyes. I raise my head just high enough in the ditch's foliage to spot the top of the grain storage tank mounted on a steel platform slightly off to my left rear. "I'm past the pen, and almost to the edge of the house."

Josh asks, "Can you get close to the house?"

"Wait one." With binoculars parting the grass and weeds, the house's front exposure reveals itself. As I scan with the lenses, I talk softly. "Brick. Wood in bad shape. Doesn't look like it's been lived in for a while. Large picture windows with open drapes. Two big-assed ornamental pots with dead plants straddle the walkway next to the front door." I describe the driveway to the ranch house's detached garage its west side.

I scuttle in the ditch another thousand miles—closer to two hundred yards. I call. "Josh. Andres. I'm past the west side property line. The two-car garage is actually a carport. One vehicle inside. It looks like its tires are flat."

At this point, the other side of Brushy Creek Road is heavily wooded. My binoculars reveal a side of the house with a door and a short concrete breezeway attached to its carport, and, in some distance behind the carport, several small outbuildings.

Josh asks, "Can you cover us from where you are?"

"No. Best guess, I'm looking in the open door to the kitchen or mud room. No movement. I'll have to get across the road and next to the wooded area."

I take a deep breath and burst from the bar ditch and across Brushy Creek Road, then clumsily dive to the ground and crawl until I hit a cedar fencepost. And wait. No sound but the rasp of my breathing, and blackbirds cawing in the distance.

Josh speaks again. "The back of the house is an unscreened,

covered porch. Sliding glass doors into the house, which are open. I think that's where those two men came from, going to the truck. Two smaller windows. Screens look knocked out."

Andres talks. "Maybe the MREs were unloaded for supper?" It's more him thinking out loud than a question.

One thing seems sure: the killers haven't posted any guards. Anger momentarily overwhelms me. These fuckers kill a whole family less than fifteen miles away and are not even worried someone will try to hold them accountable.

Now what? Long shadows envelop much of the west side of the house. I can almost see gray darkness crawl up the wall near the carport. Dusk will be on us soon. Maybe we have not thought this out very well, because we never discussed spending the night watching the place.

Hoping I blend with the shadows, I edge along the fence line to the side of the carport. Suddenly, an engine roars to life.

"What the fuck, Josh?"

He comes back quickly. "Seems they've decided to move the truck further behind the house. Wait."

The engine noise becomes louder. The truck is backing past the house. The driver's door opens the truck's brake lights blink on and off as the driver positions the truck directly behind the carport—and twenty feet from where I stand.

Josh's voice comes through my earbud. "You okay?"

I'm too close to respond except by keying the mic. The truck door slams shut, and the driver grunts. I unsling the deer rifle praying the movement isn't heard. I lean it against the west side of the carport. A twelve gauge is needed at this range. I check, then re-check to ensure the shotgun's safety is off. Water splashes on the carport's rear wall, and the driver begins to hum some tuneless melody as he pisses.

Josh says simply, "I think I can shoot the driver when he comes into view."

I want so much for Josh to take his shot. But he's using an un-scoped AK47. He's too far away to ensure a hit.

Shit. Shit. Shit. My hands are sweating so badly I almost drop the twelve-gauge. It's decision time. There is a *click* and I almost gasp. I glance toward Brushy Creek Road. Did someone sneak behind me, ready to blow my head off? I flex my knees in relief. The sound is of the driver's Zippo. He's fired up a cigarette.

I bring the shotgun up and tuck the butt into my shoulder. I turn the corner to a look of shock. The cigarette falls from his lips. Both his hands are on his zipper. "Oh, Jesus," he mutters, smoke wisping from his mouth.

I don't pull the trigger but signify with the shotgun barrel for him to raise his hands.

"Can I zip up my fucking pants?"

"No. How many of you are there?"

The driver's baseball cap flies off as one of his hands brushes by it when raising his arms. "Who are you?" His voice quivers, and I can almost smell his fear from ten feet away.

"How many are in the house? How many of you are there?" I level the shotgun on his chest.

He's Anglo, partially balding, and maybe in his forties. I recognize him as one of the two prisoners that are wanted in Nebraska. He starts to turn.

"You move, you die. Your name's Walt something or other. You and a guy named Lester escaped from the Lee County Jail, didn't you?"

This seems to give him pause. "You the law?" His right hand, heavily tatted, starts to drop. In the shadows I can't make out his eyes, but I realize he's stalling for time.

"One last time. How many?"

He grins, looks away, then dives toward me. My shotgun goes off twice, before he slams into my chest. Knocked backward, I drop the weapon as I fall on my ass. Desperately, I grab for the holstered .45 and scramble to my feet, at the same time searching desperately for the shotgun. I thumb down the safety and pull the trigger, again and again.

Both Josh and Andres are screaming into my head through the earbud. The driver is facedown, unmoving.

"I'm okay. I'm okay." I forget to key the talk button. "I'm okay. I'm okay," I repeat. The driver's right hand is under him. I almost drop the .45 as I yell at him to show his hands. Is he dead? Is he hurt? Is he pretending? I've got to know, and fast. My foot slams into his ribcage, hard three times. No sound. No movement. I give up trying to roll his body with one hand so I shove the gun in its holster, and, with two hands, grab his shoulder and push. The .45 shots weren't necessary. Buckshot raked his face away as he dove toward me, then went into his chest at the top of his ribcage. My hands feel wet, and I recoil at the blood and viscera that coat them. Frantically, I wipe them in the grass, then spot a 9 mm automatic by the dead man's side. I grab it and carefully lower the cocked hammer. *So close. So close.*

Someone yells, "Walt! Where are you? What the fuck is going on?" I recover the shotgun as the distinct bark of an AK47 fills the air as Josh sends rounds toward the voice.

Screams and curses come from inside the house. I peek around the edge of the carport. Someone is dragging a body off the back porch and into the house. I have no shot from my angle, but Josh continues firing. Sparks show where rounds smack into the house's brick exterior. The body stops moving.

I step onto the concrete walk under the breezeway and throw myself against the house. The open doorway looms like a darkened maw. How many are left? Where are they?

A spray of sparks and the low cough of a shotgun come from behind the narrow metal supports of the elevated grain storage tank. Glass shatters on the east side of the house. Andres is in a squat, his shotgun barrel weaving back and forth.

His voice is surprisingly calm. "Someone looked out a window. I don't think I got him, but who knows?".

Josh talks frantically to Andres, "Get the fuck where you've got cover!"

As if to confirm Andres' exposure, gunfire erupts from somewhere in the house. Andres turns to the safety of the tractor shed, then pauses, and instead runs toward the east side of the house. He appears to trip, then rolls onto his right side. There is more gunfire from the house, and he flops onto his back.

"Where are you, Dalton?" Josh's voice is strained. "I think they hurt Andres. Bad."

We confirm our locations. There is no way to cover all the exits to the house. Josh asks, "You see the two outbuildings my left, your right?"

"Yeah."

"Headed for the nearest one. Cover me."

The small structure, probably once housing the pump for a well, is closest to the house, and at an angle that will allow Josh to keep both the back and the side where I stand. Gunfire erupts from inside the house and follows Josh as he runs the distance from the tractor shed. He dives behind the building, then keys the mic to let me know he's okay.

I step gingerly around Walt's body, retrieve the 30.06, and, keeping the carport to my right, bolt for the front side of the house.

As I cross the asphalt driveway, something knocks the wind out of me. Involuntarily, I grab for my chest, dropping both the shotgun and the rifle as I spin backwards and onto the ground. Desperately, I try to breathe. Something is sitting on me, preventing me from moving my diaphragm. I see stars and almost blackout then feel deep pain on the right set of ribs. I gasp for air and try to sit up. The radio's earbud dangles by my side. I stuff it back in and hear Josh's voice.

"I can't see you. Dalton! Answer me!"

I wheeze out, "I think I've been shot." I look down and notice a tear in the ballistic vest in three inches below my right collarbone. Frantic, I check for blood, but find nothing. I was shot from the breezeway door into the house. And I am still exposed.

Josh interrupts my self-examination. "They're moving to the truck!"

I roll over, grab the shotgun, and turn back toward the house. A human form fills the breezeway door, and I pull the shotgun's trigger. Once, twice, three times. Then...*Shit. You dumbass, you forgot to reload!*

I am at the carport entrance, jamming shells into the shotgun as the truck's engine fires up. Whoever was in the doorway is gone, probably heading toward the truck. The truck's lights come on, and it begins to move. Josh's AK47 continues to fire, and rounds whang into the truck's metal body.

"Dalton, can you help?" Some of his AK's rounds don't hit the truck. They punch through the wood of the carport and whine off the asphalt driveway where I had lain moments before. The windshield shatters, and I hear howls, but the truck continues to roll along the back of the house. Josh appears from the wellhouse and sprints toward the retreating truck.

I clumsily run to the front of the house, hoping to meet the truck head on. The only escape route is between the east side of the house and the holding pen. I forget about the large flower-pots until I knock one into the concrete walkway, shattering it and sending dirt flying. The truck's headlights bounce crazily as it appears from the back of the house. The driver turns toward Brushy Creek Road. I am seized with madness. These bastards cannot escape! Although now slower, the truck continues to move. I toss the shotgun to the ground, jump on the driver's side running board, and blast away with the .45

through the open window until I run out of ammunition, then jump off.

The truck hiccups as it stalls and the engine dies. I retrieve the shotgun. "Josh, I've got the driver's side."

"I'm on the passenger side."

I yell out, "Get out of the cab with your hands where we can see them, you motherfuckers!" My voice sounds shrill.

Nothing. Josh comes to my side of the truck and yells, "Cover me." I keep the shotgun pointed at the driver's door as he reaches up and tries to open it. He tugs on it several times.

"Won't open," he grunts as he pries on the door handle. Finally, the door swings heavily against him as the driver tumbles out, dead.

Somehow the inside cab light still works. It reveals a bench seat, soaked in the driver's blood. Another person slumps against the passenger door. We run to that side and drag an inert male onto the ground and roll him onto his back.

Josh kicks him in the head and ribs, looking for signs of life. There are none. We run toward Andres.

Please don't be dead, amigo.

"What took you so long?" Andres' voice is weak and raspy.

Josh gasps and falls to his knees. "Where are you hit?"

Andres points and my eyes follow his finger. His lower right pants leg is soaked with blood.

"Jesus Christ, Andres. You dumb motherfucker." I continue to scream at him with curses said out of relief. I train my shotgun on the two small windows on the house's east side, but no one appears.

Josh fashions a tourniquet out of his belt and a large stick. Andres holds the tourniquet in place as Josh and I cautiously approach the back porch.

"Whoever's in there, come out!" I scream. I think I hear a moan, but it stops before I can be sure. I continue to scream. There is no answer.

Josh bobs up and down, taking quick glimpses into the darkened house, occasionally showing his flashlight trying to draw fire. Finally, we decide to enter. The body someone tried to drag inside remains face down, feet and lower legs exposed on the patio. We roll the body. Walt's cell partner in the Lee County Jail.

"Lester. This is the other piece of shit fugitive from Nebraska," I say. He's now equally as dead as his buddy. I count five entry wounds in his upper torso.

"Nice shooting, Josh."

He merely grunts.

"Our illustrious sheriff will be happy, anyway," I mutter.

"That's four. Two in the truck, the one you killed at the truck, and this one," Josh says softly.

Are there others? It takes time to clear the house safely. Stolen food and cigarettes litter the parquet covered living and dining rooms and den. Four empty bedrooms, a couple with shards of glass from broken windows. We reach a closed door to what can only be a small sewing or washroom. Josh turns the knob and ducks back as the door opens.

Something scurries on the linoleum.

"Come out, or we'll kill you," I say.

A moan comes from the room. I extend my flashlight around the corner of the door. It gets no reaction. I nod, and Josh quickly enters. Our flashlights reveal a man, clutching at his abdomen. He's gut shot.

"How many of you are there?" I ask as I rifle through his pockets, looking for identification.

He whispers, "Five."

"Not anymore, cocksucker." I throw his wallet toward his face. The driver license says he's Vincent Guerra, from Escondido. "What brings you this way from that shithole town? Thought scum from there was interested in Lincoln City."

Vincent Guerra looks at me but doesn't answer.

. "Why?" Josh asks as hit kicks Guerra in the side. "Why'd you kill them?"

Vincent Guerra groans. "The two from Nebraska. They said they knew where to find food. Us three, we've been pretty hungry. They say they need our truck. Promise us a share of what we steal. We say, 'why not?' when they ask us to go with them." He coughs and bright red blood runs from his mouth. "Didn't plan on having to kill them kids, though."

Josh screams, "Then why'd you do it, you bastard?"

Guerra raises a hand and looks at the blood on it. "Gut shot. You going to take me to a doc?"

Josh grabs Guerra's face. "Why'd you kill that family?"

Guerra's hand returns to his belly. "Don't know. Guess a man's gotta do what a man's gotta do." He pauses. "You taking me to a doc?"

Josh and I look at each other as we stand up. The AK47 and shotgun go off almost simultaneously.

A man's gotta do what a man's gotta do.

Chapter Twenty-Four

ANDRES CRACKS JOKES, MAKING LIGHT OF HIS LEG WOUND. "HELL, Dalton, if I was in the Marines in a combat somewhere over-seas, they'd probably keep me in-country to heal up. Wouldn't even get my ticket punched for a ride home."

I don't know where Andres has picked up the military lingo. He's talking shit, of course. The leg wound, hell, any gunshot wound, is serious. I let him babble on, happy it isn't anything worse. We gently elevate Andres' leg off the ground using the offloaded MRE case.

Josh disappears up Brushy Creek Road at a fast trot, intent on retrieving the ATV. The night's stillness belies the madness of moments ago. The air is cooling, and the ATV's engine starting is faintly audible, a half mile away. I look around for a moment and wonder what would have happened had our attack failed or been prolonged. The outcome would not likely have been the same. The madness of the killings is hidden in the now-welcome gloom.

The tourniquet has stopped the bleeding, but we can't leave it on more than a few minutes at a time.

As if I know much of anything. I've learned what I know about emergency medicine from the same place Andres learned his military lingo. Probably from some war movie or TV show.

"How long since Josh put this tourniquet on you?" I ask as I grasp the stick tightening the ligature.

"Five minutes, maybe?"

It's sure as hell been longer than that. "You've got a lousy sense of time." I guess it has been at least twenty minutes, but I am so rattled by what I've been a part of I haven't a clue.

"I'm going to let off on this so you can get some blood down into your lower leg. This may hurt."

Very slowly, I release the stick, allowing the tension from Josh's belt to ease. My flashlight reveals fresh blood as it blooms below Andres' knee and drips onto the ground.

"Oh jeez, Dalton. That hurts like hell."

"What? The wound?"

"No goddamit. My foot burns like hell!"

That's good, I think. It means blood flow is returning.

"Just for a few minutes, Andres." The flashlight illuminates the growing blood puddle. Time to stop the bleeding again. I re-tighten the belt until the blood flow slows to an ooze, willing Josh to return quickly with the ATV.

Long minutes later, the ATV bounces off Brushy Creek Road and its headlights wash over the two of us. Josh sets the brake, leaves the engine running, and squats next to me looking concerned. "Can we load him?"

Andres squints his eyes shut. "Sorry, buddy. Didn't mean to blind you with this thing." I turn my flashlight off. Instead of answering, I ask Josh, "You had any training in first aid?"

He shakes his head. "No. You?"

"Me either."

Josh and I exchange looks and I wonder if he shares my thoughts—that we are out here playing army, and neither of us has a clue about caring for wounds.

I pat Andres' shoulder. "Don't worry. We'll get you out of here."'

"Sure hope so." He attempts a laugh, but it turns into a grimace and he clutches his chest. I readjust the ballistic vest we've stripped off him which now serves as a crude pillow.

Josh asks, "You doing okay, buddy? We thought you'd been hit more than once."

Andres coughs, twice, spits something in the dark, and replies, "I *did* get hit twice. That first time in the leg as one of you guys was screaming at me to get under cover. Then something hit my chest and slapped me down. *Madre de dios!* Felt like a sledge hammer! Then I realized the vest had caught the slug instead of me. Decided I'd better lie down and pretend I'm dead, or I was gonna be for sure."

The explanation seems to exhaust him. Andres lifts his right hand and rubs his eyes, then extends his arm out to the side and lets it drop. I flip on my flashlight again and use its beam to do another scan of Andres' body.

"What're you doing? I told you, I'm okay!" Andres' words sound slurred. Josh cradles Andres' head as his eyes close. Yes, he's lost blood, and is probably in shock, but the slurred words and lethargy scare me.

"Yeah, but I'm bored, and want to make sure you're not lying to me. Can't trust you Mexicans, you know."

Josh gently rolls Andres onto his left side and I shine the light over his torso. He groans in pain and swings his right arm out, trying feebly to hit me.

Good. He's still with us.

"You missed, *pendejo*," I joke "Gonna have to do better than that."

There are no visible wounds anywhere on his back and buttocks. We ease him onto his back. Josh unbuttons Andres' shirt. No wounds. Just a circle of redness starting to bruise, right over the heart.

Josh gently touches its center. "Is this where you got hit?"

Andres winces. "Yeah." His voice is barely audible.

Josh shakes his head. "You are one lucky rascal. The bullet would have gone right through your heart without that vest."

I chime in. "Well, then we wouldn't be having to baby you right now, you pussy."

Andres doesn't reply but gives me a single digit salute and makes a small grin.

Good. Whatever it takes to keep him reacting.

I turn my flashlight off. "Andres."

"Huh?"

"Can you hear me? Josh and I are going to load you in the ATV and get you back to Doctor Randhawa, okay?"

Andres says something, but I can't hear him over the engine noise. He signals me to get closer. Josh and I both put our ears closer to his mouth.

"What'd you say?" Josh asks.

"Dalton, I'm hurt. Not dead. Quit yelling at me."

He's barely audible, but I laugh, more in relief than anything else. If Andres is joking, he's going to make it.

Josh says, "You're from Lee County. I don't have a clue as to how to get back to Elmhurst in the dark."

I agree and reposition the ATV next to Andres.

"Can you stand it if we put your feet on the floor?" I ask Andres.

Andres' skin is normally a dark tan. Under the artificial light of headlamps, it looks gray. I can't tell whether what I'm seeing is a man near death or the result of halogen lighting. It scares me.

He starts to shiver. "I'll try to put my feet together, but I need help."

We gently lift him.

"Oh shit," he mumbles. "Leg...foot, they hurt like hell."

We place Andres' butt on the seat and swing his left leg in.

His teeth begin to chatter. I can hear them clack together like castanets. I gingerly lift his tourniquet wrapped right leg, fully extended.

"Can you bend the knee?" I ask.

Andres says nothing but nods to show me he will try.

I bend his right knee, hoping he will ride with both feet securely on the floorboard. Suddenly, Andres gasps. I re-straighten the wounded leg as he leans out of the ATV and tries to vomit. Nothing but dry heaves. He tries to straighten up in the seat after a wave of nausea passes and instead, starts sliding off. The two of us push Andres back into the seat.

Andres' head lolls to one side. Josh says, "He's out."

Jesus, is he dying? How much blood did he lose?

The 30.06's gun sling is leather and unbuckles like a belt. Frantically, I detach it and pass it around Andres' waist, then scramble into the back seat hoping it is long enough to secure him. It is, barely.

Josh asks, "What about the leg?"

I haven't a fucking clue. "He's passed out. Maybe we can bend the knee and get that leg inside. Otherwise, I don't know how he's going to make it."

Andres' right leg is still dangling outside the vehicle. Josh's flashlight reveals fresh blood. The tourniquet isn't holding. Change of plans. We've got to get that leg elevated.

"Forget it," I tell Josh.

I unbuckle the leather gun sling. I hold his right leg off the ground and Josh somehow lifts Andres' inert body out of the front seat and into the ATV's small back seat. Still unconscious, Andres makes low grunting noises. Snot pours out of his nose and drool soaks Josh's left arm positioned under his right arm.

Josh belts Andres into the backseat with the gun sling, while I use my belt to fashion a loop for the damaged leg. Josh tenderly cradles Andres' right leg as I buckle the belt around the ATV's steel pipe roll bar. It will do. I open the loop and we lift the leg, then re-buckle the belt.

"Josh, you watch him and that leg," I shout. With Josh next to Andres in the back, I gun the engine and drive onto Brushy Creek Road.

We backtrack and then turn onto County Road 203. I floor the gas feed and the ATV soon is traveling at 40 miles an hour. With no maintenance on the rough and uneven surface, I am stupid to drive this fast. A sudden washout appears, and I hit the brakes. The ATV starts to roll onto its side, and I cut the wheel desperately into the roll. The ATV bounces to a stop, perpendicular to the road's direction.

"Fuck! You'll kill us before we get there, Dalton." Josh has both hands wrapped tightly around Andres' torso.

I flip on my flashlight. Andres' eyes are partially open, but they stare at nothing. "Jesus, are we losing him?" I don't expect an answer. Josh looks as frightened as I feel. "Sorry. I'll slow down."

I restart the engine and turn up the rough road. Five miles later, we hit the paved and striped Farm to Market Road.

"This go toward Elmhurst?" Josh asks.

I nod in the dark. "Straight into town." Although it is asphalt surfaced, I will myself to keep the ATV's speed at 45 miles an hour. I don't know the highway's condition or if there are any obstructions.

The ATV's engine coughs as we climb the hill into town, but the gas gauge shows we aren't empty. I feather the accelerator, and the engine backfires, then smooths. Houses appear in the darkness as I spot the city limits sign. Two miles further and I turn into Doctor Jagir's driveway. Josh jumps out and begins pounding on the door while I train my flashlight on Andres' leg in the makeshift sling. No new blood. I breathe a sigh of relief until I turn the flashlight on Andres face. He doesn't appear to be breathing. His tongue lolls and his pupils are fixed.

Doctor and Misses Randhawa appear behind flashlights.

"Andres was shot in the leg." My voice cracks. "We got him here as fast as we could, but I think he's dead," I begin to cry as I frantically loosen the rifle sling holding him in the seat. "Please help."

Jagir asks us with his usual lilting calmness, "Can you be so kind as to move him in the house so that I may see what I am doing?"

I grab Andres' torso under the arms and Josh cradles his legs and ass as we clumsily surmount the stairs.

Mrs. Randhawa clears off the kitchen table and holds an electric lantern for her husband. Jagir checks for a pulse on Andres neck. Obviously frustrated, he turns to me. "What is this large red spot on his chest?"

I relate what Andres said about the gunshot strike to the ballistic vest.

"Oh, my."

I mentally translate this to "Oh, shit. This is really, really bad."

A rivulet of blood streams from one side of his mouth and onto the table.

Where did that come from?

"Geez, Doc," Josh exclaims "It's a fucking leg wound. We got a tourniquet on it damned fast. What's going on?" remember the lady present, he turns to her. "Sorry for my language, ma'am."

The doctor waves off the question, a stethoscope to Andres' chest. He shakes his head, then mutters something in Hindi to his wife. She reaches in and pushes on the center of Andres' chest, in the middle of the red blotch.

Even without the stethoscope, I can hear a small crackle.

Jagir asks his wife to repeat the process, and she pushes, but this time much harder. The crunching is louder and ominous. I stare at Andres' face, willing him to breathe. Instead, more blood seeps from his mouth.

"Did you try to resuscitate him?" the doctor asks.

"No, we drove straight here. We talked with him. He joked with us. He was alive when we put him in the ATV," Josh says, sounding like he's trying to convince himself that Andres must still be alive.

"We should have done it. I almost flipped the ATV. We could have stopped and given him mouth-to-mouth. We could have done chest compressions. We didn't. We could have saved him, couldn't we?" I am overwhelmed with guilt.

Jagir shakes his head, his face a picture of sadness. "Dalton, it would not have helped your friend." He takes my hand and places on Andres' chest. "I will put your hand on his chest. No, you cannot hurt him now."

He places his hand over mine and pushes, hard. Through the skin I can feel broken bones rub against each other.

"Oh, dear God. What am I feeling, doc?"

Doctor Randhawa wearily removes his stethoscope and hand sit to by his wife. "Myocardial contusion, Dalton. Heart bruising. You say he was struck by a bullet here."

He points and Josh nods, his eyes filling with tears.

"The vest kept the bullet from entering his body"—he pronounces it BODE-ee—"but it broke bones which damaged his heart. It began to bleed into the heart cavity until the organ could no longer beat because of the pressure. As you see, he also had blood in a lung."

He sounds so clinical, so distant, until suddenly, the doctor wraps his right arm around Josh and his left around me and shaking us as he does so, says, "There is absolutely nothing you could have done to save this man's life. You must understand this." He continues to hug the two of us, repeating reassuringly, "Nothing would have helped. Please believe me."

I shrug off the doctor's hug and wipe the blood and slime

from Andres' mouth. Mrs. Randhawa hands me a damp dishrag. Josh and I take turns cleaning our friend's face and then hand the rag back to her.

She turns off the lantern. By flashlight, Jagir leads Josh and I into his den. Once again, Mrs. Randhawa provides hot tea. Little is said.

Elmhurst's City Burial Ground, as our cemetery is called, lies just north of the downtown area, its older grave sites constrained in cement borders in neat rows, between tiny streets. Large oak and elm trees, some loaded with ball moss, shade the tombstones inscribed with family names.

The large number of deaths since the EMP has added mounds of un-sodded dirt in new sections of the cemetery. Most of the mounds are marked with small wooden crosses, some with paper stapled to them identifying the dead underneath. A few are decorated more ornately. Some are lined with rocks. Some display decorations of beer cans or liquor bottles. Noticeably absent are candles. They are needed by the living now.

The funeral home long ago ran out of caskets, so six of us carry Andres' body in a plastic tarp to his resting place, not in the unshaded area of new graves, but to a site donated by a friend with an empty gravesite in an older family plot. Josh, Elsie, and the kids trudge behind us as we enter the Burial Ground.

During the night, family members dug Andres' grave. Andres' mom and dad stand quietly, along with other family members, including several of his no-account cousins. Mrs. Lujan, Andres' mom, is a diminutive woman, once full of over-sized energy. Her son's death seems to have shrunk her even tinier. Unsteady on her feet, she reaches for her husband's arm.

Mr. Lujan, once a robust truck driver, stares blankly. I remember him a full head of black hair. It's now mostly gray, shaggy and uncombed. Neither say anything. Grief seems to roll off them in waves.

Elmhurst's Catholic Church was served by a visiting priest, but he's not from around here. Too grief stricken to argue about it, Andres' family agrees when Chief Pettibone rustles up Alex Salazar, a Pentecostal preacher, to say some appropriate words.

I'm not a praying man normally but I lift up a prayer that Salazar doesn't get too windy. He's known for trying to preach people into Heaven.

The Chief must have said something to Salazar. He's often dubbed himself a "recovering Catholic," but respects the family's faith and keeps the committal short and remembers enough from his upbringing to throw in several phrases I recognize as coming from the Catholic burial service. When finished, he asks if anyone would like to share any memories of Andres. Mr. Lujan starts to say something, begins to sob, and collapses. He is gently led away, Mrs. Lujan seemingly regaining strength because of her husband's need.

It isn't pretty, but we are able to gently lower Andres' body into the grave without mishap. As people drift off, at least a dozen friends and family stay at the grave. We swap the two shovels around and cover Andres' body. The thud of dirt hitting Andres' plastic makeshift shroud is jarring. It starts to drizzle.

I am tired beyond exhaustion but need to be near loved ones. The Kaufmans are the closest I've got to anything like family. I return to my house, retrieve my bicycle and pedal to the country.

I have an infant daughter that I need desperately to hold.

Chapter Twenty-Five

As I pedal onto the Kaufman property, Gail is walking in the pasture, holding Josefina bundled in a small blanket. She doesn't notice me as I lean my bicycle against a post. The early morning rain has brought a fresh northerly breeze that carries the scents of Ashe juniper and grass. The sun has begun to dry up small puddles in the driveway. The last drops from a shed's corrugated roof make melodic tones as they hit the water surface in an old trough.

I stand and watch my ex-wife... She sings to our baby. I'm too far away to hear the words, but know they are soothing to Josefina. I cannot imagine them being anything but that. Gail wears old tennis shoes, a faded t-shirt and jeans. The t shirt is several sizes too large, and the jeans are baggy in the butt. Her arms look muscled, but thin. She's lost all the weight from the pregnancy, and more. Her red hair is pulled into a ponytail. I sense a slight tumescence and realize Gail is sexy as hell standing there with our kid.

I want to call out to her. I desperately want to hold my daughter. But Gail appears happy in a small world of her making, a world not for me to violate.

"Dalton?"

My reverie is broken by Randall Kaufman. He pushes open the screen door to the porch with an old carved mesquite wood cane, and very carefully takes the three steps to the ground.

"What're you doing, son?" He asks, then looks out into the pasture and grins. "Oh. They're something to see, together like that, aren't they?"

I nod and watch him shuffle toward me. He's thin as a rail now. His belt's tongue flops several inches and new holes show in its leather. The Kaufmans are better off than most, but still…

He hasn't run out of Doctor Randhawa's pills yet, but Randall can't help but be counting the days. His increasingly feeble walk is a painful reminder that I've struck out on locating any more high blood pressure medication.

"Hello, Randall," I say as he shifts his cane and extends his right hand. We shake and his calloused grip still feels like it is one squeeze from breaking my hand. "Came out to see Josefina."

"Boy, she's a beauty," he replies, and I can't tell whether he's talking about his granddaughter or Gail.

Gail turns and waves, says something to Josefina and walks towards us. The wind blows stray sun-bleached strands across her face. "Hey Dalton, come to see your daughter?" she shouts.

She's sunburned, and without makeup, the freckles she never liked stand out in a dusting across the bridge of her nose and her cheeks. She smiles and my heart does little flip-flops. The woman is stunningly beautiful.

"Cat got your tongue?" she asks.

I realize that momentarily I'd forgotten Josefina's presence. "Just tired is all. Sure, I want to see Josefina."

The little girl sports a tiny bow on her head. Asleep, she makes small movements with her mouth.

"I think she's hungry."

Gail lets out a guffaw. "Dalton, she's *always* hungry. You come around more often, you'd see what I mean."

Gail kisses our daughter, then sets her in my arms. She takes her dad's arm and gently nudges him toward the porch. I follow with Josefina. I readjust the blanket and her tiny hands appear, grasping. I touch one with a finger and she clings to it. For a few moments, my exhaustion leaves. Bertha appears, wiping her hands on a ragged dishtowel.

"Good to see you, Dalton."

The house blocks the north wind and it feels good, just standing in the sunlight with the child. "It's good to be here." As I say this, a warmth runs through me. "It really, really is."

Gail touches my shoulder as I gingerly find a seat on the glider, hoping not to wake my daughter. For a moment, there is no sound but the hypnotic squeak of its mechanism as I rock back and forth.

"We heard about what happened, Dalton. Sorry about Andres. You doing okay? How's the other fella, Josh isn't it?" Randall's questions come out in a rush.

I look up. The Kaufmans are staring at me. How *am* I doing? I know it may take some time to sort that out.

"Josh is okay. Just exhausted. He's with his family." I pause, wanting to add, "and I'm with my family too." The words don't come, and inwardly I feel like a coward. I'm afraid of a rejection, but more afraid that by saying so, I will commit to a status I'm not sure I can uphold.

The moment passes.

"Word travels fast," I say, wondering how much the Kaufmans have heard.

"Billy's been going back and forth to town," explains Bertha. "It was a horrible thing. To kill a whole family. What kind of animals would do that? We're glad you found the killers." She slowly shakes her head.

I'm not pressed for details, but the Kaufmans must know of the revenge exacted.

The talk becomes a monotone drone. I can't keep my eyes open.

The man taking a piss is reaching for his pistol. I raise my shotgun, but it will not come up fast enough. Suddenly, it is there and I pull at the trigger. It won't move. I haven't released the safety. Oh, sweet Jesus. The driver's gun fires and I am struck in my right shoulder by its bullet.

"Hey, you okay, Dalton?" It's Billy. He's shaking my shoulder. "You were starting to scream. You been dreaming?"

Where am I? My eyes clear and focus. I haven't moved off the glider, but Josefina is no longer in my arms. "Where is she?"

"Josefina? Gail's feeding her. Momma says you fell asleep in mid-sentence."

Panic subsiding, I ask, "How long have I been asleep?" Shadows give the sun's position as slight past mid-day.

"Guessing an hour. You wanna crawl back on one of the beds? More comfortable than this."

I want to desperately, but there are things left undone. "Thanks, but no. Gotta go." I turn to him. "We need some help." I briefly explain about the stolen food and the damaged truck. I omit any mention of the bodies.

Billy's grin creases his wide face. "Sure, I'll go…As long as you give me a ride into town in that sidecar."

We stop at City Hall so that Billy and Chief Pettibone can follow me to my house with two ATVs. I secure the BMW in the garage. Josh appears from my back door, still haggard.

"You look like I feel," I tell him.

"If I feel as bad as you look, I'm walking dead," he retorts.

He gives the Chief a ride back to City Hall. I futilely attempt to wipe Andres' blood off the remaining ATV's surfaces.

I'm leaning into the back-seat area when Billy taps me. "You've got company."

Two of Andres' cousins stand in the driveway. I know them both. They're part of his kin who stole veterinarian supplies. They also helped cover Andres' grave this morning.

"Can I help you?" Too much has gone on too quickly for me to gauge how the Lujan family feel toward Josh and me.

"I'm Frank, or Francisco," the shorter one says. "This is my brother Felipe."

He extends his hand and I shake it. Billy nods, and Felipe says, "How's it going, Billy?"

I look at Billy quizzically.

"Frank and Felipe have done some work for Daddy at our place off and on." He shakes both their hands. "Good to see you guys."

I'm still wondering why two of the Lujan cousins are in my driveway. Finally, Frank says, "We heard how you tried to save Andres. He thought a lot of you. We're here to help out."

Josh pulls into the driveway and kills the engine. After introductions, I turn back to Frank. "What do you want to help us do?"

Like everyone else, the two are aware of the Simpson murders. "Andres made us give him some of that veterinary stuff, just before the three of you went looking for the killers," Felipe offers. "We know you found the stuff they robbed. We want to help you."

I'm bone tired and less than tactful. "You guys ever steal from Mr. Kaufman when you worked for him?"

The two feign surprise at the question, but Billy comes to their rescue. "They were good hands, Dalton. We trusted them."

Frank says, "We're not here to steal. We're here to help. We were the ones who are going to fix that Power Wagon. We hear there's a truck that needs some repairs to get that stolen food back to town. We hear it's shot up some and we can help with that."

I don't believe for a minute that the two are as altruistic as they are letting on, but there is no denying we need the killers' truck. "I know there are at least some flat tires." After calling Felipe Frank, and Frank Felipe, I give up. "Francisco, you're Pancho from now on. Felipe, you by chance left-handed?"

Felipe grins sheepishly. "Yeah."

"You guys are now Pancho and Lefty." They smile approvingly and give each other a high-five.

Soon, along with Billy, they leave in an ATV. An hour later, they are back, the vehicle loaded with mechanics tools, a weird looking modified bicycle pump, patches, and baling wire. I add a metal two-gallon container with gasoline to the load. In thirty minutes five of us in two ATVs turn onto Brushy Creek Road from County Road 203.

I dread what we will find at the ranch house. We pull off the road and drive to the damaged truck. In the daylight, I see it's a sturdy Freightliner stake truck. Neither it nor its load of food supplies have been disturbed even nearly twenty hours after a barrage of loud shooting. A body lies on each side. The driver's eyes have already become tasty morsels for some scavenger.

Pancho exclaims, "Oh man, you guys shot the shit out of this thing." He seems unfazed by the dead men next to it.

"That's what scares me," says Josh. "No way we can get all this food back into town in these ATVs."

Lefty interjects, "We'll make it happen. Don't worry."

Pancho jumps out and begins unloading tools and supplies, while Lefty crawls under the truck. They're eager to start but there's something that's got to be done first.

The five of us walk around the back of the house. Black vultures are already feasting on the man I killed behind the carport.

We drag the two bodies out of the house. They are beginning to bloat, and everyone dons bandanas in a futile attempt at avoiding the stench. Josh catches my eye when we enter the room where we found Vincent Guerra, the gut-shot killer from Escondido. The two wounds caused by our *coup de grace* seem to stare back at us accusingly. The other three make no comment about the wounds to the dead man, nor the broken bits of floor tile directly below the two wounds. They are glaring proof that Guerra was shot while lying on his back. Momentarily I feel ashamed. It passes quickly, but I can tell Josh remains bothered by what we did.

Billy asks, "What now? We going to bury them?"

"No, Billy. We haven't discussed it but leaving five bodies to rot isn't a good idea. " That's what the gasoline is for."

Billy asks, "Burn them? Holy shit, Dalton, really?"

Josh adds, "We don't have the time or energy to dig a big enough grave. Coyotes, wolves, foxes, they'll dig 'em up and scatter bones everywhere."

Pancho instinctively genuflexes but says nothing.

We stack the five bodies in the swale of Brushy Creek Road's north-side bar ditch, dead tree branches interlaced between each, and pile additional deadfall on top and the sides. I carry the gasoline to the bar ditch and leave it there.

We return to the truck. Josh retrieves the opened MRE case and throws it on the truck. Somehow, Pancho and Lefty patch the punctured rear tires, and we take turns on the air pump.

The temperature is dropping as the sun moves westward toward the trees.

"Cool front," says Billy. Normally talkative, he's said little to this point.

Pancho slams the truck's hood. "Lots of bullet and shotgun holes in this *camion,* but only one nicked sparkplug wire. Amazing. Let's see if she'll fire up."

Lefty jumps in the cab and pumps the gas feed, then turns the ignition key I took when we left last night. Amazingly, the engine cranks over and remains running when Lefty drops it into an idle.

"Let's get out of here," Josh says. Pancho and Lefty load their tools into the truck's bed and hop in the cab.

No way do I trust these two enough to let them take the truck. "No way Jose," I say. "One of you guys in the truck with Josh. One with me. Billy'll take the ATV."

Pancho grins like a kid who almost pulled something over on an adult. After Josh trades places with Felipe, Josh eases the big truck onto Brushy Creek and asks, "You okay starting the fire?"

I just nod, and he turns toward Elmhurst.

I unscrew the gasoline can's cap and walk to the bier and begin splashing the liquid over the bodies. The brush covers them, and I'm relieved I can't see any features, that is until a limb, disturbed by the sloshing liquid moves slightly. A face is partially exposed. Its filmy eyes seem look at me accusingly.

I re-cover the body, then I let the gasoline soak in. I move upwind and toss a lit rag. The gasoline lights with near explosive force, and the bodies are enveloped in fire. I move away but the stench of burning flesh seems to follow me toward the other men.

As we turn north on County Road 203, flames reach at least ten feet and a dark oily smoke drifts southward.

The truck and supplies have attracted quite a crowd of onlookers in front of City Hall. Everyone is emaciated, and several men and women, stare longingly at the boxes and metal containers. The Chief has a key to the old armory. Billy and I pull up in the city's ATVs as someone starts to climb the side of the truck.

Suddenly, several people start to push against the Chief, trying to shove him out of the way, almost daring him to pull his gun. I'm momentarily shocked at the palpable rage on many faces. Billy appears from the ATV behind me and bowls into the people attempting to climb onto the truck bed.

Pettibone has disappeared under the mass of people swarming over him. Josh starts the truck's engine and begins to pull away from City Hall. Billy climbs over the truck's side and throws two men off the truck. But not before they pull several MREs from the box opened by the killers.

The crowd passes over the Chief. I run to him and help him to his feet. He looks shaken but otherwise unhurt. He shrugs me off, pulls his pistol from its holster, and begins firing shots into the air.

Except for two men fighting over an MRE, the deafening gunshots seem to shock everyone into stillness. Josh brakes, exits the truck cab with his pistol and stands guard.

Billy, large, docile Billy, climbs off the truck and joins him.

"I'm still police chief in this town," the Chief yells. "This food is going to be locked up and then rationed out. No one is going to take anything off this truck!"

The Chief is usually taciturn and calm. The anger and steeliness in his voice surprises me.

Someone in the crowd starts to demand the food be distributed immediately, and several others second this.

"Who said that?" Pettibone does not wait for an answer. He walks to the loudmouth and slams his pistol over the man's head. He crumples to the ground.

"Anyone else?"

No one says anything. Pettibone turns to me and says, "Let's get this stuff locked up."

I weave the ATV through the crowd. Everywhere I look, I see desperation on peoples' faces.

How much longer can our town hang on? Is it time to search for somewhere safer for those I care for?

WINTER

Chapter Twenty-Six

"LAST TO BUD, FIRST TO DROP THEIR LEAVES." GAIL SURVEYS THE pecan trees in the creek bottom. "That's why I've never been fond of them, I guess."

Josefina wiggles, and I gently adjust the baby carrier strapped to my back. Josie—we've taken to calling her that—is four months old and is fond of walks with the two of us.

"Maybe so, but it never stopped you from eating Bertha's pecan pies."

Gail steps over a fallen log and continues into the dry creek bed. Her tennis shoes make a crunching sound on the rocks and gravel. I am at the Kaufmans more often now. Elmhurst's situation worsens, and this place seems light years away from the gnawing concerns of daily survival there. The walks around the Kaufmans' acreage have become part of what we do, often with Josie, sometimes not. Whatever rancor left over from our previous relationship seems to have disappeared, and Gail seems genuinely to enjoy my company. Although through inflections she makes it clear that Josefina is her paramount concern, I find myself wanting her company more and more. It's a good feeling, but not without some trepidations. It hasn't been that long ago that we were hurling verbal hand grenades at each other.

We are still in the creek, but the nearly naked limbs of the pecans bend with an increasing energy that indicates a cold front is moving in. Some remaining leaves drift down, and I wonder if our daughter is warm enough.

I unsnap the pack's belt and ease the carrier to the ground. Josefina has fallen asleep. The sweat on my back is chilled by the cold and I wish I'd brought a light jacket. Josefina's head is now a mass of brown curls. Gail sits on a boulder and watches as I adjust the blanket around Josie's ears. I glance over and see her eyeing me.

"What are you thinking about?"

"What's going to happen to us, Dalton?"

I'm enjoying the rare peace and don't want to get into a discussion about something I don't have much control over. "I don't know. We'll get by." As I say it, I know that it is not the truth. Gail does too.

"Nonsense, Dalton."

Josie yawns and once again I'm in awe of the beauty of our daughter's face, her tiny nose, toothless mouth, drool, everything.

"Dalton, leave her alone. She's fine. We need to talk."

Reluctantly I leave the child and sit next to Gail. "So, talk."

"Winter's here," she starts, saying the obvious. "Is my family going to make it until spring?"

It's a troubling question and not the first time I've heard it. Despite the lack of medication, Randall's still with us, although I know the skyrocketing blood pressure will eventually kill him. Bertha is worn down caring for her husband. Billy stays gone as much as he's here, off scrounging for anything than can be traded for food.

Food. Precious food. We all need food. As beautiful and desirable as Gail is, if she offered me a roll in the hay or a hot meal, she'd remain untouched. I imagine a large hamburger, with cheese, greasy, slathered with mustard, and French fries.

She bumps my shoulder. "I bet you were thinking of food, weren't you?" "Yeah." I grin. "I don't know what's going to happen to us. And I don't know if any of us will make it if things don't get better."

What little I hear through Anson and other HAM operators doesn't bode well. Further north, there are reports of mass starvation as winter's cold takes its grip. Here, winter is normally a small inconvenience, but now? The shorter days are mostly dry, and we've had a few light freezes. A year ago, none of this would have been significant. Now, it means there are no crops to harvest.

Gail's voice drops. "My daughter," she says. "I want to see her grown up. I am not sure I will get to do that." Her face crumples as she cries. "I'm not sure *she* will live."

The idea of Josie dying jolts me. I seem to spend countless hours while in Elmhurst worrying about our daily existence and the direction things are heading, but Gail's tears once again make the fear of our future all too real.

We walk back to the Kaufman's house. Wood smoke from the chimney is a welcome smell, despite the energy expended to hew the cordwood. At the back porch, I hug Gail, then hand her Josie, still in the pack.

"I'll think of something. I've got to."

The bicycle ride to town saddens me. More houses appear deserted. Some of those won't last long. I wave at two men near the railroad tracks. They lug planks of wood torn from an abandoned house to a sawhorse. As I pass, one picks up a handsaw and begins to shorten one of the boards. Firewood. I can't blame them. There's no one to complain about it, and the structure will be transformed into something useful for warmth and cooking.

I stop in at City Hall to visit with Chief Pettibone. He still wears his Police Chief uniform but seems not to notice, or perhaps care, that his pants have a tear at one knee and his shirt is missing a button at the collar.

"How's it going, Larry?" Using the Chief's first name still sounds strange, but after the Simpson family murders and the ensuing gun battle, we've become closer.

Today, he offers none of the usual pleasantries. "Dalton, can you get Josh and Jill and what's left of the Elmhurst Neighborhood Patrol? We need to meet."

Once seven persons, we are now down to four— Josh, Jill, me, and Kevin Daugherty. Daugherty is new. An African American bachelor who lives on the north side in a small clapboard house, urged to join when Andres was killed, and two others quit.

"Sure, where and when, and why?"

"Got a message today. From your old friend Ike Belton. He wants to meet."

Whoa. "You mean he's interested in this side of town?" Ike has created his own little fiefdom on the east side of Elmhurst and made it clear he wants nothing to do with community policing, or anything else resembling cooperation with anyone not in the 'hood. "Where are we meeting?"

It turns out it will be in an old Hispanic non-denominational church on the edge of the area Belton controls. Templo de Fe is neutral ground, I guess.

The Chief continues. "He's asked that we come unarmed."

"That's not going to happen, Larry." Alarm bells are going off in my head.

I borrow an ATV. It needs new spark plugs and the engine coughs and wheezes, but it gets me back to my house. Fred Aston limps to his fence line and waves. I am amazed that he is still alive, and thankful Andres' cousins coughed up the medication to save Fred and his foot. "Jill here?" I ask.

She appears beside her husband. Jill's blond hair tints are

long gone, as is the makeup. She dresses in cutoffs, long socks, khaki shirt, and hiking boots. Strictly utilitarian and strictly business now. "I'm here. What's up?"

Josh appears and the three of us pick up our newest member, then return to City Hall. With the chief, we head to Templo de Fe, armed. As soon as we stop in front of the church, Josh takes a guard position at the church door, holding his rifle ready at port arms position. Four of us enter the darkened sanctuary together. I carry a twelve-gauge shotgun as well as my holstered sidearm. My eyes adjust to the gloom. Ike Belton stands unarmed, arms folded, where the altar once was. The altar's missing and I guess it's been cut up for firewood. Lupe Aguilar stands to one side, still Belton's flunky.

Nothing is said for a few moments and Ike looks curiously at Kevin Daugherty. "You bringing a brother? You must be serious."

"Ike, I've got a name," Daugherty retorts. "It's Kevin, remember?"

Chief extends a handshake to Ike. The ice broken, six of us exchange nods while Lupe Aguilar stands off to the side, mute. I recall my last encounter with Ike and find I am still angry of Ike's imperious condescension. And ashamed of leaving the east side of Elmhurst with my tail tucked between my legs.

"Ike," I interject, "you called this meeting. Why are we here?"

Ike seems to ignore my brusqueness. With a smile that shows two gold teeth, he says, "I asked you to come unarmed, and as you can see, I am that way. It was a matter of trust, which you seem not to have for me."

Jill speaks up. "I don't know you, Mr. Belton, but so what? Your friend over there"—she points to Aguilar—"is packing."

Ike ignores Jill. "Elmhurst is about to have a little problem, and I'm here to see if I can help."

Uh oh. This is about to get interesting.

The Chief's voice remains calm. "You want to explain that, Ike? When you say, 'I'm here to see if I can help,' I get a little curious. You've done your best not to help us so far."

Again, the toothy smile. I look around for a place to sit down, and notice Lupe Aguilar is now leaning against the sanctuary's brick wall. He has a holstered handgun. Nothing exceptional there. What catches my attention is Aguilar's shoulder strap. He reaches down and adjusts it, exposing an Uzi, with a large magazine. Two things go through my mind. First, Lupe Aguilar never had two nickels to rub together. And second, he wouldn't be packing an Uzi with its wicked firepower without Ike's permission.

As Lupe leans back against the wall, the Uzi makes a metallic noise as it rubs up against the brick. Daugherty catches my eye. He's seen it too. No doubt, Ike Belton's got other people stationed near Templo de Fe. I'm thankful we have Josh outside, his head on a swivel.

I walk over and lean against the wall next to Aguilar. I've known him for years. The rat-faced little bastard and his family moved to Elmhurst when he was fifteen. He got booted out of Elmhurst High School for breaking into lockers and stealing kids' stuff. I nod, my shotgun cradled barrel facing him.

Another laugh from Ike, and he continues, "I am here to tell you that my people and I want the keys to the armory. You all've got medicines and foods in there, and we on the east side need them."

He stops, as if awaiting a response. Nothing is said, so Ike continues. "The east side people are hungry, and they're sick. Chief, you've been preventing us from getting our share."

Pettibone's countenance becomes florid with anger, but his response is measured. "Ike, there isn't a soul in this town who hasn't had food distribution opportunities with what we *had* stored there. And Doctor Randhawa has been seeing anyone who he can get to, regardless of race, color, or creed. If they don't see him, he'll come to them." He pauses. "Except maybe for your side of town, where we hear you won't let him come. And where we hear that you try to keep people from crossing the highway to see him. So, don't play that race card with me, *Mister* Belton. Besides, there's not much of anything left in the armory now anyway."

Ike shakes his head, but before he can interject anything, the Chief barks, "We've been handing out anything and everything to anyone who needs it. What really is going on here?"

Ike looks around. "Chief Pettibone, there are only so many folks who can survive on what's out there." He motions vaguely toward the church entrance. "Not just in this town, but all over. It's time for some to move on."

I interject, "This town's sixty percent Hispanic, Ike. Are you talking for them? Because I don't think they'll let you."

"They don't get a voice in this."

The Chief asks, "You turning this into some kind of race war, Ike?"

Ike laughs. "No race issue. It's all about supply and demand. There are too many people—too much demand—and not enough supply. I aim to correct that."

We've heard talk of the gang warfare in Lincoln City. HAM reports and people from the state capital have described gun battles and turf wars in parts of the city. Killings over food. Until now, Elmhurst has been spared.

"What I hear, folks on the east side are just trying to get by, like everyone else. You and who else? You have some militia force you've been hiding?" I ask.

He looks over at Lupe Aguilar. "Lupe, he's my bodyguard. His family is from Escondido. And he's got lots of family."

Escondido? The thugs that Medrano and his men were trying to keep out of their neighborhood in Lincoln City were from that place. The ones Jacob the professor killed at the filling station also were from Escondido. Vincent Guerra, the murderer, along with two others, were from there. The uncomfortable thought crosses my mind that someone may realize that Josh and I, along with Andres, took out three killers from that city.

"I think we're through here." The Chief turns to Jill, Daugherty, and me. "Let's go."

What I'm hearing is crazy. "Wait." I walk to Ike. "Before this EMP happened, you and I used to be, maybe not friends, but cordial." I'm not sure how much I want to disclose of my encounters with the gang members originating in Escondido but tell him of my trip on my BMW to pick up Gail. "I saw firsthand what they will do. I saw them kill people in cold blood. Ike, I'm begging you. Don't invite these people into our town."

Aguilar speaks up. "You better watch yourself, Dalton." He points toward the church's entrance. "And your bro out front too. And your families too."

"Why's that, Lupe?"

"You and he and Andres, *ese pocho,* you killed three of my homies." He uses a pejorative term telling me Andres wasn't "Mexican" enough.

Oh shit. Only three people knew that the killers with the Nebraska escapees were from Escondido. Josh and I swore Chief Pettibone to silence. We never told the three helping us recover the truck and burn the bodies, and I don't remember them asking. If there were gang tats on any of the bodies, I didn't recognize them.

Bad things are about to happen, and I need to ensure they don't occur to those I love.

Chapter Twenty-Seven

THE ATV'S ENGINE IS ALL I HEAR ON THE RETURN TO CITY HALL. No one appears along the U.S. highway that separates of the predominant west side of Elmhurst from its east side. Even the few dogs still wily enough to scavenge choose to avoid this wasteland.

The shuttered businesses along the once-busy thoroughfare, Colorado Street, through town pass in splintering snippets of sensation. Johnson grass and tiny tree seedlings push through the gaps between the concrete curbing and the asphalt. The flaking paint, shards of broken glass from shot-out streetlights and broken windows aren't new, but the bleakness they portray seem to create a dimension of hollowness I've not before felt. Elmhurst, once a robust center of Lee County life, is now just a collection of desperate people and a smudge of decaying structures.

The sky cooperates in this portrayal of gloom. Today's skies are leaden, and lowering clouds threaten rain.

The usual group of hangers-on at City Hall has dwindled considerably. Too little information, too much energy expended to walk there. Those few people here now just stare as the

ATV's engine stops. Whatever curiosity they may have at the five of us seems suppressed by the ever-present malnutrition. I feel like I am attending a funeral, maybe my own. Josh hops off his position standing on the back bumper, weapon at the ready rocking the ATV. Momentarily the remaining four of us just sit. I stare at the fading paint of a handicapped parking place. I have no idea why, but I trace with my eyes the pebbled surface of the asphalt and the interruptions in white and blue paint, wondering how long before time erases the location's privilege.

"Dalton." Jill nudges me gently. "You okay?"

"No." I can't look at her.

I crawl off the passenger seat, clear the shotgun, and walk up the steps into the building. The others follow. Wordless, we move to the Chief's office. Daugherty seems puzzled, but at the same time, eager to help. He brings in extra chairs and we all sit.

The Chief takes a deep breath and blows it out, disturbing a piece of paper laying on his desk. "Anyone want to start off this discussion?"

Kevin Daugherty says, "I'm new to this. I know Ike. Anyone who's lived here for any length of time knows Ike. When I first moved to town from Chicago, three years ago, Ike and I were on a couple neighborhood committees, as the Chief knows. Working on community policing policies."

The Chief nods at the memory. "There were, what, six folks in that group, weren't there?"

"Yeah, Chief. We made some recommendations about policing, especially about hiring more minority police. I was impressed with what you tried to do. 'Course you never hired enough, but you tried."

The Chief nods ruefully. "Big cities snatched up most qualified candidates offering a heck of lot more money."

"I know you did. Ike wasn't convinced. He used the term 'brother,' a lot, and wanting me to push you harder. I didn't buy that I was his 'brother' then. Sure as hell not now. Seemed to blow a lot of smoke trying to convince me he was more important to the world than he really was."

I'm learning things about Kevin Daugherty I didn't know, but part of me wants to bolt from the meeting and be anywhere else. Somewhere far, far away. The room's air is chilly, but my shirt is drenched with sweat. My guts feel like knotted rubber bands.

Daugherty looks at me and Josh and asks, "I get that Ike and his buddies want to take over the town. But what was all that stuff from that skinny shit about you killing his homeboys?"

Jill says nothing but it's obvious to me that she's just as curious about Aguilar's remark.

Pettibone leans back in his chair and says nothing. I know he is deeply concerned, and it shows. He suddenly looks old beyond his years. I glance to Josh and he shrugs as if to say 'okay.'

"Chief knows. No one else was supposed to. The people that murdered Simpson and his family. Besides the two from Nebraska, the other three were all gang members from Escondido. Aguilar's found out, somehow, that Andres and the two of us killed them."

Jill mutters, "Oh, shit."

In the dim sunlight filtering through the Chief's office window, Josh looks ashen. I wonder if I look the same.

Josh scuffs his feet and nods. "Yeah, oh shit."

The Chief, Josh, and Jill are aware of what I'd witnessed in Lincoln City, when Gail was pregnant with Josefina. I bring Kevin up to date. "I took my motorcycle and sidecar to get Gail when she was pregnant with Josefina. The gang or gangs out of Escondido pushed right through a roadblock defended by armed citizens. I saw them execute two of the survivors. Point blank shots to the head." As I talk, I wonder whether Medrano and Jacob the retired professor are still alive. "With the help of a group trying to defend their neighborhood, Gail and I made it out of town, but not before two more of the Escondido group were killed."

When I'm finished, the Chief asks despairingly, "How in God's name can we keep them out of Elmhurst?" He doesn't wait for an answer. "This town isn't surrounded by defensive walls like in the Middle Ages. Nothing but farmland, over-grown pastures, a small river, and trees. And who's going to defend the place? You four and me? Who else even has the strength to step up, or even cares to?"

Josh says, "I'm new here, but we're on top of a hill. That's got to offer some defensive possibilities, doesn't it?"

The Chief gives him a baleful look. "Sure, we've got the river that wraps around the north and east, with a couple of bridges over it. And yeah, some areas are damned neared impassible in wet weather. And yeah, Elmhurst is perched on higher ground than the farm and ranch lands. But so what? It'd take a battalion of soldiers to defend this place." He looks defeated.

I can't deal with this right now. "I feel..." I pause. "To tell you the truth, right now I'm not thinking clearly. Why don't we all sleep on it and maybe come up with some ideas later?"

Jill isn't letting go that easily. "How much later, Dalton? You think we've got a lot of time to plan?"

I want to tell her to shut the hell up, but she's right. Neither Ike nor the Escondido gang are telegraphing their punches. Ike didn't with me the last time we met.

The Chief runs his hands through his thinning hair. "We may not have much time to prepare for this."

Josh states the obvious. "Hell, I'm betting money some of Aguilar's family and gangbangers are already here, stashed over on the east side. It wouldn't surprise me to see the bastards walking this way right now."

Instinctively, I glance out the City Hall's glass entrance. If that's the case, we're already doomed. Kevin picks up the shotgun I've just set down and walks to the front of the building to stand guard. That action by someone I hardly know gives me a sense of relief that far outweighs its effectiveness. Nevertheless, Kevin Daugherty seems a stand-up guy.

Jill softly asks, "God in heaven, what are we going to do?"

Josh cracks a humorless grin. "Preemptive strike."

For a moment, I think he's joking. He's not. Josh's smile is vulpine, and not for the first time I am glad he's on my side.

"You're kidding me, right?"

"No, Jill," I reply. "I don't think he is."

Josh confirms my statement. "I've got a wife and two young kids. I'll be goddamned if I'll let anything happen to them. Dalton and me, we did what we had to do out on Brushy Creek. I'm ready to do it again." He now has color in his face and is breathing heavily. "I came to this town looking for peace and quiet. It's been anything but that, but my family's been safe. Now?"

Jill isn't buying it. "What, you going to sneak over and shoot a couple of people and presto, the problem's solved? Are you out of your fucking mind? I've got a husband that nearly died. He's just barely ambulatory now. You don't think there'll be retaliation? And maybe not just against you, but against anyone associated with you!"

Josh roars back, "Hell, woman. Two seconds ago, you were asking what we can do, and freaking out just like the rest of us. You don't like the idea come up with one better. Until then, don't crawl up my ass."

In seconds, two people who have worked together amicably are screaming at each other. Jill's rage fills the room. She lunges at Josh, and I grab her around the waist. She reaches and scratches me across the face. I pull at her clawing hand, bending her fingers back to prevent another slash. I want to break her goddamned fingers.

Kevin is suddenly there, prying her off me. The Chief holds Josh against a wall. Jill continues to scream but now her accusations include me.

"You bastards. Don't you see what you've done?"

"Stop!" a booming voice brings stillness to the room.

I release Jill, and Kevin pushes her into a chair, placing himself between us. The Chief's voice has caught us all by surprise. Like when he took charge at the near-riot over the Simpson food stash, he seems renewed by the necessity of seizing control.

"Just fucking stop! We are unravelling. It's just what they want. Look at yourselves."

"Bitch," I mutter as I try to wipe the blood off my face with a bare hand.

Jill begins to weep. "I'm sorry. Things are getting to me."

"Oh great, now the woman starts to cry so we'll feel sorry for her," Josh taunts.

Not a good idea. Jill lunges and punches Josh in the nose. It's a solid hit.

"Son of a bitch! That hurt like hell! You broke my damned nose!"

I start to laugh. Kevin looks at me like I'm crazy, then begins his own deep laughter. Then the Chief starts. Suddenly, Josh, holding a rag to his nose with one hand, reaches out to hug Jill. Reluctantly, she accepts the embrace.

"What about me?" I ask. Jill kisses me on the forehead and says, "That's the closest you'll ever get to a real kiss from me, cutie."

This produces gales of laughter from the other four. Eventually, the laugher subsides to giggles. The Josh begins to reset his broken nose, and I gasp as I hear the cartilage crunch.

Kevin shakes his head. "Not sure I want to be around you people. Maybe Ike's not so bad after all." Which starts the laughter all over again.

I stand up and see my face dimly reflected in the Chief's window. Three gouges furrow my face. "How am I going to explain this to Gail?"

More laughter. And then, like an ebbing tide, the silliness is gone. The physical damage to Josh and me is minimal, given the cathartic effect of what's just happened. It's time to start planning.

The next hour is consumed with ideas, most of which are discarded as impractical or impossible. There are several questions: Can Elmhurst be defended, and if so how and what cost? How do we protect ourselves? Unfortunately, solving Elmhurst's issues don't necessarily include saving our lives and those we love.

My assignment is to track down Pancho and Lefty. With the availability of the truck taken from the killers, we've put the Dodge Power Wagon project on hold. Instead of mechanic work, the two have proven their value as scroungers. Billy is often with them now. I don't ask many questions. They probably wouldn't tell me the truth anyway, but I know the trio has made furtive ventures into Lincoln City.

If we are to have any chance of success, we need their help. And the help of as many more of Elmhurst's citizens, armed and willing to take on an encroaching enemy.

But first, it is time to reach our families and loved ones and to put them on notice.

Josh and Jill catch a ride ATV with Kevin. Chief uses precious fuel to drive me to the Kaufmans. En route, Pettibone offers to help explain to the Kaufmans what has transpired. I wave him off. "You've got a wife to look after, Larry."

He squeezes my shoulder as I step out of the ATV at the Kaufmans' entrance gate. Chief rarely mentions his wife. Somehow, she has withstood the cancer's ravages these last months, but her end is near. I cannot plumb the depths of his misery, both at losing his wife and facing the future alone.

Stepping around the ruts in the uncared-for track, I reassess the Kaufman farmhouse, seemingly so sturdy and timeless. Now, its wooden structure spells doom if a Molotov cocktail is splashed against it. The many windows speak to its indefensibility. The outbuildings that surround it are avenues of hidden attack.

The farmhouse holds the only people I dare consider as family. And because of my actions, their lives may be forfeit.

Chapter Twenty-Eight

"WHERE'S BILLY?"

"And a good day to you too, Dalton." Bertha holds open the porch screen door, clearly displeased.

I know I'm being rude, but I'm too freaked out to care. To be worth a damn, I have to ratchet down my anxiety several levels. "I apologize. Something's come up, and I need to find Billy."

"He's on the back porch with Randall." She steps aside as I barge past her. I feel an exasperated gust of her breath. "Josie's out near the creek with Gail, in case you're interested."

Oh, sweet Jesus. Totally unprotected. "Billy!"

Randall's thin frame is encompassed in a large wooden rocker. Cushions ease the hardness of the seat, and a quilt drapes over his shoulders. Billy sits next to his dad. The two appear as if they've been in deep discussion. Randall looks worse than ever. I pull up short, shocked by how close to death he must be.

"Hello, Dalton," he rasps, nearly inaudible. Billy puts a protective arm around Randall as I take a deep breath and shake hands with both of them.

Billy asks, "What's going on, Dalton?"

I am still taken aback by Randall's deterioration and decide he's not up to what I need to discuss. Fleetingly, I wonder if his death will make protecting the rest of the Kaufmans easier. Shitty thought, but it's there.

"Need to visit on some business, Billy. When you and your daddy finish, I'll be out front."

I turn to walk into the house, but Randall has not let go of my hand. His hand is dry and leathery, and its once robust veining is now barely visible. He stares at me with jaundiced eyes, mouth-breathing like a fish out of water.

"Good to see you, Dalton," he wheezes. I pull away, but he reaches with his left hand and places it gently over my right wrist. "Don't leave."

Billy finds a hardback chair, and I sit and take a deep breath.

"I want to thank you, Dalton." Randall gulps a breath. "For all you've done for me and my family."

Right now, I'm trying to get his family to safety, and he's slowing the process down. "I appreciate it, Randall, but like I've said, no thanks have ever been necessary." *Come on Randall, I love you, but I've got things to do.* I glance at Billy, but no help there. He's just looking at his dad with a sorrowful look on his face.

Randall lets go of my hand. He reaches helplessly for the quilt as it slides off a shoulder. "Billy, the quilt's dropped a bit. I'm feeling a draft."

Billy and I make eye contact as we both re-adjust Randall's source of warmth. Billy makes a tiny head shake. It tells me I need to stay and hear his father out. Randall settles under the quilt, coughs quietly, and says nothing. Behind me, the slap of the front screen door and Bertha's laughter announce Gail's return from her walk with our daughter. I'm drawn toward the joy of Josie's presence, but welded to my seat by Randall's insistence.

"I'm dying, Dalton."

That's obvious, but hearing Randall verbalize it hits a nerve. He has been a rock for so many years. "I know," I say. Any attempt at minimizing his words would be insulting.

Billy's eyes fill with tears as Randall continues. "Things have been tough. I suspect with winter coming on, they'll get worse. I won't last the cold. I'm just takin' up space now."

The noise inside the house has stopped and I suspect Gail and Bertha are hovering nearby. Josie emits a hunger cry, confirming their nearness, and the women retreat toward the kitchen.

"You've got a wonderful family, sir." I realize I am blinking back the sudden onset of tears. "I'll do all I can to make sure they're okay after you're gone."

"I know, Dalton. I know." He reaches a hand from under the quilt and pats Billy's shoulder. "You two, take care of my three wonderful ladies."

I nod, speechless.

"Now, you and Billy go have your talk about whatever was bothering you. We'll see you later."

"Daddy, can I help you move inside now?" asks Billy.

"No, son. I think I'll just sit here for a while."

Billy pauses, then the two of us re-enter the house. Gail hands me Josie, and I carry my daughter to the glider on the front porch. Bertha and Gail join Billy and me. Both are red-eyed from crying.

Josie mewls comfortably as she sucks on a baby bottle she's learning to grasp with both hands.

"Daddy's quit eating and drinking," Gail says.

That helps explain the suddenness of his deterioration. "Was that what you and Randall were talking about when I came in?" I ask Billy.

"He's determined not to be a burden. I've searched the bedroom without luck, but it wouldn't surprise me if he hasn't hidden some kind of pills that will speed things along."

Holy shit. The idea that Randall Kaufman could take his own life would have been, a few months ago, inconceivable. And yet, I'm not surprised. He won't be the first. There have been murmuring for weeks about people willing themselves to die. Not that it would happen here, but some have wondered whether family members have 'helped along' others taking up space and eating precious food.

And now, with winter approaching, Escondido thugs and Ike Belton want to drive out the Kaufmans and anyone else in or around Elm City not a part of their gang, almost guaranteeing their deaths.

Worse, because of me, the Kaufmans, Bertha, Billy, Gail, and even tiny Josie, may not live long enough to see that come about. I explain what's just occurred with Ike and Lupe Aguilar. "Ike's thinking he's in charge, but I wonder how long that's going to last."

Bertha asks, "We're out here in the country. We can take care of ourselves." She looks to Gail and Billy who both nod in agreement. "You can move in out here and help us."

"You all are marked people."

Billy gets a quizzical look and asks, "Why is that?"

"Lupe Aguilar." I pause, hating what I disclose. "You helped us burn the bodies of those killers, Billy. Three of them were from Escondido. Aguilar says he knows that Josh, Andres, and I killed them. He's threatened that anyone close to us…" I look at Josie and can't go on. But I do. "It gets worse if that's possible. I keep saying 'the gang from Escondido,' but I'm sure there has to be more than one group. And they'll talk, and sooner or later the group moving into Elmhurst will talk with the bunch Gail and I dealt with in Lincoln City."

Gail's face is ashen. "Oh, sweet Jesus."

I nod. "The two killed at the service station by Jacob the

professor. I was there, and a BMW with a sidecar stands out like a sore thumb. There were plenty of people who saw the two of us trying to get out of town, and even more that saw us help Medrano escape after the bad guys broke through the roadblock on the Interstate."

Billy asks, "Can't the five, uh, four of us defend this place?"

I don't know the answer to that. I don't think so but am also dealing with something I hadn't thought out: Maybe it *could* be defended by the four of us. But I've taken on responsibilities in Elmhurst. How in hell am I squaring my obligation to my family here and my promise to help defend the town of Elmhurst?

Gail speaks. "Because there won't be four of us out here. At least not all the time. Isn't that so, Dalton? You're part of that patrol, and that hasn't changed, has it?"

The three look at me. I nod but try to find another reason for them leaving their home. "This place can't be defended. It's too open, but also has too many outbuildings. It's wood. Someone throws a Molotov cocktail through a window, the place'd go up in minutes."

Gail won't relent. "And you can't be here all the time, can you? You've promised that chief of police and some others that the town needs defending?" Her voice is like acid dripping on soft metal.

I want to pinch her head off. Partly because of how she's talking to me, and partly because she's too damned accurate in her accusation.

Bertha cuts Gail off. "Stop it. Both of you." She turns to me. "Where will we be safe in town? And why?"

Hopefully, because we'll have some more people to defend various places, I think, although I can't even be sure of that. "I have a house." I explain about Josh and his family.

Gail snorts loudly, startling Josie. "Nothing about being in Elmhurst sounds worth a damn, Dalton. At least out here, we've got food and shelter. We can tear down a couple of sheds —*including* the one your Beamer's in for the moment—so no one can sneak up behind them…"

This is getting ugly. The trust I thought I'd rebuilt with Gail is coming down around my head. I turn to Billy. "I'll be back as soon as I can. Please don't leave."

He gives me a thumbs-up and the two of us walk to the shed where the BMW's stored.

"Where are Pancho and Lefty? I need anything they can give me on Ike Belton and the situation on the east side of town." I pause. "And anything you can give me as well."

"Dalton, I haven't seen either one of them in a couple of days. Sometimes I go with them. Sometimes they go scrounging on their own and I stay here to take care of family. About Ike, I know less than nothing. He doesn't like me and made it clear he didn't want me around when Pancho and Lefty were doing business with him. I haven't been over to that side of town in over a month. What'd you have in mind?"

"Honestly? I'm not sure yet. They may help us. They may not. I'm shooting in the dark right now."

Billy laughs. "Shooting in the dark. That's kinda funny."

"Not really, Billy." I swing open the shed's door, anxious to leave.

"Guess not."

The Beamer's surfaces scatter the sunlight. The motorcycle's metal surfaces contrast jarringly with the shed's unpainted wood siding and rafters, rusted metal roof, and dirt floor.

"Dalton."

"What?" I straddle the seat and reach for the ignition switch. I'm not in any mood to chitchat.

"It's okay."

"Nothing's okay right now, Billy."

"Dalton." Easy going Billy straddles the BMW's front tire, fists clenching its handlebar. "I'll look out here. I promise. I'll do what I can to settle my sister down. She's just scared and worried."

"Thanks." My voice is tight sounding. I'm angry at being braced by Gail. "She's right, Billy," I confess. "If I don't help here, I'm screwing the pooch. If I walk away from the Chief and Josh and...Ah, shit."

Billy catches me by surprise. He releases his grip on the handlebars and walks to my side, then awkwardly bends and hugs me. Over the years, I've often dismissive of Billy. I am ashamed.

I take a route back into Elmhurst on the BMW that keeps me away from the east side of town. It's late afternoon when I pull up to City Hall. Inside, Josh, Kevin, and Jill stand with eight other people I recognize from town, some Anglo, some Hispanic, and one African American. The eight, six men and two women, display an odd collection of sidearms, rifles, and shotguns. Josh introduces some, Kevin the remainder. I'm impressed with the ability to find citizens willing to help but wonder if they know what they are getting into.

The Chief asks, "How'd things go at the Kaufman place? They willing to come into town?"

I wave the questions off. It didn't go well, and no, they aren't, at least not yet. I'm not going to explain all this in front of the newcomers. He accepts my reluctance and turns to the eight. "Raise your right hands to be sworn in."

"Do each of you solemnly swear to defend Elmhurst, so help you God?"

I have no idea where that oath came from, and sure as hell doubt it'll slow down anyone wanting to cut and run.

The eight whose names already have escaped me, are assigned in pairs to Josh, Kevin, Jill, and me. Chief designates the four of us 'patrol leaders.'

"What is this, a Boy Scout troop?" I can't help but ask. "Do we get names for our patrols? If so, I want us to be named the Cougars."

Jill gets into the act. "Hell, I'm the only Cougar here. Pick another name. That's my patrol."

Josh sounds off. "Wise ass, not a bad idea." He turns to his two assignees. "We're the Coyotes!"

This whole exercise is absurdly stupid. Chances are better than good that we'll either be dead or in hiding soon. But Kevin chimes in. "We're the Panthers! The Black fucking Panthers!"

Which is funny since his patrol now consists of Kevin, a short Hispanic woman, and a pasty-faced white guy I now remember was a bank loan officer.

As if on cue, Pancho and Lefty walk through the City Hall door. I excuse myself and the three of us head toward some privacy.

"What's going on with Ike Belton?"

Lefty says, "Shit, man. What's always going on with Ike? He's being an asshole and acting like he's king of the world. Nothing new there."

"Has he been doing anything new, or hanging with different people? Any people you don't recognize?"

Lefty squirms until I speak up. "Quit it. I know you've done some business with him and could give a shit less. We need to know, and fast, what's going on over there!"

Pancho interjects, "Boss, we quit dealing with him about three weeks ago. He said he didn't like that we sometimes run with Billy. Said Billy's a spy, which is *pura mierda*. He was asking for some stuff if we made a run into Lincoln City, but, well, we didn't feel comfortable with it."

"What'd he want?"

"Guns."

"Guns. Jesus, this state has never required anyone to register firearms. There are guns everywhere. What kind of guns?"

"Military type stuff. Like AR15s and M4s. Said something about him working on Sears pins." He looks at me quizzically. "I thought Sears went out of business."

Uh oh. "You heard 'sere' pins. They're trying to convert semiautomatic weapons into automatic ones. What about strangers coming into town?"

Pancho this time. "There's always people drifting through."

Josh appears, or maybe has been here all along. "Gang bangers drift through all the time?" His tone is angry.

"Lay off for a sec, okay?" I want him to tone it down. Then to Pancho and Lefty, "You know gang tats. You know who belongs and doesn't. Have you seen any *cholos*? *Pachucos*?" I use slang for street gang members.

Lefty says, "Other than that prick Aguilar, who was acting more and more like one every time we saw him, no."

Maybe we've got some time. But how much? "Any way you guys can show up on the east side and take a look around without looking like you're checking things out?"

The two look at each other. Their expressions tell me they aren't happy with this assignment. Lefty says, "We go over there now, without something Ike's wanting to trade for, he'll know what we're doing. What's going on, Dalton?"

"Those bodies you helped us burn? Three of them were from Escondido. Their *compadres* are making a move this way."

Pancho mutters, "*Hijo de la chingada.* That town has got gangs up the ass. Lot of the members come up from Mexico too. When we make runs into Lincoln City, we steer clear of the neighborhoods they've taken over. They are mean mother-fuckers."

Lefty says, "Dalton, we'll do it for you, *tocayo*, but man, we may get our butt's shot off."

I shake my head. "No. We'll think of something different."

The two confirm Lupe Aguilar has moved out of his derelict house and into the back of the stolen Reddi-Ice truck parked behind Ike's house. "He took the doors off, Dalton. Made him a cozy little place."

I crack a small smile, the memory of the washtub full of ice and my last cold beer flooding my senses. The two look at me questioningly.

"Thanks, guys," I tell them. "Appreciate that you were willing to do that, but it's not fair to put you in that spot. In the meantime, get out there and help us recruit some folks to defend this place. We've got eight new members, but we need about twenty-five more. You guys have got kin all over the place. We need to keep the gangs out of Elmhurst."

The two fist pump me. As they leave, Pancho promises they can do that. They look relieved I didn't push them to snoop. I hope I have the information I need.

Josh watches them fire up the confiscated truck. "Dalton, I'm not going to wait to defend my family and let some fucking thugs decide when and where they're going to hit."

I nod. "We need to strike first."

Josh acts surprised that I agree with him. "Who do we strike, and how."

I remember as a kid, cutting the head off a rattlesnake. "We take out Ike Belton. We take out Lupe Aguilar. It may not stop Escondido gangs from coming, but it probably will slow them down some."

Josh's tight grin looks almost like a grimace. "Who's 'we'? Jill, Kevin, the new ones inside? Pancho? Lefty? The Chief?"

"No." I remember Vincent Guerra lying wounded inside the house on Brushy Creek Road. "What needs doing is up to you and me, without bringing anyone else into it. Maybe a little payback for Andres. Are you okay with that?"

Josh nods. "When?"

"Tonight."

Chapter Twenty-Nine

KEVIN EXITS CITY HALL AND ASKS, "YOU TWO OKAY?"

Josh nods. "Yeah, they're going to look for more folks willing to fight."

"Hmm. Think they'll be able to?" He makes a head gesture toward the departing Pancho and Lefty. He sounds doubtful.

"I think so, Kevin. Let's go inside." I lead the way back into the building. The eight volunteers and the Chief carry on a desultory conversation as the late afternoon shadows begin to blur their features.

"Dalton, Josh, Kevin, you and Jill see if we can put semblance of order to what we need to do." The Chief sounds worried, impatient, and distracted. For the umpteenth time, I wonder why he persists at a thankless and increasingly hopeless task but admire him for doing it.

Truth is, I haven't got a clue as to what to do with eight untested citizens. But now's not the time to show any equivocation. "Sure, Chief," I say. "Let's go sit outside where we can visit for a while."

A sudden gust of cold air brings down many of the remaining pecan trees' leaves. It seems foreboding. Already, the newbies cluster around their leaders. Jill introduces her Cougars as Susan and Ray. The new Coyotes introduce themselves to Josh as Vince and Rob. Kevin's Black Panthers are the puny banker, Robert, and the tiny Hispanic Andrea.

"I'm Keith." A white guy sticks his hand out. I shake it. "This here's Felipe."

I nod. "Let's work out some patrol schedules first of all."

"Whoa there." Keith puts his hand to my chest.

What the hell? Instinctively, I make a fist, but Keith smile reveals unbrushed teeth and a friendly, open face. "Everyone else's got a name. What patrol are we in, sir?"

Sir? "What do you want our patrol to be, er…Keith?"

The other three patrol leaders watch. Despite the tension, this interlude amuses them.

"Sir, how about the Armadillos?"

Felipe and others snort.

"Don't call me sir again. It's Dalton, er…Keith. Why the hell not? Yep," I turn to the others. "You virile folks can have your ferocious names. We're the Armadillos."

The Chief again explains the threats and the need for additional assistance. The eight display varying degrees of attention. Elmhurst needs more people to defend it and provide security, but really? Only Josh and I have witnessed the ferocity of our enemies.

Chief Pettibone makes his own notes as patrols and rotations are worked out. Within thirty minutes, my notepad is filled with schedules. We spend time inspecting the weapons they've brought. All are serviceable, but there is no additional ammunition for some of the calibers.

With one truck and three serviceable ATVs, how much of Elmhurst can be patrolled is not an academic discussion. For the moment, the plan is to continue coverage of as many areas east of Colorado Street, the north-south highway. After some give and take, Chief tells everyone to go home and find something to eat. No one objects.

"This is your first night, people," he says, nodding at the patrols' members. "Let's get to know each other. Learn from each other. Jill and her folks have first shift. Be back in an hour." He looks at his old Timex wristwatch. Jill and her two have serviceable time pieces. The two new Cougars nod.

"Four-hour shifts. Kevin's folks next, and Dalton, your Armadillos have the dog watch. Josh, you and your two can get some decent sleep. We all start and end here at City Hall. Questions?"

There are none.

Josh and I exchange glances. We've got other things that need our business. After handshakes and the Chief's "thanks for helping us out," the eight scatter. Some leave on bicycles; most walk.

Kevin stands to one side, kicking at a dirt clod. Hard.

Uh oh. "What's eating on you, Kevin?" I ask.

"Cut the shit, Dalton. This little kumbaya session...." His voice trails off. "You wanna tell me what you and Josh are up to?"

Jill stands with arms crossed. "Dalton, do Kevin and I look stupid? You two don't seem awfully interested about what we just did here. The two of you are twitching like you're about to wet your pants." Her face is bright red with anger. She now stands toe to toe with me, and as she talks saliva flies.

I try to push her back as I wipe my face, but she won't have it. "Don't you fucking push me."

Chief Pettibone is clearly interested, as are a couple of scraggly men sitting on the street curb fifty feet away.

This is getting out of hand, and quickly. "Let's go inside."

We tromp noisily back into the Chief's office. Once again, he settles into his chair, leans back and says, "Spill it, you two.

What have you hatched up that has got Jill and Kevin wanting to cut your throats, *again?*"

Josh subconsciously moves away from Jill as he touches his broken nose. 'We're going over to the east side of town. Check it out tonight."

"Why?" Kevin asks. "What are you going to find out in the dark?"

Jill adds, "Check it out? Check what out?" She pauses and begins to shake her head. "Oh, no, no, no."

The Chief's slouch is gone. He looks like he's about to come over his desk at us. "Sweet Mother of God! Have you lost your goddamned minds?"

Jill's face, florid with anger minutes ago, is now ashy white. Kevin, well, I think I detect a tiny smile.

"We've got someone who has demanded that we turn this town over to him and a bunch of cold-blooded killers." I look around the room. "After what we heard today, I'm open to anyone in this room explaining how reacting instead of acting will help anyone left in Elmhurst." The more I talk, the more I'm convinced that Josh's instincts are correct. I turn to Kevin. "You went out to guard the front of this building after we got back from the church. Tell me you didn't sense danger."

Kevin doesn't say anything. He looks down at the floor. "Ike and Lupe have to know that we've found several more people who say they're willing to fight. And now we've got Pancho and Lefty scrounging up more. If I was Ike, I'd be wondering if I'd made a big mistake by tipping my hand to the Chief. I'd be thinking that the sooner I can cut the head off the leadership at City Hall, the easier it'll be to just waltz into the armory, and any other place he wants to."

I want to hug Kevin. He is either one smart man, or just as stupid and reckless as Josh and me.

Chief Pettibone rocks back in his office chair. "You're probably right, but…" Suddenly, he puts his head on his hands and begins to weep.

I'm stunned. I've never seen Larry show anything but stoicism and strength. Jill steps around the desk and embraces him. He gently unwraps her arms and wipes his eyes.

"I apologize."

I'm too embarrassed for him to speak.

"My wife's probably not going to last past tomorrow. We've got our neighbors sitting with her and helping round the clock, as you know."

No, I didn't know his arrangements. I know she's dying, but I've been too involved in my own troubles to ask how he's been caring for a dying woman.

He continues. "Doc Randhawa, he's been kind enough to get pain meds, but they're gone now. Louise, she's in terrible pain now." He looks up with bloodshot eyes. "She wants to die so bad."

Christ. I even forgot her name was Louise. The Chief has brushed off questions about her so many times, I've quit asking. I'm a total asshole.

Pettibone regains his composure and looks around the darkening office. "I can't be here to help you. I need to be home." He coughs. "If you're going to do this, you'd better be thinking about what happens afterwards. What happens if you're not successful—if that's the right term? What happens if you are successful? You going to include anyone else in this soiree?"

Jill still stands beside the Chief. "And what about the eight new people? You do anything and it'll provoke a response. Were you going to let anyone else know what to expect?"

Josh and I look at each other but say nothing.

Jill scoffs, "That's what I thought." She turns to the Chief. "I've got to check on my husband, and you've got a dying wife. Let's go, Chief." Her voice drips with anger and contempt. "I'm taking the Chief home with an ATV, that is unless any of you studs disapproves? I hope when I get back you have come to your senses."

She doesn't wait for an answer. When Pettibone doesn't move, she walks out saying, "I'll be waiting outside."

I realize I've been holding my breath and let out a rush of air. The Chief stands up and shakes our hands. "Sorry boys, but you're on your own. I hope you know what you're doing."

It's clear that Jill no longer considers me a friend. It hurts. I drop into a chair and Kevin and Josh follow. Kevin says, "You two aren't going by yourselves."

Josh starts to protest. Kevin tells him to shut up.

"I've been fending for myself and not thinking much about the town." The dark-skinned man is almost invisible in the increasing gloom. "Truth be told, I'm not sure I give that much of a damn now. But what I saw over at that church scares me. I suspect that, like me, neither one you guys have any other place you can run to."

He takes a deep breath and sits quietly. The temperature in the office is dropping along with the outside air.

I wait for more and when nothing comes, I ask, "So, what are you saying?"

I sense rather than see Kevin lean forward in his chair. "I'm in. You can use another set of eyes, and maybe, more firepower."

In the next hour, a plan takes shape. Our main target is Ike Belton. Lupe is a follower, so he is secondary. We decide on a scoped high-power rifle, hoping for a clean single shot at Ike, with assault weapons as backup. I'm generally familiar with most of Elmhurst and Apple Street, and Kevin and Josh decide I will take the first shot.

I try to convince myself this will be no different that than the gun battle on Brushy Creek Road, but without success. I will aim through a scope which will magnify Ike, his torso, his face.

I will pull the trigger and kill someone I have known for many years.

Josh asks, "You okay with doing this?" We are unlocking the gun vault next to the Chief's office, and he reaches for weapons.

"No," I reply. "If either one of you wants to pull the trigger..." I pause as he hands me a Remington BDL 30.06 and a box of ammunition.

Neither says anything. This plan is my idea— mostly—and I have to see it through.

I describe Ike's house. It's been some time since he told me to get the hell out of his territory, but small-town chatter hasn't had him changing locations. As Josh holds a flashlight, I draw a map of the neighborhood and Ike's property. "Lupe is shacked up in a stolen Reddi-Ice truck with no back doors. Ike usually has a fire going in a fifty-five-gallon drum, and he likes to sit out there and drink before hitting the sack."

Kevin asks, "Where are you getting this info?"

"Pancho and Lefty," I tell them. They've been over there several times."

Josh says, "Let's hope they're right."

No shit.

We are gone before Jill and her Cougars return to City Hall. We wear Kevlar vests and hooded sweatshirts under dark jackets. We pass the courthouse and sheriff's office and pause at the burned remains of the old coffee shop on at the corner of Colorado Street and Market Street long enough for Josh and me to smear wood ash on our faces. Kevin demurs with a smile. No one has a balaclava, so we rig bandanas to hide our faces.

One last check of radio headsets, fist bumps and we continue eastward. Few houses show lights as we cross the highway into the east side of Elmhurst. No dogs bark. They've either been eaten, run off, or died of starvation. I carry the scoped 30.06, along with a .45 pistol. Kevin and Josh carry AR15s and Josh has a shotgun slung across his back. I have a set of binoculars but wish for night-vision goggles. The moon hasn't risen and there's little ambient light.

The straight-line distance from City Hall to Ike's property on Apple Street is less than a half-mile. A ten-minute walk normally. It takes us much longer. As we come to a street corner, Josh taps me on the shoulder. We freeze. Someone laughs inside a house. Another hundred yards, and soft mutters of a conversation wafts from the open windows of another darkened structure.

I calculate we are a couple of blocks from our target when a scuffling sound sends us crouching behind tall shrubbery. *What the hell is it?* Moments later, the noise reveals itself as a male, shuffling down the middle of the street. He stops, less than ten yards from us, then walks towards the Market Street curb next to us.

Has he seen us? I carefully unholster the .45, but Kevin taps me, then takes my wrist and shoves it and pistol downward. I return the automatic to its holster, wondering what he has in mind. He takes my now-free hand and guides it backward. I feel the razor-sharp edge of a heavy hunting or military knife.

I am unnerved by the stranger's appearance. Kevin shifts places with me. I pray that the man at the curb will leave. If not, Kevin is going to kill him.

Suddenly, there is the splash of water hitting the curb, and the man begins to hum. *Mother of God! The guy's drunk and pissing on the curb!*

It lasts forever. He zips up his pants and wanders off and away from us.

"Jesus," Josh whispers.

A drunk has nearly walked up on us undetected. Suddenly,

the idea that we have any chance at sneaking up on Ike and company seems absurd. Cold sweat chills me under my hoodie.

We wait until the shuffling fades away, then step out of the bushes. To the east, a small flickering light appears over nearby rooftops. I tap the other two and receive taps in return. Ten minutes later, I lean up against the rough lumber of an abandoned house directly behind Ike's property. It's approximately one hundred feet to the common back fence with Ike's property on Apple Street. I vaguely recall it from my truncated visit weeks before. I open my eyes wide, willing better vision, Google Earth, and better recall.

Josh speaks into his headset. "Once you're set, two clicks, and we'll move your way from here."

I double click my mic and get confirming double clicks back from Josh and Kevin.

I move backwards toward Market Street. Its pavement begins to slope downward, and a hundred yards away, Pine Street enters from the right. It's hardly more than a paved alleyway, hemmed in by heavy brush on both sides.

Apple Street dead-ends into Pine in less than two hundred feet.

Ike's house is the second from the corner. I don't know who, if anyone, is in the corner one. I need to get past Ike's house and then face it. My hope is that with the firelight, the high-powered rifle's scope will detect those around it. I hope. *Why in hell didn't I just bring a semi-automatic weapon, like an AK47, and let its volley of rounds supplant my loony idea of a 'surgical strike?'* Too late now. I move on.

Moving up Pine, the thought hits me: This *must* be a trap! After his threats of open warfare, there is no way that Ike will be here. Belton and his *cholo* buddies are waiting in ambush!

My heart is pounding so hard someone must hear it. I stop, squat, and take several breaths. Cool it, Dalton. *Two others are depending on you right now.* Pine Street levels out at is nears the T intersection with Apple. A line of unkempt shrubs surrounds a vacant lot cater-corner from where the fire burns. Several voices echo, then the soft *crunch* of an aluminum can being crushed.

I move to the other side of Pine Street and into a short distance not choked with trees and brush. Short of low-crawling, movement can be detected if someone looks this way. Fortunately, a derelict house's empty windows stare toward Apple Street. The empty wooden structure's timely presence allows me to move around and behind it, shielding me from line of sight on Apple Street. Suddenly, I fall flat, almost yelping in surprise and pain. At the last instant, I hold the rifle away from me, and take the ground's impact with my left shoulder— and my temple. The pain of an impact near my crotch is excruciating, and I can't remember if I've made any noise. Gingerly, I raise up, pull my right leg out of a hole, then feel around. My hands make out the arc of old brick and mortar. My pants are torn, but after a few tentative movements, the pain eases. The dim flicker of the wood fire gives barely enough light to confirm I've nearly fallen into an old uncovered water well.

I wait for my head to clear, then gather the rifle. I hope the rough treatment hasn't damaged its scope. The ground around the rest of the property is thankfully just grass. I clear Ike's street, go further along, then cross Pine Street and push into the bushes. Across the street, less than a hundred feet away, the much-discussed oil drum holds a large fire, its flickering light bouncing off the faces of several men. They sit on benches or in lawn chairs.

Once the binoculars are focused, four heavily tatted men appear, along with Lupe Aguilar. I go prone, set the binoculars down, and aim through the rifle's scope, surprised at how well it pulls in the light.

Through the headset I hear Josh's worried voice. "Are you in position?"

We'd agreed that the only response Kevin and Josh would

get from me would be two clicks when I'm ready, but clearly, I've taken much longer than anticipated. Raucous laughter erupts and I use it to cover my response. "Yes, but no Ike yet. Lupe and four others at fire."

Conversation seems directed by one person. He's bald and sports a ragged goatee. Tattoos walk up into his neck from inside a jacket and descend to cover the backs of his hands. He sits facing me in a lawn chair. He's no one I recognize from Elmhurst. He speaks sharply. Lupe seems to object to whatever is said, then slowly walks toward Ike's front door. He doesn't look happy. The man who barked the orders laughs, and the three others join in.

I have no doubt he is the leader and I decide he and the three others, all Hispanic, are from Escondido—perhaps, some of Lupe Aguilar's extended family. I shift the rifle's aim and center the scope's cross hairs on his chest. The goateed man has to die.

But where is Ike?

Chapter Thirty

THE QUESTION IS ANSWERED QUICKLY. IKE STEPS OUT THE FRONT OF his house, the screen door slapping closed behind him. Before I can train the rifle on him, he takes the concrete two steps to the ground and joins the group around the barrel fire. I release the safety with an audible *click*. Worried that the noise is heard, I try desperately to focus. The scope's magnification creates a blur of flickering light and bodies moving. Breathing into the bandana fogs the scope. Frustrated and scared, I pull the bandana down and raise my head to sort out what is going on.

Ike talks with the goateed man, but he is shielded by Lupe Aguilar, who has led the way from the front door to the burn barrel. My right eye on the scope, I inwardly plead for Lupe to step out of the way so I can get a clean shot at Ike.

There is a *thwap* as the screen door smacks wood again. Two more men step from the dim candlelit interior of the house. *Now what?*

Lupe takes a stick and stirs the fire. Sparks fly up and momentarily, its light brightens the men's faces. I count eight— Ike Belton, Lupe Aguilar, the goateed man and his three compadres, and now, these last two arrivals. They are heavily bearded Anglos. I'm suddenly thankful I didn't have a shot. The Anglos would have still been inside.

Since when did Escondido and its gangs involve themselves with white guys? Ike's collection of thugs is widening.

Josh's voice comes through my earpiece. "What's going on up there?"

Suddenly, there is a stillness. They couldn't have heard Josh through the earbud, but something has them spooked. The goateed man says something and heads swivel—toward Ike's back yard. Hands reach for pistols. Lawn chairs are pushed back and some reach toward assault weapons leaning against the house's chain link fence.

Fearing they may have detected Josh and Kevin. I pull the rifle's buttstock harder into my shoulder and again try to pick out Ike. He is taller than the men I've determined to be from Escondido, but the newly arrived Anglos are of similar build. Is that him? Yes! I think so, I begin to squeeze the trigger, but the blur of men disappears into the darkness.

I key the mic. "Everyone is heading toward the back yard. I hope you two aren't back where they can see you."

No answer. *What is going on? Dammit! I should have pulled the trigger!* The pulse in my temple throbs against the scope, so I set the rifle down and pick up the binoculars.

"We haven't moved." It is Kevin's voice.

What spooked the group, and will they come back? Unless they relax, there is no way I can get a shot. Worse yet, I haven't thought out how I'm going to get away from here.

"They heard something. They're heading your way," I whisper.

A mic click affirms they got the message. Flashlight beams bounce off trees, bushes, and wooden structures. Then laughter erupts. Seconds later, the men begin reappearing from behind Ike's house, two of them dragging a small object.

There is a yelp and I realize the 'object' is a child. The eight men, and a young boy, gather around the fire again. What the hell is a child doing out at this time of night? And what's he doing in Ike's back yard? Ike doesn't have any children—and if he did, they sure as hell wouldn't be wandering around in a darkened lot while daddy entertains thugs. This must be some neighborhood kid.

The kid looks to be around ten, but it is only a guess. With the shortage of food, it seems no one is growing as fast as they used to. Ike's screen door screeches open. I can't figure out who just went inside until Aguilar reappears with a paper sack in his hand. He gives it to the boy, who immediately opens the sack. He stuffs its contents in his mouth, and immediately spits out whatever he's been given.

Ike guffaws. "You don't like what I gave you? I told you next time I see you around here I'd make you eat dirt. How's it taste?"

Dirt. Now the boy begins to gag. He must have swallowed a bunch of the stuff.

Ike leans against his fence as the rest of the gang—I can't think of anything else to call the group— reacquire their positions around the burn barrel.

I have a clear shot at Ike and double click the mic. I'm in position and am ready—at last—to take my shot. There is a double click acknowledgment. Hopefully, Josh and Kevin are moving toward Ike's back fence. I take deep breaths and silently beg the child to finish spitting up the dirt they gave him and get the hell out of here.

"How many are there? Please reconfirm the number is six. I say again—six." Josh again.

One, two, three…, eight clicks, I respond.

"What the fuck?" Josh whispers. "You just said six, and now eight. Where in hell did the last two come from?"

One of the bearded Anglos stoops down. He comes up with a bottle of what looks like whiskey and gets a murmur of approval. He's wearing some kind of biker vest, but I can't make out any insignias or patches. His presence with Ike Belton and the rest just confirms he's up to no good.

Click, click, click. "Answer if you can, goddammit. We need to know!"

I've been too intent on watching the boy. He's quit gagging and tries to push toward the warmth of the barrel's fire. The kid's got some guts.

"Wait. Out."

A *cholo* seated in a lawn chair takes a swig from the communal bottle and offers it to the young boy. The boy shakes his head and gets slapped across the head for refusing. Momentarily, I change my aim, wanting to take that guy out first. Another of the group barks, "Get the fuck outta here," and the boy shambles off, crossing Apple Street to head south on Pine.

As he nears me, I tuck me head down. The boy is crying but stops directly in front of me. He's spotted something, and I realize he's noticed the unnaturally straight blued barrel of the 30.06, extending from the darkness.

"Hey kid. Get gone," Ike says. "What're you doing standing there? You act like you've seen something."

The boy suddenly kneels, and his head blocks out the light from the fire. He's looking straight at my hands cradling the rifle and scope. I do not dare move.

"Just some pecans someone hasn't picked up." The boy's head doesn't turn as he addresses Ike in a reedy, quivering voice. "I'm gone."

He stands and coughs then begins to move, quickly. The sound of his feet ebb as he moves south on Pine Street. I shake so hard, I can't grip the rifle. I gently lay it in the grass and roll onto my back. Betelgeuse's redness looks down through the cloudless heavens. I wonder what Orion thinks about all this. I'm losing it. I roll back onto my belly, press the mic key, and whisper, "They're all around the burn barrel. We need to take them all. They all have weapons. They all are no good."

Click. Click. "We're ready," says Kevin.

I'm sure as hell not. Adrenaline and fear compete for control of my body. I grip the rifle, confirm the safety is off, and peer through the scope, setting its crosshairs in the middle of Ike's chest.

I pull the trigger.

The noise is deafening, and the weapon's kick jams the scope into my eyebrow. I work the bolt, ejecting the spent shell, and push another round into the chamber. More gunfire erupts in a staccato of flashes that explode like a string of firecrackers. I don't look through the scope, but fire into the mass of humanity that is dissolving into individual forms. Bodies move, reaching for weapons. Again, and again, and again, and again. And the hunting rifle's internal magazine is empty. The cold has stiffened my movement, but I leave the rifle. Someone kicks over the burn barrel, and its fiery contents fly out and onto the street looking oddly like molten lava flowing from a crater. Sparks from the disrupted fire mix with the flashes of gunfire. I skitter backwards like a land crab.

Screams fill the night. Automatic gunfire sweeps the air. Gasping for air, I lurch behind a tree and feel rather than hear the impact of two bullets smacking into it. Someone pushes through the bushes I've just left, and I turn and fire toward the sound with the clunky .45 Colt.

There is a heavy sound and I realize a body had slammed onto the ground. The .45's muzzle flashes blind me, and I pull the trigger until the bolt locks open. Empty. I don't know who is on the ground, or whether they are still able to cause me harm. I fold myself behind the tree.

The sparks of muzzle flashes reach through the foliage. I recognize the rapid fire of the 5.56 mm AR 15. It is not alone. A higher pitched automatic continues to fire. And then... silence.

Well, not silence. My ears ring deafeningly.

Click. Click. "Dalton, you okay?" Josh's voice competes with the wheeze of heavy breathing.

"Yeah."

"Come our way."

Which way is that, I wonder? I shine my penlight toward the ground. A biker on his back— dead. Or at least, not moving. I kick the body and get no response. Blood blossoms from a chest wound. I kneel and roll the body face down. There are two wounds in his lower back, and I wonder whether he was coming toward me or running away from the torrent of gunfire at Ike's house. He's not in a position to answer. I retrieve a pistol. It is still useable and there are rounds in its magazine. I stuff my empty .45 in my waistband and walk toward Ike's house. Two small flashlights blink off and on. The dying embers scattered in the street reveal little of the carnage. Somewhere in the darkness, people yell and children cry.

I pull up the bandana before I cross Apple Street. "You two okay?" I ask. I think I say it quietly but am not sure as my ears haven't recovered from the blast noise of the rifle and pistol.

Josh nods silently, his faced hidden behind the bandana. "How about you?' he asks.

He's barely audible over the ringing in my ears. "I'm okay."

"Your face is covered with blood."

A quick swipe, and my hand reveals fresh blood. "The gun's recoil. Scope smacked me in the eyebrow. It's nothing." I use a part of the bandana to staunch the cut. I can't see Kevin, then realize he is moving from body to body. I shine my flashlight. A bullet struck Ike in the throat, killing him instantly. If it was from the 30.06, I shot high. He lies flat on the sidewalk, dark blood still oozing from the gaping wound.

"How many?" I ask as I catch the odor of burning flesh. A body lies partly in the scattered fire. I pull a tattooed body out of the embers and gag.

"Seven," Josh responds, his voice oddly muffled in the face covering. "You said there were eight." Shell casings, seemingly hundreds, lay in the street.

"There's one in the bushes." I point back to where I've just come from. "A biker."

"This one's alive," Kevin whispers. He points a flashlight beam toward a heavily tatted body. The *cholo's* legs are soaked in blood. A round has caught him in the abdomen. His eyes are closed. He moans softly.

"Leave him. We need to leave, and now," I say softy. We need to get away, and quickly, and without being IDed or confronted by the neighbors.

Kevin grunts, leans down. There is a muffled pop. "Now we leave," he says as he steps away from the tatted man who no longer groans.

Wordlessly, we trudge onto Pine, not taking the Market Street route back to City Hall, the weight of the dead men's weapons slowing us down. We cross Colorado Street two blocks south of our crossing to the east part of town. Jill's patrol ATV moves slowly down a side street on the west side of Colorado Street. We wait in an alleyway until it passes, then slip into a side door to City Hall, using a key I was provided weeks before. We check the front door. It is locked.

The weapons hurriedly are cleaned. They are returned to the vault, along with unexpended ammunition. All other gear we used is stowed. We strip off bandanas and hoodies. We are two hours into Jill's shift and two hours before Kevin's two Panthers arrive to begin their four-hour shift.

Our frantic efforts allow little time to decompress. I feel giddy with joy at being alive. Is this feeling remotely appropriate when we've just snuffed out the lives of eight humans? I doubt it, but a quick glance at Kevin and Josh show small smiles on their faces. At least I'm not alone.

Kevin states the obvious. "All hell broke loose. I bet most of the town heard the gunfire." He tells us how many rounds he expended. Hell, it was a full-blown war.

Josh adds, "And Jill and the Chief aren't stupid. Eight dead bodies aren't easy to explain away."

I agree, but with a caveat. "They may not like what we did, but I think we can trust those two to keep our names out of it. Pancho and Lefty may put two and two together, as well as my ex-brother in law. A lot of folks may suspect someone from City Hall had something to do with it, but that's not the same as knowing it. Besides, who is going to give a shit? Right now, we know nothing. When someone asks, we say we don't know but that we 'heard' that rival gangs were making a play for that side of town."

Kevin asks the obvious as I stack the dead men's weaponry in one corner of the vault. "How do we explain all these extra firearms?"

"We don't," I reply. "We just don't."

The two look at me dubiously.

"They know but they don't know." I reach for Lupe Aguilar's Uzi. "I'm taking this home. Grab whichever piece you think you need. The rest stay here."

"And we don't tell anyone," cautions Josh as he shifts through the guns. Some are stained with their erstwhile owners' blood. "This had to be done, but the new folks on the neighborhood patrols don't need to know. Our family doesn't need to know."

We all nod in agreement. "And no one who's still alive saw us," adds Kevin.

I'm not sure why, but I choose not to disclose the young boy's peering into the bushes. I try to convince myself that he couldn't make out my features. Or maybe because of the men's treatment of him, he'll keep what he saw to himself. Or possibly, that I'm in the company of two men who've helped me ambush and kill eight men, that I trusted them with my life, but

I'm not sure about what would happen if they knew about a poor kid who chanced to witness our actions.

"Time to disappear for a while," I say, and the three of us head to our homes, not disturbing the remaining ATVs.

There will be consequences. There always are. I hope we can deal with them.

Chapter Thirty-One

Josh and I knock gently on the back door to my house. We both have keys to the place—I gave him one when his family moved inside. Recently, Elsie has taken to wedging furniture against it as added insurance against unwanted visitors. Little interference to someone seriously intent on harm, but no doubt gives her a small measure of additional safety.

A candle in an old ornamental glass holder illuminates Elsie's hand and then her face as she places it on the shelf just inside the back door.

"Just a minute, guys," she mutters as she begins to disassemble the makeshift barricade.

Moments later the door swings open. Elsie sniffs the air. "You two reek of gunpowder and cleaning solvent."

Josh hugs his wife as I maneuver around the two, heading for my bedroom upstairs.

"Dalton. What happened to your eye?"

"Just a small cut. Why?"

"It's puffed up and turning black." She pauses as she holds Josh at arm's length. "What's been going on? Look at the two of you. Is this blood?" she asks as she points to telltale spots on Josh's shirt.

"Nothing happened tonight, Elsie. Absolutely. Nothing." Josh's voice is harsh. "Absolutely nothing."

Elsie seems taken aback, but quickly recovers. "If nothing happened tonight, and if you want anyone with half a brain to believe it, you two better get cleaned up and get rid of what you're wearing."

She picks up the candle holder. "Unlock the water, Dalton." She leads us back outside into the darkness. "And strip."

Twenty minutes later, Josh and I stand beside my rainwater storage tank, shivering as we towel off with ragged and half-clean hand towels. I scamper up the stairs, hoping the children are asleep, and shut the bedroom door. Naked, I crawl under an old comforter, trying to warm up.

The stairs creak and there is a tap on the door.

"Hey Dalton," utters Josh in a stage whisper. "You asleep?"

"No."

"Elsie and the kids heard the gunfire tonight. We're a good ways from Pine Street. If they heard it here, everyone in town did."

I'm not surprised. "Okay. So?"

"Nothing, I guess. She's a stand-up woman, Dalton."

"Heck, Josh," I say. "No doubt about it. Who else would think to get us cleaned up and rid of those clothes? Tell her thanks for me again."

"'Night, Dalton." Josh pauses. The bedroom door starts to close, then swings back open. "You okay with what we did?"

An odd question I think, remembering his earlier insistence that we do something immediately to quell the danger to our town and families. "I think I am, Josh. Haven't had time to let it sink in, I guess."

"Me too. See you in the morning." He gently closes my door and retreats down the stairs.

An old windup clock clangs my wake up call. It reads 3:30, which seems close. My patrol begins in thirty minutes. I've kept the timepiece wound up since the EMP. I shut the alarm off, groggy but pleasantly surprised that I was able to drift off into a dreamless sleep. I find some warm clothes, dress and head downstairs. Josh waits by the back door.

"Need to let you get out of the house," he says in a joking manner as he moves away furniture.

"You've been wide awake, haven't you?"

"Yeah," he admits. "Worrying about what daylight will bring, I guess."

I squeeze his arm. "Me and my new squad will probably know something before the sun's up, my friend."

Checking to ensure my .45 is secure in its holster, I ride my bicycle toward City Hall. Jill's Cougars sit on the entry steps. As I set the kickstand, Jill waves her people goodbye and walks toward me.

"We need to talk."

I point toward Keith and Felipe, shivering beside an ATV. "My Armadillos are waiting on me. Can it wait?"

"What do you think?"

"I guess not." I wave at my two patrol members. "Be there in a minute, boys." I turn back to Jill. "Hold your voice down. Please."

"All hell broke loose last night." Jill quietly bites each word off as if to spit it at me. "I had to pretend I didn't know what was going on. I made up a bullshit story about not being allowed on the east side of town."

"Well, that part's true, anyway."

Jill's face is barely visible, and I'm thankful. What I do see is suppressed rage. I envision her trying to kill me. It's certainly possible. "Take it easy, Jill."

"Like hell I will. You and Josh, and I bet Kevin too, you went over and killed Ike, didn't you? And not just him, but others as well? How many?"

It's time for me to play the hand as agreed. "I don't know what you're talking about, Jill. I heard the racket too. But it wasn't anything any of us were involved in, honest."

"Dalton, you are such a lying shit. I have access to the gun vault too. Some new firearms appeared between the time my shift started and ten minutes ago. Some AR15s recently cleaned, lots of rounds missing."

Her anger turns to disgust. "Get out of my sight. Whatever happens is on your head."

She turns and walks away, ignoring small greetings from Keith and Felipe.

I take several deep breaths and walk toward the ATV where Keith and Felipe stand. I greet them quietly. "You ready to do some patrolling?"

Keith grins his goofy grin. "That Jill lady sure seems pissed. You guys married or something?"

"Or something. Leave it alone."

Keith cackles, "Armadillos are ready, sir!"

I'm not in the mood for much levity. "Keep it down." I check their weapons, then load two AR15s from the vault in City Hall. "Let's go."

Felipe asks, "I heard gunshots earlier. Like all hell broke loose, somewhere the east side of Colorado Street. You know what's going over there?"

I'm thankful for the darkness, as my face tells a story. "No. Heard it too, but that's Ike's area. We stay out of there. He decided he was going to take care of that side of town. Not our responsibility."

"Un huh," Felipe mutters, as he stares hard at my black eye and cut eyebrow.

The four hour patrol seems endless. I answer a few questions about procedure, describe the streets and areas as the ATV rolls through neighborhoods. Mostly, I keep quiet while chatty Keith carries on a one-sided conversation with Felipe.

Sunrise finds us driving east on Market Street. As we near Colorado Street a plume of black smoke boils up angrily from the vicinity of Apple Street. Flames dance above a house fire.

"Shouldn't we check on that?" asks Keith. Yes, we should, but with my bruised and cut face I fear being recognized, despite last night's hoodie, dark jacket and bandana.

"Uh, yeah. Normally, we don't go on that side of Colorado."

Felipe becomes edgy. "There could be folks in trouble, Ike Belton territory or not, Dalton. We have an obligation to at least try and help."

We've got another hour until Josh's daytime patrol relieves us. *Shit.* "Okay, let's go. Let me grab the first aid bag from inside City Hall." I dismount and unlock the front door. I unzip my jacket and stash Lupe Aguilar's Uzi in the vault. No sense in making things obvious.

I re-lock the door, and the three of us drive the ATV across Colorado on Market. As we turn up Pine, the structure fire is evident – Ike's house. Wood smoke mixes with something much stronger. Much stronger.

A group of men, Hispanic and Black, stand with hoes and shovels, occasionally smothering ashes blown from the fire's intense updraft. A smattering of underfed women and children stare. The house adjacent to Ike's on the corner with Pine Street is fully engulfed too. I expect to see concerned faces but detect none.

Reluctantly, I follow my two Armadillos to the circle of people around the fire. A Hispanic I vaguely recognize walks up. "You guys crossed the highway to see what's going on?"

The wind shifts, and I'm overwhelmed by the smell of burning flesh.

Felipe gives the man—his name is Severo—a limp fist bump. "What happened?"

Severo sneers. "What happened? You're shittin' me, *carnal*. You just show up in town from la la land?" He doesn't wait for a response, but points to Ike's house.

"Someone greased eight dudes last night. Snuffed the motherfuckers out in like, fuckin' seconds!" He looks at me.

"You, Dalton is your name, isn't it?" He doesn't wait for an answer. "You know me."

"I do, Severo. It's been awhile."

"Well, the *mayate* that lived here and some of his asshole buddies were killed last night. You know the dude, *esse*. You're the one Ike ran out of this side of town awhile back, aren't you?"

I nod but say nothing. Severo comes closer. "What happened to your face, man? Someone hit you?"

I shake my head, praying this interrogation will end. Severo turns back to Felipe. "Whoever shot these fuckers up were *puros pinches*."

Keith has refrained from commenting thus far, but can't help himself. "Why are they assholes, man?" he asks.

Another snort from Severo. "You think this side of town's got backhoes? No rain for a month, ground hard as concrete, and the goddamned barrio's gotta smell dead bodies? Sheeit!"

I already know the answer. Keith apparently hasn't snapped yet. "I don't get it. What do you mean?"

Severo, underfed, rawboned, and angry, steps up to Keith. "I don't know you, *bolillo* boy, but you should have been here to help us."

"Do what?"

"Well, we threw the bodies in the *mayate's* house and started a fire. What else did you think? Eight bodies and the house—we clean up the bodies so there's no stink anymore, and we burn down *pinche* Ike Belton's house." He turns and spits on the pavement.

I stand behind Felipe and Keith. Unless they are psychic, they can't detect the overwhelming sense of relief that has washed over me.

Felipe asks, "Who were they? You said the black dude Ike? Who else?"

"*Ese pinche joto*, Lupe Aguilar, some of his *cholo* homies, and two white dudes. All shot to shit." Severo is getting into the narrative now. "Look over there." He points at the largest of the dark stains on the sidewalk and street. "That Ike dude took a bullet through his neck. Bled like a calf at a slaughterhouse." He spits again.

"Lupe, he and the others. Shot to shit, man."

Keith glances back at me as if some kind of light bulb came on. "Who'd do that, Dalton?"

I shrug, but Severo volunteers an answer. "Ike, he was making everyone in this barrio miserable, man. As if we weren't bad enough shape. Word was he was going to take over Elmhurst. Take over Elmhurst! This *pinche* town! Why the fuck for? We're all starvin' now. Who cares who did it, eh?"

Yeah, who cares?

The shiplap siding on the front of Ike's house suddenly falls away. Several in the crowd murmur. In what was the living room, a mound of bodies burns more brightly than the surrounding structure. Grease runs across the floor, catches fire, and drips like molten lava onto the ground. I gag.

After a few moments, Severo, seemingly unmoved, continues, "Piss me off, man. Four dudes, bandanas, all dark like. Took all the guns with 'em. Some say they ran west," he nods toward me, "Some say they had a truck and went south. *Quien sabe*?"

Keith asks, "No one knows who they were?" He sounds incredulous.

"Nah," Severo responds. "Little kid over there." He points. "He was here just before all the shit happened. He says he didn't see anything. No one did. Shit! No one here cares. 'Course if someone hooked up with those biker dudes or Lupe's family finds out, they're in deep shit."

I look toward the "little kid." A small boy, maybe ten years old, the same one who spotted my 30.06 last night, stares at the fire, then turns his head and looks directly at me and nods. Does he recognize me? I have no way of knowing, but the possibility scares hell out of me. My sense of relief turns to fear.

Severo winds down as several men yell at him to help contain small grass fires started from embers from the two houses. "Gotta go, man," he says to the three of us. Then to me, "You City Hall *patrullas* going to help with some kind of law and order on this side of town now? You gonna help us get some food? Some medicine?"

"We could use some help on patrol," I tell him. "Send some folks to City Hall, and the Chief will see what we can do."

"All right, man! Maybe we can score a little food, eh?"

I do not disabuse him of the idea that there is food to be earned. "Maybe. What about Lupe's kin? They from around here?" As if I don't know the answer.

"Nah. The *frontera*. Bunch of fuckin' gangbangers. Hope they don't show up in Elmhurst and blame us." He waves a hand to indicate the fire's attendees. "We got enough problems without that shit."

Don't we all.

Chapter Thirty-Two

I HAVEN'T SEEN FRED ASTON IN WEEKS. HIS APPEARANCE AT MY garage catches me off guard. Gaunt but not limping, he ruefully grins, "Hey, Dalton, you doing okay?"

"Sure, I guess. How's your foot?"

"Healed up. Glad I'm still alive."

"What brings you over here?"

"Jill's saying some pretty bad stuff about you and Josh." He pauses, and when he gets no response, continues, "Says you two killed Ike Belton."

I continue to stare at him. Still smarting from my confrontation with Jill, I am not the least interested in wasting time processing what we did and what we later witnessed on Apple Street. Again, I say nothing.

He shakes his head and walks away.

What the hell was that all about? As if I didn't know.

I retrieve my bicycle and lock the garage. A body wrapped in a sheet lies next to the curb two blocks from Anson Gutierrez' house. One block later, two more. Once shocking, it is oddly routine. There are few individual graves now. No fuel for backhoes, and little energy to dig into the cold ground of winter. The cemeteries are full. Chief Pettibone and Doctor Randhawa have, for the most part, been able to convince people to not bury family members in back yards, for fear of disease. Now, several men from local churches who own horses and wagons offer their services. When they get the word of a death, they take the body to a mass burial area outside of Elmhurst.

Grim.

Anson Gutierrez is outside, twisting a galvanized water pipe to which an antenna is attached.

"Glad you're here. Go inside." Anson proceeds to tell me what I'm to expect if he is successful in 'tuning.' The HAM setup hasn't changed much in the last few months, but the room is a mess.

A speaker's squawk turns into a high-pitched howl. This means something, so I yell to Anson. Minutes later, he waits for me to get out of the way, and satisfied, grunts a thank you. "What do you want, Dalton?"

I hand him an unopened can of tuna fish, the going price for information from the outside world. Anson quickly stuffs it in a coat pocket.

"For your cat." I say, just to goad him. His beloved cat has gone missing.

"Like hell it is. Little bastard got tired of me not feeding him and disappeared." He pauses. His pretense of harshness disappears. "I miss him. I hope he didn't get eaten."

"Any news?" My visits have become infrequent. Each requires some sort of remuneration, and food is scarce. There is little information that hasn't been recirculated umpteen times. His efforts to find medical supplies have dried up.

Without his feline friend, Anson has gotten even more withdrawn and crankier than usual. Of course, hunger may have something to do with it, too.

"Some, maybe." His voice carries something more than the usual reply.

"What?"

"Here." Anson hands me a notepad. "I wrote down as much as I could. Some of it made sense. Some, maybe not. Anyway..."

The entries captivate me, and I no longer hear anything as Anson drones on.

Survivalist vigilante groups in gun battles with cartel and other gangs in state capitol. Lincoln City. Fires in government buildings. More people fleeing. Lots of running gun battles in outlying suburbs.

Down below, another entry:

Scratch force of re-constituted United States Army has entered the state. Order restored in some areas in north of state. Maybe will be in Lincoln City area within a couple of weeks.

"When did this information come in?"

"During the night. What do you make of it, Dalton?"

"I don't know. Is this all you got?"

Anson is indignant. "Hmph. Came in from several HAMs. I used to get a lot of chatter from HAMs in Lincoln City. Couldn't raise any last night, which is weird. Then one came up on the net. He's the one told me about the fighting in the capital. Told me other HAMs have had equipment torn up. About the time we were talking, he told me he had to sign off, pronto, saying somebody was trying to burn up his house. Hope he's okay."

"Please, let's see what info you can get, right now."

"Daylight now, so won't get as much." Anson flips several switches, keys the mic, and sends his call sign. "CQ. CQ. CQ. Anyone in area of Lincoln City?"

Static. Then, faintly, another call sign. "I've tried raising someone there, too. No luck."

Then another call sign with the same information.

The Chief needs to get this information, and fast. I pedal off toward City Hall. The front door is open, but Chief Pettibone isn't in his office. Josh and Kevin, looking the worse for wear, sit the building's foyer, bundled up against the cold.

"Where's the Chief? We've got trouble, and I need to find him."

Josh responds. "His wife died during the night. He's taking her body to a family plot at Genesis Cemetery."

I recognize the name. It's a small private cemetery in the country a few miles south of town.

"Didn't want the body snatchers to pick her up and put her in a mass grave. We told him to take an ATV. Can't blame him."

Aw, shit. "He need help?"

"We offered," Kevin replies. "He said no. Neighbors had helped all along and would help dig the grave." He pauses. "What's going on?"

Quickly, I describe what I've learned at Anson's house. "We can expect another bunch of people heading down the highway from the capital. All hell's broken loose. Maybe far worse than anything before we've seen before."

Kevin nods. "Yeah, but it sounds like the good old U.S. of A. actually exists in some form and is trying to get back in control."

"But maybe not in time," I reply. "If armed warfare spreads here before order's restored, Elmhurst is a lost cause."

Kevin and Josh look over my shoulder and. I see Jill in the doorway. "What are you talking about now? Anything you'd like to share with the rest of us?" Her voice drips with contempt.

I miss Chief Pettibone right now.

I repeat what I have found out.

"Does any of this have something to do with what happened to Ike Belton?"

Her question catches me off guard. The information gleaned from HAM operators come from a different geographical area than Escondido, and no mention has been made about eight dead men in the small town of Elmhurst.

"No. Nothing to do with whatever happened on Apple Street. Nothing at all."

She lets out a short snort. "Wanna bet Ike's death ends up being one side's or the other's reason to come to Elmhurst?"

I don't want to be bet. I don't want to argue with Jill. After a few seconds, I volunteer to find the Chief. We need leadership now, and he's a proven commodity.

Josh makes a quick exit to find his Coyotes. Jill agrees to alert her Cougars but looks intent on saying something more. Thankfully, Kevin cuts her off.

"Hop in," he says, glancing uneasily at Jill. "I'll drop you at the Kaufman's and round up my patrol."

When we are out of Jill's hearing, Kevin yells above the engine noise, "Motherfucker, that is one pissed off she-wolf."

No argument there. I plan to get my BMW and ride to the Genesis Cemetery. Hopefully, I'll return with the Chief.

Kevin brakes, and I step from the ATV. "Hope you get a better reception here," he says.

Gail steps outside with our daughter. I'm not sure I want to face her. She's accused me of putting Elmhurst's interests over those of her family. If she's heard of the Apple Street ambush of Ike Belton, there isn't any way that I will convince her that I had nothing to do with it.

Gail meets me at the shed. Josefina is bundled up against the chill.

"Hey," I swing the shed's door open and go inside, reaching for my helmet and fasten the chinstrap. I turn the key, check the gauges, and pump the gas.

"Hey, Dalton. What's the hurry?" Gail's face is flushed. I don't know if it is anger or the cold weather. "Don't you want to see Josie?"

Of course, I want to see Josie. I cradle my daughter, wrapped in a warm blanket. It seems her features change daily, and I rue the time spent away from her. She grins and coos as I rock her gently. She is amazing.

Gail brings me back to another reality. "What's going on?"

Once again, I recite what I heard from Anson. "I've got to get the Chief. He's burying his wife, but we need him."

As I say this, it dawns on me: Anyone moving south in a warlike fashion probably will sweep through outlying farms and ranches looking for food. The Kaufman's small farm lies on the wrong side of what little protection Little Elm River provides.

My earlier warning of danger seems to be realized, just not from whom I had envisioned. I turn the ignition switch off. "Gail, we've got to get you out of here. You and the family. And now. Today."

Before she can argue with me, I start the BMW and yell, "Get everyone ready. I'll be back as soon as I can with something, maybe an ATV, maybe a truck, maybe both. But for now, your family has to come where I can protect you."

I shift into first gear, engage the clutch, and accelerate out of the shed. Gail's words are lost in the noise.

Fifteen minutes later, I find Genesis Cemetery. Its remote location, devoid of trees, creates an otherworldly gloom. In the northeast corner, several people stand around a mound of dirt. I slow and turn past the cemetery's open gate.

I roll to a stop and shut off the BMW's engine. Though helmeted, I can now hear the low howl of the north wind. A perfect setting for the Chief's grief. Someone reads from a small prayer book. I sit on the motorcycle and hope for the solemnities to finish.

After shaking hands, two men begin to spade dirt into the grave. Larry Pettibone reaches for a shovel, but is rebuffed gently, with hugs. He walks toward me.

"Why are you here, Dalton?"

I apologize profusely. "I shouldn't have come, Larry." I

haven't even allowed the man the decency of a brief time to grieve over his beloved wife's grave.

"You're here, Dalton," he says with a steely voice. "Why?"

"I got news from Anson this morning. It's not good. We need you, Chief. Now, more than ever."

His eyes are bloodshot, and he wipes snot from his nose. "I'm through, Dalton."

I take it to mean he needs some time alone. "Look, Larry. We just need some help to get organized. You're the one who can give us some guidance." Once again, I apologize.

"No. Dalton. You don't understand. Once we get back to Elmhurst, I'm clearing out." He points toward the ATV. "I'm turning in all my keys. I can't take it anymore. You're gonna have to find someone else to hold everyone's hand. I'm through."

"But who, Chief?" I didn't expect this but realize the finality of his pronouncement. "Who can do what you've done for the last months?"

The Chief pats me on the shoulder. "Time to saddle up, Dalton. You can handle things. I'll go to the neighbors' house and help them if it comes to that, but I'm done." He points to the gravesite. "Now, leave me alone. I want to be with my wife one last time."

He turns and walks away, hunching his shoulders as if to ward off the cold wind.

After a few minutes, I realize my gloved hands are numb from cold. I turn the switch and kick the BMW into life.

I've relied on Chief Larry Pettibone to be the rock we've all leaned on. Now, I've got to either step into his shoes, or walk away.

Chapter Thirty-Three

It begins to drizzle as I ride toward the Kaufman's property. I slow the BMW as I near the highway bridge over Little Elm River. Haggard people trudge southbound. Some look startled at the sound of the engine. Others seem too worn to care. I stop in the Elmhurst side of the concrete structure, chain the BMW to a guardrail, and slowly turn so my holstered .45 is visible. I don't plan to be away from the motorcycle long but no sense in tempting desperate refugees. I tromp through dead brush. Soon, I am at the bridge's abutment, looking at its concrete expanse. A raccoon waddles down off the sloped concrete. growling its unhappiness at me as it leaves its dry refuge.

The bridge spans Little Elm River on six pairs of support piers, one at the north and south ends, and four in the middle. The four center piers are on dry land, with Little Elm River sluggish and low because of dry weather, flowing between numbers three and four. Bent foliage, gouges in the gravel, and mounds of dead brush and tree limbs are evidence of Little Elm's capacity for a quick rise after heavy rains. Built in the early 1950s, the narrow two-lane bridge was slated for replacement by the State highway department. Weathered survey stakes with engineer's plastic tape are the lone evidence of that interrupted work.

The acrid smell of bird shit and mold attacks my nose as I climb the abutment. At the top, I lie flat and peer into the recesses of the concrete. Above the abutment are the beams supporting the road surface. The spaces between the beams are about three feet wide. Without a flashlight, I can't tell how far back the recesses go. I look around for a long stick to probe, without any luck. Still...I remember the pallets of fertilizer stored in George Hixson's shed.

Now to check the old iron bridge on Pederson Road on the way to Gail and her family. I will defer a look at the last bridge, on Hixson Lane until later, when, I hope, I'll find George Hixson amendable to a proposal.

I slide down the concrete, out from under the bridge and push through the wet grass to the highway. Men and women, most alone, some in small groups with children, continue their slow exodus south from Lincoln City. The drizzle is now a steady, slow rain.

I open the BMW's pannier and retrieve a raincoat, then unlock the chain securing the BMW to the railing, wipe the seat with a dry rag, kick start the engine, and begin a turn south.

Someone yells, "Dalton!"

A man runs toward me. I grab my .45 and aim it at him.

The scrawny character sports an unkempt beard and torn bib overalls. He takes off a slouch hat and raises his hands. "Don't shoot! Don't shoot!"

Instinctively, I kill the engine, climb off and use two hands to point the cocked automatic at the stranger. "Who are you?"

"It's Bob Medrano," he shouts in a raspy voice as he begins to cough violently.

"Who's Bob Medrano?" I ask. "Do I know you?"

The man spits phlegm over the side of the bridge. "You ought to. We've met before, in Lincoln City. On the Interstate." The coughing starts again.

The light comes on. "Holy hell." Medrano's appears to have lost almost half his body weight. I holster the .45 and pull off my helmet. "Sorry, I didn't recognize you." I feel like a jerk. This guy probably saved my life and the lives of Gail and Josefina.

Medrano shakes my hand, then puts his hat back on. "I was hoping I'd find a friend in Elmhurst. I need one," he says despondently.

Too many people 'need' me right now, but I can't find a way to gracefully leave the ragged-looking man in the middle of a bridge. "I've got some stuff to take care of. You said your first name is Bob? Sorry, I don't think I ever knew it." I point to the BMW. "Let me get this thing pointed south and I'll get you into town."

Bob Medrano mounts behind me. "Not many motorcycles with sidecars," he speaks over the wind noise as I climb the hill into town. "Thought I'd had some kind of vision. You aren't a Visitation of the Virgin of Guadalupe, but you'll do."

Ha, ha with the Catholic mumbo jumbo. I can't lug this guy around with me, so I pull under a carport. "What brings you here, uh, Bob? Where's your boy?" I remember a gangly teenager, Adan, hugging his father. "And your wife?"

"Dead." His face shows no emotion. Bob Medrano just stares at me. The only sound is rain pattering on the carport's metal roof.

More victims! What the hell do I say now? His stony countenance tells me to change the subject.

"God, I'm so sorry." I pause. I've got the trite and meaningless expression out of the way. Now he needs to tell me when the madness in Lincoln City will reach Elmhurst. "What happened?" I ask, but Bob Medrano has mentally gone somewhere else.

Rain disturbs the puddles on the driveway. I want to yell, "Earth to Medrano. Earth to Medrano." I settle for a wave of my hand in front of his face.

"Don't want to talk about it," he replies in a monotone.

"Sorry. But can you tell me how bad it is in Lincoln City? And what we might be looking at here in Elmhurst?"

He studies a couple with a small child shuffling by and points at them. "There are lots of folks besides me you can ask."

True. But Medrano was in the thick of defending his neighborhood. He was part of a tight knit group of committed fighters, who knew what they were doing. We need his knowledge, and I need it now.

"Can I ask one question?"

Medrano sighs. "One."

"Is Elmhurst in danger?"

"Yes."

"What do we need to do to prepare?"

He shakes his head and climbs into the sidecar and sits. He slipped into another dimension.

"You've probably got a better idea than most. But I'll drop it." I'm screaming inside. I'm not going to let Medrano zone out in lala land very long, grieving for his dead family. We've got living ones here, including my infant daughter.

"Good," he manages. "Don't. Not now. Maybe not soon." He starts to shiver. "It's cold."

"You need a place to stay." It's not a question. Medrano isn't carrying a rucksack or sleeping bag. Kapok pokes out of holes in his nylon jacket.

There's no room in my house. I can't take him to the Kaufman's. Randall's dying, if he isn't already dead. There are plenty of empty houses, but as bad as Medrano looks, he won't do well without help from a Good Samaritan. I hardly fit the bill, but I'm what Medrano's stuck with.

I'm not sure my idea is a good one, but I tell him to climb on and head to Anson Gutierrez' house.

I honk the horn and rev the engine. Anson sticks his head out the front door, looking at the two of us doubtfully. I tell Medrano, "Climb off. You need to get out of the rain." Medrano is shivering uncontrollably.

I push our way past Anson. "You've got an extra room. This is Bob Medrano. Bob needs a warm place to stay."

The static and hum of the radios in the next room fills the void left by Anson's refusal or inability to answer me. He just stares.

"Anson, I'll owe you one, but right now, let's get Bob under some warm blankets or something." I snap my fingers in front of his face. "Chop chop, Anson."

At this, Anson comes alive. Oblivious to the feelings of the soaking wet man standing five feet away, he whines, "How in hell am I going to feed him, Dalton?"

As he hears this, Medrano looks like a caged animal. He moves toward the door. I grab his arm. "No, you don't, Bob. You've got a place to stay and it's right here!" I get up in Anson's face and realize I'm gritting my teeth. "I'll get you some goddamned food, Anson. Right now, this man needs a place to bunk. And it's here."

Anson quickly loses the staring contest. "All right, Dalton. Jeez, ease up. I guess with my cat gone, I've got some room. Who put you in charge?"

Good question. Who did put me in charge?

I doubt that screaming at Gail to move, hinting at something ominous and without explaining it as I sped off, is going to cut it. The family farm's location, on the north side of Little Elm River will guarantee armed gangs sweeping down from the north intending harm will turn their attention on outlying structures—and people.

. Instead of going directly there, I head to City Hall. With the rain, I might catch Pancho and Lefty and Elmhurst's shot up Freightliner stake truck, recovered from the five murderers a lifetime ago. They seem inseparable. The Chief has always locked up the keys to lessen the chances of the two outlaws disappearing with it on one of their many scavenging expeditions, or at least the ones they can't justify as beneficial to Elmhurst. As a consequence, the two are usually found close nearby.

The raincoat protects my upper body, but my pants are soaked. A slight north wind drops the temperature and a shiver runs through me. I climb off the BMW. Behind City Hall, the shot-up Freightliner stake truck sits unattended. I unlock City Hall, then head to where the Chief kept—the past tense feels weird—the truck's keys.

For many years, Chief Pettibone has been a fixture in Elmhurst. He's survived goofy city councils out for his job, disgruntled citizens unhappy with some police action, and cocky young officers testing his leadership. He's outlasted all those things. But now, the EMP's strain and his wife's illness and death have brought a good man down. It is as if his spirit has already vanished from the building, even though his announcement is only a few hours old. The weight of responsibility he must carry hits me suddenly, and hard. I am quickly in a very dark place inside; I feel crushed by sadness and fear of failure. Staring into space and seeing all the horrible imaginables, I scream at the walls of City Hall, "Shake it off! Get a life, Dalton."

I feel marginally better. Now to find Pancho and Lefty.

I don't have to try. Lefty appears out of nowhere. "You need us to do something, *jefe?*"

"Follow me to the Kaufman property. We're going to load that family up and get them into town." Once I'm convinced Gail and her family will cooperate, I intend check out the Hixson Lane bridge, and more importantly, try to convince George Hixson that a crazy idea roiling my brain might work.

Pancho is suddenly at his *compadre*'s side.

"*Pues*, how much stuff they going to put on the truck?"

It is a good question. Pederson Road's flimsy iron bridge over Little Elm River is load limited for a reason.

"Not enough to worry about." Chief Pettibone drives up in an ATV. I guess he's done burying his wife. "Start heading that way," I say as I walk toward the Chief.

"Here are the keys, Dalton." Larry Pettibone's raincoat is shiny with rain. "I'll walk back to my house from here."

I start to say something but before I can get any words out, he hands me a ring of keys. "These are for City Hall, the gun safe, the armory." He points them out as they lay in my palm. When he finishes, he folds my hands around the keys, and simply says, "Gotta go now. God bless you."

And walks away not even giving me a chance to offer him a ride home. The Chief's words at the cemetery echo through my mind: "Time to saddle up, Dalton."

Pancho and Lefty are at the City fuel depot. I watch to ensure the truck gets no more than the few gallons allowed, lock the pump and tank, then follow them as the truck splashes over the crappy streets on the northeast side of town.

The rain and gray skies have sucked out what little color is left in the neighborhood. The remains of vegetable gardens, with what they produced long picked, appear as clumps of dirt and soggy dead leaves. I shake off the images and turn onto Pederson Road, suddenly mad as hell at myself.

"Saddle up, you dumbass." I'm talking to myself, but maybe it's necessary. The stake truck's brake lights come on as Pancho eases it over the old bridge. The bridge seems to groan as the truck's weight shifts the timbers as it passes.

The drop down to Little Elm River at Pederson Road is steeper than at the highway to Lincoln City. The water must cut through rock here, so there is less space for floodwaters to push into. In better times, there is a beauty to the chasm and its lush darkness. As a kid, this part of the river's path was spooky. There was less warning here of a sudden rise. Less chance to get out of the path of the water quickly. Which made sneaking out and tempting fate by swimming in the deep pools even more enticing.

There's a zigzag trail we used to take as kids. It's still there, but now slick as hell. I fall on my ass in the wet grass, finally finding shelter from the rain under the bridge's metal and wood floor. No telling what's in the shadows. I realize I'm grinning like a kid seeing presents under a Christmas tree. If I can find someone who knows what they're doing, we can blow this rickety structure to kingdom come.

Pancho and Lefty are standing on the Kaufman back porch, visiting with Bertha. Lefty holds Josefina, rocking her back and forth. I pull the motorcycle into the shed and splash through the mud. There is nothing in the bed of the truck.

What the fuck! I swallow my anger as Lefty hands me my daughter.

He grins, "Dalton, this little girl, she is so pretty. Thank God she looks like her mother."

And, oh, is she beautiful. She's changing before my eyes. I rock her back and forth, then quickly shed my raincoat after her little protests when water drips on her forehead. For a moment, all is right with the world.

I savor the oohs and aahs of Pancho and Lefty. Bertha's silence returns me to another reality. Her face is swollen from crying. She dabs at her eyes.

"Is he...?"

She just nods. I hand her Josefina, and quietly go to the bedroom. Randall's pallor is gray with death. Gail and Billy are on either side of his bed, still holding their father's hands.

Chapter Thirty-Four

RANDALL KAUFMAN HAS BEEN A PRESENCE FOR MUCH OF MY ADULT life. The grayness of his dead body doesn't diminish my grudging admiration and, yes, love, for this occasionally difficult man. He lived according to a code of honor and decency that challenged me and on more than one occasion, shamed me. I admit that I aspire to it, if only to myself.

Gail and Billy acknowledge my presence silently. I put my arm around Gail's shoulders and feel her body mold itself to mine, I'm not sure if it is her acceptance of my comfort or is merely cold.

While I want to continue in this poignant family moment, the fact is that I am very anxious for the remaining Kaufmans to kick it into high gear and get their asses across the Little Elm River. The longer I look at Randall, the more I wonder how fast I can get him into the ground. Not exactly touchy-feely, but it is what it is.

Most who could fled Lincoln City within the first few weeks. Survival of the fittest has meant ruthless extermination in many cases, and slow death from malnutrition and hunger in others. Medrano and others leaving now have somehow survived the anarchy, rioting, looting, and fighting for disappearing food and supplies.

Now, the madness of Lincoln City is moving our way. I have a plan that might work to protect Elmhurst, but first, I've got to get Gail and my daughter Josefina into a place where I can protect them. It strikes me suddenly—I care much more for the survival of my daughter than Gail. It's not that I don't love Gail. It's just that this beautiful baby girl is higher on my priorities. Maybe that's the way it is with all parents. Or maybe, it's just that, along with my thoughts about Randall, it confirms what I've told myself for years. I am an asshole.

So be it. I've got things to do.

I disengage from Gail with a reassuring hug and return to Pancho and Lefty and Bertha. It's time to talk turkey.

"Some very bad people are coming toward Elmhurst, Bertha." I explain what is being reported by HAM operators. "Your property is on the wrong side of the river. Please, consider what I'm saying."

She appears skeptical, but to my relief does not walk away as I plead with her. Whatever Bertha decides will sway Billy and Gail. Half an hour later, I am making headway.

My relief at her acquiescence so soon after Randall's death is diluted by a sense of guilt—I'm pleading that she leave her beloved homestead, and ensure that Gail and Josefina, and Billy, do the same.

Randall will be buried on the property. I promise that will happen before we leave. I ask Pancho and Lefty to start digging a grave.

"You gonna help us, Dalton?" asks Pancho.

I have to find George Hixson, but promise I'll be back as soon as possible. Bertha gives me a doleful glance, and then pats the two men's arms. "Billy will help."

Placated, Pancho and Lefty give her reluctant nods. They aren't enthusiastic—the cold rain continues without interruption. Digging a grave and loading a stake truck in this weather is not going to be any fun. I tromp through the mud toward the BMW, and then stop.

"Shit," I say. "This ain't gonna work." I turn, head to the Kaufman's implement shed.

Billy appears. "What're you looking for?"

"Shovels. Four of them."

He rustles around in the gloom.

Some twenty yards from his house we begin to dig. The rain has softened the first six inches of the dark clayey soil, which adheres to everything. Below the six inches, the soil is rock hard. Randall's grave isn't going to be any regulation six feet of depth After an hour, we have managed three feet. Bertha, cloaked in an oversized raincoat, appears.

"This will have to suit my husband under the circumstances. I think he and the Good Lord will understand." She peers into the shallow grave. "This gumbo needs a backhoe. You boys have done enough. Let's carry Randall here."

Pancho, Lefty and I wait outside while Billy kicks off muddy boots and follows his mother into the house. Soon, Billy appears with his father's diminished body, wrapped in a sheet, over his shoulders.

Gail holds an umbrella, mostly over Josefina and Bertha, as Billy allows me to help lower Randall into the grave. Two inches of water has run into the hole. The white sheet becomes translucent with the wetness and Randall's corpse eerily begins to appear through its covering.

Gail sobs quietly as Bertha recites the Lord's Prayer. Finally, Bertha tries to shovel in the first dirt. It sticks to the blade, refusing to drop. She mutters, "dammit," hands me the shovel and retreats to the house. I'm not sure what to do, until I hear Bertha's wails of anguish.

Gail hands me Josefina and the umbrella, takes the errant shovel from Pancho, and shakes muddy clods onto her father.

She hands the shovel to her brother, retrieves Josefina, and follows Bertha into the house.

Ten minutes later, a sea of mud is the only evidence of the grave. No headstone, no cross.

Pancho and Lefty follow Billy into the house where Gail hands them ragged towels. The packing begins.

Ten minutes later, I drive by City Hall. There are people standing inside and under the protection of its portico. I want to stop and see how others are doing with their assignments, but I will be asked too many questions. My plan for defending Elmhurst is still so amorphous, and I have no idea if any of it will work. I continue west on Main Street until the turnoff to Hixson Lane. Once out of Elmhurst, I lean the BMW into a slight turn and drop toward the Little Elm river bottom. I gear down carefully as I approach the slick surface of the bridge over Hixson Lane. It is a steel and concrete span by Lee County built sometime between the iron structure on Pederson Road and the Lincoln City highway bridge.

I gently brake at the bridge's south entrance. Little Elm River hasn't risen, but it is now is turning muddy from runoff. I want to crawl under it like I did on the other two bridges but decide against it. The embankment is steep and wet. I'll probably fall on my ass without accomplishing much. I realize that with my complete ignorance of explosives, I'm wasting my time.

Minutes later, the BMW splashes through deep puddles at George Hixson's gate. Wisps of fog have begun to settle in swales. The gray mist gives George's buildings an otherworldly look. I stay in first gear and slowly pass the shed that I hope houses the fertilizer. The shed's large wooden door is closed against the weather. I pull under a tree near the house and dismount.

"George! You here?"

No answer. I walk toward his barn. No sign of him. The Dodge Power Wagon, still unrepaired, sits mutely under a siding.

Where in the hell is George?

Seconds later, the barrel of a gun is jammed against my neck. "Don't turn around, whoever you are! Where'd you get that motorcycle?"

"Goddammit, George. It's me, Dalton." My heart pounds like a nail gun operated by a speed freak.

"Hell, so it is." He lowers a .44 magnum revolver with a seven and a half inch barrel. "Not taking any chances these days."

"Christ, George. You scared the shit out of me with that goddammed cannon."

He's draped in an army poncho, camouflage, jump boots and a boonie cap. George leers at me. Water drips from its brim and into his scraggly beard. I can't be sure whether he really didn't recognize me, or whether he's just screwing around with me. Or maybe both.

"Can we get under cover?"

"What?" he scoffs. "You don't like this weather?"

"No," I reply. I ask again, and grudgingly, George uses his handgun to point toward the barn. Once inside, he strips off the poncho and cap, grabs two wooden chairs, and says, "sit."

I squish into one of them, take a breath, and begin. "I came to warn you."

"About what?" he asks.

Lincoln City, anarchy, swarms of armed men heading toward Elmhurst. I launch into the same speech I gave Bertha Kaufman. After ten minutes, George sits back and says nothing.

"George, I'm concerned. You're on the wrong side of Little

Elm River. There's no way you can defend yourself here." I sweep my hands around. "This is bald assed prairie. You need to get somewhere you can defend yourself."

Hixson seems unimpressed. "Like Elmhurst, eh?"

"Exactly!" I exclaim, hoping he's starting to come around. He remains mute, so I press on. "Aren't you worried?"

He begins to laugh. "Dalton, you are a finagling son of a bitch. You couldn't give a rat's ass about me or my place."

I'm pissed. This isn't going the way I'd hoped. He's nailed me, fair and square, but I try to demur. It doesn't work.

"What the hell are you here for, Dalton? What do you want from me? You made me a deal for my old Power Wagon, and never followed through. I'm still waiting for the fuel you promised." He leans to one side and lets loose a huge fart. "Damned beans. I'm eating too many of them and not much else."

With no wind the rancid odor hangs in the moist air. "Hell, I've seen you twice since this EMP. First time, you yahoo me out of town. Second time, you're out here begging me to give you that old truck." He points to where the Power Wagon still sits. "You send them two Mexican fellas out here. Not that I've got anything against them folks. But after two visits assing around out here, your compadres never came back. Now you're back again with some horseshit story about people and a city I don't give a rat's ass about."

I wave my hand trying to push the fart's smell away "Are you sure you didn't shit in your pants?"

George's eyes get squinty. "I'll ask you again, Dalton. What is it you want from me?"

"Can I ask you a question or two first?"

"Maybe."

I point toward the shed, remembering how he bridled when I had asked about its contents the last time here. "Was that ammonium nitrate fertilizer I saw last time I was here?"

"No."

Shit. Shit. Shit.

"Why?" George sounds marginally interested.

I am dog-assed tired. I lean forward and put my elbows on my knees. "I had a plan. Elmhurst is damned near defenseless. I'd hoped you could help, but…"

"Help, how, Dalton?"

I glance over. Suddenly, George Hixson's face is on the same level as mine.

"Blow up bridges."

"What in hell do you know about explosives, Dalton?" George snorts. "I'll bet the only thing you've ever exploded was a Black Cat firecracker."

"Wrong." I play along. "Got ahold of some M80s one time. Damned near blew my fingers off." I stand and reach for my helmet. "Gotta go." I have no idea what I'm going to do now, but I'm too deflated to listen to this right-wing nutcase give me any more grief.

"Dalton, sit down." George disappears into the gloom of his garage. I turn and see a Model T truck, and a disassembled Reo. Curious, I do as he says.

Moments later, he reappears with several books. They are softbound, and all are covered in plastic sheafs. He wraps his poncho around them and walks quickly to his house. I follow.

Inside, he drops the bundle of books on a large table in the living room, lights several kerosene lanterns, trims their wicks, and kicks a chair in my direction.

"Sit."

I sit.

He sifts through the books, then hands me one. "This is an Army Field Manual." I look at the cover. *FM 5-25, Explosives and Demolitions.*

My heart begins to pound. "George Hixson, what are the rest of these books?" I'm smiling so big my face hurts.

"More FMs and Army munitions guides."

I pick up one. A Bureau of Mines circular entitled *Explosives and Blasting Procedures Manual.* "Where in the hell?"

"Dalton, you are a self-absorbed ass. I spent twenty-five years in the Army Reserves. Retired as an O-5. My branch was Ordnance."

I dimly remember that George is a veteran but haven't ever given it much thought. I certainly was not aware he'd attained the rank of Lieutenant Colonel. Reeling a bit, I ask, "Will you help me? Blow those bridges?"

"Maybe. But it'll cost you." The grumpy bastard leers at me.

"How much, and what?"

"I'll tell you later." He pauses. "Now, tell me about the bridges."

"But, if it's not fertilizer, what does it matter?" I gesture toward the shed.

"Shit, Dalton. You asked whether it's fertilizer." He laughs. "Well, technically it is, but that stuff is a few thousand pounds of ammonium nitrate prills."

"What's are 'prills'?"

"Pure pellets of ammonium nitrate. Mix that stuff at a 95% to 5% fuel oil, or diesel, which I've a storage tank full of, and you've got ANFO"—he pronounces it 'an-fo'—"The stuff they use to blast in mines."

This rascal seems to know what he's talking about. I let him rattle on.

"You ever heard of Oppau, Germany?"

"No."

"1921, BASF, big chemical producer, still in business today— well, maybe not after this clusterfuck caused by the EMP—but, anyway, they had the stuff in piles. Didn't think it was explosive. They had ammonium nitrate in big huge piles. Blew half the town off the map. Texas City, 1947. Freighter full of the stuff blew and wiped the harbor off the map. Hell, boy, I could go on and on."

He grabs a lantern and hands me one. "Be careful now."

We walk in the rain to the storage shed. I start to go inside. "No. No. No. Let's not tempt fate, Dalton." He points. "There's your 55-pound bags of prills."

Hixson's sudden enthusiasm is more than a little bit troubling. An Army ordnance officer, pure ammonium nitrate, and manual after manual on how to build bombs and explosives.

"George, why do have all this stuff if you weren't going to use it as fertilizer on your acreage?"

He holds the lantern high. Its hot metal top sizzles as the rain hits. "Son, you don't want to know."

I turn and look at him closely. The lantern's dim light white cheeks and the rictus of a smile contrast with his unkempt gray beard and dark piercing eyes. Suddenly, George Hixson is not just weird, he's downright spooky.

Chapter Thirty-Five

ABOUT A MONTH AGO, CHIEF PETTIBONE RECEIVED INFORMATION about some unusual deaths on Spruce Street, and since I was pulling a shift for the Elmhurst Neighborhood Patrol, I drew the short straw.

The large wood and brick house sits back off the street on a heavily wooded two-acre tract. A human scavenger, hoping to find food or weapons, and not detecting any life, broke in the front door.

A grandmother, her daughter, and the daughter's three kids were dead, laid out in the kitchen like a display of caught fish. The mother had placed white napkins over the faces of her children and the grandmother. After she'd poisoned her family, she hadn't bothered to cover her own face when she'd blown her brains out. On the kitchen countertop was an empty prescription bottle that had contained a narcotic pain reliever, and a Bible with the more bizarre portions of the Book of Revelation underlined in red ink.

And that's how the place became available. Being squeamish isn't an option for desperate people, so the interior was rummaged through thoroughly, despite the bodies' presence, but not otherwise damaged. The family wasn't local, so there were few to mourn their deaths when buried outside of town. The grandmother was old. Her death was perhaps inevitable. Her daughter, the mother of the three kids, chose her fate, so not much sympathy there., But the children—none was older than twelve. Their chance at survival was stolen from them by some apocalyptic wacko dispensing poison to confirm her own end time vision.

Am I pissed? Fucking A, I am. Robbie and Jose, the scraggly kids next door to Anson—Guillermo has somehow managed to keep those boys alive. Josh and Elsie's kids, David and Sarah, are thin as rails but still healthy. Josefina is receiving enough nutrition, thank God. Quite a few children have died, but many have not. Doctor Randhawa said the dead kids showed signs of malnutrition but weren't anywhere near death. They had a chance and were robbed of it.

Several of us lugged the bodies out of the house to the street for burial at the makeshift cemetery outside of town. I hope someone prayed for the kids' souls.

Now, the house sits empty. And is three blocks from my house. More importantly, it's on the right side of Little Elm River.

I boarded up the front door as soon as the bodies were removed, hoping I would convince the Kaufmans to move into town. I even went to the few houses nearby still occupied and passed along that I booby-trapped the place. It's worked. I may be pissed off, but I intend to take advantage of the situation.

The place is habitable, albeit with an occasional whiff of bad air. I'm not going to tell Bertha or Gail about the three dead kids. They might get the heebie jeebies.

Pancho and Lefty are unloading the stake truck as I arrive. There's no sign of Gail, Billy, or Bertha, so I pull under the structure's carport and park. I kill the engine and walk inside.

Kerosene lanterns cast their pale warm glow in several

rooms. Josefina is wrapped in baby blankets on the sofa, two side pillows securing her sleeping form. Billy appears from a bedroom where Gail and Bertha are carrying on a quiet and intense conversation.

"Can I come on back?" I ask.

Billy gives a wave, and I enter the hallway.

"We're here, Dalton," Gail says. "We're taking you at your word that this is what's best." She pauses. "Don't let us down."

The last comment draws an exasperated look from Bertha. "Take it down a few notches, daughter."

The two unpack quilts and clothing onto a double bed. After Bertha's quick hug, I join Billy in the kitchen.

"We brought something into town that might help." He points toward the back yard, a small smile on his face.

Curious, I return to the carport and then through a gate in the chain link fence enclosure. A cow and two calves stare vacantly, before returning their attention to bales of hay.

"Holy shit, Billy. Where in hell? How'd you get them on the truck?"

Lefty joins us. "Miss Bertha insisted we bring them. Was keeping them in a trap down by the dry creek—which by the way isn't so dry anymore. The cow is pretty tame. We led her to the truck with a rope."

Billy adds, "She balked a little, so we used a come-along to pull her up into the truck. The calves aren't weaned, so they followed her up the ramp."

The three creatures present mixed blessings. They can be killed and butchered, and in the cold of winter much of their meat can be preserved by drying. But all around this place are hungry people, some on starvation rations. If the cattle's presence is known, hell will break loose.

"Wow." Saliva begins to fill my mouth. A meal of fresh beef is making me feel giddy. "I had no idea."

"Momma isn't anyone's fool," Billy says. "She's hand fed

these for a while. I guess she figured we'd need the food at some point. In the meantime"—he points at the cow's udders —"your daughter has had some fresh milk."

Where in hell have I been? "I thought Gail was nursing her."

"Shit, Dalton. Like Gail's gonna have a lot of extra nutrients to keep that up. You really do have your head up your ass."

"Did anyone see you drive up with these animals?" I hope against hope the rain and the heavily wooded lot have kept prying eyes away from the place. "If anyone did, they'll be here before dark, and we'd better be prepared to kill or be killed." I stare frantically into the rain.

"Dalton, *calmate, hombre.*" Lefty points to the bed of the truck. "We cinched the momma up to the front rail, pushed her babies in, and then packed boxes around them. We went out Sims Ranch Road, wound around and came over the bridge on Hixson Lane. It was wet out there."

"Thanks, Felipe." I breathe a sigh of relief that they didn't cross Little Elm River on the Pederson Lane bridge and come through most of Elmhurst.

"What? You remember my real name, Dalton? *Hijole!*"

"And Pancho is really Francisco, or Frank," I say.

For some reason, this exchange seems uproariously funny. I start to giggle, then erupt into belly laughs.

Pancho steps out of the house and says, "What're you laughing about?"

Which gets all three of us laughing. Gail steps to the doorway with a lantern, and peers out. "You guys just smoke dope or something? We need help. There's stuff still on the truck getting soaked."

I laugh so hard I start to choke. It feels good.

Eleven men and women, the Cougars, Black Panthers, Coyotes,

and my Armadillos, sit quietly in City Hall's council chambers. Someone's brought a kerosene lantern, which barely dispels the gloom of the meeting room.

I draw a crude map on the whiteboard and circle the three bridges. "In order to defend our town, we've got to keep any armed force coming down from Lincoln City on the other side of Little Elm River."

The room is icy cold. As I speak my breath condenses in the chill air. I haven't eaten in eighteen hours. People huddle in jackets.

A few head nod. Mostly, I get vacant stares. "Look around. No way, with four patrols, are we going to be able to do it. Suggestions?"

"Throw in Pancho, Lefty and Billy Kaufman. That's three more," Josh says.

"You saw Severo, over on Apple Street," Ignacio, one of my Armadillos, adds. "He sure as hell didn't like Ike or Lupe or those bikers. I can ask him and some others to help. I bet that'd be good for another five, at least."

Yes, I remember Severo. Scrawny and pissed off. Not exactly a model citizen but he's alive, he's here, and he'll probably help.

"What about Medrano?" Josh asks. "The guy you met on the bridge. The guy from Lincoln City?"

. "Bob—that's his first name, Bob's a basket case right now. Something, he won't say what, killed his wife and son." I re-tell my encounter with Medrano while retrieving Gail. "I wish we had the others that were with him. They've got grit."

Jill sits, arms crossed, staring at me. I can't take it any longer. "Jill, you want to add something?"

She unfolds her hands. "Yeah, I do. Twenty or so people aren't going to have a whole lot of luck stopping a bunch of bad guys intent on taking over Elmhurst."

Jill pisses me off, and I snap back. "Well, Jill, how about

twenty-one? How about your husband, Fred? He's mostly healed up, isn't he?"

Jill stands and gets in my face. "Who made you king of the world, Dalton?"

"Shit, Jill. You take over if you want. I'll try to get Gail and my daughter out of this fucking burg and let *you* sort this mess out."

We stand toe to toe, both with fists clenched.

"Stop it, you two!" Kevin stands. "Sit down, Jill. Dalton, shut up." The black man isn't large, but something about him is a commanding presence.

Jill sits. I shut up.

"Now that that's out of the way, Dalton, how about sharing some good news with us. The Chief's gone. I'm too new here and not stupid enough to take on the job. As far as I'm concerned—no offense, Jill—Dalton's in charge. You might not like what we did, but tough shit. It's done. It's over with. And it worked."

Quite a speech from an otherwise quiet and reserved guy. Several of the new squad members look puzzled at his statement. He turns to them.

Oh, shit. He's going to spill the beans about our Apple Street ambush.

He doesn't, merely adding, "Before the Chief helped Dalton form these patrol groups, decisions were made. They have absolutely nothing to do with what's going on now." He pauses, looks at Jill. "Do they?"

Jill, visibly calmer, nods in agreement. I'm relieved by her reaction, and with his giving me credit for the patrol groups. I don't know Kevin Daugherty well, but he's got stones.

Kevin sits down.

Josh pipes up. "Okay, Dalton. What's your plan?"

I need to make things right with Jill. "I apologize to Jill, and to the rest of you who saw this. It's my bad."

Jill makes the next move. "Mine too. Sorry. Let's hear what you've got to say, Dalton."

I turn to the whiteboard and point to the map. "In order to get to Elmhurst without swinging way west or way south, anyone coming from Lincoln City will have to cross any of these three bridges." I circle the bridge on the Lincoln City-Elmhurst highway, the Pederson Lane iron bridge, and the Hixson Lane Bridge. "These are the chokepoints. If we stop them, we might have a chance."

"'Might have a chance'?" Someone, I don't catch who, mutters. "What the fuck does that mean?"

"I'm Andrea," the short, slender Hispanic with the Black Panthers stands and raises her hand. "Stop them? Who's them? And for how long?"

The first thing someone in charge needs to do is keep those working for him informed. I've flunked. I'm tired of apologizing but do it anyway.

"Let me start with the new information we've received from HAM radio operators."

Ten minutes later, everyone knows about as much as I do. Anson's HAM messages, and Bob Medrano's appearance on the highway. Some of the squad members appear nervous, and I expect them to walk out.

"Before anyone leaves, please. Hear me out."

The fidgeting stops.

"Does anyone know George Hixson?"

As if on cue, a flash of lightning brightens the council chambers, followed less than a second by the loud reverberation of thunder.

"Close," mutters Keith, my wiseass Armadillo.

"No. It's God," says Robert, the puny banker, who is part of the Black Panthers. "No one likes George Hixson. Not even God."

Susan, the new woman in Jill's group, agrees. "No shit, Sherlock. He doesn't like women."

Andrea chimes in. "Nor us Meskins." She turns to Kevin. "And if he doesn't like us brown people, he sure doesn't like you black folks."

"If it's any comfort," I say, "he's not too warm and cuddly with white folks either."

"So why are we talking about him then?" Josh asks impatiently. "What's he got to do with helping us?"

I grin. "He likes to blow things up."

Chapter Thirty-Six

KEVIN ERASES THE WHITEBOARD. JOSH, KEVIN, AND JILL BEGIN TO create duty rosters for the three outposts planned for the Lincoln City sides of the bridges. The radio headsets, so useful in the Brushy Creek Road and Apple Street ambushes, are re-checked. Remarkably, the batteries still show they are over half charged. I'm planning three outposts. The city has five complete sets in its inventory. Let's hope that will be enough radios and battery charge. My concern is whether their range will be too short. They must be able to communicate with some sort of command center on the Elmhurst side of all three bridges. We'll do some tests to see whether the manufacturer's promised three-mile range is realistic. I sure hope so.

I'm dead on my feet and chilled to the bone, but I need better information on Lincoln City. Rain collects in large puddles and runs into the storm sewers. As I pull up to Anson's house, shapes stir under blankets on the covered porch next door. I wave, and two heads peer out of the bundles. It's Guillermo Sosa's two boys, Robbie and Jose. I'm relieved the boys are still alive and idly wonder where Guillermo has found enough food for his family.

The boys' heads disappear under their blankets. I wonder why they are outside. Probably the family's small single-wall house isn't any warmer on the inside. At least now, there are distractions for the boys, like a motorcycle sloshing through the puddles.

"Hey boys! You guys stay warm!" Two disembodied arms appear and wave as I tromp to Anson's front door. It's closed and locked. I pound on the side of the house. "Open up, Anson. I'm freezing my ass off!"

Floor joists creak, and seconds later, Anson unlocks and opens the door. "C'mon in, Dalton."

I push past him. Two kerosene lanterns cast a deceptively warm glow. The place is icy cold.

"Dalton, you gotta do something about that guy you made me take in," Anson starts, before I even shed my raincoat. "He's weird."

Oh shit. Now what?

"He just lays in the bed. He hasn't moved. He just stares at me when I check on him. He's spooky."

"What do you care if he's spooky? Has he done anything? Is he hurting you, Anson? Is he damaging your precious house?" I don't have time to deal with this.

Anson rocks back a bit acting like I've hurt his feelings. Fuck him. "Well, no, but…"

"What's going on with Lincoln City right now? That's why I'm here, Anson."

I glance into the bedroom. Bob Medrano is covered with blankets. He stares at me. I wait for him to blink. He *is* spooky.

"See? Told you so."

"Bob. Bob? You okay?"

He blinks. That's it.

I shake my head. "Anson, talk to me. I need to know what's going on in Lincoln City. What have you heard? What's going on up there?"

It comes out in a torrent. "Slow down, Dalton. I've got problems with my rig right now."

I guess rig means the HAM equipment. "What problems?"

"You notice any sun out there? No solar power. No wind either. I've even rigged up one of those." He shoves the venetian blinds away on a window. A crude wind turbine's blades stand motionless. "If you haven't noticed, this rain's coming straight down. My batteries are low, low, low. Only been able to stay on for a few minutes. Then have to shut her down."

Uh oh. "When's the last time you were on the air?"

Anson looks at a windup clock that reads 5:20. "Just before noon."

Crap. "What've you heard?"

"Not much more than what I told you the last time. Some big fires, but the rain's knocked a lot of them down. Flooding in low lying parts. Two CBers with illegal rigs—well, I guess nothing's illegal anymore—were on the air with a shitload of wattage. First time I'd heard them. Whoever's running them seems to be part of some kind of shake-and-bake militia. Kept talking about taking back Lincoln City from the cartels. Kept bragging about how tough they were...Then they went off the air."

"Christ! Anything else?"

"Mostly, what I heard before. Gangs spreading out from the capital. Lots of nasty stuff." Anson shakes his head. "None of what I've heard is pretty at all."

"What about Elmhurst?"

Anson just stands there shaking his head.

I grab his arm. "What about Elmhurst?"

Anson stares off into space.

"What about Elmhurst, goddammit?"

"Jesus. Let me go, Dalton. You're breaking my fucking arm!" Anson's voice rises upward in a whine.

I let go, and Anson rolls up his sleeve. My hand has left a livid red and purple mark on his scrawny arm. "Jeez. I'm so sorry, Anson." And I am. "Sorry. I'm just a little stressed I guess."

"A little? You're almost as weird as the guy in my bedroom." He pushes me away. "Chill out man."

I apologize again. Anson runs his hand through his long greasy hair. "Don't blame you, Dalton. What I'm hearing is fucking bad. People getting burned to death. People killing people. Women getting raped. Sounds horrible." He pauses. "But, no. Nothing about Elmhurst. Except…"

"Except what?" I scream. "Except what?"

"Something about some groups planning a move south to take over new territories." He slumps into a chair. "That's all I got, before…"

"Before what?"

"Before juice ran out and I lost the transmission." He looks up, grimacing. "Sorry, Dalton. I've let you down." He begins to cry.

"Aw shit." He looks pathetic. "No, you haven't, compadre. No, you haven't." Too late, I realize how fragile Anson is. And why most of his human contact is long distance. "I'm sorry. You've been gangbusters, man. You've got us this far with great information."

And he has. If gangs move south, the nearest town is Elmhurst. I give him an awkward hug and open the front door. The rain gutter is rusted through, and water splashes into the house.

Bob Medrano stands in the bedroom doorway, wrapped in an old quilt. "I heard you."

How could he not? "And?"

"Your HAM friend here." He points to Anson. "He's not much of a host, but he's worked his ass off trying to find out what's going on." He stares at me, glassy eyed. "You need to be nicer to people."

Anson gets a smirky look on his face. "Yeah, Dalton. You need to be nicer to people."

I want to smack him. Instead, I close the door.

"Glad you're back with us, Bob. Care to add anything?"

Ten minutes later, I've heard enough from Bob Medrano to convince me we are running out of time.

By the time I'm back on Spruce Street, the Kaufmans' household items are off-loaded and under cover. The stake truck hasn't moved. I pull under the carport and go inside. Pancho is holding Josefina as he sits on the sofa. Lefty is in the kitchen, looking restless. A small Coleman stove perches on the countertop, water in a pan heating over its blue flame.

Gail appears from the bedrooms. "Hey Dalton. Want some coffee?"

"Does the Pope shit in the woods?"

That comment draws a roll of the eyes. She spoons some dried crystals into a mug and adds hot water. It smells unbelievably wonderful.

"Thanks." I burn my lips on the first sip, but I keep drinking. It's gone too soon.

"Another?"

My exhaustion seems to leave me. Either the caffeine or the little touch of normality has restored some strength. Billy enters from the back yard enclosure. He carries a small bucket of milk which he hands to his sister.

"Not much, sis, but it'll get Josie another day down the road." He pulls off his slicker, howdys me, and pulls out a chair at the kitchen table. "What's next, Dalton?"

"We head to George Hixson's place."

Pancho and Lefty grunt in disapproval.

"Why there, Dalton?"

"You'll see."

I take the lead on the BMW. Twenty minutes later, Pancho, Lefty, and Billy pile out of the truck in front of George Hixson's fertilizer shed. Its door is open. In the darkness, the plastic fertilizer bags remind me of misshaped lower teeth in a Halloween mask. Hixson appears from his garage, waving a flashlight. I pull forward and onto a concrete slab near his house. The others park the truck in front of the barn door. Cold rain pelts us as we scamper under cover.

"Hello Billy. Sorry to see you're tied up with these yayhoos." George shakes Billy's, then accepts Pancho's and Lefty's extended hands. I'm relieved.

"Let me show you what I've got." George leers at me as he motions us toward a fifty-five gallon barrel. Its top has been cut out and is partially filled with ammonium nitrate prills. Beside the drum are its contents' three empty plastic bags. On George's workbench, a U.S. Army Field Manual is held open by a claw hammer.

George moves to the bench. With the contrasting lights and darks of the meager lantern light, I'm reminded of a mad scientist. All he needs is a white lab coat instead of bib overalls.

"I've got plenty for you gentlemen—I use the term loosely— to do." He taps on the book. "Not complicated really. Like a cookbook." George points toward the driving rain. "I need more drums. They're over by that old Power Wagon. Bring every one you can find."

Shit. I'm so exhausted I am seeing double. I almost ask if I can crash for a few hours in George's house. Billy, Pancho, and Lefty head into the weather while I stand next to the work bench.

"What are you waiting for? You too high and mighty to help out?" George says as he follows the others.

I tromp back into the rain.

We recover twenty barrels. Most are empty. Some, by their odor, have dregs of some sort of petroleum product.

Billy asks, "What do we do with the gunk in the bottom of some of these?"

"Leave it," George responds. "Whatever's in there won't hurt what we're doing. In fact, it may help."

George's assortment of metal saws, pry bars, chisels and hammers are now employed. Four hours later, the drums are topless and the barn stinks of metal and old oil.

"Now we load the rest of the prills on your truck," George pronounces.

"What are 'prills'?" asks Billy.

"Fertilizer pellets," I answer. There is a collective groan.

"All right, you pussies. All right." He disappears into the rain with a lantern. I doze off listening to the other three bitch about the work.

"Up and at'em."

Billy's whoop startles me awake. Pancho and Lefty have already joined him at the workbench. I struggle to clear my head while climbing off the concrete floor. A large plate of hard sausage, cheese and crackers is being attacked. Despite my exhaustion, I shove my way closer.

"Sweet Jesus," mutters Billy with a mouthful. "I'm in heaven."

Pancho and Lefty step away with two handfuls apiece. I take their place and shove three pieces of sausage into my mouth. "Venison?" I ask, but with my mouth full, I'm not sure I can be understood. I don't care.

Off to one side, his right arm resting on the lip of a barrel stands George. He's grinning like a shit eating possum.

I nod my thanks. He grins at me, and then loudly asks, "Who wants a beer?"

You can hear a pin drop.

George points to Lefty. "Come with me."

They return moments later with a wooden crate containing brown bottles of varying shapes.

"Home brew," George announces. "Made it about a year ago. Shouldn't kill you." He waves a bottle opener around, then pops the top off a bottle. Yeasty brown foam rises out of the bottle. It's the most beautiful aroma I've ever smelled.

"Two apiece," he pronounces as he drains the open bottle. "We've got a full night of work ahead of us. Don't want you bastards drunk." He pauses. "Especially you two." He points to Pancho and Lefty. "I hear you Mexes can't hold your liquor."

If he wants a fight, he's disappointed. Pancho merely drains a bottle, burps, and says, "When this is over with, I'll show you who can drink. I'll put your *bolillo* ass under the table."

Uh oh. Billy takes his beer and quietly sets it on the bench. Lefty shifts uncomfortably. I wait for George's explosive temper to erupt. Instead, he breaks into a devilish laughter, and reaches for another bottle. "Hell, when we all blow ourselves to kingdom come, the good Lord will have hell sorting white and dark meat anyway."

Before moving the rest of the ammonium nitrate prills, George concentrates on the one drum already partially filled. "We need to mix in some diesel fuel," he announces, and takes a plastic fuel can. "But not too much."

He talks to himself as he flips a page in the Field Manual, and then slowly pours diesel fuel over the prills. "Start mixing, boys." He hands a wooden canoe paddle to Billy.

For the next hour, Elmhurst's stake truck moves back and forth to George's shed, moving sacks of ammonium nitrate. Three more canoe paddles appear, and soon, there are seventeen barrels full of prills. When dry, ammonium nitrate is odorless, but the dust creeps into everything I'm wearing and I begin to sneeze helplessly.

Then, George tosses the empty plastic bags outside, and the few remaining prills inside them interact immediately with the water. The stuff smells awful.

"Why'd you do that, George?" Billy asks. "You can cut that stink with a knife."

George grunts, "Keeping you boys awake is all."

Rain and chemical smell be damned. I have to step outside to clear my lungs of the dust. As my eyes clear, the scene inside takes on the macabre. Three dust covered gnomes stir fifty-five gallon cauldrons of an evil brew. George splashes past me toward his house.

"Follow me," he yells over his shoulder.

He disappears into the living room's darkness. I stand in the doorway, afraid to trip or stumble over furniture. "Where are you, George?"

Grunting sounds emanate from some recess in his house. "Here, help me. This thing is heavy." A light beam waggles its way across the room until George appears, holding a penlight in his mouth and a wooden crate in his hands.

I take it from him.

"What is it?" The crate is heavy.

"Dynamite. Well, actually, military grade dynamite. A lot more powerful than the original stuff. Seventy-five percent RDX and other goodies."

"Damn. Is this stuff dangerous?" I have no idea what RDX is, but figure if George 'liberated' it from the US Army, it's deadly.

"Nah. Not like it is right now."

"Is this going to set off the ammonium nitrate?"

"Ammonium nitrate needs a secondary explosion for it to be worth a shit."

"Secondary? What's the primary?"

"Blasting caps." He turns toward his kitchen. "Those little buggers are touchy as my last wife. I'll install those later."

Chapter Thirty-Seven

IT'S DAWN WHEN I STOP IN THE MIDDLE OF THE HIXSON LANE Bridge, turn off the BMW's engine and step to the upriver railing. I watch Little Elm River push against the bridge's concrete piers. The road surface vibrates under my feet. It's as if Mother Nature is doing her best to remove the manmade hindrance. I hope George Hixson's concoctions will help her along.

The river is out of its banks, and the muddy water gulps as it reaches hungrily in newly created whirlpools. Dead trees and trash are pushed unrelentingly in the flood. A dead deer circles in an eddy. Two feral pigs disappear under the bridge, their legs pointing in the air, their bodies bloated like hairy balloons.

Then, something else.

I want to look away, but don't. The body of an unclothed woman moves downstream headfirst. Her hair seems to move away from her downward facing body. She nearly collides with a pier, then is swept to one side and out of my sight. Where did she come from? Whose mother, wife, lover, was she? Did she float out of a grave, or was she killed and thrown into the water? I shake my head, as if that will dispel further thoughts.

I turn onto Spruce Street and stop at the lane into the Kaufmans' new shelter. As the BMW idles, I peer down the lane. A tendril of smoke wafts from the house's chimney. Good. Billy's found some dry firewood. I imagine the fire's warmth, and want desperately to check on Gail, Josefina, and Bertha. That will have to wait. I tap the motorcycle's shifter, ease into gear, and drive to my house. Josh appears as I swing up the detached garage's overhead door.

"How'd it go?"

"Seventeen barrels complete with diesel and fertilizer, and dynamite. Blasting caps and safety fuses ready to be inserted. The devices look evil as hell, but I don't know…" My voice trails off.

"You look like shit. Go get some sleep, Dalton."

I squeeze his arm in a thank you. "Too much stuff to do."

"Bullshit. You're no good to anyone if you die of exhaustion." Josh pulls the garage door down and we are engulfed in darkness. "I'll get you up in a few hours."

I want to ask about progress on the outposts, the radios, and additional help. My words are mushy, and Josh steers me toward my back door.

"You're not making any sense. I'll fill you in later. We're making progress."

David and Sarah play in the dim light from the dining room windows as I stagger up the stairs. I strip off my wet clothes, but before I can fall into bed, Elsie is at my bedroom door, holding a quilt.

"Wrap up in this, Dalton. You look half frozen." She retreats downstairs.

Josefina chokes on something. I reach desperately, and begin pounding on her tiny back, trying to dislodge whatever it is. She turns blue. Gail screams at me. She wrenches my arm away from my dying child. "It's your fault! It's your fault!" Josefina looks at me with gentle, blue eyes, as if to tell me that I am forgiven. I wail uncontrollably.

"Hey, Dalton. Wake up!"

Someone is tugging on me—hard. "You're screaming. Wake up." It's Josh.

"Christ!" It is pitch black outside. "How long have I slept?" I am drenched in sweat.

"Not long enough, but things are starting to happen. We need you down at City Hall."

The nightmare's horror slowly dissipates. I dress as Josh holds a small flashlight. I find a work shirt and pair of jeans in a rancid pile of clothes. As Josh and I tromp down the stairs, I scratch at my beard. It itches like hell and I wonder if I've got nits.

Elsie re-barricades the backdoor as Josh and I stumble into the rain.

"Is this ever going to stop?"

"I hope not," I reply. "At least not for a while."

"You taking the BMW. I'm on a bicycle?"

"I guess." Seems selfish, me zipping through the rain on a motorized transport while Josh pedals. "You wanna ride sidecar?"

He doesn't hesitate. "Sure. Just don't kill me with this contraption." We push the motorcycle out of the garage, and he climbs into the sidecar. "I feel weird in this thing."

"Quit your bitching." I engage the clutch, shift into gear, and lean into the turn, rounding the jury-rigged outhouse built over the sewer main in the middle of the street. The usual smell of shit isn't present. I hope the rain is sluicing away the accumulated human waste beneath it.

Main Street is dark, with clouds shrouding any moonlight. I pull into the City Hall parking lot. Someone armed with a rifle stands as if guarding its front door, which hasn't happened before. Josh uncoils from the sidecar, cursing its cramped space, and the two of us climb the steps to the front, around the sentry, and walk inside.

"What's with that?" I ask. "New security? Something you, Jill, and Kevin came up with?"

"You'll see." Josh turns on a flashlight, and we walk into the council chamber. Four or five shadows materialize, and I recognize two as patrol members. Another human lies flat on the floor.

Josh shines his flashlight on the prone figure, then reaches down and pulls a rag out of its mouth.

"Fuck! You bastards soak that thing in gasoline, or what?" The voice catches me by surprise. It sounds like that of a woman. I look closer at a face partially hidden by layers of clothing as I scratch my facial growth subconsciously. A beardless face appears.

What the hell?

Josh pushes the woman into a sitting position. Her hands are zip-tied behind her.

"Cut me loose, goddammit. I can't feel my hands anymore." Her breath has the stink of a heavy cigarette smoker.

Josh leaves her on the floor and the two of us settle into chairs nearby.

"Ain't ya gonna cut me loose?" When we don't answer, the woman coughs. "At least let me have a cig."

I'm still puzzled, but this is Josh's show. He toes the woman in the arm. "Cigarette? We haven't seen many of those in Elmhurst. You, on the other hand stink like you've been able to get all you want. You need to brush your teeth."

The woman shakes her head, and the sweatshirt hoodie falls away, revealing a porcine face and a crude butch haircut. "I said, cut me loose."

Josh waves an arm toward the back of the room and Vince, one of his patrol members, comes forward, then lays out a Tec 9 machine pistol with a fifty-round magazine on the far end of a large conference table. It's fully loaded. Several unopened packs of Winston cigarettes also appear.

"We found this on her." Josh pauses. "Alex Salazar, the Pentecostal preacher that spoke at Andres' funeral discovered her. He and his cousin were snooping around. They smelled cigarette smoke coming from the burned-out building—the old La Riata Bar that caught fire a few months ago. Hell, no one has any tobacco around here anymore. Turned out, it was her, smoking cigarettes."

I remember the place going up. It perches on the side of the hill a quarter mile south of the Lincoln City highway bridge, with a great field of view of both the Little Elm River crossing and the northern portions of Elmhurst. Someone had built a cook fire that they let get out of control. Its roof collapsed. Last time I'd checked, no one was using the building. Interesting, but there must be more to this. There is.

"She'd rigged a tent, had a backpack with plenty of MREs and water. She tried to knife the good preacher when he walked in. He's tougher than you'd think. Knocked her unconscious. He and Severo—you remember him from the Apple Street fire —turns out they're cousins, but who isn't in this burg—trussed her with some rope. Anyway, here's what else they found."

With a dramatic flourish, Vince places high dollar binoculars and a walkie talkie handset, along with extra batteries, next to the Tec 9. The radio is a Midland X Talker handset. This is quality. The X Talker has a range of nearly forty miles. I turn it on. Its battery shows a 90 percent charge. The LED lights up with a choice of twenty-two channels. The hissing noise tells me it survived the EMP. I thumb through the channels. Nothing but atmospheric noise until I get to Channel 17.

Then, "Hey, Dana, you hear me? What's the status? What are we looking at in Elmhurst? Come back."

I stare at the woman. It's hard to read facial features in the gloom, but her full cheeks and round face tell me one thing already—she's not suffering from any malnutrition.

"Your name Dana?" She glances away when I ask.

She recovers, and sneers. "Fuck you, country boy. I'm just passing through. I don't have a name. Don't know what you're talking about."

"You haven't missed any meals, have you? Stand up."

Vince pulls her to her feet.

"Cut her hands loose."

Josh looks at me quizzically but produces a clasp knife and cuts the plastic binding. Dana, if that's her name, looks toward the Tec 9.

"We're letting you get some circulation in your hands." I point my .45 at her head. "One twitch in the wrong direction, and I'll splatter your brains all over this room."

She acknowledges my threat with a nod and begins to knead her hands. Every finger has at least one ring on it. One ring in particular catches my eye.

"Dana, where'd you go to college?"

She closes her hands into fists. "Didn't. Why?"

We sit her in a chair and tell her to extend her arms on the conference table. On her pudgy middle finger, a heavy gold Texas A&M class ring glints as the flashlight rays hit it.

"Take it off."

Dana tugs on the ring and bangs it on the table. Class of 1982. Inscribed inside is the name 'John Ellis.'

"Where'd you get this?"

"Found it."

Josh points to her other hand. "Take a look at these."

Dana's pinkie and ring finger on both her hands are festooned with women's engagement and wedding sets, all with large diamonds.

"Find these too?"

Dana says nothing.

The others in the room crowd around. Josh and I exchange looks. "Dana, were any of these rings taken from people still alive? Or did you kill them first?"

"I...I didn't kill anyone." Dana is adamant about this, but a momentary pause before her denial is telling.

Josh and the others pull the rings off her fingers and gather them in a pile. They aren't gentle. Josh suddenly laughs. "Dana here, she's a cross-cultural kind of person." He shines his light on a woman's college class ring. This one is from the University of Texas.

We need information from this repugnant creature. "Dana," I begin. "I want you to look at me." She turns her away.

"No. That won't do, Dana. I want you to look me in the eyes." I grab her chin and squeeze her cheeks— hard.

"Oww. Goddamn. That hurts." Her head turns and she squints at me.

I continue, "Please tell us what's going on. We're a small town, and we think you are helping some bad folks coming our way. Am I right?"

She looks away. "I'm not telling you anything."

"Josh, where are your zip ties? Let's get Dana secured again."

She winces as her hands are re-secured.

"You people can't scare me. My folks are heading this way in a couple of days, and they'll cut me loose. Doesn't matter that I got caught."

"This is where you're wrong," I respond, glancing at Josh. He nods. We both heard 'in a couple of days.'

"If you don't cooperate with us, we..." I pause. "No, I will personally put a bullet in your gut and watch you die before that happens. I won't shoot you in the head. I will ensure that your death is a slow and painful one."

Dana puts on a tough act, but I sense she's crumbling inside. "How do I know you won't anyway?"

I look around the room. "We will lock you up. But I swear to you in front of all these people that if you help us, *and* we defend our town successfully, I will set you free when it's over."

"Okay," she mutters. She looks around as if for assurance. Several heads nod. "Can I have that cigarette now?"

Josh lights a cigarette and puts it in her mouth. It wags up and down as she talks.

"They're the Free Americans," she begins, disassociating herself from the marauders. "They've got most of Lincoln City under control. Now they're wanting to expand their territory." She takes a long pull and blows smoke at my face. "That's why they're coming this way. They've got plans, they say, to move onto other cities, but can't go south down the Interstate. The Mexican gangs and cartels got Escondido and other cities near the border sewed up tight. This town is in the way to other parts. Just a pimple on the ass of progress." She effects a belligerent pose. They've got enough people and guns to blow this place off the map."

"Why are *you* here?"

"They gave me that radio." She nods toward the end of the conference table. "Told me to check this place out. Tell them if there's any danger."

"Why you?" Josh asks.

She shrugs. "Guess they needed someone they could trust. That knew about Elmhurst."

I'm puzzled, and Dana sees it. "Used to live here until about five years ago." She gives an address I recognize on a familiar street. "'Course, I wasn't supposed to get caught."

Josh asks, "Why are they worried about Elmhurst?"

Dana coughs, takes another draw on the cigarette. "They got vehicles. Trucks, some jeeps, some homemade armored cars. Gotta get past that river so they can keep going." She pulls on the cigarette, and a half-inch of embers appears. "Word is the old U.S. of A. has got itself an army of some kind headed into the state. Free Americans may not stay free, or alive, if that army shows itself strong enough to take back Lincoln City."

An hour later, we know what she knows, I hope.

"Oh, one more thing, Dana. If any of what you've told us that proves false, all bets are off."

Dana asks for another cigarette. Josh sticks another on in her mouth and lights it. After another long draw she asks, "How am I gonna have any control over that?" She expels smoke as she whines.

I ignore her question.

If Dana is telling the truth, we've got at most three days before Elmhurst will be attacked by a polyglot group which dubs itself the "Free Americans." I have no idea what the hell that title has to do with a gang of murderous scavengers.

We lead her out into the rain and walk her the two blocks to the County Jail. Sheriff Leonard Baird's staff has long since ceased to exist, but his jail is usable. The cells are empty, so Josh selects one far away from the exits.

"Jesus Christ! It's as cold as a witch's tit in here. I'll freeze to death. And I can't see a damned thing."

Three pieces of tow chain, and three Master locks ensure that, without help, Dana's not going anywhere. We toss in a book of paper matches and a few cigarettes—the rest have already been shared out—and promise some blankets.

Out of Dana's hearing, I whisper to Josh, "Let's check this place out."

He follows as I wander out of the jail area and into the various offices.

Keeping my voice down, I point to the steel reinforced inside doors and small exterior windows. "Would this be better to defend than City Hall, or even the Lee County Courthouse?" It's a rhetorical question. I already know it is.

Josh nods. "Haven't thought about it, but yeah." He pauses. "Only problem is, if we end up having to defend a strongpoint, what are the bad guys going to be doing to Elmhurst? I mean, if I was them, I'd tear the town up and ignore us."

"If we get to that point, I suspect we'll just be saving our own skins, and maybe not have a choice."

As we slosh back to City Hall, Josh asks, "I guess I can see not trusting her with that radio, even with a gun to her head."

"Josh, I'm not sure I'm doing the right thing there. Someone's got to suspect she's been caught."

"Maybe not," he replies. "She'd steal the pennies off a dead man's eyes. For all they know, maybe she just kept heading south."

"Hope so. We're flying by the seat of our pants."

"What are we going to do with her, Dalton?"

"Let's see how this plays out before we decide."

He glances over at me as we climb the steps at the City Hall. "She's done some bad stuff, Dalton."

"Yep."

We both know what needs doing.

The word is out that we are about to be attacked. As dim daylight pierces the rainclouds, women and men trickle into City Hall. Bundled against the weather, most are not recognizable. Some tote shotguns, others carry rifles. A few have pistols and knives under jackets and raincoats. Patrol members ask the people to stack weapons in the foyer. There's not going to be enough room in the council chamber as it is.

The council chamber has no outside windows, and quickly becomes redolent with unwashed bodies and wet wool. Kevin and Jill have placed two Coleman lanterns on the conference table. Their light and the occasional flashlight flickers off those adjusting clothing or finding a place to stand or sit.

Finally, the influx trickles to a stop. I introduce Kevin, Jill, and Josh, then thank the people for coming. "Elmhurst is in danger of being attacked. You all know or suspect that, or you wouldn't be here this morning. I doubt if any of you trotted down here in the rain just for fun."

This gets a few nervous titters of laughter.

I explain about guarding the bridges into town, about the need to create observation posts on the Lincoln City side of Little Elm River, about the "Free Americans" and its intention to move south out of the capital. Mostly, I emphasize the need to defend Elmhurst. After twenty minutes of talking, I open it up for questions.

Someone asks the about how well armed our enemy is. My answer is that we don't know. Someone asks about the Free Americans group makeup. I expand on what Dana's given us.

"From what we understand, this group is a mishmash of bikers, anti-government survivalists, gang bangers, etc." The council chamber is filled with a mix of Hispanics, Anglos and Blacks. "These folks are killers and rapists, and they come in all sizes and colors."

Perhaps I imagine it, but some appear relieved they won't be put in the position of defending against one ethnicity. I know I am.

"How long do we have to hold out?" yells a woman. The question stirs the crowd. No one has said it, but they can't help but wonder whether what we are doing is an exercise in futility.

Bob Medrano appears in the council chamber doorway. He still looks spooky but seems to be holding it together. A voice behind him shouts, "I can answer that." Anson Gutierrez gently pushes around Medrano. "The United States armed forces have moved into our state. They are northeast of Lincoln City about two hundred miles."

Several whoops and a smattering of applause echo in the room.

Someone asks, "When will they get here?"

"I'm a HAM operator, as most of you know," Anson describes what he's heard. It is hopeful, but vague. He fields questions like a professional baseball player. This is a side I've never seen before. I catch myself grinning with pride at Anson's performance.

After an hour, everyone is restless, so I finish up. "You are here because you're willing to fight. If that's not the case, leave now. Go home to your families and children. It won't be held against you. This is serious."

I pause. No one moves. A smartass in the back hollers, "This is just like the Alamo. Ole Dalton's like William Barrett Travis. He's drawn his line in the sand and no one's stepped over it! Let's hope we don't go the way those poor bastards did."

More laughter. Then we ask everyone to step into the foyer. We need to collect names, determine who has been in the military, who's a hunter. We'll make assignments on experience and weaponry.

The crowd moves into the foyer. Salazar, the preacher, and his cousin Severo, fist bump me. Fred Aston, Jill's husband, shakes my hand as he limps past me. Something in my throat catches, and I blink away tears.

The room thins out. Billy Kaufman walks by, followed closely by someone smaller. As Billy shakes my hand, the figure, oddly familiar, pushes past him. I get a glimpse of red hair under a hoodie.

"Gail!"

She turns. "You weren't supposed to see me, Dalton."

Shit. "Where's Josefina? Why are you here? You can't be here." It comes out in a rush. I pull her back into the near-empty council chamber.

"I told her you wouldn't like it." Billy apologizes. "But she's determined to help."

I grab her shoulders. I am afraid like I've never been afraid before. "You can't, Gail. You just can't. You've got a child to take care of."

Gail pushes back the hoodie and shoves me with both hands. "So do you, Dalton! So do you! Momma is taking care of Josie right now. Quit worrying about it." She is now toe to toe with me. "You don't control my life. You tried while we were married, and it didn't work. It won't work now. We've got a town to defend, Dalton. I intend to pull my weight." She is breathing fire. "Now get the hell out of my way. I have to get my assignment." She stabs a finger into my chest. "Just." Stab. "Like." Stab. "Everyone." Stab. "Else."

And walks out.

Chapter Thirty-Eight

KEVIN CLIMBS IN THE BMW'S SIDECAR AND THE TWO OF US CROSS the main highway bridge over Little Elm River. A few souls walk south from Lincoln City. Some wave or cup their hands to show their need for food. Some shy away from the motorcycle's engine noise. Most seem too miserable to pay any attention to the rare sight of a functioning motorized vehicle as it passes them the other way. All are pitiful.

Hoping for recent information from Lincoln City, I wave down a man and woman, and stop. The woman has a ragged plastic poncho draped over her and carries a wadded-up blanket. As we get nearer, I see the blanket swaddles an infant.

"Excuse us," I begin. The man and woman eye us cautiously. They have no reason to trust anyone. I introduce myself and Kevin. "We're from Elmhurst, just over the bridge. Can you tell us what's going on in Lincoln City?"

"It's bad," the man says. "The place is a war zone." He points to the woman and child. "We were expecting a baby. Afraid to travel before our little girl was born. My wife and I almost waited too long to leave. We're able to avoid the gangs and get out last night. I'm not sure how."

As he speaks, the woman seems about to collapse. Her baby makes a weak mewling sound.

"She's hungry, mister," the woman says. "And dirty. And cold. We just need to keep going." She stares at me. "We've got to get out of this rain so I can try to nurse her."

Josefina is blessed with safety, warmth, and shelter. but this child has none of that.

Kevin and I can't stop what we need to do, but maybe I can help. I pull my small notepad out of my breast pocket. Kevin removes his hat and uses it as a shield. I manage to scribble a note without the paper getting wet. "Give this to the first person you see in Elmhurst," I say. "God bless you."

The woman tucks my note inside her bosom, and they trudge southward.

Kevin has a Motorola radio headset on, and continuously talks and listens as we continue to leave the small family behind. I check the motorcycle's odometer. Hopefully, radio's specs are correct about its range of three miles.

A mile past the bridge, the highway dips slightly and Kevin taps me furiously. I stop the BMW as he shouts, "We had good contact 'til that dip."

Careful not to slide off the wet road surface, I turn around and slowly move back toward Elmhurst. Less than a quarter of a mile later, Kevin taps for me to stop. "Good contact. They can hear me and they're coming in loud and clear."

Despite the rain, there's good visibility here toward Lincoln City. This is farm and ranch land, mostly level ground, with few trees. Good views north, but little cover or concealment.

Kevin points a few hundred yards to the east. "That stand of trees. Let's see if the radio'll transmit and receive from there."

We leave the BMW on the road, unstaple a barbed wire fence with pliers, and slog through mud and wet grass. Moments later we are in a copse of live oaks. Kevin keys the mic, mutters something, and then gives me a thumbs

up. This location will have to do. We return to the motorcycle with as much haste as we can muster. I unlatch a
pannier and remove a red towel. I tie it to a fencepost to
mark the location. We'll put one group of lookouts in the
oak trees.

"I sure hope whoever we put out here can make it back
across the bridge before getting cut off," Kevin says.

"Or get themselves killed," I respond. "*I sure hope we get
the explosives set and blow the bridge before we have to put
someone out here.*" I wonder where George Hixson and his
bombs are now.

I get my answer as we approach the bridge over Little Elm
River. The city's large stake truck sits in the middle of the
highway on the Elmhurst side. As I carefully downshift, Jill
steps down from the cab. She carries an AR15 at the ready.

The motorcycle idles a few yards from her. In the rain, it's
hard to read her facial expression. I glance at her weapon,
hoping it's safetied. I kill the bike's engine.

Kevin climbs out of the sidecar and mutters, "Oh, shit. I'd
better get out of the line of fire."

Ha Ha.

He steps to the edge of the bridge and leans over the
guardrail. I want to look too but need to give Jill some
respectful attention. Our recent truce is fragile.

"Hey, wet enough for you guys?" My question isn't a great
way to ease the tension. In fact, it sounds ridiculous.

She shows a smile. It looks more like a grimace. "Soaked to
the bone, Dalton. And freezing my butt off."

I pause, relieved by the response. "How's it going?"

"We've just started. I don't know how long this one will
take, but your explosives guy said you wanted this bridge
rigged first."

Returning to the BMW, Kevin says, "There's a bunch of fifty-
five-gallon oil drums sitting near the abutment. I haven't met

George Hixson. Is he a weird scientist looking white guy? That fool's not wearing any rain hat. What a dumbass."

I can't help but laugh. Kevin's description is apt. "Yeah. What else you see?"

"Hell, Dalton. I'm not holding you hostage," Jill says. "I'd like to check out what's going on too." She turns to Kevin. "You mind guarding the truck? We'll swap out."

Kevin shrugs and Jill hands him the AR15. She and I step down the slope to the concrete abutment. Grass uprooted by the human traffic has turned the path muddy and slick. Halfway down, my feet come out from under me.

"Shit!" Now I'm soaked to the skin and covered in muck.

Jill erupts in laughter. "Serves you right for being an a-hole."

I bite my tongue, wipe my hands through wet grass to remove some of the mud, and walk underneath the bridge. Five drums butted up end to end, are secured by nylon ropes onto the narrow shelf at the top of the abutment's concrete slope, directly under and perpendicular to the bridge's beams. They extend across its width, but don't jut out onto the concrete wingwalls.

"Like what you see?" Hixson cackles.

"I'm not sure what I see, George."

Hixson points to five more oil drums. "We'll roll three more up there and tie 'em tight with the others."

"Are those lines the safety fuses?" I ask. Strands of red-colored cord loop between the barrels.

"Hell no, son. That red stuff is Primacord. Detonation cord. It ignites so fast it acts as an explosive. A few wraps around a tree and set it off —blows the tree apart. Great for land clearing. No, the safety fuse is that thing." He points to one strand of black cord running from underneath the bridge embankment where it is tied off to a tree.

"Safety fuse is waterproof. It's got a rate of burn of…" He mentions centimeters per second. I do a quick calculation.

"So, when that safety fuse is lit, it'll take about, what, a minute to get to the explosive?"

"About right." Hixson nods his approval. "Of course, someone has to have the balls—figuratively speaking only, ma'am—to light the fuse. Hope no one's shooting at whoever you get to do it. Hope whoever you get to do it can run like hell."

Me too.

"Are these things prepped with dynamite and the blasting caps already?" Muscling around the volatile mix spooks me.

"No blasting caps yet, Dalton. I may be crazy but I'm not stupid. I'll get them all in place, then prime the whole bunch." The drums' tops have been reattached with wraps of gray duct tape, and three inches of dynamite protrude from each bung, which is also wrapped in duct tape. He points to spacing between the drums. "I've rigged them so I can reach where I need to."

Jill interjects. "You said three. That's makes eight. What about the other two drums?"

"Hah! You noticed. Obviously, you are smarter than Dalton, and prettier too, not that that he is much to compare to." He turns and walks toward the river, waving at us to follow. He pats the concrete on a support pillar.

"This is called a pier. One we'll set here, and the other one over there." He points to the downriver pier. "Sandbag 'em—if we have time—to force the explosive power inward. Should take this Elmhurst side of the bridge down." He reaches inside his raincoat and pulls out a notepad. "These figures tell me, if I've calculated right, that this arrangement should blow this span to hell and back."

Little Elm River, out of its banks, is rising fast. George stuffs the calculations back inside of his raincoat, then turns back toward the efforts at the embankment. The wind swirls and water pouring down from the road surface is blown onto his head.

"Shit and damn!" Hixson shakes the water from his hair and beard.

"Do you have a rain hat?" Jill asks. "You look miserable."

"Can't see to help with that damned thing over my head." He walks back toward the embankment and begins barking orders. Pancho and Lefty have recruited five other men. They tip a barrel onto its side and begin inching it up the concrete. The process is painful to watch. Six inches. Reposition. Six more inches. Hold. George screams encouragement as he uses a huge pry bar as a crude chock at the end of each push upward. I squeeze in with the men and somehow, another barrel of high explosives is anchored.

Jill and I return to the road surface and Kevin disappears underneath the bridge. Jill climbs into the truck cab and motions for me to join her. "Get out of the rain for a minute."

There's so much to be done, and I'm not comfortable being in close quarters with Jill, but a respite from the wet and cold overcomes my reluctance. I slam the door behind me. In minutes, the windows fog up from our body heat and humidity. I crank down the passenger side window. A gust of wind blows rain in, and I roll it back up.

"Cold and miserable out there."

"Yes, it is." She pauses, then says softly, "That was a nice thing you did a few minutes ago."

"Huh?" I don't get what she's talking about.

"The couple with the baby. We'd just pulled up. The woman showed me your note."

"Oh, yeah." I mutter. "Were you able to point them in the right direction?"

"Yes. Told her to keep the note. Gave her the address and told her to ask Doctor Randhawa for some baby formula. I know he's got some stashed for extreme cases. And I think that little baby qualifies."

"Didn't know what to expect. The baby….Well, reminded me of Josefina, I guess."

Jill turns toward me. "You aren't as hard as you try to make out, neighbor." She touches the sleeve of my coat. I want to reach over and take her hand, and just hold it. I don't, instead remaining motionless.

Jill's hand retreats, she coughs, and puts her hands on the steering wheel. The moment has opened the door to my memories of her desirability. And like that, it's over with.

I'm suddenly overcome with exhaustion. My eyes close in a blink. Suddenly, Jill shakes me awake.

"Hey, Dalton. Wake up!"

"Huh? Sorry. Did I go to sleep?"

"Duh. How much sleep have you had?"

I try to concentrate, but the pieces aren't coming together. Finally, I shrug. "Gotta get out of this cab. Too warm." I push the door open and nearly fall to the street.

Kevin appears and he and Jill shake their heads. No doubt it's something about me. I crawl onto the motorcycle, kick the engine over, and motion for Kevin to come on. He waves me off, rubs his butt to show it's sore, points to me and makes the sleeping gesture with his cheek tilted onto his two hands. No time.

The rain has eased into a slow drizzle. A cold fog encompasses everything, dropping visibility to less than a hundred yards. Elmhurst is suddenly cocooned in silence. We've put out listening posts on the far side of Little Elm River, but with crappy visibility and the fog muffling most sound, there's the possibility that whoever is manning them will be surprised and not be able to warn Elmhurst before being taken out.

No one has bitched about pulling a shift across the river, and Kevin's using one of our ATVs to run the roads entering Elmhurst from the north. Besides relaying people to our outposts, he is probably going further north. Granted, using a Motorola radio to relay to our lookouts can extend the distance for early warnings, but it's not worth it. By doing so, he's potentially in even more danger than anyone. An ATV is noisy. He's chancing getting his head blown off. I just chewed his ass out for doing this, and he promised he won't do it anymore. I don't believe him.

Do we blow the bridges before we know it is necessary? Take the chance that any assistance coming from outside the state won't have access to our little town? Or do we just do it, and quit worrying? It's a crap shoot.

Anson Gutierrez is my go-to guy. Beside his sometimes-faltering HAM power sources and equipment, we've entrusted him with the Midland X Talker taken off Dana the gang banger. We can't move Anson or his equipment, so I swing by his house way too often for updates.

"Anything new?"

"Anson, how are you? Can I get you anything? No, Dalton, but thanks for asking." He points toward the extra bedroom. "Those are normal salutations, Dalton." He snorts, "I'm busy, and your very weird buddy, Medrano, snores like a freight train. So fuck you and the horse you rode in on."

I ignore the sarcasm and feel a twinge of sympathy. Bob Medrano does snore very loudly. No way in hell could I sleep in the same house with that racket.

"When'd he show back up?" I did not notice Bob the last time I checked in with Anson.

"Dalton, the guy's almost like the walking dead. He'll be okay one minute, then put on his raincoat and disappear. Next thing you know, he's back and asleep. Only way I know he's back is when the snoring starts again."

"It'll get better."

My trite and ridiculous comment gets another snort of disapproval.

"Anyway, what have you heard?"

"Nothing on the HAM, except more reports from the northeast part of the state about U.S. Army moving this way. No specifics as to how far, if at all, the Army has moved since we got the reports a couple of days ago. Some chatter on that Midland. Just guessing but seems like it's from a stationary location inside Lincoln City. That Midland does have a nice range to it. Talk about weather slowing 'things' down—whatever 'things' are. And, seems someone is wondering where their lookout is. Didn't mention any names or locations, but a good guess is that woman you have locked up."

"Nothing else?"

Anson gives me an exasperated look. "Dalton, you think I'm holding out on you. For Christ's sake, you and everyone else need to give me a fucking break." He's on a roll. "Or you come man these radios. My butt is sore."

I mutter an apology and leave. I've worn out my welcome. It's time for someone else to check in with Anson.

I step back into the rain and onto my BMW. The engine kicks over. The warmth from the engine against my legs and the patter of rain against my helmet and raincoat are hypnotic. I'm falling asleep on a damned motorcycle in a cold rainstorm. Keith's suggestion suddenly is a mandate. I must take time to sleep.

My first thought is to check on Bertha, Billy and, especially,

Josefina. But that entails more effort than I can muster up. I opt instead for the privacy of my own bedroom. I pull into my garage and enter the house's back door. It's not barricaded, which means Josh is with his family. He, Elsie and their two kids huddle under several blankets. David and Sarah giggle as they sing nonsense songs. The flickering candlelight casts them as angelic.

"Come join us for a minute, Dalton," Elsie gestures toward a chair. "Know you guys are crazy busy, but a little family time will do you good."

I thank her but beg off and slog up the stairs to my bedroom. Besides, I can't for the life of me come up with a nonsense song that doesn't contain foul language.

Moments later it seems, Elsie yells, "Hey, Dalton! Don't know how long you want to sleep, but thought I'd better wake you up."

"Thanks," I yell down the stairs, and hurriedly dress.

At the bottom of the stairs I ask, "Where's Josh?"

"He's been gone for a couple of hours." Elsie grasps my arm. "I've only got one husband, Dalton. Please. Please. You all be careful." She suddenly hugs me. "God bless you."

Stunned, I step out the back door.

I go east on Main Street, pass City Hall and, two blocks later, slow at the courthouse square. I turn into the parking area in front of the Sheriff's Office, and stop to check on our prisoner. I pull open the front door, step into the darkness, and yelp loudly. Something hard and round is pushing against my neck.

"What the hell?" I manage to squeak out.

Two flashlights snap on and I recognized Kevin's Black Panther squad members, Robert and Andrea.

They offer quick apologies. "Sorry, sir. We've been told to guard this place."

"Well, you scared the living shit out of me," I exclaim. "Kevin put you guys here?"

Robert responds, "Him and Josh said we need to make sure no unauthorized person gets in, and no one messes with the prisoner."

Andrea's eye roll is evident, even in the near darkness. "I'd like to 'mess' with that pig."

"She behaving?"

Andrea shakes her head. "She's a nasty one, but'll turn on what she calls charm trying to get us to unlock her cell."

Robert chimes in. "And we don't have the key. But she won't shut up."

The two escort me back to the cellblock. Dana lies on the cell's steel bed. It's cold, damp, and there's no mattress to guard against the metal. She sings and hums a song I don't recognize but stops when the flashlight beams play over her.

"Hey, it's the big shot! You come to let me out?" She steps to the cell door.

"No." The cell reeks of urine. Dana's pissed in a corner.

"No bucket to piss or shit in. No mattress. No blanket. What about that, what'chacall it, Geneva Convention? Please, can you make this a little more decent?" Her voice takes on a gentle, pleading tone.

I turn, and with Robert and Andrea, walk toward the office area. Dana's charm offensive ends quickly. "Come back here you motherfuckers!!! Let me out, or I'll rip your heads off and shit down your throats!" She beats on the cell door with her fists.

"Wow," is all that Robert can muster up.

"Yeah," I reply. "Wow."

No one is present at the Pederson Road's rickety bridge, but tire tracks and footprints say Hixson's merry band has been here. I dismount. A black strand of safety fuse leads to a lone tree, about fifty feet from the bridge, where it is tied off. There are large pecan trees further on, which would provide a whole lot more protection. The fuse would have to burn longer, but still… If the Lincoln City Bridge fuse will take about a minute, then this one will be about twenty seconds. Someone with balls and nimble feet will be needed here, too. I carefully work my way under the bridge, following the safety fuse. The river is a long way down, and one misstep…Somehow three oil drums have been tucked under the Elmhurst side. Red Primacord peeks out from between them. The contraption looks downright evil.

Both the main bridge and Pederson Road's bridge appear to be ready to be blown up.

The rain stops as I ride toward Hixson Lane. I'm not sure why, but George has saved his namesake bridge for last. Flash-light beams flicker back and forth in the gloom of late after-noon. Several voices, but mostly George Hixson's, echo from underneath the bridge, overcoming Little Elm's angry torrent of noise.

"Move that Goddamned drum further up, you lazy bastards!"

"Fuck you, you white-assed motherfucker!"

Oh, shit.

I crawl under the bridge abutment. Pancho and George Hixson are in a stare-off. George may be the mad scientist, but Pancho is capable of pounding sand up George's butt. Lefty and five others stare, as if hoping for something to happen.

"Hey!"

George breaks the stare first. "What, Dalton? You taking up for this lazy Mex?"

"Shut up, George. Both of you back off." I pull Pancho away. "What's going on?"

Pancho responds while stabbing a finger toward George's

chest, "I'm tired of this *bolillo* barking orders. We're all doing the best we can. I'm going to kill this old bastard."

Everyone is on the ragged edge. I step between them. "Pancho, everyone knows—including George—that we can't get this done without you." I turn to George. "Don't we?"

Surprisingly, George nods in agreement. "Yeah, the sumbitch is working his ass off." He pauses. "Sorry, Pancho. You're all right."

Pancho grins, obviously surprised by the concession.

"For a Mexican."

Before Pancho can flare up again, George abruptly reaches over and embraces him.

Oh, wow. Never seen that before.

Pancho looks around, then returns the *abrazo*. "Okay, you *pinche gringo*. Let's get this thing done."

Three oil drums have been secured under the bridge's Elmhurst-side abutment. Another one is on its side, ready to be shoved and rolled upward to be yoked with them.

Everyone sits in the relative dryness of the bridge's shadow, taking a breather. I turn to George. "Four drums here, three at Pederson, ten on the main bridge. That's seventeen. That's all we made. Is it going to be enough?"

George cackles. "It's going to be fun to find out, won't it?"

"Not really, George. I don't think I'd trust your calculations if you were remotely normal, and not some weird mad scientist."

He glares. Uh oh. I've gone too far. I now expect he will make me and by extension, Elmhurst, pay for my mouthiness. Instead, George turns his flashlight on again and says, "One more barrel to roll. Then we can take a break."

With groans, Pancho and three of the men position the drum for rolling upward and into place. Two others man ropes, ready to tie it into place. I join the four on the drum and we begin the process. George, like the lead of gandy dancers, begins a cadence for rolling, resting, re-securing, and repeating the process.

We reach the top of the abutment—it is not as high as the main bridge's—and the nylon ropes hold it in place as it is lashed in. George leans an aluminum ladder against the concrete, climbs to the explosives' location, and begins the arming process. Blasting caps, Primacord, and finally, safety fuse. Several of us shine flashlights as George finishes up at the oil drums.

I remember George hadn't placed blasting caps at the Lincoln City bridge explosives earlier and ask him about it.

"The other two bridges are ready to blow, now, Dalton. Set the caps after I've gotten everyone a safe distance away. Wanted to make sure everyone is safe, you see?"

I look at his box of blasting caps. "What? You arming this thing now with us around now, George?"

"Getting dark."

So much for his safety concerns for the seven of us.

"Where you going to be tonight, George?" I ask.

Hixson tossed down the safety fuse roll, moves a leg onto the ladder's next rung down. And misses.

Before anyone can react, he desperately grabs for the ladder as he falls backwards. He lands awkwardly in the darkness.

"Well, shit," he mutters.

Relieved, we reach to pick him up. Someone shines a flash-light on George's face. It is ashen under his heavy beard. His eyes roll back in his head as he slips into unconsciousness.

Pancho shines his flashlight downward. George's right leg has an unnatural bend it, between the knee and hip. "Oh, shit, Dalton."

Oh shit is right.

Chapter Thirty-Nine

As I crouch at George's feet, Pancho and Lefty squat and make a two-handed seat, then lift George off the dirt. His head lolls and he grunts in pain. His leg lies grotesquely twisted. I lose my grip and his foot hits the ground. I feel and hear bone rubbing on bone. *Christ!* I choke back the gorge in my throat.

George's eyes flare open and seem to focus on my face accusingly. He makes an almost silent scream of pain, and then his eyes flutter as he lapses back into unconsciousness.

The embankment is muddy, slick, and steep.

"We've got to figure a way to get him up to the truck," I say. The words sound ridiculous even to me. "Suggestions, anyone?"

One of the men clambers up the hill and returns with a filthy quilt. He pulls off his poncho and lays it and the quilt on the ground at the bottom of the embankment. "Put him on this and we'll pull him up the hill."

The seven of us try to keep George's lower body somewhat stable as we scramble up the muddy embankment to the road surface, my raincoat now a cradle for the damaged limb as we slither upward. Lefty and the crew jump in the bed of the stake truck and crowd around George. Pancho crawls into the cab, gets behind the wheel and promises he'll drive as carefully as possible. I race ahead on the BMW.

Doctor Randhawa comes out of his house with a flashlight. He barks something at his wife and commands us to bring George inside. Once inside the front door, he guides George's unconscious form onto the kitchen table. "Put him here." Mrs. Randhawa has cleared its surface. George groans, and then begins to vomit uncontrollably.

"It's the pain," the doctor says. He produces scissors and we cut George's pants and long johns off. "Femur broken." The break is a few inches above the knee. The upper part of the femur bulges just below the surface of the skin. A sliver of the lower portion has pierced the surface, its whiteness obscured by blood and tissue.

"Mary Mother of God," exclaims Pancho.

"Yes," Doctor Randhawa says. "Her help is needed here. This is called an open fracture. It is very serious." A staccato burst of Hindi with his wife and soon she returns to the room with rags, alcohol, and a doctor's bag. Mrs. Randhawa uses a Q-tip and cleans the wound, paying attention to the bone fragment. She pulls small cloth fibers from the wound. Every time she touches the bone, he moans. Pancho's and Lefty's act like a Greek chorus, gasping, and muttering, mostly in Spanish.

"Jagir, my dear," Mrs. Randhawa says, still concentrating on wound clearing, "please tell these good people to shut the fuck up. They are most distracting."

Wow. That's a new one.

The chorus of sighs groans and *madre mios* immediately stops.

"There are nine of us here," the doctor states after a nod from his wife. "We have no pain medicine. I will give you instructions on what to do. If I am blessed by the Holy Mother of your God, this man's bones will be put together without a mishap."

He pauses. I can't help but ask, "And if not?"

"We will tear open blood vessels, possibly an artery. Or damage the tissue. Or not be able to join the bones. Without x-ray, it is, as you Americans say, a crap shoot."

I'm reliving Andres Lujan's death on this same table. Perhaps acknowledging it, I receive a gentle pat on the shoulder. "We have the opportunity to do better this time, Dalton." *Dole-tun.*

Ten minutes of instructions and I am holding onto a rope tied to George Hixson's ankle. Four men hold George under his armpits, and Pancho and Lefty drape themselves over his abdomen.

"Do only as I tell you. Nothing more and nothing less," Doctor Randhawa says, as he and his wife hover over the open break. "Ready?"

Shit no, I'm not ready. Nor is anyone else in the room.

"Begin to pull, Dalton."

George's body begins to thrash.

"Hold this man down, damn you!" This from Mrs. Randhawa.

"Pull. Pull. Hold," the doctor says. Whatever he is doing to George's leg isn't gentle. The two Randhawas chatter in Hindi, and then suddenly the doctor says, "Very slightly ease your tension on the rope, Dalton."

The instruction comes as a relief. My hands are sweating so badly from the tension I am about to lose my grip. Doctor Randhawa pushes on George's leg above the knee. George's face is so white it reflects the dim lantern light. He is completely unconscious. Cocked to one side, a frothy drool seeps from his mouth.

Mrs. Randhawa asks, "Where does this man live? Does he have help?"

Shit no, lady. No one can take more than five minutes of the grouchy bastard. "He has no one. He doesn't live in town."

We carry George into the den. A foam mattress is produced from somewhere. Mrs. Randhawa speaks to the group. "Someone will need to assist us until you can figure out what to do with him."

Pancho assigns two of his helpers. They make no complaints about staying out of the rain and in the relative warmth of the doctor's home. I wonder what they'll think once George returns to consciousness and pain.

As I don my raincoat, Doctor Randhawa quietly says, "Dalton, I can sadly assure you that unless your friend receives IV antibiotics, his wound will become infected."

I shake his hand, nod, and step out into the darkness.

───────

I follow the truck to City Hall. The sky is pitch black. The rain has resumed as a light mist. We tromp inside. Jill is huddled under a blanket, her head encased in a Motorola headset. She speaks to someone, nods, then makes notes. Pancho, Lefty and their remaining crew members trudge into the council chamber, and plop down in chairs or the carpet.

Josh and Billy drive up in an ATV. They nod brief greetings barely visible in the gloom, then slump into chairs. Josh holds the Midland Talker.

"We heard about Hixson," Jill says.

Josh asks, "How bad is it?"

"Bad," I reply. "But maybe not Andres bad."

"Good. Not sure we can deal with another like that."

I want to change the subject. "Good thinking, putting people at the jail."

To my unasked question Jill responds, "We've got people out across all three bridges. Three people per location, all armed. All the radios work." She stops, then says, "Thanks" into her headset. She writes something down and turns back to me. "That's Kevin. He's in the other ATV, going back and forth. Everyone's on a four-hour shift."

I nod. "Who's out there now?"

She rattles off three names for Hixson Lane, three more at Pederson Road, two north of the main highway bridge.

"You said three. Who did you miss?"

"Gail. Gail Kaufman."

Aw, damn, damn, damn. I know better than to berate Jill. "Let me guess. She created holy hell until you agreed to use her, didn't she?"

Jill pulls the blanket closer. "All I can say, Dalton, is that you seem to like bitchy women."

"I notice you used plural 'women.'"

Which gets a smirk.

Billy looks at the floor. "I couldn't stop her, Dalton. She says she'll pull her weight."

"Like taking care of an infant isn't pulling her weight? Or taking care of her mom? What the hell, Billy?"

"Billy isn't at fault here," Josh says quietly. "We're all busting our asses. He and I've been taking our lookouts and making sure the bridges are manned. You need to lay off."

"Sorry. I apologize." Josh's rebuke hurts, as does the pain on Billy's face, but that's the best I can manage. "Thanks for everything." I just want to find a warm place to curl up and sleep. I walk toward the Council Chamber. Maybe there's some room on the floor. What seems like moments later, Jill shakes me awake as she talks on the headset's mic.

"What?"

She snaps her fingers and motions me to follow her.

Woozily, I stand and look around. Everyone else in the Chamber is still sound asleep.

"Where are they now?" Jill asks someone, then nods. "On the way." She stands. "Let's take your motorcycle. I'll fill you in. We need to get to the main bridge ASAP."

I start the BMW as Jill shouts, "Kevin just roared by the lookouts. Didn't even try to pick 'em up. Told me there was just no time. Gail's got the headset. They've spotted movement."

"That SOB! He left three people behind! What about the other bridges? Any word on those?"

"Nothing. Everything quiet, except for distant sounds of engines that must be from the Lincoln City highway."

"Shit and damn." I return to the Council Chamber and scream for everyone to load up. "And make damned sure you've got your weapons with you. Meet us at the highway bridge."

In minutes, Jill and I are at the south end of the highway bridge over Little Elm River. The truck and Josh's ATV beat us to the bridge. The whine of an ATV's engine indicates Kevin's approach. He's driving fast. Too fast for the wet surface. As the ATVs headlights hit us, he pulls up.

"We've got company coming, and fast. We've got to blow this bridge."

I start to say something about Gail and the two other look-outs. Kevin grabs my arm, puts his mouth close to my ear and says, "If I'd tried to stop, they would have killed me and taken the ATV. If I'd even slowed down, they'd have figured out where Gail and the others are hidden." There is urgency in his voice. Kevin's look is one asking me to understand reality.

I nod. "You had no choice, my friend."

And he didn't. I remember our trek to the copse of trees and back through the pasture. Unless Gail and the other lookouts had left their hiding spot and been waiting to be picked up, which they weren't.

As if reading my mind, Jill hands me the Motorola headset. "She wants to talk to you."

I don the headset. "Gail?"

"Dalton, blow the bridge. There are a lot of vehicles and people heading to Elmhurst. They're at a walking pace but will hit you within twenty minutes."

"What about you, Gail? Where are you?"

"We're still in the woods and haven't been spotted. I don't think we will be."

"Is there any way you can get back across the bridge before they get here?" I know the answer but am groping for hope.

"No way, Jose." She pauses. "Blow the bridge, Dalton."

"I can't." I look at Billy. I want to hand him the mic so he can talk sense to his sister, but he shakes his head, pulls back the charging handle on his AR15 as if to ensure it's loaded. No help there.

"Blow the fucking bridge, Dalton! Try to keep the Pederson Road bridge intact. I think we can cut cross-country." She mentions properties adjoining the Kaufman farm. "It's getting light, but don't forget, I grew up around these parts."

Jill has a look on her face that tells me she knows what is going through my mind. After a few seconds of silence, Gail's voice comes through the headset.

"Dalton, I'm signing off for now. We've got to skedaddle. Don't worry about us. Just do what needs doing."

I key the mic and get nothing.

I bury my face in my hands. I can't protect Gail. She may be captured, maybe killed. I look at Jill, dimly lit by the dawn, as if she has a solution.

"I'm sorry, Dalton. I am so sorry."

Bob Medrano appears, holding an AR15. I've forgotten about him and his presence jars me. He breaks into my anguish. "Hey, my friend. I hear motors. We gonna try to keep 'em from crossing?"

A quick glance at our small armed group confirms to me how pathetic we look. Bob's not confided in anyone about what happened to his wife and son. "Those people." I point north. "They get to Elmhurst, it's going to be awful, isn't it?"

His eyes well up with tears, but he says nothing. He doesn't need to.

"Pull everyone back." I don't have any idea what the blast area will be. That is, if the explosive charges work at all. "Get back at least to the wall at La Riata."

Pancho says something to Lefty and the others. They just stand there.

"NOW!"

Jill asks, "What about you? Can you make it back before this blows?"

I pat the BMW. "I sure as hell hope so."

Medrano says, "I'll cover you."

Josh interrupts. "Medrano, I'll stay with Dalton."

"Not this time. This is something I need to do."

I shrug. Medrano's family is dead, and maybe he needs this more than Josh does. There's no gunfire, yet, but I don't argue with him. Josh hands the Midland X Talker to Jill and explains. "Got it from Anson. Figured we'd need it closer to hand than at his house."

He leaves in the ATV, enroute to the Pederson Road bridge and the small group of defenders there. My gut twists: I should be heading there to help find Gail. I almost say as much, but Josh is already walking away.

People scurry into the back of the stake truck, or cling to Kevin's ATV as the vehicles move back from the bridge.

Moments later, Medrano and I are at the tree where the safety fuse is tied. I feel around in the layers of clothing and nearly panic when I can't find the butane fire starter used to start charcoal barbecue briquettes.

"What?" he asks.

"Can't find the lighter."

"Dalton." He shakes me. "Dalton. Take a deep breath."

Nodding, I do as he tells me. And find the lighter stuck in an outside coat pocket.

"Whew. Thanks." I untie the fuse and hand the end to Bob. "You ready to run like hell?"

He shields the fuse's end as I strike the lighter's trigger. "How much time we got, Dalton?"

"A minute...maybe. I think."

"Do it," he says, and I hold the butane flame to the fuse end. Smoke and a snake-like flame begins to flee down the fuse. The reaction is more sudden and violent than I expect. For a moment we just stare at the quick process eating up the fuse.

"Drop it, Bob. It's supposed to be waterproof."

He does and we run to the BMW. I jump on the kick starter. "C'mon baby, don't let me down."

The motorcycle's engine over-revs as I twist the throttle. I ease off, squeeze the clutch, and tap it into gear as Bob climbs into the sidecar. I glance back, looking for the fire speeding along the fuse and see nothing.

Something causes sparks on the highway to my right. What is it? Another spray of sparks, and then an eerie *kawhowowowow*. "Holy shit, that's a ricochet!" I scream. "Those fuckers are shooting at us!" I still haven't let off the clutch. I peer toward the bridge. Nothing. "Shit. Has it gone out?"

Medrano yells, "What'd you expect? A friendly wave? Doesn't matter. If we stay here, we'll get blown to pieces. If it went out, we stay here, we get shot down like dogs. Move this thing, Dalton!"

Tracer rounds leave ominous trails in the air on both sides of us. I don't need any further encouragement. I let out the clutch.

The BMW climbs the hill toward Elmhurst. Five hundred

feet later, everyone is huddled behind a rock wall by the ruins of the La Riata bar.

"Forty. Forty-one. Forty-two. Forty-three," Bob counts as I kill the engine.

I start to push the motorcycle toward the cover of the wall. Bob helps until he hits "fifty,' then says "fuck it" and dives for cover.

It's my prize possession. I love this bike!

I keep pushing when a silent wall of air tears me away from the handlebars and throws me upwards and the world turns white. Then there is a horrific sound that feels like a force of its own and slams me onto the pavement. I've been thrown thirty feet from the BMW, which now is canted awkwardly on its side, the sidecar's wheels spinning six feet about the ground.

The bridge is engulfed in smoke and dust. Someone yells "Get down!" I wonder why until a chunk of concrete smashes into the sidecar and rebounds toward me.

Oh my God. It worked. It actually worked.

"Dalton!" It's Bob Medrano. "Get your ass over here!"

My brain isn't putting things together well. I don't understand where 'here' is, until he runs over, grabs me, and drags me toward a rock wall. As I run, bits of concrete and rock rain down. Something hits me on the top of my head. Hurts like hell.

Everything is happening in slow motion. As Medrano propels me toward the relative safety of a wall, I am aware of the roar of the river. Or is it my ears? The first span no longer seems to exist.

Jill says something into the headset mic, but I don't understand it. She moves away from me and keeps talking. Pancho, Lefty, and the others start to peek over the stone wall.

"Hijo de la chigada!" comes from someone.

"Sweet Jesus!" says Medrano.

Suddenly, I am afraid for everyone's safety. "Get down! They're shooting at us!"

Medrano pulls me up. "Maybe they will soon, Dalton, but not right now. You gotta see this."

The dust cloud is abating. Elmhurst's main highway connection to Lincoln City has been severed. George Hixson's oil drums attached to the piers dropped the south end of the middle span of the bridge into the river also. *Unfucking believable.*

Chunks of concrete, some at least two feet in width, are strewn on the approaches to Little Elm River. The road surface is peppered with debris. On the collapsed middle span, a *Road Warrior*-looking truck dangles, its fall to the river interrupted by rebar tangled in its back axle. Scattered among the bridge's detritus are darker objects I can't make out.

"What are those?" I ask.

Bob Medrano has a huge grin on his face. "Bodies," he says.

Someone starts to clap. Another lets out a joyful scream. Suddenly, Pancho grabs me and starts to dance around. We are in a frenzy of glee at having destroyed an engineering masterpiece and killed a whole lot of people. *Weird.*

The exhilaration slowly dies. *What about Gail? What about the other bridges?* I have to find Jill.

"Where's Gail?"

Jill keys the mic. "Gail, do you read me?" She turns to me. "Nothing."

"May I have the headset?" I ask.

Jill hands it to me, then waits as I key the mic.

"Gail, Dalton here. If you hear me but can't talk, just key your mic."

Click. Click. Click.

"Are you heading toward Pederson Road? Click once if yes. Twice if no."

Click.

"Are you being chased?"

Click.

"Do you think you can make it to the Pederson Road bridge?"

Click. Click.

Shit.

Chapter Forty

THE BMW SIDECAR IS A TOTAL LOSS. UNLESS I CAN GET THE motorcycle upright and detach the sidecar, I'll need another form of transportation. Absurdly, I wonder where I left my bicycle.

There are tools in a pannier to detach the appendage. Without the sidecar, the bike won't track right, but I need wheels.

"Help me pull this thing over so I can get it going," I shout.

"Whoa, amigo. This isn't a repair shop." Bob Medrano pulls me back to the relative safety of the rock wall around La Riata.

"Goddammit! I need to get to Pederson Road, *NOW*."

"Maybe so, but you're going to get your butt shot off before that can happen." As if to emphasize his point, bullets whack into the upended sidecar, punching holes through it inches from my head.

"Well, shit, Bob. No need to showboat." I'm trying to be a wiseass, but I'm scared shitless. Together, we give the BMW a desperate shove and it falls back onto the road leaving a trail of oil and gasoline.

A green dot touches Bob's forehead and I dive, knocking him to the ground. "Laser scope!"

The bullet vibrates the air where Bob had stood before the *crack* of a rifle shot arrives.

Bob and I lay in the lee of the rock wall in a puddle of the BMW's oil and gasoline.

Bob looks at me blankly, then mutters thanks.

A viscous liquid splats on my raingear. I look up and point.

"What?" Bob asks.

The boxer engine's left cylinder is cracked. Oil dribbles out from around the head gasket. We are lying in a gasoline puddle being thickened by the BMW's life blood.

"I almost got you killed for nothing, Bob. That engine's a goner."

Whatever distraction our episode with the motorcycle has provided is supplanted by the angry roar of gunfire from the north side of the bridge. Occasionally, a bullet breaks off a chunk of the wall's structure, but so far, it does not appear to have been penetrated. Bob and I move closer to the defenders huddled under its protection. Occasionally, someone will stick a rifle or pistol over the wall and shoot blindly in the direction of the noise, but no one seems eager to take the time and chance at death by exposing himself and actually aiming at someone.

Jill holds the Midland X Talker taken from Dana, the lookout now locked in the County Jail. It comes alive.

"Dana, you hear me, you fucking bitch!!! Where are you? What the fuck is going on? You were supposed to warn us."

The voice is that of a gruff Anglo, gruff and sounds angry. Jill turns the volume down.

"You can almost feel this guy's spit coming through the airwaves," she chuckles.

We don't key the mic, and for a moment there is nothing but a slight atmospheric hiss.

Then, "Goddamn you, bitch! Where are you?"

I am so hyped up I can't resist. I grab the Midland and key the mic. "Dana here," I say in a falsetto. "Sorry, what were you saying?"

A momentary pause. Then, "This ain't Dana. Who the fuck is this?"

I drop the falsetto. "Hey, you piece of shit! Sure are a lot of dead motherfuckers on the bridge. Come any closer and we'll kill a bunch more of you scum." I'm shouting into the mic.

"Where's Dana?"

"Dana? The skag with the rings on her fingers from all the dead people. Is that the Dana you're talking about, asshole?"

"What's your name?"

"I'm just one of the Elmhurst defenders. There are a lot of us here, and you need to fuck off. We're armed. And if you haven't figured it out, we're not letting you come through this town."

"Where's Dana?" the Anglo male asks again.

"She's nice and secure. Why? You banging her? Because she is sure ugly as sin. You two deserve each other."

Josh looks at me strangely.

"What's your name, loudmouth?"

"Just call me Leroy. What's yours?"

"The name's Chuck, peckerhead." His voice is suddenly and eerily calm. There is a deep laugh. "Well, 'Leroy,' you remember 'Chuck' because you're going to use my name when you beg me to stop as I skin you alive."

"Well, Chuck, if you want to see Dana again, you'll hightail it out of here. Don't you know the United States military is headed this way? They'll look forward to cleaning house on scum like you. You might want to think about that. The Army on one side, and us on the other. You linger here much longer, it's gonna get mighty unpleasant for you and the trash you're with."

Then it hits me. That's why this mob is heading south. To get away from the Army. Holy shit! We've blown up one of their escape routes! That means they are desperate, and we've just made them more so. I've got to get to Pederson Road and hope that Gail's made it to the bridge.

"Uh, you do have a way with people, Dalton," Kevin opines.

"Yeah, probably not. I messed up. Sorry." Maybe baiting the bull isn't such a good idea.

"I'm not worried" Kevin coughs a small laugh. "When Chuck asks who's 'Leroy,' I'll just point and say that you forced us to defend this shithole town."

I hope he's kidding. "This'll hold them here." I need to get to Pederson Road's bridge. I pray that Gail has escaped across it.

Kevin's ATV is parked behind the remains of south wall of La Riata. We stay low as we scramble to get around the edge of the building. Rounds smack into the burned-out structure. Some make nasty whines and whirs as they ricochet off rock and masonry.

Jill, headset on, suddenly screams "stop!"

Kevin and I hunker down and I lean around the edge of the back wall. "What?"

"Lookouts. Hixson Lane. They just made it back across the bridge. They've got company. Bad guys about a half mile behind them."

"Tell them to blow the bridge, Jill. We'll head that way."

Jill nods and speaks into the mic, "Light it. Now!"

Gail will have to wait. If Chuck and his gang succeed in crossing Little Elm River, all our lives will be forfeit. I need to check on Hixson Lane. As Kevin and I speed that direction, I suddenly blurt out, "Oh no."

Kevin eases around a corner as he responds. "What now?"

"I cannot remember whether George Hixson armed the explosives before he fell."

"Oh, shit, Dalton."

As we near the bridge gunfire erupts. "We may be up shit creek. I've watched George arm the explosives, but not paid a lot of attention to the process."

As we drop down the hill toward the Hixson Lane bridge and Little Elm River human forms appear just north of the river. Some are prone, some stand. All are pointing firearms. Continuous crackling of automatic weapons sounds.

Kevin steers the ATV into cover behind several large pecan trees. Rounds smack into the tree trunks. Some hit leafless branches, and a shower of small limbs hits the ATV's roof. Where is the group guarding the bridge? As if in answer, someone waves at us and yells, "Stay down. They're shooting at us."

No shit. I un-safety my AR15 and join our meager force. I count six or seven, all shooting, more or less, at the people gathering near the north side of the Hixson Lane Bridge.

"Why are you still here? Did you light the fuse?" I demand of one of them.

"We lit, ran back and waited. Nothing happened."

Several vehicles cautiously approach the Hixson Lane Bridge. Each is flanked by three or four armed persons on each side. If we can't blow the bridge, Elmhurst is lost. I jump out of the ATV.

"Cover me," I yell. For a few seconds, people stare at me without responding. "Cover me, goddammit!! Don't just pull the trigger. Aim at them and shoot the fuckers!"

I start to run down the hill and slide down the muddy embankment. Kevin accompanies me, despite my insistence that he stay with the ATV.

Once under the bridge, my eyes try to adjust to the gloom. Kevin asks, "Everything okay?"

"Somehow, I'm not shot, if that's what you mean. How about you?"

He pats himself down. "No. God is in His heaven."

I start to climb the concrete to the oil drums, then glance toward the dirt at the base of the concrete. "Aw, shit!"

"What?"

I slide back down and carefully open a small wooden box. Inside are the blasting caps, wrapped in waxed paper.

A bullet, then two, smack into the concrete at the bottom of the embankment. Kevin yells, "Someone must be leaning over the bridge."

He's wrong. It's the bad guys on the north side of the river shooting at us from *under* the other side of the bridge. At least five of them.

Thunk. Thunk. More rounds punch holes in the oil drums.

"What do we do now?" Kevin asks in a shaking voice.

"I don't think bullets will set the explosive off." Hell, there's dynamite inside the drums of fuel oil and fertilizer too. I have no idea what I'm talking about. "Kevin, we don't need two of us getting killed. Get the hell out of here."

He ignores my plea and carefully unwraps the blasting caps. "Do your best, Dalton. Do your best." Kevin produces a sharpened plastic dowel from the blasting cap box, his small flashlight, hands them to me, then grabs my weapon and ammo. "You don't need this, and I can use another firearm. He stations himself behind a concrete pier and begins firing in a steady tempo. The sound is painfully loud.

Now, less gunfire from the people under the bridge. Some rounds ricochet off concrete abutments, some smack into the wet ground on each side of the bridge. Another *thunk* as one penetrates an oil drum. My butt clenches. I stick Kevin's flashlight in my mouth and carefully climb to the oil drums. Illumination makes clear what George was about to do when he broke his leg. Each drum full of fuel oil and fertilizer has several dynamite sticks bundled together just under the barrels' tops, visible through the open bung. Trying to tune out gunfire and dread, I select one drum, take the plastic pointed dowel and auger a hole in one of the dynamite sticks, then carefully push the cap in the dynamite.

There's a small pause in the firing. Kevin's managed to scare several of the shooters into vacating the area under the north side of the bridge. One body lies still. Another shooter is down, writhing on the ground.

"Nice shooting."

Kevin hands me a six-foot strand of black safety fuse.

"Where'd you get that?" I ask.

"Leftovers, I guess," Kevin replies, then turns and sends several rounds toward the enemy. The bridge begins to vibrate as one, then two, then three vehicles start over it.

I've armed one drum. There is no more safety fuse. The detonation cord strung between the other barrels remains unattached. Right or wrong, Kevin and I have to move, and fast. I remember the lighter in my coat pocket. "Six feet is not much time before it hits the blasting cap," I yell at Kevin. "Get the hell out of here."

"Not leaving until you do."

"Okay, but run like hell." The bridge creaks as the vehicles edge toward the Elmhurst side. Footsteps. People following in the relative safety of the vehicles send bursts of gunfire south-ward. I hear nothing from the Elmhurst guards. They're either dead or withdrew to safety.

I light the safety fuse.

"Holy shit that thing goes fast!" exclaims Kevin, and we both break for the embankment, clawing upward toward the road surface. Suddenly, Kevin grunts and falls backwards. I reach to grab him, but he rolls back down the hill. I glance toward the fuse, barely spotting it as it creeps up the concrete embankment toward the oil drums.

"Kevin! Come on!" I pull on him. There's no response. His eyes are wide open. He's been wounded, or maybe killed. More rounds hit around the two of us. I glance up at the bridge.

Several train rifles on us. "Kevin," I scream as I try to lift him. I reach to drag him, and blood pours out of his mouth.

Why haven't I been hit? As if in response, something smacks into my right side, knocking me onto my ass. I clamber to my feet. I've got to get away from the bridge. Here, I'll be blown to bits. I struggle to run down toward Little Elm River.

Oh, dear Jesus, is Kevin Daugherty dead? I splash into the muddy eddies at its banks as bullets spank the water's surface.

Suddenly, I am thrown into the water from the pressure wave of an explosion. My mind only has time to realize that the drum has blown. My face and eyes sting badly as I smash into the floodwaters of the river. Before I have time to react, I ingest an unknown amount of filthy water. I fight for what I think is 'up,' although I'm not sure. As I surface, something hard hits me on the back of the head.

BOOM!

For a second I can't tell if it is an explosion or my head breaking in two. I try to take a breath, succeeding only in sucking water into my lungs. I'm drowning, and part of my brain calmly acknowledges this. At the same time, another part tells me to fight like hell. I cough, then catch a lungful of air before the current pushes me down again. This time, my body is prepared, and I don't try to breathe under water. Up again, facing upstream and I reach and wipe water moisture out of my stinging eyes. It is more than river water. My hand is streaked with rivulets of watery pink blood.

I paddle fiercely but feel strength ebbing even from the few moments in the cold water. I push away small branches following me downstream. More blood and water in my eyes, and through the blur, perceive that Hixson Lane Bridge is no more.

I think I've been hit by a chunk of concrete from the exploded bridge. Or maybe smacked by a floating log. I don't know, but now I've got to figure where I can get out of the raging waters. I try to sweep the river away so I can face downstream, then stick my feet out in front of me. Better, but my left side spasms.

Up ahead and sooner than I ever could believe possible is the Lincoln City highway bridge. The explosion that blasted the first span had dropped a portion of the second span into the water, constricting the flow and increasing its speed. I kick furiously toward the shore. Broken concrete protrudes from the water and I push toward an eddy. Rebar extends as if to offer a handhold. I grab it with my right hand, and the water's strength slams me into the jagged concrete. I cannot hold on, and bounce against the jagged chunks until the current speeds me under the remains of the bridge.

Someone waves at me. I have no idea who it is. But humanity's nearness seems to offer hope despite the odds. I raise an arm to wave back.

And then the person and bridge disappear. I'm in the deepest and narrowest part of Little Elm River, where we kids were warned never to swim or float. I try to remember if there is any kind of take-out point near Elmhurst. Soon, I'll be swept under the last connection to town—the Pederson Lane Bridge. That is, if it hasn't been blown.

I hope it has. In the rush of water and pattering of rain, I haven't detected any explosion. It's collapsed steel structure might offer something to grab onto.

My head swivels back and forth between the bluffs. Vaguely familiar outcroppings are much, much closer to the water than I ever remember.

Jeez, I'm hauling ass. My arms don't work very well. "I'm going hypothermic—big time." That I say out loud. My voice reassures me I'm still alive. There are clay bluffs on each side, with most of the vegetation now submerged.

The dim shape of Pederson Road Bridge is dark against the gloomy sky.

Shit. It's still intact. I'm suddenly pleased, as Gail and the other two lookouts are trying to escape by this route. I'm not sure I really care about Elmhurst, and my strength is ebbing fast.

Suddenly, someone yells. My name?

"Dalton! Grab the rope!"

This is a hallucination. No way anyone'd dare be down here. No way anyone would know I'm here.

"Dalton! Grab the fucking rope!"

Something splashes in front of me. Nylon rope? I grab. Or try to. My hands don't have any strength. I furiously take a wrap around my body and try to tie the loose end to make a loop.

My body is jerked tight in the rushing water. It digs into my left side and I scream. The pain is beyond imagining. My head goes under the water and I cannot raise it. I'm running out of breath.

Then, the force of the water eases and I rise above the river's flow and gasp for air.

"You've got to help, Dalton!" A woman's voice. Then a man's. "C'mon. Kick hard."

I am up against a steep clay bank. Hands pull me part way out of the water.

"Kick, dammit!" The woman's voice again. I realize Jill is part of the group trying to save me. I start to slip back on the bank's slick surface. "Kick, kick, kick!"

"Trying to," I say. Or think I do. I'm not sure. Somehow, someone or several someones have pulled me onto a narrow ledge, usually halfway between the Pederson Road Bridge and the Little Elm River.

I look upward. Billy and Fred Aston pull me upward as Josh begins coiling the rope.

What the hell is this? Old home week? Where'd these two come from?

Jill's hands are bloody.

"How?" I ask.

Josh replies. "The people at Hixson's bridge saw you go in. Thought you might be alive. Jill spotted you at the main highway bridge, but you were going too fast. She headed here."

I begin to shiver uncontrollably. "Where's Kevin? Gail?"

Josh looks away. I slip into unconsciousness.

Chapter Forty-One

My arms are being pulled out of their shoulder sockets, and every bounce and jostle ravages the pain in my side. My eyes flutter open. I am being dragged through mud and grass. I realize I am still alive! How did that happen?

"Hey, easy!" I choke out. "Hurts like hell!"

There are no apologies. Only mutters of "Faster, dammit. Faster." What the hell is going on? Then I remember—Chuck and his cohorts are trying to get into and through Elmhurst. We've blown two bridges, but the Pederson Road old steel girder span remains intact.

But why am I being dragged like so much meat through the mud, in the middle of a driving rainstorm? Sharp reports, some high, some of a lower pitched sound. Gunfire?

Yes. And a lot of it. Reality returns to my muddled mind. Someone is shooting real bullets at my saviors. The underside of the bridge looms closer and closer as I'm pulled up the steep side of the river's gorge. Barrels of explosives appear, jammed together like suckling pigs under its connection to Elmhurst's side of Little Elm River. On level ground, whoever is dragging me stops, wheezing from exhaustion, while others let loose in a fusillade of various calibers.

Now on level ground, my feet bounce in the gravel and asphalt of Pederson Road's tarmac. My guts feel like they are being pulled out of a hole in my side. The Lane's old iron bridge leers at me. Two people hoist me onto another's back, and that person—Billy?—sets off in a clumsy run toward a stand of pecan trees two hundred feet or so from the bridge.

"Blow the goddamned bridge! Get away! You'll die if you don't," I say. Or maybe think. What comes out of my mouth is anyone's guess. Each bounce causes excruciating pain from my right side, the one a bullet struck seemingly eons ago. Through the pain I try to remember where the fuse is tied for the explosive. My head bounces on Billy's back. When my eyes clear momentarily, I see people advancing across the bridge.

I'm dropped into the muck behind a huge tree. On impact, I scream from the pain. No apologies. Hands reach down, grab my jacket, and shove me against the tree in a sitting position.

Someone fires a weapon, deafening my right ear. I am in the middle of a maelstrom of screams, shouts, and gunfire. Words filter through the cacophony. The reek of mercury fulminate from exploding primers is everywhere.

"Shoot the fuckers!"

"Trucks coming across!"

I want to see what is going on. An attempt at twisting around proves fruitless, and I grunt in pain as I wobble and fall on my side.

Then, "NO! Fred! Don't!"

My right cheek is in mud and water. I raise my head and realize our safety in the stand of pecan trees will soon prove illusory. On the Elmhurst side's approach to Pederson Road bridge is a mishmash of the poor neighborhood's small frame houses. The structures end at the pecan trees we now seek cover in, some two hundred feet from the river's steep embankment. The trees' access to water has allowed them to grow to enormous heights and widths. But there are only about a dozen of them.

Blinking furiously to clear my eyes, I recall that George Hixson did not run the safety fuse to this far. Why not? Sensing George's perverse sense of humor, maybe he wanted to ensure 'towns people' were brave enough to cross an open area to light the fuse. The reality is probably more prosaic. The six-foot strand Kevin handed me at the Hixson Lane Bridge explains it. Not enough safety fuse. Whatever the reason, this bridge's detonation depends on the fuse looped around the lone tree fifty feet from the bridge's mouth. It is light-years in distance from our cover.

Jill—I realize it is her I'm hearing—screams like a banshee. "Fred! Don't. Come back."

Someone darts toward the bridge.

Pop. Pop. Fred Aston, her husband, staggers drunkenly as bullets strike him. He's barely covered half the distance.

Where in hell did he come from?

Billy takes up the cry. "Stay down, Fred! Stay down!"

Brown and grey grass, dormant with the winter's cold, stands as high as two feet in places. Fred disappears into it, then raises his head slightly.

Josh screams, "Cover him! Cover him!"

Several attackers are already on the Elmhurst side of the bridge, prone in the tall grass. This is the last chance to cross Little Elm River, and the attackers are aware of the possible danger lurking underneath this rickety steel structure. One man, in cammies and a hoodie, low crawls to the end of the bridge and seeks cover from the bridge's guardrail which extends some fifteen feet from the bridge's end. The guardrail of the highway safety type is a later addition to the Pederson Road bridge. It is solid and is bolted to wooden poles set in concrete. It sets too low to crawl under. He swings a leg over the guardrail and rolls over the top. His head mists with brain matter and blood. He drops straight down. Billy laughs and cackles. "Another one."

Four trucks move slowly onto the span's shaky structure. Armed men creep behind the trucks, using them for cover. In a macabre dance, Fred gets to his knees, then stands and begins to stumble forward. He is now only a few feet from the fuse's knotted end.

Billy aims his scoped deer rifle, calmly squeezing off shots and calling out, "Another one. And another one." Others fire as fast as they can pull triggers. I am mesmerized by a horrible beauty of Fred's selfless rendezvous with death. He pulls something from a pocket and steps to the tree. And is slammed to the ground by another bullet.

We let out a collective moan. He must be dead.

Instead, Fred lunges upward and wraps his arms around the tree, hugging it to stay erect. Wood chips fly as the attackers renew the intensity of their fusillade. Fred squeezes something. Nothing happens. Then again. And again. At this distance it is hard to make out, but it must be a butane lighter. In a slow-motion ballet, his right hand moves it toward the fuse. A small puff of white smoke appears and begins its relentless travel down the tree's trunk and toward the bridge.

Screams indicate that the attackers have witnessed the fuse's being lit. In seconds, it seems as if the small tree is nearly cut in two by bullets, not aimed at Fred, but at his creation. The fuse's quick advance appears to outpace the lead slamming into the tree. Small limbs from the leafless tree rain down, as a multitude of bullets aimed too high to be effective.

Fred Aston has no chance at avoiding the fusillade. He turns toward us and grins. And is struck in the head and torso by multiple rounds. He slumps and is hit again, and again. His body crumples lifeless at the tree's base.

Jill keens in wordless anguish. Elmhurst defenders' gunfire slackens, until Josh screams, "Keep shooting!"

Billy gasps, then mutters an uncharacteristic curse. "You sorry motherfuckers." His large-bore deer rifle booms again. "And another one."

Three of the four pickups, with plate metal welded across their windshields and radiators, clear onto the Elmhurst side and move into positions on either side of it. The fourth one stops on the bridge just short of the Elmhurst side to offer cover to a group of armed men.

A convoy of mismatched vehicles, including armed contraptions, line up to move onto the Pederson Road bridge's wood planked surface. Under the sharp barks of gunfire, the bridge moans with their weight as, one, then another, inches onto the span's wood planked surface.

Several gang members, indistinguishable in bulky jackets and rain gear, sprint from behind the truck providing cover and clear the bridge.

BLAM! One jerks, throws his arms wide and falls face down. He doesn't move.

"And another," intones Billy as he works the rifle's bolt and a hot brass casing spins onto my neck.

Josh appears beside Billy. "We need to move," he shouts. "We're about out of ammunition. We've got to fall back and fast or we'll get wiped out."

There *is* no fallback position.

Billy nods and squats over me. "You gave it your best, Dalton. Think you can move on your own?" I can barely hear him over the ringing in my ears.

I prop on an elbow and grunt. "I'll try." I move my legs and the throbbing in my side explodes. My body starts an uncontrollable shiver.

Billy's look of concern is confirmation that I'm not going anywhere without a lot of help.

The bridge still stands. We have failed.

As if they understand this, the Free Americans or whatever they call themselves, increase their rate of fire. One, acting like a military squad leader, barks unheard orders with accompanying hand signals. Four attackers rise and rush forward. Someone scores a hit, but the other three go to ground twenty yards closer to us. Then another four scurry forward, passing the first three that survived and who are now in prone firing positions. None of the four seem to be hurt as they dive into the underbrush on either side of Pederson Road's narrow surface.

"Give me a gun!" I scream. I can barely take a breath with the pain but have to do something to try and help. No one pays me a bit of attention. "Give me a fucking firearm!" I scream.

Billy unholsters a semi-automatic pistol and hands it to me. "You might want to save the last bullet," he says.

"What for?"

He turns away and peers through his scope. I suddenly get it. He's telling me suicide may be a better death than what I can expect from horde advancing on our position.

"Leapfrogging closer," Josh yells frantically. "Billy, can you take one out on the next move?"

Another ejected shell casing tumbles, burning my cheek. I want to move, or scream, but I feel totally useless. And the huge pecan's trunk is the only thing saving me from sure death.

"No," responds Billy. "I've killed two trying to get under the bridge, and they're still trying."

I wonder why they bother. If the bridge were to blow, it would have happened by now...

Futilely, I point Billy's 9 mm pistol in the general direction and pull the trigger. Then a concussion wave hits me milliseconds before the overwhelming sound of the ammonium nitrate explosives detonating.

An enormous cloud of dust seems to encompass the bridge. Chunks of wood planking soar above the grey and brown cloud. Shredded steel scissors through the air. Bodies, some seemingly whole, others in pieces, fly in all directions.

The bridge jackknifes into the gorge taking what remains of people and vehicles with it. The explosion's shock waves bounce along the deep cut in the Little Elm River's passage like echoes of thunder after a nearby lightning strike. Over the top of this is the bright-sounding snap of steel bending and breaking.

Then, silence. On the other side of the river, a few bent trusses expose their jagged and severed ends. Would-be attackers stand motionless around their line of stranded vehicles.

A ragged cheer erupts from several in the trees. I let out a whoop and immediately regret it. Despite the rain, dust seems to hang motionless over the severed span. An immutable part of Elmhurst no longer exists.

In the tall grass, a man in a heavy brown jacket raises up and turns to view what has happened, and Billy's rifle barks. The man's head explodes. I look around. Jill stands, seemingly transfixed by her dead husband's body. She picks up an AK47 and begins to fire. My hearing is spent from the gunfire and explosions. I barely notice the report of the weapon but am awed at the cool deliberation with which she fires, re-levels, aims, and fires again. I follow the weapon's barrel and find her target. Each round smacks into the muck in the area where one of the last four attackers went to ground. He is not visible until she drops a magazine and reloads. A man in knee-high wet-weather boots takes his chance and starts to clumsily scramble toward a truck's armor-plated safety. Jill fires two shots, both connecting. A rubber boot comes off one foot as the man spins and falls onto his back, raises a hand limply, then becomes inert.

Despite the ringing in my ears, the crackle of gunfire tells me others are emulating Jill. Mud and water splashes near other hidden prone bodies and soon, the remaining squad of leapfroggers flees to the rear of the three trucks. They are stranded on the Elmhurst side of Little Elm River. Their only chance now is to overpower our small group here.

Billy turns toward Elmhurst. He looks confused, then begins to laugh. He looks down at me. "Can't you hear it?"

"Hear what? I can't hear a fucking thing." I can hardly understand his words.

"The city's truck! It just pulled in between some of those houses—about five back—toward town. We've got reinforcements!"

The Free Americans' pickup trucks, all old and ragged, have no welded plate as defenses to their beds and I spy no movement as bullet holes appear there.

I expect the vehicles to move toward our position with the remaining invaders using them as cover. So far, it hasn't happened. Idly, I wonder if Chuck is in one of the trucks cabs.

Billy's rifle sounds again, and this time, I deflect the spent shell casing limply with my hand. It splashes and sizzles in the water next to me. He points to one of the trucks. The tiny slit in the sheet metal covering the windshield is shattered. The driver's door on the truck's side opens and a body falls out.

"And another one," Billy mutters.

Josh takes notice and commands, "Aim for the drivers' slits." Bullets begin to whang into the steel. One driver shifts into gear, and the truck lurches forward, but instead of coming directly toward the trees, it steers onto the thin tarmac of Pederson Road, its driver seemingly intent on escape. A MAC 10 with the twin drums of a hundred-round magazine extends out of the driver's side window and lets loose a spray of .45 bullets. With no time, nor any realistic ability to take cover, I empty the 9 mm as the truck roars by. I have no idea if I have done any damage.

A staccato of automatic gunfire erupts from behind us. The

truck slows, drifts into a bar ditch, and begins to burn. Three of the remaining thugs are left without a shield and Billy takes advantage to down another Free American.

Still half deaf, I feel rather than hear feet pounding in the sodden soil. Painfully, I roll enough to see Bob Medrano, Pancho, Lefty, and several others moving carefully through the trees toward our position.

Oh, sweet Jesus. We did it.

But where are Gail and the other two?

Chapter Forty-Two

THE FIRE REACHES THE BURNING TRUCK'S GAS TANK. WITH A whoosh, it explodes. The driver, already wounded, lunges from the cab, on fire. His scream is other-worldly in its agony. Mercifully, Billy and others shoot the man and his body slams against the burning vehicle, then falls smoking in the wet grass. I am thankful to be upwind.

A bullet strips out a chunk of the pecan tree, and Billy yelps in pain. I swing my attention back toward the remaining enemy on this side of the Little Elm River. Billy drops his rifle as he clutches his head. Instinctively, I grab it and somehow keep the barrel out of the mud.

Oh, dear God. Not Billy. I grab his pants leg with my left hand and scream at him to stay behind cover. He squats on the ground, blood streaming from between the fingers of the hand clutching at his temple.

"Billy! You all right?" I somehow manage to rise to my knees and wonder where the pain in my right side has gone. It returns like an electrical shock. My vision dims, and I lean into Billy's heavy jacket. Josh continues to scream commands. Some

I comprehend, others are too garbled by the confusion and my hearing loss.

A wave of nausea passes as I half-cradle, half lean on Billy for support. "Talk to me, Billy. Are you okay?" His blood soaks my right hand that I have draped over his back, then mixes with water in the mudholes. I want to yell for help, but everyone is sending round after round into the enemies' trucks on this side of the river.

Jill calmly pulls the AK47's trigger. The weapon bucks upward as the bullet leaves the barrel. She waits, then shoots again, as if wanting each bullet to count. Bob Medrano isn't as methodical. In seconds, he burns through a thirty-round magazine of AR15 ammunition, then hits the release button and slams another magazine in, chambers a round and empties that mag, too.

"Stop shooting!" Josh yells. Someone behind the riddled pickup trucks waves a dirty white cloth in the air. "They're surrendering."

A few desultory rounds are fired, and then, silence. Or at least, I think so. My ears are so traumatized I am not sure.

"Step away from the vehicles and walk this way," Josh screams. Two heavily bundled figures appear, half-carrying a third. They start the two hundred or so feet toward the pecan trees. As they near, Pancho steps out to escort the three in—and then dives into the mud as bullets splash and zip near him.

Jill yells for everyone to remain where they are. "You okay, Pancho?"

"*Hijo de la chingada! Esos putos trataron matarme!*"

Lefty breaks into nervous laughter. "*Pues*, bro, don't be such a dumbass! Stay down!"

"Those shots came from across the river," Jill exclaims. "Stay back. Stay under cover. We don't need any more people hurt."

As the two thugs drag the third one toward where Josh commands them to move, I look over at Billy from his right side. He raises his head. A wood splinter protrudes from his left temple.

I begin to retch uncontrollably. Stomach acid, dirty river water and bile burns my throat. I clutch my injured side and cough out a scream of agony after each convulsion. My vision fades, and I see Gail holding Josefina. She smiles as she hands me our daughter. Bertha Kaufman erupts in laughter at something Randall has just told her. As I cradle Josefina, Gail holds out a mason jar drinking glass, full of iced tea. She gently touches the sweating, cold glass to my forehead. "Thanks for all the hard work you did around the place today," she says. I smile.

"Dalton! Dalton!"

Someone shakes me, and I cough violently, and am again wracked with pain.

"You okay?"

"Bob? What?"

Medrano hands me a bottle of water. "Drink. You zoned out on us for a sec."

The dream. So peaceful. I want to go back to it. Instead, I take a swallow, and realize I haven't eaten since.... I still clutch Billy's rifle.

"Billy?"

Medrano nods and I realize I've been draped over Billy's body. He has a six-inch splinter stuck in his head.

"Aren't you dead?" I ask.

Two bloody inches of pecan tree protrude, giving him the appearance of having a small horn growing out of his skull. The remaining wood is imbedded from the corner of his orbital bone to his left ear, where a sharp splinter punctures the entry of its canal. I ignore the gore, amazed that it did not pierce his skull, only pushing just under the surface of the skin.

Billy grimaces. "Naw. I'll live. Got a hell of a headache though."

"You look like shit, Billy. And you weren't that much to look at before you grew a chunk of wood out of your head."

Medrano interrupts. "We've got business to finish here, so cut with the compliments."

Two bearded Anglos stand spread-eagled against pecan trees, on the side away from the river. A third, bloodied from the waist down, lies face down with his arms extended perpendicular to his body. Josh holds a pistol at his side, as Lefty strips off the men's' rain gear and jackets and frisks them. Lefty pulls out a small pistol from one of them, and then a small slapjack, a nasty club made of lead pellets sewn in a leather pouch. Pancho, disheveled and muddy, grabs the slapjack from his compadre and whacks its owner's collarbone with it, producing a howl of pain. No one interferes.

"*Que pasa, cabron?*" Pancho snarls. "You gonna use this to hurt someone here in Elmhurst?"

The injured man wisely says nothing. The other man still standing has been stripped down to his filthy union suit and crosses his arms over his shoulders as he shivers. In comparison to the folks defending Elmhurst, he looks well fed. Too well fed. Next to Lefty is a growing collection of pistol belts, ammunition, and clothing.

It's been, how long now since the bridge blew? A lifetime ago, but perhaps just a few minutes. I insist on trying to stand erect. With Medrano's help, I am able to do it. The wound in my side oozes blood, but the flow is nowhere as heavy as it has been. Maybe a good thing, but I'm not so sure. It might just mean I'm fresh out of blood.

The rain stops and a fresh north breeze clears the air of any reminder of the Pederson Road bridge explosion. I focus on our enemies, stranded on the other side of Little Elm River. Pederson Road is a "hogback" road with no shoulders and deep bar ditches on either side. It is almost impossible to turn around on the narrow asphalt, even in dry weather. Several vehicles are attempting the feat now. There seems to be no coordination of efforts. A woman wildly gesticulates to the driver of an old pickup truck, its cab ladened with welded armor. She is inaudible to me over the sound of the river, but is screaming wildly, as the truck makes several small turns to arrive perpendicular to the narrow road's surface, and then slides uncontrollably into the flooded bar ditch.

Further back in the line of vehicles, tires smoke as an old sedan tries to push another car backwards to make space for its attempt at turning around. Suddenly, puffs of smoke appear and four or five sharp *craaacks* sound. The driver of the car being pushed opens the driver's side door and points a rifle at the sedan. The passenger side door opens on the old sedan and a gunfight ensues as he returns fire.

"Jesus Christ," mutters Medrano. "They're turning on each other." He smiles.

The Midland X Talker comes alive. Jill has its volume cranked up. "Hey, you people from Elmhurst. You copy?" crackles through its speaker.

Rather than respond, Jill looks at Josh and asks, "Do we talk?"

Josh looks to me, but before anyone can formulate an answer, the radio comes alive again. "We know you've got a Midland X Talker. You took it off Dana. So I know you can hear us. You might want to hear to what I've got to say."

Oh shit. I recognize the voice. It's Chuck. The Chuck who I taunted after we blew the Lincoln City highway bridge.

"I can't talk to him," I tell Josh. "But someone ought to."

Jill shakes her head. "I can't. I haven't even seen my dead husband's body." She hands the radio to Josh. "It's on you."

Josh key the mic. "We're here."

"You blew these bridges. It may take us longer, but eventually, we'll loop around, north or south, and come back. We're going to kill every one of you sorry motherfuckers."

Josh stares at the Midland. "This is bullshit. Why is this bastard wasting time threatening us?" He keys the mic. "Okay, thanks for the warning but what do you want?"

As Josh talks, I lift Billy's deer rifle using its scope to try and spot Chuck. I'm so unsteady that I cannot make out any image long enough. Chuck could be one of the men milling around the tangle of vehicles trying to move away from Little Elm Creek, or he could be concealed somewhere.

"Dalton, you couldn't hit your ass with both hands right now." Bob Medrano reaches for the rifle, and I don't have the strength to resist him.

The mic comes alive. "We've got three of your people over here. Thought you might want to see what we do to them."

Oh God. The only three people I can think of are Gail and the two others in the outpost near the Lincoln City highway. They didn't make it. Gail was right, of course. She knows the land between the highway and Pederson Road. I don't know how, but they must have been nabbed somehow.

Before keying the mic, Josh looks at me. His face mirrors my own feelings of bone chilling fear. I bend over ignoring the pain in my side and take deep breaths as my vision once again narrows with darkness. Lefty appears and grabs my right arm. Jill rushes and grabs my left.

"I'm okay. I'm okay," I say. "It'll be okay." I babble words with no connection to reality.

Before he keys the mic, Josh asks Bob Medrano, "Can you get a bead on whoever's on the radio over there?"

"Trying." Medrano stands on the side of a pecan tree, using a knot on its truck to steady the bolt action weapon and its powerful scope. Then, "Uh, oh. Three people being pushed up from back in the line of trucks and cars. Two men." He pauses. "And a woman."

"Who has binoculars?" I ask. "I need to see."

Jill hands me a pair. I try to focus the eyepieces. "Where?

Where?" I don't spot the captives. "Where do I look?" Then I detect the movement toward the remains of the Pederson Road bridge.

Please, God. Don't let it be Gail.

Chuck's voice shatters glass in my mind. "We've got these three who were snooping around. I'm sure they had something to do with you blowing that bridge. You killed a lot of my people. We're going to show you what we can do to yours."

"Stall for time," I say. "We've got to save them." I can't think of a damned thing.

Through the binoculars, I see two men pushing the three toward the precipice that once was the beginning of Pederson's Road's link to Elmhurst. I lower the binoculars.

"Oh, shit, Dalton," Josh mutters. "Who are the other two?"

Jill responds, "One of my Cougars. His name is Ray. I can't remember who the third one in the group is. I feel like a shit. We should all know who they are."

Lefty chimes in. "One of my cousins. Name is Raul Pruneda. On my mom's side. He worked for the county."

Josh keys the Midland X Talker. "We've got three of yours over here. And we've got Dana. We can trade."

Chuck pauses. I silently pray that he and his group will take the deal and go away. As the seconds tick by, I will him to form the words that will end this nightmare.

"C'mom, c'mom, c'mon," Bob Medrano whispers. "Take the fucking deal." He speaks more clearly to those gathering around Josh and the radio. "He's got to know he's in deep kimchee. The U.S. Army is about twenty miles out of Lincoln City, and nothing has slowed those forces down."

"What?" This from Jill. "How do you know that?"

"Your HAM guy. Just before the bridge blew. Not many aircraft right now, but the ground forces are already in the northern suburbs of Lincoln City. They catch up with this scum, it'll be lights out."

Josh keys the mic. "If you don't know this, Chuck, you guys are about to meet up with the United States military. Best thing you can do is take our deal and get the hell out of here. We've got a jon boat on this side with paddles. We'll make the first move and bring your people to you."

Still nothing. I don't recall any boat.

Then, "Those four don't mean shit to me and mine. Do what you want to with them."

This can't be happening.

Jill grabs the binoculars out of my hands. "Oh God," she mutters as I hear a soft *pop*. Even without binoculars, I can see what's happened. One of our three has just been executed. The body slumps, then rolls off the precipice, disappearing down Little Elm River's steep embankment.

"They just killed Ray," says Jill softly. Curses and moans emanate from several people.

I say a silent prayer of thanks that it wasn't Gail, unable or unwilling to acknowledge the selfishness of my gratitude.

"That's the first one," Chuck barks over the radio. "Who's next? The man, or the red-headed woman?"

Bob Medrano says something to Jill.

"What?" asks Josh.

"I think I've got the Chuck guy located. Should I try to take him out?"

At least one, and maybe more of the enemy stand behind Gail and Raul Pruneda, using them as shields.

"Fucking A," screams Lefty.

Billy's deer rifle booms. Gail and Pruneda are forced to the ground and I can't tell if they've been murdered.

"Any luck?" Josh asks.

Jill continues to glass the other side. "He got someone, but I'm not sure if its Chuck."

The Midland X Talker comes alive. Dammit, it's Chuck. "Nice shooting, but you killed the wrong guy."

Gail and Raul are forced up and another *pop* reaches us. Pruneda's body arches backward, then falls face down the embankment.

I lunge at Josh and grab the radio. "Chuck, this is your buddy Leroy. Remember me? I'm the guy you said you would skin alive. Are you such a pussy that you'd kill a woman? I'm headed toward the river. Trade that woman for me and do what you want with me."

Snot runs uncontrollably out of my nose as I try not to sound as horribly desperate as I feel. "I'll make it easy for you. I'm walking toward the bridge now. You can kill me in the open. Just spare the woman. She's the mother of a three-month-old baby."

Josh starts to say something but doesn't. I look at the Jill and the others. They are now just a blur of faces and shapes. I nearly double over with pain, then step from the cover of the pecan trees and begin the walk toward Little Elm River.

I stare at Gail but cannot distinguish any features. I walk past the tree where the fuse was tied. Fred's body is a dark shape in the sodden grass at its base. At the bridge's abutment, I stop. I don't bother to glance down at the wreckage in the chasm.

Now I can see Gail clearly. She looks scared but defiant as she is held by someone from behind. Her eyes do not leave my face. I want to tell her I'm sorry for everything I've fucked up. I want to tell her what a great mother she is to our daughter.

Gail nods, and I sense her forgiveness.

Then, she suddenly drops, exposing her captor.

I hear a *pop* of a pistol shot, just as Billy's deer rifle booms.

Chapter Forty-Three

I AM TRANSFIXED. MY EYES REFUSE TO TURN AWAY FROM THE horror.

Gail's sudden movement had been intentional to expose Chuck to her brother's scoped deer rifle. Her captor's body doubles over as the bullet smashes through his torso. Driven back by Billy's shot, Chuck's body then lurches upward as more rounds from our side of the river find their target. Puffs of blood spray from bullets appear on his chest, neck, and his forehead. The Midland X Talker flies away from his hand.

Gail lies eerily still in a grotesque shapelessness, blood pooling around her head.

"Gail!"

I stagger out of the trees and then am at a full sprint running toward the ruined bridge's abutment, as if is possible to cross Little Elm River's chasm. The twisted metal girder at its edge has been pushed vertical from the explosion. It affords me some support, and I wrap my left arm around it to remain erect. I continue to scream Gail's name. God! She's got to be okay!

The metal pings—then again, and I feel vibrations caused by bullet strikes. I try to duck down, but the pain in my side is too intense. The staccato beat behind me increases as Elmhurst's defenders fire round after round across Little Elm River.

On the other side, there is a flurry of movement. More drivers struggle to turn vehicles around as rifle and automatic fire peppers the area. Windshields shatter. Bullets ricochet off a truck's armor plate. Deflected rounds whine, or tumble end over end with oscillating wobbles. I can't see if Gail has moved at all.

A flatbed pickup stalls in the bar ditch. The driver tries furiously to return to Pederson Road's surface, smoking his tires in the mud. The truck suddenly bursts into flames, and the driver shoves open his door. Suddenly, he flings his arms upward and falls backward, then disappears into the bottom of the bar ditch.

Over my own anguished keening, I hear, "Get down, Dalton! Get down!" I am slammed to ground from behind, and howl in pain.

"Dammit, Dalton. We're not going to help you fulfill some goddammed death wish. Stay down!!"

Bob Medrano lies on top of me. My weak struggle to stand is no match for his strength.

"Stay down, fool!"

Bob's breath is rank, and I idly wonder if he's brushed his teeth. As if any of us have lately. "Give me room to breathe," I plead. "I'm starting to black out."

He rolls to one side, one hand on my shoulder preventing me from moving my head upward. "I don't trust you not to keep your fucking head down."

"Gail's dead. I don't want to live," I mutter, blinking my eyes furiously, hoping that it will keep me from slipping into unconsciousness.

"Tough shit. You've got a child you're gonna have to raise. You check out now, you are nothing but a coward. So stop your whining."

Bob's dead wife and teenaged son come to mind. He's living through worse that what I'm dealing with. He hasn't checked out. I shut the hell up.

A bullet plows into the dirt two feet from where I lie, and Bob pushes my face down harder. Mud clogs my nose and I begin to sneeze. My right side hurts so badly I grab my nose and squeeze it, trying to stop the next eruption. It doesn't work.

I scream as I cough. "Oh shit, it hurts so bad."

"Where?"

"My side, where I was shot, you idiot," I reply.

"When?"

I realize Bob wasn't part of the crew that dragged me out of the river. As gunfire is exchanged, I haltingly tell him about Hixson Lane. I begin a sentence, then lose my train of thought. I am warm and weirdly comfortable. I just want to go to sleep.

Bob's hand rummages around my waist, then my crotch and legs.

"You feeling me up, Bob? At a time like this?" Although the gunfire has slacked off, this is suddenly so damned funny.

He sticks a blood-slick hand in front of my face. "Jesus, Dalton. You *are* bleeding pretty bad."

I'm relieved that I've still got some blood in me. "Yeah, that's what happens when you get shot."

A bullet smacks into a creosoted support, the treated wood spattering Bob and me.

"Crap," Bob barks. "Splinters."

He takes his hand off my head as he digs detritus out of his eyes. I take the opportunity to raise up. As the remains of the Free Americans desert, there are fewer gunshots now. I put my head down and fall asleep.

Seemingly, moments later, someone lifts me from under my arms.

"Hey, what's going on?" I mumble.

A voice—Josh's—weaves its way into my blood-deficient

brain. "We're getting you to Doctor Randhawa." His voice is urgent. "Please help us."

I push up on my rubbery legs. As I am dragged, I glance to my right. Jill holds Fred's bloody head in her lap and uses a rag to wipe his face.

"Josh, stop for a sec," I mumble, not expecting his cooperation.

"K, but just for a second, Dalton." He doesn't add anything, but his voice reflects his concern.

Bob and Josh make a cradle with their arms and carry me to Jill and Fred. Fred's eyes stare blindly at the heavy clouds. Jill gently pushes his eyelids closed. If not for the bloody marks of bullet wounds on his body, I'd confuse him for someone sleeping.

"Jill, I'm sorry." I don't know what else to say.

She rocks back and forth, as if unhearing.

"C'mom, Bob," Josh urges. "We need to get going with this guy."

"Wait!" Jill looks up at us. Her face is streaked with tears. "I'm sorry too, Dalton. That was awfully brave what you tried to do just now."

We turn away, and Bob and Josh grunt as they carry me toward the city's truck.

"She's right, you know," Bob says as I am pulled upward onto the truck's bed. "You tried."

I don't acknowledge his comment. Whatever I did wasn't nearly enough. I've lost Gail. Josh pats my shoulder. "See you later. Bob, I've got the ATV. Gotta take care of some stuff."

The ride back into Elmhurst is excruciating. Bob cradles my head, and when Pancho hits a bump, screams at him to "slow the fuck down!"

I black out, then come to as the truck creeps along Main Street. A small crowd gathers at the front door of the Sheriff's Office. An ATV sits next to abandoned patrol cars.

Uh oh.

"Stop!" I scream, and grunt in agony.

Bob pounds on the truck cab and echoes my command. Pancho eases to a halt.

"Bob, is that the ATV Josh just took?"

"Looks like it. Why?"

Before I can respond, Josh leads Dana outside. He is followed by her guards, Robert and Andrea. Dana has her hands secured behind her. Josh carries a yellow electrical extension cord.

"Stop them, Bob," I croak. "Josh is going to hang that woman."

"Can't say as I blame him. She's part of that sorry lot, isn't she? Maybe time for a little justice, after what I've just seen."

I want Dana dead too. But something has changed. There's no need for this now. Elmhurst is secure. If she hangs, we are no better than the Free Americans.

"Bob, give me your gun."

He looks at me like I'm crazy. "You're lying in your own blood, about to bleed out. What're you gonna do, amigo? Shoot your friend?"

I don't know, but there's been too much death. "No more. No more." I grab at his pants leg frantically. "Please," I beg.

Josh doesn't even look our way as he tosses a length of extension cord over a pecan tree's lower branch.

"Stop," I try to scream. But am not heard. My voice is only a whisper.

Bob shakes his head. "I've got my own ghosts to deal with in Lincoln City, dammit." He sighs, then lets loose a stream of AR15 bullets up in the air.

A woman dives to the ground. A male onlooker screams.

"Josh," Bob barks. "Please stop that and come over here."

Reluctantly, Josh drops the makeshift hanging rope and walks to the truck leaving Dana with her minders. A dark stain shows she has soiled her pants. Pancho kills the engine, opens the cab door and stands on the running board, watching us.

"Don't, Josh. Just don't." I plead.

"You and I agreed what we needed to do, Dalton. Now I'm doing it."

I try to lift my head but see stars. Pancho climbs onto the truck bed, squats down, and props me up by my shoulders.

"Times have changed. Circumstances have changed." And maybe, just maybe, I've changed. But I don't say that.

Josh looks doubtful. "The bastards killed Fred. They murdered Gail." His eyes are bloodshot, and his voice vengeful. "She's scum, Dalton. You know that."

This is too much. "Josh, not now. Not ever. You'll regret it."

He shakes his head in disgust. "I'm so goddammed mad." He smacks the flat of his hand on the bed of truck. "Dammit, Dalton. Just, dammit."

He storms off, but not toward the pecan tree and wire. Something in his voice tells me he's not sure about his plan to lynch Dana.

"Please. Please. Don't." I black out.

People heft me off the truck and into Doctor Randhawa's house. As they carry me up the front steps, I hear a distant *whop whop whop,* and look up into the clouds.

Helicopters? No way. I'm hallucinating.

I'm laid out on the dining room table. Mrs. Randhawa begins to cut my clothing off, while the doctor checks my vitals. I find the process very interesting.

"Am I going to die?"

"Probably not," says Mrs. Randhawa in her lilting voice. "We will just have to prevent that occurrence."

She sounds so reassuring. I start to drift off, ignoring the frantic efforts of the two, when it comes to me. I've just seen a large sheet covered body lying in the Randhawa's front yard with familiar looking boots poking out. "What happened to George Hixson?"

"Mister Dalton, please be quiet. We are most busy," The doctor sounds pissed, or maybe just worried.

"George didn't make it, did he?"

Mrs. Randhawa finishes cutting off my pants, which he hands to Bob Medrano. "I am sorry to say, Dalton," *DOLE-tun* as she pronounces it. "Mr. Hixson seems to have had a stroke. He is no longer among the living."

"Well, shit," I manage, before darkness envelopes me.

SPRING

Chapter Forty-Four

DESERT CAMOUFLAGE WITH ITS TAN ON BRINDLE MARKINGS FLIT across my vision several times. The fabric appears clean and pressed. People dressed in these oddly marked clothes don't stink with body odor. I am sure I even smell perfume on one of them.

I drift off into darker scenes. Of Gail, who does not roll down the river's steep embankment, but lays slumped in an expanding pool of blood and brain tissue. I scream, or think I do, but as something pricks my arm, the warm syrup of forgetfulness returns.

I emerge, befuddled, to a cacophony of oddly normal sounds. A woman laughs. Two men converse. My nose itches—horribly. I try to lift my right hand. It is pinioned to something. My left hand isn't, and I reach, clumsily scratching. And pull away a cannula. There is a slight hiss as I focus on the two plastic stubs. I'm on oxygen.

Lifting my head is laborious. I'm in a hospital bed, its head raised slightly. My right hand is secured by a strap to the bed's steel framework. I compress my abs trying to reach the strap with my left hand, and immediately grunt in pain as something in my abdomen objects strongly.

Oh, yeah. I got shot.

"Well, howdy, young man." A salt-and-pepper haired man leans over me. "Glad to have you back with us." He doesn't try to reattach the cannula. He's dressed in military cammies but wears a white jacket with a name plate. 'Major Jonas Wilkins MD.'

"Doc," I croak. "Where am I?"

"Right now, you're in the United States Army's 155th Combat Support Hospital, in what's left of Lincoln City."

"How long?" I manage.

"About three weeks now," the doctor replies, as he looks at a computer printout on a clipboard. "You about bled out before you got medevaced." He smiles. "Bullet in the gut with septicemia. Understand you were exposed to a bunch of nasty river water after you were shot. We had to take a bit of your liver out. Fortunately, that's doable. Then had to induce a coma and chill your body down so we could fight the infection." He pauses, pats me on the shoulder and puts the cannula back in my nostrils. "You're a lucky man."

He starts to leave, and I grab him. "Can you untie my other hand?"

"Oh, yeah, I guess we can now, as long as you behave. You were grabbing at your wound and that's just our way of keeping you from ripping off your dressing."

I have so many questions, but Doctor Wilkins is gone before I can begin to formulate them all. As he leaves, I realize I'm in a ward of what looks like it's a retrofitted school classroom. There are at least thirty other beds in the well-lit and warm space. All the other beds are occupied, except for the one directly across from me. Its sheets are taut and a folded blanket rests atop them.

I have so many questions. Mostly, I am alone—and awake—

with guilt and shame. I was helpless to stop the cold-blooded murder of three people, including the mother of my child. Visions of the bullet destroying Gail's brain tissue will not go away. A bedside monitor begins to beep loudly. A woman, also in cammies and white coat walks quickly to my side.

"You okay?" she asks.

I nod, but she ignores the response and pushes a stethoscope against my chest. It's cold. "Your heart is doing some galloping, Mr. Kirby. What's upsetting you?"

The pressure cuff on my arm inflates. It cuts off circulation in my right arm, then releases. The woman looks at a monitor.

Mister Kirby. How does she know my name? I haven't heard it used in—how long now?

"BP is high, but we'd rather have it that way than on the low side." She pauses. "The good doctor say something to upset you?"

I shake my head and feel tears welling and running down my cheeks. "No. It's just that…"

She gives me a sip of water and pulls up a chair. "I can give you a sedative if you need it?" It's in the form of a question.

I want desperately to accept but shake my head no. I don't know why, but I have to start dealing with Gail's death. And Fred's. And Andres'…And Kevin's. And George Hixson's. And so many others. I ask the woman her name. She tells me. Tells me she's a nurse called up "when things went to hell in a hand-basket," that she's from Helena, Montana, and that some parts of the country were spared the worst of whatever happened.

I'm interested but my mind wanders off. I interrupt her. "I need to see my daughter."

She frowns, nods, and tells me she'll see what she can do about it. "In the meantime, there's someone here to see you. Are you up to a visit?"

"Who is it?" I reply, not sure I want to be seen by anyone besides my daughter.

She glances at a slip of paper. "Someone named Medrano. Says he's a friend of yours."

He most definitely is. "Yes, please."

She admonishes me again that the visit is required to be short. "And don't get riled up where we have to worry about your vitals."

"Yes, Nurse Rached."

She walks away in a huff. I doze off, pleased with myself for evoking her reaction.

"Hey, amigo."

Bob sits on the empty bed. "Damn, Bob, you're all cleaned up."

He laughs, and noticing my dry lips, lifts a cup with a bendable straw for me to sip.

"You come from Elmhurst?"

He shakes his head no. "Dalton, I'm back here in Lincoln City. Got things to do."

I forget to ask about how he got here with the bridges, and Bob just tells me that, "he caught a ride with the Army."

I can't imagine what his reasons for returning may be and tell him so.

"I've got cousins here. Lots of them. And uncles and aunts. And things to set straight." ,

Bob is clearly healthier now, but the haunted look still lurks. "Do I dare ask what you need to set straight?"

He pats my shoulder and laughs. "No violence, Dalton. I promise."

Images of his wife and son come to me. I'm not sure I believe him. "Thanks for helping save my life."

"That's what friends do, and you are my friend. We'll see each other again."

I hope so. He gives me a gentle *abrazo* and walks away. I begin to cry. The damned bedside monitor goes off—again.

I've slept again, thankful that there are no dreams this time. I am roused by two male NCOs.

"Time for you to try to get moving," one says. "We don't want your muscles to atrophy, and we don't want you getting pneumonia."

With much coaxing of reluctant limbs, I manage to sit up on the side of the bed and nod toward the empty bed. "Every other bed seems taken," I say. "What happened to this one?"

The question isn't answered. Instead, the taller NCO merely notes that, "It'll get filled pretty soon." The two give each other a look that tells me that whoever was in the adjacent bed is dead.

Tethered with a support belt and using a walker I make it out of the ward and into a hallway. It's still festooned with grade-schoolers' artwork. With a white backless gown, a catheter and IV port, I must look pathetic.

Instead of returning to the ward, the two NCOs guide me to what is normally a cafeteria. Fold-up tables built for school kids occupy most of the room. The Army has cleared an area for more comfortable seating away from the raised stage. Institutional looking straight-back chairs and a couple of sofas form a large square.

"You've got some visitors, so we'll help you get situated here. It's a hell of a lot more comfortable than there in the ward." They lower me into a wooden armchair. My side hurts like hell. The sergeants disappear, promising to get me in twenty or thirty minutes.

A double door opens from the hallway and Bertha and Billy Kaufman enter. Bertha pushes a pram. Josefina is sound asleep. I try to stand. It doesn't work. Instead, Bertha reaches into the pram and carefully sets my daughter in my lap. She is beautiful beyond imagining. I cradle her and she opens her eyes and smiles. Tears drip onto her perfect nose. They're mine.

Billy grins, the angry purple of the jagged wound's suture marks making him look like a movie pirate. Bertha sits quietly. I find myself avoiding both of their eyes as I respond to Billy's questions about my recovery. Soon, the questions flutter to a halt, and an awkward silence descends over us.

"I'm glad you're going to be okay," Bertha manages. "Josefina needs her father."

"I'm so sorry, Bertha. I'm so sorry." It's all I manage to get out.

Billy clears his throat. "Gail's buried next to daddy. We think she'd want that."

"I would like to have been there," I say. I don't mean it. Not at all. "To help." I turn again to Bertha. "I'm so very sorry."

She shakes her head. "Gail made the choice. You didn't. I know what you tried to do. I know you tried to protect her." Suddenly, she stands, walks to me and cradles my head to her bosom. "Whatever you may think, Dalton, her death wasn't your doing."

A dam breaks inside and I begin to sob.

Doctor Wilkins doesn't fit my notion of a military doctor. He is from a small town in central Missouri, also spared the worst of the EMPs' damage and chaos.

He is friendly and chatty. "I'm not Regular Army," he tells me, as if reading my mind. "They paid my way through med school, so I owed them six years of my life, then reverted to the Reserves. God willing, when this clusterfuck is over with, I'll get back to my family and my private practice."

"We're going to discharge you, Dalton." He laughs. "With instructions to take care of yourself. Hygiene and all that.

Maybe the United States, such as it is now, will get the grids up so there'll be some running water and electricity so those instructions may not sound so nonsensical."

I'm comfortable listening to him. Then he asks, "Are you with the bunch that blew three bridges into Elmhurst?"

"Yes." I don't add anything.

"Three bridges? Three goddammed bridges? With fertilizer bombs? Whoever thought that up and whoever put that together is a fucking genius. Incredible."

Yes, it does sound incredible. Maybe someday I'll feel like talking about it. Now, I just want out of the hospital.

Josh comes to take me home in Elmhurst's stake truck. "Some folks have actually been able to get more vehicles running," he says. "Won't do them any good right now. No fuel. Refineries shot to hell. Pipelines out of commission."

I'm not sure 'home' is the proper description for Elmhurst, but it is where my house is. I'm mostly healed, or so I'm told, but there will be more months before I am officially out of the woods. Had the Army not showed when it did, I would be like so many others—moldering in some unmarked grave. If it weren't for Josephina, I would wish I were dead.

"Things are looking up, Dalton," Josh says as he slowly drives toward Elmhurst. We chitchat about what's happened in my absence. Talk of restoration of electrical service and water and sewer—eventually. "All the emphasis now is on the big cities. Looks like we are on our own until Elmhurst is on some-one's radar."

I want to ask about Bob Medrano and so many others. And I want to ask about Jill. Josh finally gets around to it.

"Jill's having a rough go," he says.

No surprise there. "Watching your husband sacrifice his life like that can't be easy," I reply. "Where's she staying?"

"She's still next door. Still helping out around town. She's helping us with a garden in your back yard—I hope you don't mind, but we've used the space next to her fence and put in some vegetables."

He glances over at me like he's wondering about me and her. I remain stony countenanced. There is no 'me and her.' I've been interested in Jill, but then any red-blooded man would be. She's not shown anything but anger or contempt for me. Inwardly, I cringe at what I'm thinking, which is that Fred's self-sacrifice has set the bar impossibly high for any man. And that I'm an asshole for letting my mind drift there to begin with.

Five miles north of the Lincoln City-Elmhurst highway bridge it suddenly dawns on me: the bridges were blown but Billy and Bertha somehow made it to Lincoln City with Josefina. Josh is driving a truck as if it will cross Little Elm River.

Josh begins to laugh. "Wondered when you'd wake up," he says. As we near the blown highway bridge, he slows to a crawl. There's a makeshift steel structure spanning the bridge's blown sections. It reminds me of a World War II Bailey bridge, and I say so.

"Compliments of the U.S. Army combat engineers," Josh replies.

"Damn." I hold my breath as we creep over the gap. A sign says *Maximum Speed—5 mph.* Josh takes it at no more than two.

I stare out the window as we climb past the burned-out remains of La Riata Bar.

The BMW motorcycle with its damaged sidecar has been righted and pushed away from the highway's—Colorado Street's—surface.

"No one's taken my Beamer."

"It's not that some haven't tried," Josh replies. "But the side-car's shot, and the engine's all screwed up."

"Oh, yeah. Forgot." The machine's demise seems so long ago.

"If you're still interested in keeping it, we'll get it moved back to the house," Josh says. "Things been too hectic to deal with it, but maybe things will settle down."

At the intersection of Colorado and Main Streets, Josh slows and turns to me. "Thanks, Dalton."

"What for?"

"Stopping me from hanging that woman. I've got enough to deal with, without that on my conscience."

I pat him on the shoulder, relieved. "Don't we all, Josh. Don't we all."

As we turn onto Main Street and pass City Hall, I am aware of people enjoying the spring-like day. And there are more people on the streets. Some folks wave as the truck passes them. Some actually smile. Probably my imagination, but everyone looks like they've gained back a few pounds. There's still a long way to go.

"MREs are getting old, but I've never been so happy to have them. We've even gotten some airdrops of powdered milk and infant formula," Josh notes. "C'mom. I want to go by your house. Some folks want to give you a hug before I drop you off."

We pull up to my garage. The outhouse we built is still standing over the open manhole. For some reason, its presence is reassuring, which makes no sense. I bark a laugh, and Josh smiles.

"Good to see you laugh, Dalton. Yep, we're still using it."

I wonder about the trek there to an upstairs bedroom, then sigh. I'll be staying with Billy and Bertha at the Spruce Street house. It's a single-story structure—easier for that sort of thing. More importantly, I will be with Josefina.

Josh parks in the driveway. Elsie and the Cerveny kids, David and Sarah, rush up and give me hugs as I gingerly climb out of the truck cab.

"We're glad you're back, Dalton," says Elsie. Her kind nature is well ingrained in David and Sarah. Josh is a rock, but silently I'm glad they are more like their kind-hearted mother.

"Come see the garden," urges David. "It's going to be a good one!"

He and his sister grab my hands and tug me toward the west side of my property. Five neat and weedless rows show the beginnings of what promises to be lush.

As David and Sarah chatter excitedly about who planted what, the Aston's screened back door slaps against its jam. Jill appears, and walks toward the fence's gate.

"Hey, Dalton." Her voice sounds tentative.

Is she as uncomfortable as I am?

"Hey, Jill."

She walks around the edge of the garden and hugs the Cerveny children. "Glad you're back home. Sorry I didn't come visit. It's just that…well…."

Her voice trails off. Elsie and Josh, with their children, begin to hoe lightly at the other end of the rows. Jill and I stand four feet apart. Her eyes are sunken with a darkness around them I've never noticed, even in the leanest of times.

We talk mostly about how she's managing without Fred, but there is no tenseness. I watch her and realize I have something that, hopefully, will allow me to focus on the future. I have an amazing child I desperately want to watch grow up. Jill and Fred were childless, and I'm not aware of any close family nearby. For most of their marriage, she struck me as the stronger partner. What can she look forward to now?

My legs get wobbly on me. "Can we sit down? I'm still a little shaky."

She takes my arm in hers and steadies me. We sit on a

wooden tree swing. A soft breeze rustles new growth on the yard's unkempt bushes. Jill pushes out and the swing begins to move.

She takes my hand, and for a while, we sit and rock back and forth.

The End

About the Author

Dalton's Run is the second novel by Todd Blomerth. He is a retired state district judge and former prosecutor and criminal defense attorney.

His debut novel, *Border Crossfire*, was released in 2020. In a remote Texas border region, Kickapoo County Deputy Purdy Kendricks has plenty lining up to do him in: booze, brutal cartels, the DEA, the unforgiving terrain, a past that needs confronting and a family that needs protecting. Not to mention a couple of scores to settle.

His non-fiction book, *They Gave Their All: Stories of the Caldwell County Men and Women Who Gave Their Lives During World War II*, tells the stories of the Caldwell County, Texas men and woman who died in the service of their country in World War II.

He and his wife Patti live in Lockhart, Texas.

The author welcomes comments or suggestions about his books. He may be contacted at: **blomertht@gmail.com**

Also by Todd Blomerth

Novels

Border Crossfire

Dalton's Run

Non-Fiction

They Gave Their All: Stories of the Caldwell County Men and Women Who Gave Their Lives During World War II.

Made in the USA
Columbia, SC
18 July 2021

42031849R00252